M
JONES

THE EMPTY MIRROR

ALSO BY J. SYDNEY JONES

Hitler in Vienna (2002)

Frankie (1997)

Viennawalks (1994)

The Hero Game (1992)

Time of the Wolf (1990)

Tramping in Europe (1984)

Vienna Inside-Out (1979)

Bike & Hike (1977)

THE
EMPTY MIRROR

A Viennese Mystery

J. SYDNEY JONES

Minotaur Books ♯ New York

This is a work of fiction. All of the characters, organizations, and events portrayed in this novel are either products of the author's imagination or are used fictitiously.

A THOMAS DUNNE BOOK FOR MINOTAUR BOOKS.
An imprint of St. Martin's Publishing Group.

www.thomasdunnebooks.com
www.minotaurbooks.com

Library of Congress Cataloging-in-Publication Data

Jones, J. Sydney.
    The empty mirror / J. Sydney Jones.—1st ed.
        p. cm.
    ISBN-13: 978-0-312-38389-3
    ISBN-10: 0-312-38389-4
    1. Murder—Fiction.   2. Klimt, Gustav, 1862–1918—Fiction.   3. Serial murder investigation—Austria—Vienna—Fiction.   4. Criminologists—Fiction.
5. Vienna (Austria)—Fiction.   I. Title.
    PS3610.O62553E47   2009
    813'.6—dc22   2008029825

First Edition: January 2009

10 9 8 7 6 5 4 3 2 1

To my wonderful wife, Kelly Mei Mei Yuen, soul mate and love of my life, who makes it all worthwhile, and to our four-year-old son, Evan, who generously granted me breaks from our playtime to write this book

ACKNOWLEDGMENTS

Thanks first go to Alexandra Machinist, an agent of wit, intelligence, grit, insight, determination, and loyalty. You are a writer's dream come true. Also a round of applause to Peter Joseph, an editor whose enthusiasm for this project was palpable in every query and edit. Additionally, Peter's able assistant, Lorrie McCann has earned this author's best regards for her efficiency and good humor. The stellar and thorough copy editing of Steve Boldt, under the very able direction of production editor Bob Berkel, proves once again the importance of the old adage that the devil is in the details. My book-savvy daughter, Tess Jones, also added encouragement in the early stages of this project as did writing buddy supreme, Allen Appel. Finally, thank you Thomas Dunne, gentleman publisher, for seeing the promise and potential in this work.

PART ONE

Real hate has only three sources: pain, jealousy, or love.
—Dr. Hanns Gross, *Criminal Psychology*

PROLOGUE

She hurried along the darkened, cobbled streets, angry and full of self-recrimination. If she hadn't missed the last tram; if Girardi had invited her to his pied-à-terre instead of pleading early rehearsals; if she had only taken her friend Mitzi's advice to drop that pompous little jellyfish of an actor and sleep with Klimt instead. So many ifs.

A man tipped his hat to her at the corner of Kärntnerstrasse and Graben. "How much?" he asked.

Couldn't blame him really; not many respectable girls out alone this late, and half the whores in Vienna plied their trade at that intersection. But it unnerved her, being mistaken for a prostitute, and she turned into a jumble of unfamiliar, darkened lanes behind Stephansdom before she had intended to, eager to get to her lodgings in the Third District.

Now there was nobody about; as quiet in Vienna at ten thirty as it was in her little village in Vorarlberg. She felt a sudden shiver of fear. The newspapers were full of reports about a mad killer on the loose in Vienna, about bodies dumped in the Prater amusement park. Another shiver rattled her body.

She picked up her pace and took her mind off such thoughts

by remembering what she had achieved so far in her young life. The muddy streets of her village in Vorarlberg seemed like another world. It had taken her three years to steal enough pfennigs from her father's wage packets to finally buy a third-class ticket to the capital, escaping said father and his black moods. She never looked back, seizing her opportunity like a life raft, and she had made it. Lover to the most famous actor in Vienna, model to the most famous painter. But if her papa ever saw one of her portraits . . . Not much danger of that, though; never took his nose out of his beer.

She thought of Klimt as she hurried along. He had eyes that penetrated. That bloke could look at you so he made you feel naked, even when you already were. As if he saw inside you. Cold his studio was. Made her all goose bumpy. But when she complained, he told her that was the way he wanted her; made her nipples perk right up did the cold, just the way he needed for his paintings. Clever old dog that Klimt. *Call me Gustl,* he said. And no funny business, though she knew he wanted her.

Suddenly she realized she'd become lost. Wasn't sure which way was which in the narrow and dark lanes. She saw a pulsing glow of light to her left and took that street. The light came from a canvas tent over a manhole cover; men working. That seemed safe. She followed the glowing light, but as she passed the manhole, she found nobody about. Must be working below. She shuddered at the thought. A terrible life working in the sewers.

"Fräulein."

She spun around at the sound of the man's voice. Then, seeing who it was, she smiled in relief.

"Oh. Hello."

Those were her last words.

ONE

Wednesday, August 17, 1898—Vienna

D amn that Gross, he thought as he sat restlessly in front of his untouched breakfast, a blank sheet of folio staring at him reproachfully from the desktop.

Advokat Karl Werthen was at loose ends this morning. The lawyer usually reserved the breakfast hour for writing. To date he had published five short stories, tales of "interrupted lives," as he liked to describe them.

Today, however, he had appetite neither for Frau Blatschky's excellent coffee nor for the antics of his foppish protagonist, Maxim, and the mysterious woman in the checkered mask he had met at the Washerwoman's Ball. And it was all the fault of his former colleague from Graz, the esteemed criminologist Doktor Hanns Gross, with whom Werthen had had dinner and a subsequent conversation last night. By his very presence, Gross had made Werthen realize that such scribblings were a poor substitute for real action and adventure. Werthen suddenly saw his literary ambitions for what they were: vain attempts at adding spice into his otherwise stodgy life. After all, his creations were far from art; merely clever little stories of amorous boulevardiers which the young ear-nose-and-throat man Dr. Arthur Schnitzler wrote much better, anyway.

Damn that Gross.

He should not be too hard on the criminologist, though, for truth be told this was not the first time in the last six years—since giving up criminal law in Graz to establish himself as one of Vienna's top men in wills and trusts—that Karl Werthen had wondered if he had made the right decision. Had he been too rash in his decision, too self-sacrificing?

He was distracted from these morose thoughts by a ruckus in the hall outside his sitting room, followed by an urgent rapping at the white double doors.

He glanced automatically over his shoulder to the Sevres clock on the marble mantel. Too early for the first post.

"Yes?"

The door opened slowly. Frau Blatschky, red-faced, peered around it, then stepped timidly into the room, chapped hands digging into the pockets of her freshly starched apron.

"A man here to talk with you, Herr Doktor," she began.

He was about to remind her of his sacred breakfast hour when the door behind her was thrust more widely open and a thick, stocky man burst into the room. His short hair was disheveled, his beard in need of a trim, and he wore a violently magenta caftan that hung down to his sandaled feet.

"Werthen!" the man thundered, his working-class Viennese accent clear even in this two-syllable pronouncement. "I must see you, man."

"I believe you are doing so, Klimt," Werthen answered calmly, smiling at Frau Blatschky to indicate she might withdraw.

"I told him you were at breakfast," she murmured, pursing her lips. Werthen nodded at her, smiling more broadly to let her know it was not her fault. "That is fine, Frau Blatschky. You may go."

As she left, she cast the intruder, the noted and notorious

artist Gustav Klimt, the look an exasperated mother might give a delinquent son.

"The damned constabulary," Klimt bellowed as the door closed. "They're making a mess of my studio. You must come."

"Hold on, Klimt. Why would the constabulary be at your studio? A moral's charge perhaps?" Werthen decided he would take out his peckish mood on the obviously distraught artist. "One too many nude society ladies adorning your canvases?"

"Fools," Klimt spluttered. "They say I murdered the girl. Imbeciles. She was my lovely Liesel, the best model I've ever had. Why would I lay a hand on her?"

This turned Werthen's mood from irritable to curious. "Murder?"

"Haven't you been listening, man? Liesel Landtauer. Sweet Liesel."

"Start at the beginning," Werthen said, standing now and motioning the painter to one of a pair of Biedermeier armchairs by the fireplace. Klimt eyed the delicate chair warily, but finally thrust his bulk down on the damask cushions. Werthen joined him in the other.

"Now, what are the police saying has happened?"

Klimt rubbed thick fingers through his stubbly hair and leaned back in the chair.

"They found a body this morning. In the Prater."

"Not another one?"

Klimt nodded. "Some lunatic out killing people and dumping their bodies in the Prater, and now they want to go and hang it all on me."

Werthen knew all of Vienna was in the thrall of a series of four murders—five now, it appeared—over the past two months. In fact he and his friend Gross had been discussing the crimes just last night. Respectable newspapers, such as the *Neue Freie Presse* and the *Wiener Zeitung,* had reported the killings, but did not involve themselves with sordid details or speculation. The more scrofulous press, however, was quick to mention "certain mutilations" of the corpses, leaving the imagination to run riot. These same papers called the perpetrator "Vienna's Jack the Ripper." Each of the bodies had been found on the grounds of the Prater amusement park in Vienna's Second District, in the very shadow of the giant Ferris wheel, the *Riesenrad,* constructed to celebrate Franz Josef's fiftieth jubilee as emperor.

Gustav the Ripper? Werthen doubted it. Klimt was capable of a crime of passion, perhaps, knowing the man's history, but not of the cold and calculated butchering of five innocents. However, the constabulary did not know Klimt as Werthen knew him; they could only follow procedure. And procedure meant they investigated first those people closest to the victim.

Even as he thought this, Werthen realized he was experiencing a tingling sense of euphoria, becoming caught up in the web of criminal law once again.

"Obviously they have not charged you, or you would be in custody."

"Well, they're poking their noses around my studio. Asking all sorts of absurd questions about Liesel, whether she posed in the altogether or not. But of course she did, the cretins! How else do you paint a nude? Dab a couple of dubious breasts on a male model like that pansy Michelangelo did?"

"Calm down, Klimt. What are they accusing you of?"

"One of the plodders found studies for my *Nuda Veritas,* my sketch for the first issue of *Ver Sacrum* last spring. They say it resembles Liesel. Bravo for a fine deduction! It should resemble Liesel. She modeled for it."

Werthen remembered the nubile, sweet young thing Klimt had portrayed on the cover of the Secession's magazine had outraged Viennese respectability. The girl/woman stood there completely naked and apparently completely unconcerned about it. Long tresses partly covered her breasts; she held a mirror in her right hand. Werthen had especially liked the symbolism of that empty mirror. What will modern man see in that looking glass, the searing light of truth, or merely a reflection of his own simpering vanity?

But he thrust such aesthetic considerations aside for the moment. "Answer my question. Are they accusing you of her murder?"

Werthen's tone of voice finally broke through Klimt's panic. The painter leaned forward in his chair and placed his hands together at their stubby fingertips and played them like a concertina.

"Well, not exactly. But they're making an awful mess of things. Werthen, I didn't even know the other four victims."

"Who is this young woman then?"

"I told you. A model."

"But why should the police come to you? Was she your lover?"

Klimt squashed the concertina, gripping his fingers together now as if in prayer. "She was meant to sit for me last night, but she begged off at the last instant."

The artist did not answer his question about the extent of their amorous relationship, Werthen noticed, and once again the lawyer felt a frisson of delight. Though it had been years since he had last questioned an unreliable witness or suspect, he was happy to note that his skills and instinct were still intact.

"Liesel sent a message that her roommate was ill and that she had to tend to her," Klimt continued. "Lord knows why she felt she had to lie to me. Some young suitor, I imagine."

"And why is it you think she was lying?" Werthen asked.

Klimt shrugged. "Simple enough. I was out getting bread, and when I was coming back, I saw the very roommate just leaving my building. She was delivering the note, so she could hardly have been ill enough to require Liesel's ministrations."

Relaxing now, Klimt looked over his shoulder at the two half-moons of flaky *Kipferl* butter rolls lying untouched on the breakfast tray.

"You going to eat those?"

How could the man worry about food at a time like this? Werthen wondered, losing his patience and reserve. "Here, take one."

He got up, placed a *Kipferl* on a linen napkin, and handed it to Klimt, who wolfed the roll down, dribbling crumbs onto his beard and caftan.

"Why so hungry? Did you miss your usual at the Café Tivoli?" Werthen rejoined Klimt in the chairs.

Werthen knew the painter's schedule: arising every morning at six to walk a ten-kilometer circuit from his apartment (which he shared with his unmarried sisters and widowed mother) in the Westbahnstrasse out to the Habsburg summer palace of Schönbrunn, and stopping off en route at a café of the old school where he feasted on pots of strong coffee laced with hot chocolate and creamy white peaks of *Schlag obers* along with fresh rolls piled with mounds of butter and jam. Then back to work at his studio in the Josefstädterstrasse, just doors away from Werthen's own apartment building.

Klimt looked sheepish at Werthen's question.

"Well, *did* you miss your breakfast?" Werthen pressed. Noticing Klimt's reticence, he continued, "You weren't home at all last night, were you? Is that the problem, then? No alibi?"

Klimt stood suddenly, the folds of his caftan catching on the arm of the chair and nearly upsetting it. He passed to the window and looked down into the sunlit street four stories below, rattling his fingers on the sill.

"Too many alibis," he muttered into the window, then swung around to face Werthen. "But none of them will I use. They'd be the end of my poor mother. And there's Emilie to consider."

By whom he meant Emilie Flöge, Werthen knew. She was the younger sister of Klimt's sister-in-law, a woman more than a decade his junior, with whom he had been carrying on a romance now for several years. After the untimely death of Klimt's painter brother, Klimt had taken both women under his protective wing. Gossip had it that the satyr Klimt had not so much as kissed the young woman, keeping her instead enshrined as his pure and virginal ideal of womanhood.

"You must explain, Klimt. I am, after all, your lawyer. Such information stops with me."

Klimt sighed, eying the second *Kipferl*.

"Please, do be my guest," Werthen said, but sarcasm was lost on the painter, who gulped this one down as quickly as he had the first.

"Sure you wouldn't like some coffee to go with it?"

"You're a true friend, Werthen," Klimt said, again missing the lawyer's ironic tone. He poured himself a cup from the white Augarten porcelain coffeepot. "No whipped cream about, I suppose?"

Werthen made no reply, wondering once more why he should have a soft spot for this barbarian. But he knew the answer: because the man drew like an angel.

"It's like this," Klimt said, sitting again, an incongruous pinkie held out delicately as he sipped the coffee. "I have a special friend. She lives in Ottakring."

Werthen maintained his silence. He was not going to make this any easier for Klimt by guessing the obvious: a working-class mistress in the suburbs with whom he'd passed the night.

"She *and* my young son, as a matter of fact."

Werthen could not prevent a surprised arching of his eyebrows.

"Yes, I was with her last night. Her and the boy. Now you see why I can never use them as an alibi. The shock would kill poor *Mutti*. I told her I was working late on a commission and would sleep in the studio last night. And Emilie . . . well, she, too, would be devastated, humiliated."

"And what if the police charge you with this young woman's death? How far are you willing to risk your neck for the sake of propriety?"

Klimt set the cup down on the silk carpet and slumped back in his chair. "Might it come to that?"

"I don't know. But we should plan for all eventualities. These Prater murders are begging for resolution."

Klimt shook his head. "I couldn't do it. Not to Mother . . . But you believe me, don't you, Werthen? I'm not the killing type."

Werthen nodded, but without enthusiasm, remembering how he and Klimt had first begun their association: The painter had been arrested and charged with assault and battery.

"What is your friend's name, Klimt? I may need to talk to her."

"My God, you, too? Is everyone turning against me?"

The painter thrust himself out of the chair again, almost knocking over the cup of coffee, and began pacing up and down the room.

"Relax, Klimt. A formality. I am a lawyer, a trained skeptic."

"Plötzl. There. I said it. Anna Plötzl, 231 Ottakringerstrasse, apartment 29A."

"Good," Werthen said, leaving his chair and crossing to the cherrywood writing desk, which also served as his breakfast table. There he pulled out a pen and notepad from the top drawer to write down the information.

"I assume you have more serviceable alibis for the other nights in question?"

Klimt looked at him blankly. "What other nights?"

"Of the other Prater murders, Klimt. If the homicide of Fräulein Landtauer is similar to those others, then you are either guilty of them all, or guilty of none, right?"

A light seemed to go on behind Klimt's eyes. "Right," he said eagerly.

"Then . . . ?" Werthen prodded.

"I'm thinking. What were the dates?"

Like much of the rest of Vienna, Werthen had those dates fixed in his mind. "The night and early-morning hours of June fifteenth, June thirtieth, July fifteenth, and August second."

Klimt screwed up his mouth in thought. "You actually expect me to recall what I was doing months ago? Is it really necessary?"

"Do you keep a diary or journal?"

Klimt shook his head, suddenly crestfallen.

"Never mind, Klimt. We'll deal with that later. For now, I advise you to stay away from your studio until the constabulary has left. It will only make you angry, and we do not need any altercations with the police. I assume they showed you a warrant?"

"They waved some legal-looking document in my face, if that's what you mean."

"Go home, Klimt. Take a nap. Tell your mother you're coming down with the grippe."

"There's work to do at the Secession. We have our first exhibition next month, and the builders are still hammering away."

"That's fine. Go to the gallery then. But stay away from your studio until I find out what is going on."

Klimt looked relieved. "I knew you would take care of things, Werthen. You're a prince of a man. And they say lawyers have no souls."

A half hour later Werthen, looking tall, lean, and fit in a linen suit and brown derby, stepped out into the bright sunlight of Josefstädterstrasse. He began whistling a tune from Strauss's *Die Fledermaus*. It was very unlike him to whistle, and from an operetta at that, but he could not help himself.

He felt buoyant and alive. This Klimt business had done it. It was so clear to him now. For the past six years he had been suffering a sort of long-term malaise, having given up the adrenaline excitements of criminal law.

Last night's talk with Gross had begun this realization: It made him see—by comparison to Gross—how boring and stifling his life had become.

Gross's 1893 publication, *Criminal Investigations,* had made his name in Europe and America; this very year would see publication of a companion volume, *Criminal Psychology*. He had also just started a monthly journal, *Archive of Criminalistics*. In demand everywhere, Gross was visiting Vienna for a few days on his way to his new posting as the first chair of criminology in all the Habsburg realms, at the University of Czernowitz in Bukovina.

A large, florid man in his early-fifties with a pencil mustache and a fringe of graying hair around a bald pate, Gross had been animated last night over dinner as he regaled Werthen with his latest cases. Then he had surprised Werthen with the news that he had seen the corpse of the fourth of the Prater victims, a favor arranged by a former assistant of his from Graz, Inspektor Meindl, who was now quite high up in Vienna's Police Presidium.

Gross could not tell Werthen of the horrible wounds inflicted on the body, for he had been sworn to secrecy by Inspektor Meindl. "Morbid" was the only comment the criminologist would permit himself regarding the disfigurements.

Werthen knew the importance of such secrecy: When the killer was finally brought to justice, only he would be able to confess to the exact nature and methodology of his crimes. Still, Werthen had been amazed to find himself disappointed at being denied such insider information; astounded to realize he was taking an interest in such matters again.

And now, Klimt's visit reconfirmed that he had only been marking time the last six years. He *needed* the adventure of criminal law in his life. And the hell with what the Werthens—Maman and Papa—expected from their firstborn.

A lark, he told himself. He would take a vacation from his stodgy law practice.

Indeed, he had already done so, having closed his office for the August holidays last week. He was due at the family estate in Upper Austria in several days, but until then, why not a bit of adventure?

Coming to Klimt's building, he entered the massive street door and went into the courtyard, an oasis of greenery in the midst of the city. Klimt's studio stood in the garden that lay in back of the main building, and Werthen could quickly see that the police were done with their searches, but that a burly officer was still stationed outside the door of the studio. Werthen tipped his hat at the officer, his mass of reddish brown hair catching highlights from the sun. The man nodded his thick head curtly, sweating in his heavy blue serge uniform.

"Something gone amiss here, Officer?"

"Painter chap." The policeman jerked his head backward toward the studio. "Never know what they might get up to."

"Indeed not," Werthen agreed. "A rare strange breed, the lot of them."

But Werthen could get nothing more out of the taciturn policeman, so he went back to the street and headed toward the center of the city, whistling as he walked jauntily along, tipping his hat to female passersby, making way for a large pram at the corner of Landtauergasse, buying a single red carnation for his buttonhole at the florist shop at the Landesgerichtstrasse intersection.

Yes, by damn, he was beginning to feel alive again. And what a fortunate coincidence that his old colleague Gross was in town to initiate his awakening. Or was it coincidence at all? More like fate? He chuckled at the notion. Fate was something he had not contemplated in many years.

Now, still whistling, Werthen was headed toward Gross's hotel, for the criminologist would surely be as interested as Werthen himself in this new development.

Gustav Klimt, the bête noire of Viennese painting, a possible suspect in the Prater murders!

TWO

Gross was not at his hotel—the Bristol on the elegant Ringstrasse. The concierge indicated to Werthen that the great Herr Doktor had inquired as to directions to the Kunsthistorisches Museum this morning before departing and was not expected back until luncheon at twelve thirty.

Though the day was heating up, Werthen decided to walk. The plane trees planted along the new Ringstrasse had finally reached a height to provide shade for strollers on the broad sidewalk. He knew where to go once he reached the museum. The Brueghel room was to the right at the top of the grand marble staircase. Overhead, parts of the foyer ceiling had been painted by Klimt before he had given up the classical style.

Gross stood apart from the groups of visitors who were conscientiously listening to museum guides running through their usual anecdotes about the Flemish painter. The criminologist, Werthen knew, could add a tale or two to their repertoire, for he was an ardent student of Brueghel's. Under the name Marcellus Weintraub, Gross had published a much quoted monograph on stylistic irregularities in the early paintings of the Flemish master, but kept such artistic passions from the light of day. It would not do for an examining magistrate to be too closely aligned with the subjective arts, he had told Werthen on the one occasion the topic of his avocation had come up.

Now here Gross was, all six feet and one inches of the man, examining at close range the human comedy as seen in Brueghel's *Children's Games.*

Werthen approached his old friend from the back and was about to tap his broad shoulder when Gross, without turning, said, "Don't mince about, Werthen. Is this coincidence or have you sought me out?"

Gross closed the Moroccan-leather notepad he had been writing in and slipped it into his jacket pocket.

"The latter," Werthen replied as Gross turned reluctantly away from the painting to face him.

"Adele does insist I stay up on the arts," Gross said.

Werthen smiled inwardly. "Is that so, Herr Weintraub?" Gross had obviously forgotten that, prodded by a second after-dinner slivovitz, he had once confided his love of Brueghel to Werthen.

Gross had the good grace to appear sheepish caught in the lie. But it was a short-lived embarrassment.

"Get on with it, man. What is so important that you track me down here? Not that I am not pleased to see you again." Uttered with an air of palpable displeasure.

Werthen drew him to one corner of the gallery, away from prying ears, and told him of Klimt's misfortune and of his own commission to clear the painter's name.

Gross clapped his large hands together like a hungry man sitting down to dinner. The resulting slapping noise attracted the critical attention of several dowagers among the gallery visitors.

"Excellent," he pronounced in a voice loud enough to draw disapproving shushes. He charged on, unaware of his audience. "I assume you are enlisting my help?"

"If you have the time."

"Time!" Gross boomed out, earning him further hushes. "But

of course I have the time for a real investigation. I am not due in Bukovina for days yet."

Gross bustled out of the gallery headed to the main staircase, Werthen following behind. At the top of the staircase Gross suddenly stopped.

"How to proceed, eh? That is the question now, isn't it, Werthen?"

"Absolutely," the lawyer agreed.

"I perceive several lines of inquiry. First, of course, would be to ascertain if our painter chap has alibis for the other four murders."

"We are working on that. Klimt, however, keeps no journal."

Gross plunged on. "Never mind. Plenty of time for that. Regardless, there is still the question if Herr Klimt is culpable of this latest outrage. A *crime passionnel,* as our French friends would have it. He kills his model and lover in a jealous rage and then comes out of his violent stupor to discover what he has done. Now he is terrified. The instinct for self-preservation takes control. In order to cover his crime, he dumps the body in the Prater to make it look like the other murders."

Werthen found himself nodding; it was, after all, a possibility.

Gross made a clicking sound with his tongue and wagged a forefinger in Werthen's face. "There is, however, an easy enough verification of that. Lead me to a telephone, will you, Werthen. I have a call to make."

They caught one of the new *Stadtbahn,* part-underground and part-elevated train, in back of the museum and detrained at the Alserstrasse stop. From there they walked several blocks in the direction of the General Hospital. Gross made no explanations and Werthen was determined not to ask their destination. The streets were full of traffic and strollers, and Werthen's nose stung from the acrid stench of horse dung. Vienna, Werthen observed not for the first time, was truly a city locked in another time.

A handful of automobiles were to be seen—and heard. Mostly traffic was still of the horse-drawn variety; even many of the omnibuses and streetcars were powered by horse.

Such conservatism was modeled by the emperor himself. No fan of technological progress, Franz Josef had never ridden in an automobile; telephones were scarce in the Habsburg palace, the Hofburg; and imperial secretaries were disallowed the use of the newfangled typewriter. At Franz Josef's insistence, all correspondence—including his own—was laboriously hand-written.

Soon they reached the main drive of the hospital grounds. The General Hospital loomed in front of them, as big and gray a building as ever swallowed the hopes of man, Werthen thought. In the background was the squat, sandstone *Narrenturm*, Fools' Tower, used until only just three decades before to house the insane in pitifully medieval conditions.

Gross led the way to a side entrance of the main hospital building and past a gray-uniformed, gray-faced guard who exactly matched his surroundings and who apparently knew the criminologist by sight.

"Back again, is it, Herr Doktor?" the man asked.

Gross nodded. "I expect you'll have a message from Inspektor Meindl from the Police Presidium?"

"That I do, sir. Fine day for a visit. Cool down there. Like going into a cathedral."

Werthen followed Gross past the guard, finally realizing their destination. The phone call the criminologist had needed to make was obviously to his former colleague Meindl, who had cleared their visit to the morgue. Once inside, Werthen was struck with a smell so spit-and-polish clean that it was downright obscene.

They took the stairs down, and the temperature dropped with each subterranean step; a natural form of refrigeration, just as the guard said. ABTEILUNG I was the first door they came to on the left.

"This is it," Gross said, giving a light rap on the door before entering.

Inside were two rows of tables topped with marble slabs, each slab with a small trough built around it and a drainage hole at one end. Some tables were empty; their beige marble was scratched and dull from constant scrubbing. Others bore a body atop, covered in thick, off-white muslin. The floor was tiled in pale yellow. A window high up on one wall cast murky, greenish light into the half-basement; away from the window, gas lamps hung from the ceiling at several junctures.

Bent over one of the slabs, a pathologist was up to his elbows in blood, peering into the stomach cavity of a cadaver. Werthen caught his breath and also a large gulp of the stink filling the room: chemical preservative and human decay. Bile stung the back of his throat, and he quickly averted his eyes from the autopsy in progress.

"Inspektor Meindl telephoned, I believe," Gross said to the pathologist, who had not bothered to look up from his work as they entered.

"Table seven," the doctor said, his eyes never leaving the corpse he was working on.

It was the table farthest from the window, and the body under the sheet was smaller than others in the room. Gross, an old hand at the morgue, threw the sheet back without ceremony. A young woman lay before them. Her body, once so vital and fresh and pink, was now absolutely and startlingly white, Werthen observed. There were no obvious signs of violence, though there looked to be a scar upon her nose. Her lips that might have kissed young men were so white as not to be distinguished from the rest of her facial features; nipples meant to suckle children had lost their color as well and were now gray and slack. The only color at all was a splash of auburn hair splayed about her head and another forming a triangle at her groin.

Werthen felt like a voyeur looking at the unfortunate young woman. Then came a flood of memory.

"Mary," he whispered.

Werthen was not sure he'd actually spoken the word, but this poor young woman did powerfully remind him of his dead first love. She was about Mary's age when they were engaged, he reckoned. Then the old familiar sadness crept over him, the loss and grief and guilt for not having been there when she needed him. Working all day and most of the night to establish his name in Graz as a criminal lawyer, he had not even realized how sick she was until the last days of her confinement at the tuberculosis sanatorium in the Semmering Alps. Marie Elisabeth Volker, who loved the Anglicized form of her name, who laughed at Werthen's seriousness, who tousled his hair and made him feel so very young and alive, who gently chided him for spending more time in the company of cat burglars and safecrackers than he did with his own fiancée.

Truth be told, neither his parents' expectations nor his own need for an easier, safer way to make a living had caused him to leave criminal law. No. It had been Mary's last words to him at the Semmering sanatorium.

"Poor Karl," she'd whispered, her cheeks abnormally flushed, her auburn hair splayed out upon the pillow. "Ambition is a fine thing, but you will miss me. Someday you will understand the opportunity we lost."

And so, after her death, he had quit criminal law, the one thing he could blame for coming between them. He had gone into the more refined and sanitary field of civil law as a sort of penance. Now, looking at this poor young woman on the slab in front of him, he felt a tightness in his chest. Mary had been right: He did miss her.

Gross had meanwhile stripped off hat and coat and set to probing the body with his large and rather hairy hands. He pinched the mouth, opening the lips, but was unable to unclench the jaw.

"Relatively fresh one," the criminologist said casually. "Rigor mortis has not yet worn off."

As he said this, the young woman's nose suddenly fell off, revealing pink cartilage and two gaping holes. Werthen gasped, but Gross merely sighed and righted the stub of flesh as if it were clay on a modeling statue. He examined with the same sort of dispassion the woman's ears, hands, feet. The farther down the body Gross moved, the more Werthen felt he must get air.

Thankfully Gross seemed to have no interest in knowing if sexual violation had been part of the crime. Instead he returned to the head, lifting the onionskin eyelids to peer into the lifeless pupils, then turned his attention to the corpse's neck.

"Just so," Gross muttered to himself. "You might want to take a look at this, Werthen. The killer's signature."

Gross adjusted the woman's head—careful to unseat the severed nose first—exposing the carotid artery on her neck. There, midway up the neck, was a small, clean cut that went through flesh and yellow fat and sinew.

Werthen swallowed hard, nodding.

"I assume this incision was made," Gross said, "after she was dead." He readjusted the head, but it flopped over to the left.

"That is, after he broke her neck," Gross continued. "Just like the other four victims. The second cervical vertebra has been cracked like a walnut. The cause of death." Gross replaced the nose. "And this bit, too. Noses cut with a single clean swipe and then left somewhere on their persons."

Werthen swallowed again. This was not the adventure it had seemed just a couple of hours ago. But at the same time the resemblance of this victim to his fiancée made the case all the more urgent. He would find the murderer of this poor girl, a proof of his love for Mary.

"If she was already dead, why the incision?" Gross asked, but it was rhetorical. He waved his hands over the whiteness of the corpse.

"To drain the blood," Gross answered his own question. "All five of them were squeezed as dry as a shirt on laundry day."

Werthen made no reply. He only wanted fresh air now.

Gross replaced the sheet. Slowly he slipped his coat back on, donned his hat, then looked at Werthen with cold, clear eyes: "The work of a madman, you surmised last night. Do you still believe that?"

Werthen managed to find his voice. "Who else could do such a thing?"

Again Gross caught him in his penetrating gaze. "There may be other explanations, my dear Werthen."

As they left the autopsy room, the pathologist had moved on to a new corpse.

Gross cut away quite happily at the sausage on his plate, then piled a miniature dripping haystack of sauerkraut atop it before plunging the heavily laden fork into his mouth. Werthen sipped at his glass of mineral water and tried to gain appetite by watching the lunchtime crowd around him in the *Gasthaus*, but it was not working. A schnitzel sat on the plate in front of him as lifeless as the corpse on the marble slab.

Their trip to the morgue had made Gross late for luncheon at the Bristol, and the criminologist had insisted on a heavy lunch. Thus, Werthen had taken him to the Schöner Beisl, a pretty little restaurant tucked into a side street not far from the university; the sort of place he normally loved, so full of bustle and hearty cooking smells coming from the kitchen. But he could not get the dead girl out of his mind. The way she had blended with Mary, as if his fiancée were trying to reach out to him from the grave, to speak to him through another's death.

"Not hungry, Werthen?"

"A stomach for such sights takes some developing," he responded.

Gross, whose ample midriff had forced him to unbutton his coat before sitting, was deaf to double entendre. He merely tucked into the *Burenwurst* with renewed vigor.

After lunch, they strolled through the newly completed Rathuas Park, smoking after-lunch cigars and admiring the spray of the fountains. They could hardly discuss the matter in the crowded confines of the *Gasthaus,* but full of wurst and a digestive schnapps, Gross was all volubility.

"Now you have seen," he said. "This latest victim fits exactly the pattern of the other killings. Which means either your painter friend is guilty of all of them or none."

"He is not *my* painter friend," Werthen said. "He is a client. And I concur. Highly unlikely that he is the killer."

"We still have a line of inquiry regarding that. The mistress in Ottakring, I believe it was."

Werthen nodded.

"A bit of a postprandial walk would be in order, I think," Gross said. "And as the stomach does its work, perhaps our brains can also be enterprising. Now that you have seen, do you have any theories beyond that of a madman at work?"

"The letting of the blood," Werthen said suddenly. "There is a strange resonance in that."

Gross cut his eyes at his companion. "Yes?"

"I seem to remember one of your cases. Was it in Pölnau?"

"Aah." Gross sniffed appreciatively. "You surprise me, Werthen. You've been keeping up with my career."

"Well, yes. I suppose that is one way to look at it. However, as I recall, the murders were all over the papers at the time. One could hardly ignore the affair."

"Remember the particulars?" Gross asked.

"Two—or was it three victims?—in the small Bohemian district near the village of Pölnau. Each of them strangled and drained of blood. There were those who immediately labeled the murders ritual crimes. Yourself among them, if I recall rightly."

"Presented with certain facts, one is dutybound not to discount them simply because they might be uncomfortable."

"Jewish ritual killings, in fact," Werthen continued.

"I am not an anti-Semite, Werthen. After all, look at our friendship as proof of that."

"Oh, but then I'm so very assimilated. I recall you saying that my surname sounds absolutely Aryan and my fair complexion and height also lend to the confusion."

"Well, they damn well do," Gross spluttered.

"What was it you once called me? 'The Golden Boy,' I believe. As if Jews have to be some grotesque physical caricature of the hunched and grasping moneylender. Well, we Werthens try to blend," Werthen said flippantly.

He recalled with no little vehemence his father's insistence on his son's learning the ways of a gentleman, which meant endless hours on horseback over the hills of Upper Austria, agonizing sessions with a fencing master, and entire weeks in the fall and spring lost from his studies in order to tramp over hill and dale in search of chamois and wild boar. Against his will, young Werthen had been turned into a fine physical specimen and a crack shot, yet he always longed for a life of the mind.

"It was the grandfather's choice of surnames," Werthen added. "That of his former employer, in point of fact. There have been no religious Jews in the Werthen clan for decades. Just good Protestants."

Gross, a Catholic, made no comment, and they walked on in silence for a time, watching the antics of a long-haired dachshund that had escaped its leash and now ran rings around its parasol-wielding mistress.

Werthen and Gross had developed their bantering manner from long association in Graz. After losing an early case to the prosecutor-cum-criminologist, Werthen had become a disciple.

He sought Gross out privately after the trial and told him what a fine job he had done and how he wished to learn from his copious experience. Gross for his part had been flattered and took Werthen under his wing. The young lawyer had become a frequent visitor in the charming flat that Frau Adele Gross so expertly managed in Graz's inner city.

In between generations of the family, as it were, Werthen became a confidant to their troubled young son, Otto, who was thirteen years Werthen's junior; Hanns Gross was seventeen Werthen's senior. Werthen thus acted as their go-between in the difficult age and helped guide the young boy intellectually before the boy reached his majority.

Gross had been grateful for Werthen's intercession, for Otto and father Hanns did not have a comfortable relationship. So wise about the psychology of the criminal, Gross was seemingly ignorant of the proper way to conduct human affairs. Hanns Gross was far too imbued with the military rigor of his forefathers to appreciate the extreme sensitivity and perhaps neurasthenia of young Otto. Werthen, on the other hand, was only too familiar with such a life lived on nerves, for his own younger brother, Max, had been consumed by such hypersensitivity. Max had ended his life in a most Austrian manner, shooting himself at the grave of his beloved muse, the playwright Grillparzer. Werthen was determined such a fate not be Otto's. He was pleased to learn the younger Gross was now in his final year of medical school.

Such history served to bond Gross and Werthen. Where others saw the blustery criminologist as merely pompous, Werthen had an appreciation for his weaknesses.

The yapping of the boisterous long-haired dachshund brought the lawyer's attention back to the here and now.

"I do hope, Gross, that you are not making a similar hypothesis about these killings," Werthen finally said, turning away from the canine amusement. "The Pölnau affair was not your brightest hour. In fact, if memory serves me right, the murders were found to be the result of local jealousies, and the blood was drained to divert suspicion from the postmaster, the actual killer."

"Yet I maintain that it is our duty as examining officers to investigate wherever the evidence and clues lead us."

"Even if it leads to anti-Semitism?"

"It *is* said the Jews use human blood for their unleavened bread, matzo, at Passover," Gross replied with his Socratic voice, as if trying to incite debate.

Werthen stopped dead in his tracks. "You can't be serious! Ritual murders? But this is almost the twentieth century. Pure poppycock."

"The bodies were found in the Prater," Gross said. "The Jewish district."

"You can't actually believe this. I may be assimilated, but I'm still a Jew and I find such theorizing highly offensive."

"I am examining the case," Gross said evenly. "I take nothing on trust. Science is my guide, not superstition. What I know is that there have been five victims thus far, two male and now three female victims. Ages disparate, from eighteen to fifty-three, as was their social standing, from middle and lower-middle class to upper class. To date the only common thread we have in all the murders is the method of killing, the draining of the blood after death, the severed noses, and the location where the bodies were found. I deduce, therefore, that we are looking for someone, most probably a man, who is strong enough to break people's necks and handy enough with a knife or other very sharp instrument to make similar incisions of the carotid. That is what I know thus far, Werthen."

"But why the disfigurement of the nose? How could that be linked with some ritual slayings?"

Gross merely smiled at him.

"I see." Werthen nodded. "A reverse signature of sorts, is that your theory?"

"Excellent, Werthen. You really do have a first-class deductive mind. You should never have given up criminal law. That is exactly my line of thought. What is the expression? 'As plain as the nose on your face.'"

Gross waited for an appreciative smile from Werthen for his pun, but got none.

"After all, what is the one caricature we associate with the Jew but his hooked nose? Thus, to cut off the noses of Aryans would be some kind of sadistic revenge. In fact, a Jewish signature."

"I hope you're playing devil's advocate."

Another shrug from the portly criminologist. "I merely state one possible avenue of investigation."

"And I assure you, Gross, that Klimt is neither Jewish nor an anti-Semite."

"Neither, as it turned out, was the perpetrator of the Pölnau murders," Gross said with a wry smile on his lips. "As you so eagerly reminded me. But it proved an effective diversion from the truth for a time."

As Werthen made no reply to this, Gross plunged on, "I see a myriad of difficulties in this case, my friend. Speed is of the utmost importance. France may be renowned for its *affaire Dreyfus*, but I assure you Austria has its own homegrown fanatics in that sphere, many who hail from my own region of Styria," Gross said. "There are Schönerer and his German nationalists; even your newly installed and esteemed mayor, Karl Lueger, and his famous dictum, 'I decide who's a Jew.' If the details of these deaths were reported in the papers, it would take no time for such anti-Semites to turn them into ritual murders. Jew killings. With a mayor who spreads hatred of Jews from the political pulpit, there is no telling what might come of it all. Pogroms. Who knows?"

Werthen still made no reply. He did, however, take exception to Gross's description of Lueger as "esteemed." The man whom the lower-middle classes loved to call Handsome Karl was in fact a mountebank, ready to play to the masses with his brand of anti-Semitism. That the mayor, thrice denied confirmation by the emperor because of such beliefs, had initiated a cradle-to-grave form of municipal socialism hardly made up for such demagoguery.

"So you see, Werthen," Gross blustered on, "we may be working under the gun here. I need to solve these murders before the public gets wind of them. Before some enterprising newspaperman ferrets out the information and publishes a story in the foreign press."

"Actually, what you *need* to do, Gross, and what I hoped to convince you to do, is prove my client innocent of this latest outrage," Werthen said.

"Well, it comes to the same thing, doesn't it?" Gross stopped dramatically. "Either he is innocent of the fifth murder, or your good client is in fact guilty of all five murders. That is the only way he could know the killer's signature method."

Werthen felt the chill of a goose crossing his grave. He was no longer so certain approaching Gross had been a good idea. Perhaps his own involvement in such an affair was also ill-advised. Two generations it had taken the Werthens to disguise their Jewish roots. Would this investigation link him forever with the Jews? Yet the innocent girl lying on that marble slab had moved him. He had not been prepared for such emotion; it had quite overwhelmed him.

THREE

On the long *Strassenbahn* ride out to Ottakring, Gross regaled Werthen with his trained observational skills.

"You of course noted the distinguishing characteristic of the pathologist at the morgue, I assume, Werthen."

Werthen had been too affected by the smell of death to notice anything about the man other than that he was covered in blood up to his elbows.

"Can't say that I did, Gross." The streetcar passed over the Gürtel, the second ring road delineating the outer districts of the city. Suddenly the housing tracts became bigger, grayer, and dingier; worker tenements thrown up in the past several decades with none of the grace or serendipity of the buildings in the districts between the Ringstrasse and the Gürtel.

"You sure?" Gross sounded honestly surprised. "Try to reconstruct the room at the morgue, Werthen. Visualize the furniture, the lighting, and then narrow in on the pathologist so concentrated on his work that he did not bother to vet us. Can you not see some very distinguishing characteristic? A hint: It was red."

"I'm sure the man does not have blood on his arms at all times, Gross." Werthen was growing exasperated with this game.

A pensioner wearing a Tyrolean hat and seated just in front of them turned round and stared at Gross and Werthen with rheumy eyes.

Gross tipped his derby hat at the inquisitive old man, returning to the subject at hand.

"No, no, Werthen. A birthmark, not blood. In the shape of a crescent, and located on his left temple in plain sight as we entered."

The old man continued to gawp at them as Werthen closed his eyes for a moment, re-creating the autopsy room in his imagination. He saw the pathologist's hands at work in the viscera of a cadaver, then let his mind work its way upward on the man's body. Suddenly the telltale birthmark appeared.

"Why, Gross, you're right! The man did have a birthmark, and in the shape of a new moon." Then to the old man, still craning his neck backward: "Would you care to join us?"

The man faced forward again with a disgusted snort.

"No reason to be rude, Werthen," Gross said.

Werthen raised his eyebrows at this remark, for Gross was usually too oblivious of the feelings of others to even know when he was being rude.

"At any rate," Gross continued, "you should learn to notice such things, Werthen. Take me. I've trained myself assiduously in that finest of visual arts: being a reliable witness."

Gross gestured with palms outward at Werthen. "The words may seem a contradiction in terms, I know. More times than I care to recall I have had cases fall apart because of witnesses who were too easily influenced by afterthoughts; who wanted notoriety and were willing to say whatever was needed to attain it; who were even color-blind. Did you know that fully five percent of adult males cannot tell red from blue?"

"Once again, Gross, you impress one with your breadth of knowledge."

Gross caught the sarcasm in Werthen's voice. "Sorry if I'm

boring you, old man." He straightened in his seat next to Werthen. "By the way, the pathologist had no birthmark. Just goes to show you how suggestible we all are."

The old man in front of them let out a derisive snort.

They rode the rest of the way to Anna Plötzl's apartment in silence.

She lived at the end of the J line, near the Ottakring cemetery. The tenement at 231 Ottakringerstrasse was the same as five others in the block on both sides of the narrow street: five stories tall and badly in need of sandblasting. The front door was open and no nosy *Portier* was on duty to check the comings and goings of tenants.

Inside, the building was dark and cavernous: Three different staircases led to the upper stories. Staircase A was on the left. By the second landing, Werthen realized that the apartment numbering had nothing to do with which floor the apartment was on. Anna Plötzl's apartment was at the end of the hall on the fifth floor. As they knocked at her door, Werthen made a silent prayer that she would be at home. He had no desire to make a second trip to Ottakring to verify Klimt's alibi.

The door was opened on the third knock by a tiny woman who was obviously expecting somebody else. Her smile turned to a frown when she saw them.

"What do you want?"

"My good lady." Gross swept his derby off his head and nudged Werthen to do the same with his. "We have come on a mission from your good friend Herr Klimt."

"Gustl sent you?" Her face screwed up in suspicion. She was so unlike the ethereal females Klimt portrayed on his canvases that Werthen wondered what the artist could ever have seen in her. She was somewhat hunched as well as flat-chested as far as he could see, and with a shadow of dark fuzz over her upper lip.

"He did, indeed, madam," Gross replied, but she only pinched her face more, her eyes tiny, wary slits.

Werthen produced a card. "I am Herr Klimt's lawyer, Fräulein Plötzl."

She took the card in a hand reddened and rough from washing, most likely her former profession, assumed Werthen.

"What's he need a lawyer for?"

"Perhaps we could come in and discuss matters more fully," Werthen suggested.

A door opened across the dimly lit hall, and a face peered out at them for a moment. Then the door closed quickly again.

"What matters would that be?" she asked.

Behind her a little boy tugged at her skirts. She thrust a foot at him. "Not now, Gustl. Go play. *Mutti*'s got business to do."

She looked at the card again, then up and down the hall.

"You better come in."

They did so, but got no farther than the doorway, which opened directly onto a space that obviously served as living room, bedroom, and dining room all in one. A crucifix hung over a double bed, unmade, with sheets and comforter spilling onto the floor. Children's blocks were scattered on the bed; more were to be found underfoot. In the center of the room was an oval table of indeterminate wood whose chipped surface was covered with dirty dishes, scraps of papers with childish doodles on them, and a soiled chemise.

The domestic mess made Werthen feel ill at ease. He did not want to be privy to this part of Klimt's life.

"What's he gone and done he needs a lawyer?" she asked again. Then sizing up Gross, she added, "Two lawyers."

"We have come to help," Gross began, but this only increased her innate fear.

"He *is* in trouble then. I don't want any part of trouble."

The child, sickly looking rather than robust, hid behind a daybed in the far corner of the room. He was the antithesis of Klimt, with frail-looking limbs, sallow complexion, and smudges of dark under his eyes.

Werthen jumped in, "There is no trouble, I assure you. We have only come to ascertain . . . that is, assure ourselves—"

"I know what 'ascertain' means. No need to talk down to me. I read books."

She gestured at a bookshelf in the corner by the boy.

"I am sorry. I didn't mean to be impolite," Werthen went on.

Gross, meanwhile, moved to the bookshelf in question and picked out a volume. "Interesting."

"I like my books," Anna said.

"But to return to the question at hand," Werthen continued as Gross thumbed through pages. "Perhaps you could assure us that in fact Herr Klimt was a visitor here last night."

"I can assure you of no such thing. What do you take me for?"

"I believe you are a friend of Herr Klimt's?"

"Friends are one thing. He comes sometimes to draw me. Just my face, mind you. Nothing improper."

"Of course not. And yesterday?"

She puffed out her lips. "I don't think I like your incineration, Herr High-and-Mighty."

"This is no time for false modesty," Werthen said, finally losing patience with the woman. "Klimt needs your help."

"So he is in trouble after all. Why'd you lie to me? No. I want none of it. You two, get out now." She grabbed the book out of Gross's hands and shooed him toward the door.

"Please, Fräulein Plötzl—"

"It's *Frau* Plötzl. Can't you use the eyes God gave you? That's my son there."

"And his father?" Gross said.

"That's no business of yours. Now get out before I scream for help. Fancy gents like you don't want the complications that'll bring, I tell you."

"*Mutti*," the little boy said from the corner. "When is Uncle Gustl coming?"

"Out!" she yelled. "Now!"

They did as they were told. Once they regained the street, they could only look at one another and sigh.

"What does that leave us with?" Werthen asked.

"I imagine she will come around if Klimt himself were to ask her, but that would rather taint her testimony. Lower-class morality. It's enough to make you weep at the human race. Here is a woman compromised on all counts: She has a bastard child by a lover who will hardly say her name in daylight, yet she is worried about her reputation being besmirched if said lover is in some kind of 'trouble.' I tell you, Werthen, sometimes it is enough for me to want to give up on humans altogether and raise monkeys."

"I will simply assume Klimt was telling the truth when he said he was with her last night," Werthen said. "He was mightily embarrassed by this alibi. I now understand why."

"We do not, however, come away empty-handed." Gross retrieved a slip of paper from his coat pocket. Unfolding it, he presented it to Werthen, who saw that it was a crude pencil sketch of a gnomelike bearded man very much the image of Klimt, with horns on his head and a forked tail. The block-lettering signature at the foot of the sketch was unmistakable: KLIMT.

"Where did you get this?" Werthen asked, handing the paper back.

"In the book I was looking in at Frau Plötzl's. It is an interesting choice of reading, but I highly doubt it is the good Frau Plötzl's. This sketch would indicate it belongs rather to Gustav Klimt."

"So the man reads. He is not an artistic barbarian, after all."

"I gather not. Or then again . . ."

"Please, Gross, no coyness. What was the book?"

The Man of Genius."

"By Cesare Lombroso?"

"The very," Gross said. "One of my predecessors in the field of criminalistics, though I do not altogether agree with or approve of his theory that criminality is inherited. In some cases, yes. But the Italian depended overmuch on the physical defects which he held demonstrate the criminal type. For example you, Werthen, with your high cheekbones and rather hawklike nose fit two of the physiognomic categories for criminality, but I have never met anyone with less of a criminal nature in my entire career."

"I thank you for that, Gross."

"But it is interesting reading for your artist friend, don't you think?"

Werthen had not read the book himself, but knew of the theme: It argued that artistic genius was a form of hereditary insanity, and Lombroso went on to identify a baker's dozen of types of art that he characterized as "the art of the insane."

"One wonders if Herr Klimt found his own art categorized in the book," Gross said with a wan smile. "It does give us something to think about."

It was late afternoon by the time they arrived back in the center of Vienna. They transferred to a second tram that took them to Karlsplatz. There was today, as on most days of the summer of 1898, a large crowd of onlookers taking up position around the construction site at the far eastern end of the square, on Friedrichstrasse. Holes had courteously been drilled at various levels into the wooden wall surrounding the site to accommodate the varying heights of spectators. Now that the construction had reached heavenward, however, such holes were no longer necessary. Eyes were all focused on the very top of the cube-shaped building, at a gigantic ball of laurel leaves rendered in bronze. From a distance, however, the ball took on more the aspect of a giant golden cabbage or cauliflower. Pedestrians stopped midstride to shake their heads in wonder, to elbow one another jocularly. "It's those crazy artists at work again," they would say.

"It looks very like a tomb," one big-bosomed matron, lorgnette to her eyes, was saying as Werthen and Gross briskly passed, headed toward the entrance of the new building.

"Werthen," Gross finally called out. "Why so secretive? Where in the name of Mary and Joseph are you leading me?"

"You'll see," Werthen said, not slowing his pace. It was his turn to play *magister ludi* as Gross had done at the morgue, and truth to tell, he was enjoying it.

He presented his card to the red-nosed guard at the main doors and was waved on into the large entry hall of the building still under construction. Dust filled the air; the chatter of workmen and the percussion of hammers assaulted the ear, making Gross cover his with his hands.

It took only a moment for Werthen to spot their man. He was still dressed in the flowing caftan with intricate flower design embroidered on it. He seemed as at home directing carpenters and wall painters as he was behind the easel, as if he were the architect and not one of the artists who would show their work in this new gallery.

Werthen led the way to Klimt, who was busily showing a worker how to get the desired texture on the white walls.

The painter saw him out the corner of his eye before the lawyer could greet him.

"Werthen. At last. What kept you?" The painter took Werthen's frail hand into his meaty paw and squeezed it tightly.

"We had to—," Werthen began, but was interrupted by one of the thick builders, who was sweating under a black bowler hat. He gesticulated at a sheet of blueprints he held, spluttering something incomprehensible at Klimt, who moved aside with him for a moment.

Gross took the opportunity to tug on Werthen's sleeve.

"What is this chap?" Gross nodded derisively at Klimt in his caftan. "Some sort of Mussulman?"

"Actually, he's our client."

Gross pursed his lips so fiercely that they became two white lines under his mustache. "You could have told me earlier."

"Yes, I suppose I could have. More fun this way, though."

Klimt finally eased himself away from the builder and shrugged at them by way of apology.

"Klimt, let me introduce a colleague, here to help. Dr. Hanns Gross."

Klimt turned to face the man, much taller, but not half as brawny as the painter.

"*The* Hanns Gross? The criminologist?"

Gross suddenly beamed, Werthen noticed. "The very one," Gross said.

"Wonderful," Klimt said, and with that he embraced the criminologist. Gross stood stiffly, hands at his side, allowing the hug, but blinking indignantly over Klimt's shoulder at Werthen.

"We've had some difficulty with your friend in Ottakring," Werthen said, looking around them to make sure no one was eavesdropping.

However, Klimt did not seem anxious to find some more private place to talk. The constant din made by the building crew masked their conversation, anyway. Plus, here Klimt was in the company of his peers; there was no public image of propriety to maintain.

"She says I wasn't with her last night?"

"She refuses to say one way or the other. Once she discovered I was your lawyer, she decided it was not wise to be known as your acquaintance."

Klimt put a bear's paw on Werthen's shoulder. "She'll come around. Life has not been easy for Anna. She needs to learn trust."

"I am sure she does, Herr Klimt," Gross said, coming into the conversation, "but meanwhile, perhaps we could simply verify your alibis for the other nights in question."

Klimt looked to Werthen for assistance.

"I said we would deal with this matter later. Now is the time. We need you to concentrate on the dates I gave you, June fifteenth, June thirtieth, July fifteenth, and August second."

The first three murders had set all of Vienna buzzing and turned many of its citizens into amateur detectives. The killings had at first come at regular intervals: Maria Müller, washerwoman, found on the morning of June 15. Then a little over two weeks later, on June 30, the body of Felix Brunner, a pipe fitter, was found. When a third killing happened on July 15, all of Vienna thought they could see the pattern of the crimes, for not only was this killing spaced fifteen days from the last, but it was also a person of the working class. This third victim, Hilde Diener, seamstress and mother of four, had taken the dog out for the night walk and never returned home. Her body was found in the Prater, like the others. (The dog had never been found.) Thus, all the deaths were fifteen days apart, the victims were of the working class, and they followed another pattern, as well: first a woman, then a man, then a woman.

The gutter press had encouraged the populace to play detective, noting that the next crime was probably due on July 30, and that men should now be on guard.

In the event, the night of July 30 had passed without incident, except for three separate cases of assault and battery. Lone men, self-appointed deputies, placed themselves as bait near the Prater. Each carried some weapon: a heavy truncheon, brass knuckles, or a walking stick with a stiletto hidden within. Approached by strangers, these three had gone on the attack. The result was the concussion of a schoolteacher from St. Pölten who was in Vienna for vacation and, having become lost, was seeking directions to his pension; the broken left arm of a petty thief and well-known pickpocket who worked the streets near the amusement park; and the stabbing injury of a constable who was dressed in street clothes in an attempt to apprehend the killer.

Next morning, the city communally sighed in relief, thinking perhaps the killings were finished. Three days later, however, the killer struck again. This time the victim was indeed a man, but not of the working class. Alexander von Fliegel was a manufacturer who had gained membership in the nobility through his wealth rather than family. Werthen had no personal knowledge of him, but knew another lawyer who was acquainted with the man. Von Fliegel produced a popular face cream for women, Tender Skin, and had factories in Vienna, Linz, and Graz. He had been out for a night on the town with several colleagues. The last these friends had seen of him, he was a bit the worse for drink, wobbling down the Weihburggasse, lighting a cigar. He was going to walk off his inebriation, he told them. His body was found next morning, August 2, in the Prater.

Klimt was frowning, attempting to recollect his whereabouts on those dates. Finally, he shook his head. "I'll have to ask Emilie. Perhaps I wrote a postal card to her on one of those dates."

Gross and Werthen exchanged looks.

"It's our way of staying in touch, even if I do not have the time to see her. Beautiful cards. From our own Wiener Werkstätte."

"I am sure they are, Herr Klimt," Gross said. "And I am sure you see the importance of such verification."

"Yes. Herr Werthen already explained that if we can show I didn't kill the others, I didn't kill Liesel. So these mutilations the press speaks of, there must be a consistency to the wounds, to the killer's technique."

"Along those lines, yes," Gross averred.

"I would feel better about a positive defense."

"You seem to have a sense of the law, Herr Klimt. I mean, you knew me by name. And I am not such an egoist that I do not realize that the name of 'Gross' is hardly a household word."

"I do a fair amount of reading," Klimt said with a bearish grin.

"Including Lombroso, it would seem."

Klimt's grin disappeared. "How do you know that?"

Gross handed the sketch to him. "Found inside a copy of *The Man of Genius* at your . . . friend's home."

Klimt opened the folded paper, looked at the sketch, chuckled lowly, then crumpled it into a ball and tossed it onto a rubbish heap in the middle of the floor.

"Do you consider yourself a man of genius, Herr Klimt?" Gross asked.

"Sometimes I do, yes. I confess. But at others, I feel a sham. Have you ever felt that way, Doktor Gross?"

But Gross only smiled at the question.

As they left the construction site, Gross was shaking his head.

"What are we to make of the man? Flounces about in that outsized tutu, fancies himself a genius beyond the bounds of society, yet defends the honor of his shabby lady love."

"A complex individual to be sure," Werthen said.

"You never mentioned, Werthen. However did that man come to be your client?"

"An act of professional charity on my part, I must confess."

Their conversation was interrupted by street urchins tugging at the hem of Gross's morning coat. He sent them scurrying with a brusque wave of the hand. The two men left the carnival atmosphere of the building site, and Werthen continued his explanation.

"As a younger man, Klimt was a bit feckless. But my, could he paint, even then. Got himself into a spot of trouble 'going to Trieste.'"

"Whatever for? And why Italy?"

"His phrase only. Not the city but the street, Triesterstrasse, here in Vienna. A major traffic artery for teamsters bringing goods into and out of the city. Whenever Klimt's artistic muse failed him, he would take himself off to Triesterstrasse and pick a fight with whichever driver he first found abusing his draft animals. Said it freed his vital juices to be in a bit of rough-and-tumble."

"And he was charged with?" Gross asked.

Werthen shrugged. "Grievous bodily harm, I'm afraid. Broke a man's arm with his bare hands."

"Like cracking a walnut," Gross muttered.

"I proved it was self-defense. The man had a knife."

But Werthen could only think of the strength of the man, the bone-breaking ability of the painter.

FOUR

Werthen was at his desk earlier than usual, anxious to write up his notes on the events of the day before. This morning there was no interruption of his coffee-and-*Kipferl* routine, and after forty minutes he realized that he was enjoying such writing far more than he did his short stories.

Just as he was finishing his second cup of coffee, there was a knock on the double doors of the sitting-room-cum-study, and Frau Blatschky peeked her head in timidly, then entered.

"A visitor, Dr. Werthen."

He glanced automatically at the clock. Too early even for Gross, he thought.

"A woman." She said it with faint disapproval. Had she approved, the visitor would have been labeled a "lady."

He could not imagine who it might be. Shaking his head, he said, "Send her in, Frau Blatschky."

A woman entered the room in a graceful sweep of fabric and sinew, all youth and beauty, her skin alabaster, almost translucent. Her hair was done up in a fashionable frizz bound by a lavender scarf.

"Herr Werthen. Finally." Her voice was soft, almost a whisper.

"May I be of service, Fräulein?"

Suddenly he recognized her from the Klimt paintings. "Fräulein Flöge."

She nodded at his recognition.

"That will be all, Frau Blatschky."

The housekeeper gave a final disapproving glance, then pulled the doors shut behind her with extra force.

"Gustl has been arrested," the woman, clearly in distress, blurted out. "They came for him at his apartment and took him away like a common criminal in front of his mother and sisters. You must help, *Advokat* Werthen."

He was astounded and for a moment quite speechless. Then he recovered his wits and his lawyer's bedside manner.

"We will get him out," Werthen reassured her. "After all, the police could have no case against him."

"You mean his alibi, Fräulein Plötzl."

Werthen tried to hide his further surprise.

"Please, counselor. Gustl's affairs are an open secret to all of Vienna."

"He was trying to protect you," Werthen said, relieved that he would not have to battle Klimt's misplaced sense of propriety.

"But he cannot know that I know." Her voice might have been no more than a whisper, but it breathed determination.

"I don't think *you* understand, Fräulein Flöge. Herr Klimt has been arrested for murder. His life may depend on an alibi."

"And I do not think you understand, Herr Werthen. A man is a man. His word must mean something or he is nothing. We all know that Gustl is less than perfect. It is just that *he* doesn't realize that. I for one will not take that away from him. Surely the police cannot believe he is a mad killer. We will take our chances, thank you very much."

"We?"

She merely looked at him, her alabaster skin bearing a faint skein of glisten over the lips. She was hard as nails, but also playing a game. A risky game, a gambler's game.

"It is Gustl's decision. I am here to ask you not to try and convince him otherwise."

"Does his mother know of his . . ."

"Infidelities?" she offered. "Of course. But not of his bastard child."

She said the word with a harshness that spoke volumes about her true feelings.

"She is a weak woman. Her heart. News of such a thing might—no, surely would—cause her harm. It is Gustl's decision, *Advokat* Werthen. We must both honor that."

"The fools," said Gross, seated in a straight-back chair in the office of Inspektor Meindl at the Police Presidium overlooking the plane trees of Schottenring. "They're playing to the press. What evidence could they have against him?"

"My position exactly," said Meindl, a diminutive man, even smaller than Werthen remembered. He sat behind an expanse of cherrywood, nestled in an immense armchair that looked as if it might have done service to a medieval potentate, all of which made the man seem even smaller than he was. On the wall behind him was the usual photographic portrait of the emperor, muttonchopped and scowling; next to it was a smaller portrait in oils. This depicted a noble-looking head topped by a shock of white hair. Just at the bottom of the frame the artist had hinted at the vast chestful of medals that the man wore. Werthen knew who this man was immediately, for he was almost as recognizable as the emperor himself: Prince Grunenthal, the éminence grise behind Franz Josef. That the picture was in oils suggested to Werthen that the prince might well be Meindl's sponsor, which would account for the man's meteoric rise in Vienna.

"That there is the possibility of some mistake is why I welcome this visit." Meindl smiled at Gross, ignoring Werthen.

Today he is on our side, Werthen thought. Who knows what tomorrow will bring?

Meindl was clean-shaven and pink-cheeked and wore a pair of the newly invented spring-bridge, tortoiseshell pince-nez. "I strongly advised against a too precipitate arrest. But the criminal police are, as you note, Doktor Gross, under the gun as well as understaffed. The citizens want results. They demand results. And your Herr Klimt *seemingly* presents an easy target. An outsider, someone who flaunts bohemian behavior, who insists on leaving the official art league to set up his own gallery. All artists are a bit unstable then, are they not?"

"So he is to be tried for being an artist?" Werthen said. "Absurd. I see no real evidence."

"There is the matter of the bloody rag found in his studio," Meindl replied, still focusing on Gross.

"A bloody rag does not a crime scene make," Gross noted. "We are still several years away from determining whether such blood is even human in origin."

"Klimt says it is his cat's," Werthen added. "The cat in question got in a fight recently. It lost."

Meindl pursed his lips. "Then why was the rag hidden?"

"Hardly hidden," Werthen protested, finally getting Meindl's direct attention. "It was among a bag of rags Klimt uses to clean his brushes. And if it was actually the blood from the unfortunate Fräulein Landtauer, don't you think he would have destroyed it?"

"Absolutely," Gross concurred. "If anything, one would think the presence of the bloody rag proves the man's innocence. He has nothing to hide."

"Perhaps it was his bizarre form of a memento of the victim." Meindl smiled with thin, saurian lips.

"I assume you are familiar with my writings on blood, Meindl?" Gross said. "The difference between venous and arterial blood splattering? Were Klimt to have opened a victim's artery in his studio, even a dead victim, there would have been a clear splatter pattern. The human body holds five liters of blood more or less, and much of that would have found its way onto the walls and floor of his studio. Quite a cleanup job, yet your men found no other traces of blood besides this rag."

Meindl nodded. "I was not saying I agreed with the criminal police, simply that there are questions that require answers."

"We can produce the corpse of the animal," Werthen said, advancing the attack. He had had a hurried consultation with the painter in his cell at the Landesgericht prison before coming to this meeting with Meindl. Klimt had obviously been distraught, but still cogent enough to dismiss the charges against him.

"Klimt says he buried it under the apricot tree in the studio garden," Werthen added.

"Which proves nothing," Meindl replied sharply. "Herr Klimt could be more clever than any of us give him credit for. Perhaps this is all a feint, a ruse."

"I thought you said you advised against his arrest," Werthen said.

"At this juncture, yes. But we may well find further evidence. To be fair, this murder is the only one with loose ends vis-à-vis the people who knew the victim. In the other cases wives or husbands could all account for their whereabouts at the time of the murder. In Fräulein Landtauer's case, however, the man closest to her, Herr Klimt, cannot account for his whereabouts."

"Or chooses not to," Werthen added.

"Or chooses not to," Meindl allowed. "Which amounts to the same thing."

"You assume Herr Klimt was the girl's only 'friend'?" Gross suddenly asked. "Have you spoken to her roommate?"

"Surely these murders presume someone with more strength than a mere slip of a girl," Meindl replied.

Gross grimaced and shook his head as if disappointed in his former apprentice. Werthen, however, understood what he intended.

"He means that Klimt has told us that Fräulein Landtauer sent a message to cancel their sitting the night she was murdered. She said that she had to take care of her sick roommate. Klimt knew it was a lie, though, for he saw the very roommate leaving his premises after delivering the note. That Fräulein Landtauer felt it necessary to concoct a lie with which to cancel her appointment with Klimt implies a guilty conscience. Perhaps she was seeing another man that evening?"

"That is obviously another matter that needs to be gone into," Meindl said with a sigh. "I understand that the investigators visited the girl's residence, but found nothing untoward."

Meindl sighed, releasing the pince-nez and rubbing the bridge of his nose. "Understand my position. I am not in charge of this case, but I do care about the reputation of the Vienna constabulary. I contacted you this morning, Professor Doktor Gross, as I knew of your interest in the case." A beat, then a grudging nod to Werthen. "And of yours, counselor. I am willing to share with you what we have thus far discovered if it will help to prevent any future embarrassment. Such assistance, must, of course, be in the strictest confidence."

"Of course, Meindl," Gross said.

Ever the careerist, thought Werthen. Meindl was in self-preservation mode. Though Klimt was a painter, he still had some powerful friends. Half the society women in Vienna were said to have sat for him, and in their altogether. These women clearly had persuasive powers over their husbands, for Klimt had also won prize public commissions, creating a series of controversial paintings for the new university entrance, among others. The criminal police surely did not know whom they had in custody; they were thrashing about madly looking for some kind of scapegoat, some success, however temporary.

Meindl, however, *was* aware of the stature of the man they had in custody, Werthen knew. Heads might roll over this arrest, and his would not be among them if Meindl could help it. If

Gross, using information supplied by Meindl, could solve the case, proving Klimt innocent, then Meindl would surely take the credit. Then again, if Klimt was actually proven the guilty party, Meindl's machinations might well go unnoticed, as he had pledged Gross and Werthen to secrecy. Either way he won. No wonder the man had risen so far in the Presidium, Werthen thought. He knew exactly how to maneuver through the system. Such talent would not go unnoticed by a man such as Prince Grunenthal when searching for protégés.

"There is something none of us is mentioning," Gross said.

"And that would be?" Meindl asked.

"The drained blood, the severed noses," Gross prompted.

Meindl replaced his pince-nez. "Yes. One of our inspectors was examining that angle as well. Running down any leads there might be on extremist Jewish groups."

Werthen shifted uneasily in his seat, feeling his blood rise.

"There's not much in that avenue of thought, however," Meindl quickly added.

Gross had the temerity to look disappointed, Werthen noticed.

"There is something that did turn up in that context, though," Meindl said, consulting the file on the desk in front of him. "One of the few connections we were able to come up with between the victims. Two of them had employed the services of a local nerve doctor of Jewish heritage."

He passed a piece of paper to Gross, who handed it to Werthen. He read the name and address: Doktor Sigmund Freud, Berggasse 19.

But first they had a more urgent visit to make. Liesel Landtauer rented a room from a Frau Iloshnya in Vienna's Third District. Uchatiusgasse was a long and undistinguished street, not far from the Landstrasse *Stadtbahn* station. It was named after one of those curious nineteenth-century autodidacts, Baron Freiherr

Franz von Uchatius, an inventor and military man who once ran the Vienna Arsenal. Among his inventions was a primitive projector for moving pictures that predated the American Edison's by fifty years. He gained military renown and a general's rank for his invention of steel bronze that proved effective in casting military weapons. However, when one of the cannon cast from this metal exploded while being demonstrated to the emperor, Uchatius took the Viennese way out and killed himself.

Werthen, a student of his adopted city, was tempted to regale Gross with his own fund of knowledge, but doubted the criminologist would be amused. Instead, he followed Gross to number 13, where the building concierge was busy mopping the hallway. Inquiring directions of her, they were sent to the third floor, to apartment 39. Gross, who was claustrophobic, ignored the elevator in service and took the stairs, huffing mightily by the time they reached the third floor.

Gross bore an official letter from the Police Presidium, given him by Meindl, that convinced the landlady, Frau Iloshnya, to let them into Liesel's room.

"Her roommate, Helga, was so shaken that she left for her parents' in Lower Austria," the lady explained. "She cleared out all her things. Otherwise, the room is the same as poor Liesel left it before her . . ."

"Yes, quite," Gross consoled her with a timid patting on her upper arm.

"She was a good girl, no matter what the papers are saying."

The tabloids had already picked up the story of Klimt's arrest. The afternoon editions hit the streets early, with headlines declaring a LOVERS' QUARREL GONE BAD and BEAUTY AND THE BEAST. The latter paper juxtaposed a photograph of the bearlike and rather demonic-looking Klimt against his sketch of Liesel for his painting *Nuda Veritas*. A newspaper artist had clothed the parts of the body that might offend the good Viennese burghers.

"I am sure she was," Werthen told her.

"Anything I can do to help convict the man," she said. "Anything."

As far as Frau Iloshnya knew, Werthen and Gross were on police business, not attempting to prove Klimt's innocence.

She led them to a small room at the back of the apartment, giving out onto a light shaft. The room was dark in midafternoon. Looking out the window, you could just catch sight of one green branch of a chestnut tree in the courtyard of the apartment building. The room contained two single beds with iron bedsteads; crucifixes hung over the beds. A wardrobe was against the wall opposite the foot of each bed; the door to the one closest to the entrance stood slightly ajar. Gross opened it and discovered it empty.

"Helga's," Frau Iloshnya said. "I don't think she is coming back. She was quite distressed."

As Gross busied himself with a minute examination of the contents of the second wardrobe—the police had already made a cursory inspection and come up with nothing—Werthen tried to keep the attention of the Frau.

"We would appreciate any information you might have about Liesel. Do you know if she had many friends?"

The woman shook her head so vehemently that a strand of white hair dislodged from the bun she wore in back and dangled over her forehead.

"She and Helga stuck together," she said. "Both worked at the same carpet factory."

Gross, overhearing this, shot Werthen a skeptical look. They knew that Liesel had quit this job soon after arriving in Vienna. For the past six months she had made a living as an artist's model, working primarily for Klimt. Gross's look alerted Werthen to take anything the landlady had to offer with a grain of sand. She clearly did not know her tenant.

"No men in her life? She was by all accounts an attractive young woman."

"She was a decent girl," Frau Iloshnya all but shouted.

Gross had climbed atop the one chair in the room and was busily inspecting the top of the wardrobe now, Werthen noted.

"I did not mean to imply otherwise, *gnädige Frau.* But there is nothing improper, per se, dear lady, about having a gentleman caller."

"Not under my roof, I assure you," she said huffily.

To hell with it, Werthen told himself. He would get nothing but trouble from this old bat.

He took her arm and gently but firmly led her to the door. "Thank you so much for your help," he said, moving her out of the room. "We will leave everything as we found it."

She looked surprised, then annoyed, and was about to protest.

"We can let ourselves out," Werthen quickly added, and closed the bedroom door in her face.

"I think we might have something here, Werthen," Gross said, his arm reaching far back on the top of the wardrobe. He nodded as his probing hand touched something, then he produced what appeared to be a packet of letters tied with a red ribbon. He blew on the letters, but no dust came off. He climbed down and sat on the bed.

"Perhaps our Liesel has left us a clue." He unwrapped the packet and opened one letter after another, scanning the contents quickly, until he came to the last letter.

"Aah. Now matters become more interesting."

He handed the letter to Werthen, who read it quickly, nodding at Gross. "This does put a new wrinkle in things, I warrant."

"Perhaps it is time to pay a visit to the theater," Gross said, a twinkle in his eye.

The *Strassenbahn* delivered them twenty minutes later at the Burgtheater.

Werthen was a student of the hypocrisies of late-nineteenth-century Vienna. The building projects of the Ringstrasse had, in particular, informed his short stories, giving a backstory that spoke of sham and artifice. The new ersatz buildings of the Ringstrasse were all gussied up to symbolize their function: neo-Renaissance opera as the home of the arts; neoclassical parliament as a tip of the hat to Greek architecture and the home of democracy; the neo-Gothic Rathaus, symbol of burgher wealth. Here in front of him was the Burgtheater with its lyre-shaped auditorium that was intended to recall the Greek origins of drama. Great on symbols were the Viennese.

The Burgtheater was one of the most egregious monstrosities of the Ring, Werthen thought. Sixteen years in the building, with continual cost overruns spiraling the initial assessment, the Burgtheater or Court Theater—with decorative ceiling paintings by Klimt, among others—opened in 1888 to great fanfare, with four thousand electric lightbulbs illuminating the exterior. Though even now, a decade later, electrification of the city was still a long way off. The night continued to be illuminated by gas, unlike in other European capitals, where electricity was fast becoming the norm. The lyre shape of the theater created a space, according to an actor and critic for the *Neue Freie Presse*, that was an "ornamentation-choked mausoleum which makes performing a misery for me as well as for my colleagues." Speech could not be heard nor actions seen in this performing arts theater. To top it off, the designers had even gotten the symbol wrong: It was not the lyre, but the reed pipe or *aulos* that symbolized the origins of Greek theater. In the event, the acoustics and the sight lines were not improved until just two years ago.

Werthen put such thoughts aside as he followed Gross wordlessly round to the side stage entrance. Here the criminologist presented his letter from the Police Presidium to a skeptical doorman who'd seen every trick in the book employed to get in the stage door to secure autographs from one of the stars.

"Herr Girardi, if you please," Gross said to the man. "Official business."

It didn't help that their business was with the star of the day. The doorman, muttonchopped and flatulent, annoyed that his afternoon wurst break had been interrupted, squinted hard at the card.

"Be quick about it, man," Gross said impatiently, employing his hectoring, prosecutorial tone. "If you don't believe me, you can ring up the Police Presidium. I suppose you do have a telephone here?"

The doorman grunted something unintelligible in their direction, then waved his hand down the hall to the left, obviously indicating the direction of Girardi's dressing room.

The newspapers, Werthen knew, claimed that Girardi was, next to the emperor himself, perhaps the most famous person in all of Vienna at the moment. However, if you personally asked the man or woman in the street whose autograph they would rather have, you might well find nobility coming in a distant second to the stage. A master of dialect, a fine comedian and actor both in drama and operetta, Girardi was something of a phenomenon. His way of dress had infected the city and even saved him from incarceration in a lunatic asylum. Gossip had it that he and his former wife, a volatile actress, had a fearsome marriage, locked in mutual hatred. She had tried to get rid of him by having a doctor, sight unseen, pronounce her husband insane. When the attendants had come to take him to the asylum, they had mistaken a fan lurking outside the actor's house for Girardi himself, for the man was dressed exactly like the actor, right down to the signature straw boater. Known as a folk actor for his roles in popular drama and comedy, Girardi was making his debut at the fustier Burg in a Raimund production. This was a special royal presentation for the emperor, family, noble friends, and visiting Prince of Wales from England, as the Burgtheater and other theaters and concert halls of the city were normally closed from July to September.

Girardi had, like a star in the firmament, his own field of gravity. Even Gross, in Graz, had, apparently, heard of "Der Girardi."

Gross rapped on the star's door.

A voice from inside called out in French, *"Entrée."*

Gross swung the door open wide revealing what appeared at first sight to be the interior of a glasshouse. Flowers were everywhere, roses popping out of vases, violets and lilies worked into celebratory wreaths, bunches of carnations of every hue, and potted plants as well—elephant ears, ferns, and palms in brass tubs. The perfume of the various flowers hit them like an olfactory hammer and held them in the doorway momentarily.

"Yes? What is it?" The large voice came from an exceedingly small man—smaller even than Meindl—all but hidden by purple chrysanthemums in a faux Ming vase set upon a dressing table. The man gazed at them in the reflection of his mirror. His face was as white as that of the corpse in the morgue. However, in Girardi's case the whiteness was achieved by artificial means.

Werthen now understood the reason for part of Girardi's fame: not even gone two o'clock and the man was already getting into makeup. It seemed his whole life must revolve around the theater.

Gross quickly introduced himself, referring to Werthen only as "my colleague."

Girardi stood, muttering, *"Enchanté,"* and looked awfully silly in his opera pumps. He eyed them with a cunning sort of suspicion; an actor assuming the role of discerning speculation. "How may I help you gentlemen?"

"Sorry to trouble you, Herr Girardi. It's the Landtauer matter. Fräulein Elisabeth Landtauer," Gross said.

Girardi changed roles—now he was the shrewd bon vivant.

"Liesel? Dear girl, I know her well. You could say that I *have* known her, in fact." His impeccable Burgtheater German suddenly became infected with the twang of Viennese dialect. Girardi's timing was perfect: a raffish grin came right on cue.

"Are you gentlemen acquainted with her?"

Werthen and Gross exchanged momentary looks.

"Then you don't know," Gross began. "You haven't seen the papers?"

Girardi slowly began to lose his stage roles; a human expression briefly peeked through his masks.

"I do not follow the news before a performance. It unsettles one. What's this about?"

"It is my sad duty to tell you that Fräulein Landtauer is dead. . . . Murdered," Gross added.

For an instant Girardi thought it was a joke in poor taste. He was about to protest the badness of taste, but then saw the pained look in Werthen's eye.

Girardi's hand groped blindly in back of him for the chair at his dressing table, and finding it, he slumped down onto it.

"How?" he muttered barely audibly.

"Someone broke her neck," Gross said, a consoling hand on Girardi's shoulder. "It was instantaneous. She felt no pain."

As silence reigned in the dressing room, the sounds from outside became louder than ever: shouted commands, last-minute hammering on sets, a contralto singing somewhere in the auditorium for God knew what purpose.

"It can't be," Girardi finally said. "There must be some mistake."

Gross shook his head. "I'm afraid not, Herr Girardi. She has been identified."

Girardi looked straight ahead. "When?" Then he looked up at Gross. "What time did this happen?"

"Sometime between midnight and three the night before last. The medical examiner could not be too certain."

Girardi was holding his head in his hands and cupped his eyes. He made a sudden jerk, as if pulling a marionette's string on his own body, straightened in his chair, and clenched his jaw.

"Why have you come to see me about this? How could you even know we were . . . friends?"

Gross produced the packet of letters. "The young woman

saved your letters, you see. The most recent indicates that you were together the night in question."

"Correction," Girardi said, rising once again, a tiny puffed-up rooster ready for a fight. He put his hand out for the letters and Gross obliged him, handing them over.

"She wanted to be together Tuesday night," Girardi continued, slipping the packet into a drawer in his makeup table. "But I sent the girl packing after a light dinner at Sacher's. You may not know it, but I have a premier tonight. Liesel thought it unimportant enough, to be sure. But a man of my age needs sleep more than dalliance for several days before such a performance."

"What time would that be, sir?" Gross said.

Girardi shook his head at the criminologist, not understanding.

"That you sent the girl packing, that is?"

The actor puffed out his lips in contemplation. "No later than eleven. Perhaps quarter past. Ask the waiters at Sacher's. They saw us depart. She on foot, I'm afraid. A trifle miffed at me—refused the *fiaker* I called for her. Just set off into the night like—"

"Yes, sir? Like what?" Gross said.

"Inconsiderate thing to say under the circumstance, but just like a tart. A woman of the night. There are always quite a few of them prowling the streets of an evening."

"And you then went home?" Gross said, reaching for the notepad in his pocket.

"Yes. My valet can vouch for that, if you're wondering. Though I must admit I do not much care to be interrogated like this just prior to a performance."

Werthen could see that the shock was wearing off now. Girardi looked at them both with suspicion.

"And who are you chaps, after all? Not the police, obviously. Are you reporters? I'll have you thrown out." His hand moved to a pull cord next to the dressing table.

"We are trying to establish the unfortunate victim's movements two nights ago," Gross said, stopping the actor with his stentorian tone. "No, we are not reporters. I am Dr. Hanns Gross, formerly of Graz."

This brought not a speck of recognition from Girardi.

"The slightest thing can help in such cases," Werthen quickly chimed in, trying to smooth things again.

Girardi sighed. "Well, talk to that painter chap of hers, then. She was supposed to see him in his studio that night, but came to supper with me instead. See him and find out what he was doing Tuesday night. A broken neck, you say. Well, that man's built like a brick privy."

"This won't do," Gross kept saying as they plodded off along the Ring, the sun bright overhead.

"Intolerable," Gross spluttered again. There was impatience in his voice: desiring commiseration and not getting it.

"What is it now?" Werthen finally asked.

"That jumped-up blacksmith. Mistaking me for some damnable reporter in a celluloid collar. He is from Graz himself and does not even know I am one of the foremost names in criminalistics. That I have written textbooks, founded a journal, advised monarchs and constabularies alike."

"Nerves," Werthen said. "His premier tonight."

This comment, however, did nothing to mollify Gross.

"Telling me my job, 'Go find the painter chap,' he says. Acting high-and-mighty."

"He seemed genuinely surprised to find the Landtauer girl was dead."

"Hmmm."

"But why did you give those letters back to him?"

"I doubt I would repeat the kindness," Gross said, then shrugged. "What do they prove, after all, other than that Girardi is a plagiarist? Tender cooings of love, all expropriated from Shakespeare's sonnets or Lessing's romantic verse. But the Landtauer girl would surely not have known that; lucky if she read the tabloids or the penny dreadfuls."

"They are proof of a liaison," Werthen argued. "Perhaps she was leaving Girardi for Klimt and not the other way round?"

"We would hardly need the letters as proof of their affair. I am sure Herr Girardi would be only too happy for the world to know of that. Such conquests feed the ego. And the Sacher is certainly a public enough rendezvous. We can check his alibi in due course, but I am sure Girardi's story is true. He simply sent the girl packing."

"To her death," Werthen added.

Gross made no reply, but strode along more quickly in the direction of Schottenring.

"So where does this leave us?" Werthen asked, following.

Gross replied over his shoulder, "With just enough time to see a certain nerve doctor before sitting down to a hearty dinner, I should think."

In the event, Doktor Sigmund Freud was not at home. His practice was closed for the month of August, a sign announced. He could, in an emergency, be reached at the Pension zum See, Altaussee, Salzkammergut. The sign was dated August 10; Sigmund Freud had therefore not been in Vienna the night of Liesel Landtauer's death.

"Well, I'd say we've earned ourselves a drink before dinner this busy day," Gross said as they stood examining the sign outside Berggasse 19. "Pity, though. I was looking forward to discussing my work with the man. Heard he is developing some new therapy for nerve patients. A talking cure, he calls it."

"That so?" Werthen, who had himself lain on Freud's couch, said nothing. If Gross could have his secrets, then so could he.

FIVE

They were meeting him at the Café Landtmann near the Burgtheater; the choice of the venue was their guest's. Werthen was still objecting as he and Gross sat at the small marble-topped table to await the arrival of Theodor Herzl, one-time dandy, feuilletonist, and playwright, and more recently founder of Zionism and author of *The Jewish State*.

"Meindl himself said that the Jewish angle was not worth investigating," Werthen reminded the criminologist.

"Since when did you take traveling orders from Meindl? I believe you once accused him of having a second-rate mind."

Gross's elephantine memory could at times be annoying, Werthen thought. Especially when it dredged up uncomfortable truths.

The more Gross became obsessed with the possibility of a Jewish ritual crime, the more Werthen's latent Jewishness came to the fore. He thought it had been well buried by education, money, and conversion to Christianity, but suddenly it reared up in him like an unbidden dragon. He bristled at the suggestion of Jewish blood-letting; it had in fact been the Jews who had suffered, who had lost their blood at the hands of the Christians of Europe for centuries.

Gross had called in a favor from another former student, now an editor of the *Neue Freie Presse,* where Herzl had, until recently, been an editor and essayist. This former student managed to talk Herzl into a brief meeting in the midst of his hectic work life. Scheduling an interview with Herzl to discuss ritual killings or to look for leads to radical Jews capable of such deeds seemed the basest act of demagoguery on Gross's part. Werthen had not credited him with such behavior.

Yet Werthen was going to attend the interview, for his curiosity had gotten the better of him. Herzl's was one of those names that drew public attention in Vienna of late. It was only days away from the Second Zionist Congress, to be held in Basel, and Herzl had assembled Jewish notables from around the world to help plan the new Jewish state, either in Palestine or Argentina. Werthen wanted to know what drove such a man; how he could go from assimilated Austrian to the spokesman for the Jewish state almost overnight?

He recognized Herzl at once as he came through the double doors of the café. He was not a large man, but his long, thick beard was imposing. It gave him the air of a biblical patriarch. Herzl conferred with the headwaiter, Herr Otto, for a moment and was directed to their table. Gross and Werthen both stood to greet the man.

"Good of you to come on such short notice," Gross said, extending his hand to Herzl. "I know you are a busy man, what with the Zionist Congress and your own writing." He motioned Herzl to the bentwood Thonet chair set aside for him.

Introductions were made, and when Herzl made the usual polite response, *"Es freut mich,"* Werthen was almost shocked by the dissimilarity of his appearance and voice. The imposing patriarch, impeccably dressed in a dove-gray suit which looked to have been tailored by the noble firm of Knieze on the Graben, was suddenly diminished by a voice only a few registers below a castrato's.

Gross did not seem to notice, but charged on with a quick discussion of the murders they were investigating. Herzl allowed that he had read of some of them in the papers.

"I have not, however, followed the matter closely, as I have been rather pressed for time of late."

High or not, the voice had resonance and force. He spoke slowly, as if each word held special import, or as if he may once have stuttered and was working through his block with each utterance. The overall effect was rather hypnotic for Werthen; it made one hang on each word.

"Indeed, I am not sure how I can help you in your inquiries, gentlemen," Herzl said.

Werthen glared at Gross, whose eyes were fixed on Herzl. "It is a matter of a possible Jewish connection," Gross began. Then he described more exactly the wounds inflicted on the victims and the draining of their blood.

"I see," Herzl said. "Jewish ritual killings, is that it?"

"Exactly." Gross always enjoyed being in the company of men or women who demonstrated intuitive and intellectual abilities, for whom he did not need to spell out each word.

"Or the appearance of such," Werthen quickly added.

"My esteemed colleague makes an important point. Or the appearance of such. Tell me, Herr Herzl, do you know of anyone specifically—"

Here it comes, Werthen thought. He was about to interrupt, when Gross surprised him.

"—who has a grudge against you? Anyone or any group that might want to discredit Zionism or the Jewish people by such a charade of bestial crimes? Anyone who may have made a threat, verbal or written, to you or your organization of late?"

Werthen felt his scowl being replaced by an admiring glance at Gross. The criminologist smiled benignly, awaiting an answer from Herzl.

Herzl chuckled beneath his breath. "Where should I begin, Doktor Gross? How long a list do you want?"

"A man in your position surely comes to have a sixth sense in these matters. I assume you can discern the merely ignorant from the seriously malevolent."

Herzl nodded. "It is, unfortunately, a skill I have learned to hone. I will have my secretary prepare a list of those we have already noted as serious risks. Where may I send it?"

Gross gave him his room number at the Bristol.

As he was preparing to leave, Herzl said, "Have either of you gentlemen read my *Jewish State*?"

"I haven't had the opportunity," Werthen replied. "But I shall, I shall. . . . Tell me, Herr Herzl, how is it you came back to Judaism?"

"You are Jewish in background, *Advokat* Werthen?"

"I am, yes." Werthen found a sudden pride in this admission.

"Then you know as well as I the subterfuges one makes regarding his origins. The desperate attempts to fit in gentile society, to deny any influence that heritage might have on one. You are perhaps aware of my early career as a playwright and ambitious young dilettante. But when I covered the Dreyfus trial in Paris for the *Neue Freie Presse*, I came to realize that no matter how hard we try, we will always be outsiders in European society. Now I look upon my early life as something of a waste. I was mere refuse waiting to be transformed into something useful."

Herzl sat in silence for a moment, as if he had said too much.

"Hardly a waste, Herr Herzl," Gross said. "In my provincial outpost of Graz, I was brought into contact with a wider world by your writing. The 'Palais Bourbon, Pictures of the Parliamentary Life of France' series was, in particular, inspiring."

Herzl nodded solemnly at the compliment. Werthen, too, was amazed that the criminologist ever found time to read anything but forensic reports.

"Still, I personally see those as wasted years," Herzl replied, addressing them both. "In ways the Jews of Europe are the refuse of human society, just as I once viewed my own life as refuse. I therefore see my personal transformation as a model for the collective transformation of the Jews. Read, if you have the time, my short story 'The Inn of Aniline.' It is all written there. I now long only for a life full of manly deeds, which will expunge and eliminate everything base, wanton, and confused that has ever been in me."

After Herzl had left, Werthen and Gross remained at the table for a time, planning their next move.

"I need to confer with Klimt again," Werthen allowed. "Perhaps he has ascertained his whereabouts the nights of the other murders."

"Capital idea," Gross said. "As for me, it's a visit to the Police Forensic Department, a guest of our esteemed Inspektor Meindl. They have arranged a viewing of autopsy photographs for me."

He said it with the obvious relish most people would reserve for a night out at the theater or at a restaurant.

"Research for an article for my *Archive of Criminalistics*," Gross said with heavy irony.

Meindl's cover story, Werthen assumed. The man was not going to stick his neck out too far, lest his head be chopped off.

They arranged to meet at the forensic lab after Werthen's interview with Klimt.

Werthen paid the bill, then, before donning his hat, said, "I noticed you gave Herzl your address at the Bristol. Does that mean you are not leaving for Czernowitz as soon as planned?"

Gross looked at him from hooded eyes. "Nor do I see you boarding the train for your parents' country estate, my dear Werthen. Not while there is work afoot."

Werthen hesitated, wondering if he should broach the subject, but finally plunged ahead.

"You took me off guard with your line of questions for Herzl. I feel I owe you an apology."

"Don't be absurd, man. So you mistook me for an anti-Semite. I've been taken for worse. And it was not to protect your delicate feelings that I did so. No, indeed. The crimes are an obvious provocation, as you suggested. Either committed by a fanatical anti-Semite, or by some other very clever chap who wishes to muddy the water, to create diversions and false leads."

"I am glad you think so."

"Make no doubt about it, however. There is such a thing as ritual killings. See the next issue of my *Archive of Criminalistics* for a long article on such Afro-Caribbean syncretic religions as Santeria, voodoo, and Palo Mayombe. Ritual murder plays a dominant role in those beliefs. As I say, just because a fact is abhorrent does not mean we should ignore or deny it."

Werthen was shown into Klimt's cell at the Landesgericht prison, a cramped and airless space he shared with two unsavory-looking characters who, Werthen knew, were also charged with murder. In their cases, however, he could imagine the accusations bore some semblance to reality. They had the unhealthy pallor, the suspicious cast to their eyes, and the arrogant aspect of career criminals.

The guards herded these two out so that Werthen could conference with his client. But as they left, the taller and meaner-looking of the two stared at Werthen.

"You take good care of him, hear? I keep telling him he needs a real criminal lawyer, but Gustl's the loyal sort. Don't let him down."

"Move on," a guard said, prodding the man with his nightstick.

"It'll be fine, Hugo," Klimt told the man. "Not to worry."

Werthen waited for the cell door to slam shut behind the guards. "'Gustl'?"

"I seem to have made some friends. Actually, good enough chaps in their own way. But they never had a chance in life. Hugo for instance. His dad was killed working in a textile factory. No compensation for the family, and with the breadwinner gone, his mother was forced to rent out her body when Hugo was just a boy. He heard and saw everything. He was working the streets as a pickpocket by the time he was seven."

"Yes, I am sure these men have a wealth of stories. Enough to inspire a Stifter or a Grillparzer."

"It's given me a new outlook on life," Klimt said, his eyes shining. "And I thought I had it hard when my father died and I was left to take care of the family."

He beamed as he spoke. In fact, Werthen thought, the man had never looked healthier, as if he were actually enjoying his incarceration.

"But now to the matter at hand," Werthen said. "Have you been able to trace your movements for the dates in question?"

Klimt sat on the metal bunk bed and patted the mattress next to him for Werthen to do the same.

"Afraid I'm not being much help to you, old friend. Emilie has looked up the dates in her diaries, and it seems every time I was working late in the studio. Alone. But then I was there most nights for the past few months finishing the Sonja Knips portrait and also putting the final touches on my *Pallas Athene*. Deadlines, deadlines, as if I were a bookkeeper and not an artist."

Werthen rubbed his brow.

"Is this bad? Aren't you and Gross any closer to finding the real killer?"

Werthen brought Klimt up-to-date with their investigation.

"But if this Meindl fellow believes I am innocent . . ."

"I didn't say that," Werthen quickly put in. "He is simply looking out for his own career. Playing both sides for now."

"Well, then," Klimt said cheerily, "perhaps the list Herzl sends will prove some help. I'm innocent, remember? They can't condemn an innocent man."

Just then a door slammed and a subsequent thudding sound came from down the long prison-block corridor.

Werthen made no notice of the sound, but by the sudden look

of despair on Klimt's face, he realized that the painter knew what that sound meant: The guards were trying out the gallows for an execution scheduled later that day.

Gross was still examining an assortment of photographs spread out on a long table in a corner room of the forensic lab when Werthen arrived. Afternoon sunlight poured in through north-facing windows, a swath of golden light filled with nervous dust motes. Gross was using a powerful magnifying glass to look at the photos, so intent on his work that he did not hear Werthen come into the room. It was a full ten minutes before the criminologist put the lens down and noticed his colleague.

"What is the good word from Klimt?"

Werthen shook his head. "No alibis for any of the dates. But he seems to be enjoying his enforced holiday. Have you found anything?"

"Nothing more than confirmation of what I already suspected."

"Which is?"

"Take a look at these." Gross aligned five photos, all displaying the same patch of neck, and all with a single cut.

"These are the carotid wounds on each of the five victims. Thank whomever that the Vienna forensics people have read my work and taken advantage of the power of photography. There are excellent sets of autopsy photos for each of the victims. As of today, four of the victims have already been buried, so without these prints I would never have been able to make such comparisons."

"They look like very similar cuts," Werthen said, using only his naked eye.

"Indeed, very similar," Gross said, handing him the magnifying glass.

Werthen examined each cut in turn.

"In fact," Gross said, "almost identical, wouldn't you say?"

"Yes," Werthen said, putting the lens down, "but then I'm no expert."

"I am and I say they are so similar that they could only have been made by the same hand. And a trained one at that. Either this killer has trained as a surgeon, or he is a professional killer with a large degree of experience."

"You can tell that from cuts?"

"Incisions," Gross corrected. "And, yes, I can. There is nothing tentative about these incisions, no puckered flesh or abrasions where the killer made probing attempts. I assume also that our killer is right-handed, for the incision is deeper on the right side of the cut than the left. Ergo, the incision was started there and drawn across the artery in one smooth, sure stroke. Additionally, I surmise the instrument used was a scalpel or perhaps a cut-throat razor, for no knife blade can be sharpened to the precision which these cuts demonstrate. Which also lends to the argument of a trained doctor or physician having a hand in these killings."

"Or a barber," Werthen joked, then frowned, taking in Gross's last comment. "A hand, you say?"

"The victims were first murdered, their necks broken, and later the blood was drained. The killer then need not necessarily have drained the blood himself. There could be more than one person involved."

"This grows more convoluted by the hour, Gross. Shall I add to the convolutions?"

"Be my guest," Gross replied.

"It struck me walking here that there may be an alternate explanation for these crimes. What if Herr Klimt is the real victim?"

Gross squinted his eyes, nodding. "Then all of these murders were just to make Klimt look like the guilty party."

"The thought did arise," Werthen said. "It would take somebody close to the painter, who knew his schedule and the fact that he had no alibi for any of the murders. Which means any of dozens of fellow artists."

"Jealousy," Gross pronounced, "can rear its ugly head in all fields of human endeavor. I assume by leaving the official art league and founding the Secession, our Herr Klimt may have rubbed some of the more academic painters the wrong way."

"Enough to kill five innocent people to seek revenge?" Werthen asked, testing his own hypothesis.

Gross shrugged. "I have uncovered vile perpetrators with even less motivation."

"Between Herzl's list and Klimt's associates, we'll be investigating half of Vienna."

"If it comes to that. Easier might be tracking the weapon."

"How many scalpels and razors could there be in Vienna? Isn't this just another needle in a haystack, Gross?"

"Not at all, dear friend." Gross put the magnifying glass to his eye again and pointed out the incision on the picture marked M5. Using the sharpened point of a lead pencil, he indicated a section of the wound at about the midpoint.

"Examine this part closely, if you will. Tell me what you see with the edges of the wound."

Werthen gazed through the glass at the incision, focusing and refocusing on the marked section. Finally he saw what Gross's trained eye had discerned.

"Seems to be a light feathering of the flesh."

"Excellent, Werthen. Exactly what it is. But not discernible in the other four victims."

"I assume you put this down not to a change in perpetrator, but rather to a change in instrument."

"Again, spot on, Werthen. You follow my methodology exactly. The length, depth, and shall we say boldness of the stroke does not change in the five victims, only the appearance of the light feathering."

"This would be Fräulein Landtauer's, the most recent?"

Another nod from Gross.

"Perhaps the blade needs sharpening?"

"No, my friend. I am a student of such esoterica as blades and guns. I believe our man has come into possession of one of these newfangled serrated scalpels the British firm of Harwood and Meier has been experimenting with. Serrated blades leave such feathering, and for that reason the technology has not heretofore been used for scalpels, intended for clean, easily repaired cuts. The Harwood model, however, boasts added septic protection as a trade-off for the light feathering. Whereas our man was using a traditional steel scalpel or razor before, he has recently switched to the serrated scalpel. And that is, I guarantee you, Werthen, hardly a needle in a haystack. To my certain knowledge, there are only a handful of distributors of the Harwood and Meier blades in this country. We will start then with the distributors and work back to the purchasers. Even if stolen, the blade in question had to originate somewhere."

He had followed the tall lawyer back from the prison to the building that housed Vienna's forensic laboratory. The dandified lawyer had no idea he was being tracked; an amateur for certain. He was also getting into water that would soon engulf him and his professor friend. For the moment, they were simply paddling about, testing the water. He smiled at his metaphor. That was good, just paddling about, but sometimes even amateurs get lucky, hit the right current.

For now the two were no threat to him or to his *operation*.

Another smile slashed his gaunt face. He really was being clever today. *Operation*, indeed. It was nearing the end, though, and he felt a kind of sadness at that thought. These murders had been a challenge worthy of him.

He looked up again to the windows of the forensic laboratory and shook his head.

No, they were not a threat. For now.

SIX

The foehn wind blew in overnight from the Southern Alps, scorching the city in its dry blast, fraying nerves, and sending hats flying.

Werthen slept in and was still nursing a hangover by lunchtime. He and Gross had gone to a *Heurige,* a wine tavern, in Sievering, one of a string of wine villages on the outskirts of the city. There they had downed numerous glasses of Neuburger wine and dined on cold cuts of pork, bowls of cheese spread, and pickled salads. Werthen had forgone the old Viennese recipe for avoiding a *Heurige* hangover: a piece of rye bread spread with drippings or schmaltz to coat the stomach. It had been too hot for such a prophylactic, and now he was suffering for it.

He was due to meet Gross in the afternoon to continue their search for the salesmen of medical instruments, but before then, he had to get his physical ship in order. Gross had, of course, held his wine well last night, not once bursting into song, as Werthen had felt compelled to do when the Gypsy band played a popular ditty at their table. That he knew the lyrics to such a tune was a surprise to Werthen, but it was hard to avoid these things. *Fiaker* drivers were forever whistling well-liked tunes or singing the lyrics as they drove their carriages; counterpeople at the bakeries and the fruit shop in Werthen's district were also avid devotees of the more rough-and-tumble popular culture. Though he seldom did his own shopping, Werthen did come into contact with all sorts of people.

Osmosis, he told himself now, as he left his apartment building headed for his local café for a restorative lunch. The popular culture seeps into one's very pores unbidden.

Just outside his building he was given a *Grüss Gott* by Frau Korneck, the building *Portier*. He tipped his hat at her. As if to prove his osmosis theory, she was humming a tune from a Strauss operetta as she swept the sidewalk in front.

Werthen crossed the street, playing back the scene last night with the *Zigeuner* band at the wine house. No. Most definitely he had not danced. That was some kind of blessing, at any rate. He had merely sung, though painfully off tune. Then he further recalled a vision of Gross watching him, bearing one of his enigmatic smiles that could signify anything from mild enjoyment to contempt.

His irritation was compounded when, reaching the Café Eiles, he discovered it had begun its annual two-week summer closure yesterday. Werthen had not kept abreast of such things, for it had been his habit to spend much of August with his parents. And then he was reminded of a further duty: he would have to telegraph his parents and let them know that his arrival would be delayed even further. Though, truth be told, he did not look forward to that visit for a number of reasons, not the least of which was his parents' infernal attempts at matchmaking.

"*Advokat* Werthen?"

He had been so consumed with his own thoughts and concerns that he had not noticed the man approaching him. He was a tall, rough-boned-looking fellow, dressed in a heavy suit completely inappropriate for the weather, and he wore no hat. His face was weathered from the sun and he looked unaccustomed to his stiff clothes. From his demeanor and the cut of the suit, it was obvious to Werthen the man was from the country.

"Yes," Werthen responded. "May I help you?"

"I'm sorry to bother you like this, but, you see, I was told I should look you up."

The man's heavy accent confirmed to Werthen that he was indeed from the country, and most probably from the far west: Tyrol or Salzburg.

"You have the better of me," Werthen said. The man squinted at him, not understanding. "You know my name, sir, but I am ignorant of yours."

The man quickly wiped his right hand on his trousers and held it out to Werthen.

"Name's Landtauer. Josef Landtauer."

It was Werthen's turn to squint now. A sudden gust of warm wind almost blew his derby off his head, but he steadied it with his hand.

"I've come to town to collect my daughter. Liesel."

They found a *Gasthaus* with a shady garden near the Rathaus and ordered beer with the daily special, smoked ham and sauerkraut. They sat at a table beneath a massive chestnut tree that seemed to breathe coolness over them.

Once the waitress—clad in a powder blue dirndl in the style of Lower Austria—set the orders in front of them, they resumed their conversation.

"Perhaps first you should explain why you want to visit Herr Klimt," Werthen said.

Landtauer, as they were looking for an eatery, had explained that yesterday, arriving in the city from his native Vorarlberg (Werthen had been close in placing the accent), he had gone to the prison to visit Klimt, but had been told by the jailors that only family or his legal counsel was allowed access to the prisoner. In the event, they had supplied Landtauer with Werthen's name; a quick examination of the new telephone directory at a post and telephone exchange had supplied him with Werthen's office address, where there was a phone, as well as his home address, even though he had no phone installed as yet at his apartment. Too shy to call on the lawyer without introduction, Landtauer had been pacing up and down the street wondering on what course of action to take when Werthen left his apartment and Landtauer heard the *Portier* address him by name. He had simply followed, still unsure how to approach the man, he'd explained.

"It is a rather odd request, you must admit, Herr Landtauer."

"It's not like you think," the large and ungainly man said as he tucked into his meal. "My Liesel, she wrote back to me and told me what a kind man Herr Klimt had been to her. A real gentleman, she said. The way she described him in her letters, I figure the fellow can't be a murderer."

Landtauer's eyes began to tear up as he said the last word. He took a swig of the foamy beer as if to chase away the sadness.

"I cannot tell you how sorry I am for your loss, Herr Landtauer. From everything I have heard, your daughter was a wonderful girl." Werthen was always at sea in such situations; he hoped his white lies provided solace. The words echoed hollowly to him, though.

"She was, *Advokat* Werthen. A true angel of a girl." Landtauer wiped a rough sleeve across his watery eyes. "Her mother died when she was just a wee one, and I raised her on my own. Raised her to be honest and God-fearing. I'll be straight with you, I never wanted her to come to the capital. Knew she'd be exposed to wicked people and wicked ways."

For a moment another emotion other than sorrow showed in the man's eyes. Then he quickly took another gulp of beer. Werthen joined him.

"Have they released your daughter's body?" Werthen asked.

The big man nodded solemnly.

"Then leave it at that, Herr Landtauer. Take your daughter home and bury her. Seeing Herr Klimt will not help your grief. I can only assure you I also believe him to be innocent. I and my friend Professor Doktor Hanns Gross are working to find the real culprit. That person or persons will be brought to justice, I swear that." Another white lie? Werthen wondered. After all, his first and primary obligation in this matter was to secure Klimt's release and freedom. What came after that, well . . . ?

"I wish I could just leave it at that," Landtauer said. "But I feel honorbound to visit the man my daughter praised so highly. It's like an unpaid debt. I couldn't rest easy knowing I hadn't seen it through."

He fixed Werthen with a pleading look. "You'll help me, sir, I know you will. You, too, seem like a kind gentleman."

They ate on in silence. Finished, Werthen dabbed at his lips with the linen napkin, folding it again neatly and placing it by his plate, knife and fork resting side by side at a diagonal to signal his completion. Meanwhile, Landtauer soaked up the last of the meat juices with a thick slice of rye bread.

"First time I've had a real meal in days," he said, eyeing the scraps still remaining on Werthen's plate. "Ever since getting the news. Local constabulary knocked at the door just as I was sitting down to lunch. It's been a nightmare ever since, I can tell you."

Werthen nodded at the waitress for the bill, and the big man struggled a change purse out of his coat pocket.

"No, please. Allow me, Herr Landtauer."

Werthen placed the correct amount plus a generous tip on top of the bill. The buxom waitress flashed him a smile as he and Landtauer left the restaurant and came out into the glaring sunlight of Reichsratsstrasse. A Saturday afternoon in the midst of August, the street was virtually deserted. Half of Vienna was off taking the waters at a spa or hiking in the Alps, while Werthen was left sweltering in Vienna and looking into the pleading eyes of a man who had just lost his only daughter. Words alone could not console, he knew.

"It can only be a short visit, Herr Landtauer."

The man grabbed Werthen's hand and shook it vigorously.

The Landesgericht prison was in back of the Rathaus, a few blocks away. Werthen led Landtauer to the registration, where he signed his own name and added "plus guest."

"They've finished lunch," the red-nosed desk sergeant told Werthen. "Just coming back to their cells. Be a few minutes."

They waited at the registry, Landtauer pacing back and forth, his thick-fingered hands held tightly in back of him. Poor man, Werthen thought. His daughter's loss had to be a terrible blow.

Finally a warder came to take them to Klimt's cell. Klimt, lounging on his bunk, tipped a forefinger at Werthen and looked quizzically at his companion.

"Wait here while I explain matters to Herr Klimt," Werthen told Landtauer.

"Just want to shake his hand," the man said. "Tell him that. For being so good to my Liesel."

Werthen patted his shoulder. "I'll let him know."

Inside the cell Werthen quickly explained the man's presence.

"Well, bring him in, Werthen, by all means," Klimt said volubly.

Werthen turned to Klimt so that his back was to Landtauer, outside the cell; the man could neither see his face nor hear him.

"Perhaps it is best just to say hello through the bars. I don't personally know the man. He seems honestly devastated by his daughter's death, but—"

"Nonsense," said Klimt emphatically. "I will see the man face-to-face and with no bars between us. Then he'll know I could never have killed his daughter."

Klimt shouted to the guard outside the door, "Well, what are you waiting for, Officer? Show the man in, please."

Klimt's two cellmates, who had been listening to the conversation, swung their legs off their bunks. Hugo, the taller one, said, "You think that's a good idea, Gustl?"

"The man's lost his daughter," Klimt said over his shoulder. "It's the least I can do."

"Seems dodgy to me," Hugo said, glaring at Werthen.

The cell door swung open and Josef Landtauer entered, a grateful smile on his lips.

"Herr Klimt," he said, closing on the painter, who held out his hand to the man. "This is from my daughter."

The man simultaneously closed the cell door behind him and pulled his hand from his pocket to produce a knife. He lunged at Klimt.

Werthen, seated on the bed between the two men, acted out of instinct. He thrust a foot out and Landtauer tripped over it, falling onto his face in the cell. Hugo leaped from his upper bunk, crushing the man's knife hand underfoot. Landtauer groaned in pain, but this only seemed to infuriate him further. He tossed the inmate off his hand like so much firewood and was on his feet again before the guard could get the cell door unlocked and come to their aid.

"Put the knife down," another guard shouted from outside the cell.

"You bastard," Landtauer spit at Klimt. "You killed my Liesel. You're going to pay."

Klimt crouched as if to do battle with the man.

"Guard!" Werthen shouted. "Do something."

The first guard was still fumbling with his key in the lock while the one behind him was attempting to get a clear shot at Landtauer. However, Klimt was in his way.

Landtauer swiped the knife at Klimt, who managed to parry the thrust. The painter tore the blanket from his bed and quickly wrapped it around his left arm.

"I didn't kill her, I swear," he said to Landtauer in a surprisingly calm voice. "Put the knife down, man, before someone gets hurt."

"You fiend, beast, animal," Landtauer growled. "You defiled my little angel."

Landtauer made another lunge, which Klimt blocked with his wrapped arm, but the knife managed to cut through the thin blanket, leaving a streak of red behind.

Just as the guard was bursting through the cell door, Hugo jumped on Landtauer's back, ripping at his eyes with long, bony fingers. Landtauer screamed in pain, twisting his body and flailing with both arms. He finally managed to stab Hugo in his left thigh, but by then the guard had drawn his weapon and put the cold metal of the barrel next to Landtauer's temple.

"Enough," the guard said. "I'll use it. Now drop the knife."

Landtauer stared around him like a caged animal, his eyes wide and his breath fast and shallow. Suddenly he crumpled into a ball on the floor, the knife clattering beside him.

Werthen quickly kicked the knife aside, and the guard put handcuffs on Landtauer, now blubbering incoherently. As the guard lifted the man to his feet, Werthen saw a familiar-looking piece of newsprint in the inside pocket of Landtauer's coat. Werthen reached in and removed the paper, unfolding it to discover the front page of one of Vienna's gutter tabloids. This one had run a picture of Klimt next to the sketch of Liesel as *Nuda Veritas*.

Landtauer seemed to come to himself for a moment seeing the page of newsprint. "I would have killed the little bitch myself rather that let that pig sully her." He thrust his head around to look at Klimt as the guards dragged him from the cell. "May you rot in hell, you piece of filth!"

"Sounds like a busy afternoon" was Gross's first comment when, later that evening, ensconced in Gross's suite of rooms at the

Bristol, and poring over the evidence thus far collected, Werthen told him of his misadventures.

"It was all my fault."

"Nonsense," Gross said, scanning the enemies list Herzl's secretary had hand-delivered that afternoon. "You warned Klimt. It was only his own misguided sense of duty and honor that put him in jeopardy."

"I should never have taken Landtauer to the prison. But he seemed genuine to me. So much for my ability to read my fellow man."

"I wouldn't be too hard on yourself, Werthen. I am sure the man's grief *was* genuine, whatever its origin. And even the lowliest villager can demonstrate an animal cunning in times of crisis."

"I tell you, Gross, Girardi could take lessons from our Josef Landtauer."

"Speaking of whom," Gross said, "I had the opportunity to check on his story this afternoon. The headwaiter at the Sacher remembers him in the company of a young woman the night in question and that they left separately."

"At least one of us has been doing something productive today." Werthen sighed audibly.

"And how is Klimt and his criminal protector?"

"A superficial wound for Klimt, though he was shaken by the incident. Prison is no longer such a lark for him, that is sure. And his newfound friend Hugo has secured a cushy place in the sick ward for the time. Perhaps it will even work to his credit when he is brought up on murder charges himself, that he stopped a homicide in the Landesgericht."

"Landtauer, I assume, is a guest of the state?" Gross said, laying aside the list and returning to a perusal of a Vienna telephone directory.

Werthen nodded. "Klimt refused to press charges, and the police were willing to simply put it down to the effects of the foehn."

Vienna's sirocco, a warm wind that blew off the Alps, unnerved the steadiest of men. Surgeries were not performed during these winds; the presence of the foehn was a legal defense in some cases, to Werthen's chagrin. "But I requested them to contact the constabulary in Vorarlberg first and ascertain whether Landtauer had any history of violent behavior. It was quickly enough discovered the man was infamous for the way he beat his family. The police there in fact suspected him of beating his wife to death, though they could not prove it. His daughter Liesel, it seems, ran away from his abuse the first chance she could get. The Vorarlberg police say Landtauer has been a laughingstock ever since the penny press splashed Klimt's nude portrait of Liesel all over the front pages. Not able to even show his face at the local *Gasthaus*."

"So Landtauer was avenging himself rather than his daughter when he attacked Klimt," Gross surmised.

"It would appear so."

Gross shook his head. "Charming man, Herr Landtauer. But, let us put all this behind us, right, Werthen? No real harm done."

"Once the newspapers get wind of this, they will have a high old time." The lawyer sighed, leaning back in the rococo chair and sipping from a snifter filled with fine cognac. One thing the ruckus had done: cured him of his hangover. "The gutter press will be trying Klimt in its pages now, most likely turning that hideous paterfamilias Landtauer into a national hero and Klimt into a despoiler of young virgins."

But Gross was no longer listening; his attention, briefly diverted by Werthen's tale, was again fully focused on the long refectory table he'd had installed in his rooms. Spread out upon it were photos of the victims that Gross had borrowed from the forensic lab and lists of possible suspects supplied by Herzl and compiled by Werthen of Klimt's possible rivals and enemies.

There was also a list sent by special messenger from Inspektor Meindl, which contained names of political dissidents and anarchists who were being watched; according to Meindl these people might be interested in stirring up trouble of any sort that might lead to a revolution. Gross dismissed this as poppycock, but Werthen decided to examine the watch list closely for possible suspects, only to be alternately amazed and amused by those who had made the list: everybody from hardened Italian anarchists to homegrown critics of the government such as Herzl and the socialist Viktor Adler.

Next to these were stacks of notes in Gross's precise and minuscule hand, a playbill from the Burgtheater advertising the Girardi performance, and the Vienna telephone directory for 1898, which had dozens of bookmarks gummed in place.

Later that evening, they met another former colleague of Gross's from his Graz days. Richard Freiherr von Krafft-Ebing, chair of the psychiatry department of the University of Vienna. Werthen, too, was familiar with the man, for he had been director of the Feldhof Asylum near Graz until 1889, when he was summoned to Vienna to become director of the State Lunatic Asylum. Then in 1892 he took the chair in psychiatry at the University of Vienna vacated by the death of Theodor Hermann Meynert. Werthen knew Krafft-Ebing in his role as forensic psychiatrist, who both aided in developing profiles of suspected criminals from the specifics of their crimes, as well as championed the cause of what was becoming known as diminished capacity. For Krafft-Ebing, those who committed crimes because of mental illness should not be held accountable for such crimes. Instead, he proposed the novel concept of treatment rather than punishment, a course that would never, Werthen thought, find a basis in law.

Added to this, Krafft-Ebing was among the foremost researchers in syphilis and its side effects, a believer in hypnotism as a possible treatment for mental problems, and a pioneer of the study of sexual deviancy. His 1886 book, *Psychopathia Sexualis,* documented hundreds of cases of what Krafft-Ebing termed masochism, sadism, and other deviancies, including homosexuality, incest, and pederasty. Despite that Krafft-Ebing had written the case histories in Latin to avoid sensationalism, the textbook had still become an international bestseller, which never ceased to embarrass this prudish man. It was said that the sale of Latin dictionaries increased tenfold in Germany and Austria at the time of the first publication of *Psychopathia Sexualis.*

Krafft-Ebing hardly looked the part of a social revolutionary. He was of medium height and dressed conservatively. His graying and thinning hair was cut short, and his beard trimmed to a sharp V under his chin. His eyes were the most distinctive thing about the man, Werthen thought. They were gray-green and full of a kind of luminescence that seemed to come from within.

He was kind enough to act as if he remembered Werthen, but the lawyer doubted it. Krafft-Ebing and Gross were, however, fast friends as well as colleagues.

They met at the Griechenbeisl, a favorite of Werthen's in the First District, and after a few minutes of small talk and study of the menu, Gross got down to business. They were seated in one of the private booths, so they could speak freely. Gross explained to the psychologist the crimes they were investigating, detailing minutely the wounds to the bodies of each of the victims.

The first course arrived, and Krafft-Ebing, obviously not put off with such graphic details, happily attacked the liver dumpling floating in his consommé.

"No signs of sexual interference, I take it?" he asked.

"None whatever. Though . . ."

Krafft-Ebing, seeming to understand Gross's unspoken reservations, said, "I quite agree. Such wounds could be a sign of inversion on the part of the killer. Inspired by certain deep-seated neuroses, sexual in nature, but which are released asexually. Which means that the killer keeps his deviancy well under control. He . . . I assume you suspect a male killer?"

Gross nodded, forking some cucumber salad into his mouth.

"*He,*" Krafft-Ebing continued, "would be a person no one could suspect of deviancy. Outwardly, he projects the picture of decorum and balance. Inwardly he seethes. This makes your work that much more difficult."

"You are describing half of Vienna," Werthen joked.

"Do not misunderstand me," Krafft-Ebing said, his eyes burning a hole in Werthen. "Sexual feeling is the root of all ethics. However, sexual feelings, misguided, can also be the most damaging impulse known in society. It is not to be taken lightly."

"That is why you are here," Gross said, his demeanor also having taken on a new gravitas.

As if satisfied by this avowal, Krafft-Ebing went on, "The nose is intriguing. The obvious inference—further enhanced by the draining of the blood—would be a Jewish ritual murder."

"We *had* wondered about that," Gross said, raising his eyebrows at Werthen.

"As I say, that is the obvious inference. However, my research in syphilis suggests another possibility." Krafft-Ebing took a moment, dabbing his lips with his linen napkin.

The three were silent while a serving girl, under the direction of the tuxedoed headwaiter, delivered the house specialty, *Pariser Schnitzel,* made with paper-thin cuts of fresh veal.

When the girl left, Krafft-Ebing continued, "Modern systems of treatment with mercury have led to progress, but still fifteen percent of the male population are estimated to be infected with the disease. We all know famous examples of those who have suffered and died. Most notably here in Vienna, the painter Hans Makart."

Krafft-Ebing paused for a moment to cut a trim bite of schnitzel and pop it in his mouth. Werthen was growing impatient with the man's account, wondering what this might have to do with their own case. Gross, however, the lawyer noted, was nodding his head appreciatively at the psychologist.

"The disease proceeds in a step-by-step pattern," Krafft-Ebing began again. "The first stage is characterized by a chancre sore that develops about three weeks after contact with an infected person. This is followed by skin rash, headache, fever, and enlarged lymph nodes about two months thereafter. The second stage. At these early stages, the disease is easiest to treat, but many ignore the symptoms, which eventually go away. The infected person may live a healthy, normal life for another year, or perhaps even ten, before the tertiary stage begins. Here begins the degeneration of the nervous system, the infection of the cardiovascular system, disorders of the spinal cord, general paralysis." He shook his head. "A horrible disease, to be sure. Gentlemen, I still hold that sexual feeling is the root of all ethics rather than the root of all evil. When manifested for its true purpose, procreation, sex is a gift from God. Yet when used for sordid enjoyment or perverted ends, then . . ." He spread his hands.

By now, even Gross had grown impatient for the psychologist to connect this long aside with the business at hand.

"And you believe that syphilis plays a part in these crimes?" Gross prompted.

"You have heard of the One Hundred Club perhaps?"

Both Werthen and Gross had to shake their heads.

"A cynical association if there ever were one," Krafft-Ebing pronounced with venom in his voice. "A society of upper-class men—I refuse to call them gentlemen—who wear what they term the badge of sexual honor. Roués and debauched members of society's elite who have been infected with syphilis and proudly display its ravages. Many of the members are forced to wear leather noses, for in the late stages of the illness, the bacteria eats away at cartilaginous areas, including joints and the nose. It is said that Archduke Otto, younger brother of the heir apparent, Franz

Ferdinand, is a prominent member of the One Hundred Club. Young virgins are brought to the celebrations of this perverted group and are infected."

"Scandalous," Werthen blurted out.

"Inspired!" Gross exclaimed, exhibiting a contrary emotion, though not at the activities of those debauchees, but rather at Krafft-Ebing's insight. "They are in fact 'thumbing their nose' at society, is that it Freiherr?"

"Afraid so," Krafft-Ebing replied. "The 'noseless ones' has become, in fact, a bit of street argot for sufferers of syphilis. If I were to hazard a guess, I would say that you should be looking for someone suffering from syphilis, though in stages early enough to enable them still to function. The disease has affected the mind but not yet the musculature. Far from being a Jew seeking revenge on non-Jews, your killer may well be a victim of *Treponema pallidum* with a twisted sense of persecution, wreaking a terrible vengeance on those not infected."

SEVEN

G ross or Werthen could achieve little on the sacred Sunday in
Vienna. Shops and businesses were closed; if there was no
chicken in the pot for many Viennese, then at least they had a day
free from the cares of the workplace. For Werthen it had been a
day of rest, copying out his notes for the progress of the case thus
far. Gross had, however, kept himself busy with a minute examination of the lists of possible suspects, and with familiarizing
himself with each of the firms handling the Harwood and Meier
serrated scalpel.

On Monday they paid visits to the three firms distributing Harwood and Meier cutlery and surgical products in Austria, for each
had its Austrian headquarters in Vienna. Breitstein und Söhne was
located in Vienna's Third District only blocks from where Liesel
Landtauer had resided. This connection had not gone unnoticed by
Gross, and he had thus chosen it as his first visit.

The director of the firm, the only Breitstein son, despite the
"Sons" in the firm's name, received them in his third-floor office.
A large, effusive man, he was sweating heavily on this hot and
humid day, for the foehn had now been replaced by a stifling
heat wave without the hint of a breeze. The clopping of horses

hooves and the rumble of wheels over cobblestone came from the open windows in the large office. Breitstein sat at his large desk and gestured Gross and Werthen to armchairs facing him. A small gallery of black-and-white photographs hung on the wall directly in back of the director.

Gross had again used his letter from the Police Presidium as an entrée and explained that Breitstein's assistance was needed in an official inquiry.

"Can't imagine how I can be of help to the police," he said with a nervous laugh.

Werthen had often noticed the seemingly guilty behavior of perfectly innocent people when faced with a police visit.

Gross attempted to put the man at ease, Werthen observed, for the criminologist taught that it was better to have witnesses relaxed than nervous. People were unreliable at their best; with their nerves on edge there was no accounting for what they might say just to please an interrogator.

"I am sure you have a wealth of information that you might share with us, Herr Breitstein," Gross began. "A man in your position, running a company such as this, there is no telling the sort of information you accumulate. Of course, to you, much of it might seem inconsequential. You do not mind, I hope, if I therefore direct your attention to certain specifics."

Gross's garrulous words seemed to have a sedative effect on Breitstein, who leaned back in his chair and began losing the pinch lines around his mouth.

"It is true we see a bit of life in our business," the director said. "Sales is a world requiring the ability to read the customer, to understand human nature."

"Exactly." Gross beamed at him. "You have a large sales force?"

"Seven in the field and three secretaries here in the office. When I took over, there were only four salesmen."

"And handling the medical instruments line," Gross said. "How many would that be?"

"Just two." Breitstein nodded. "Binder. Gerhard Binder. Been with the firm for six years now. Bright lad. And Maxim Schmidt, an old company hand from my father's time. In knives and cutlery we've got three, and another two in razors and tonsorial devices. Do you need their names, as well?"

Gross nodded. "Perhaps I will start with your salesmen in surgical equipment. Your firm represents Harwood and Meier products, I assume?"

"Indeed. That would be Binder, then. He is our sole representative for Harwood and Meier. The finest Sheffield has to offer. Sheffield steel holds its blade twenty-five percent longer than German steel, did you realize that, Doktor Gross?"

"A handy piece of information to have at one's disposal," Gross replied, and the man nodded, a fleshy grin on his face.

Werthen more closely inspected the pictures on the wall in back of the director now: Breitstein's face was grinning out of a dozen or so photographs of shoots: one showed a small aviary of dead birds stacked one atop the other; a black bear lay dead in a second with Breitstein placing a triumphant foot on its back; a chamois made a limp sacrifice in a third. In yet another, Werthen thought there was a familiar face in the background, but was too far away to recognize detail. It was one of those tantalizing glimpses that tease the brain thereafter, for he quickly returned his attention and focus to the conversation at hand.

"And you also represent the new Harwood and Meier serrated scalpel, if I am not mistaken?" Gross continued.

"*Serrulate* scalpel, yes."

"Ah," Gross made a mental note of the technical name for the scalpel.

"The blade is scored," Breitstein explained, "but not sawtooth in form."

"Indeed." Gross raised his eyebrows at Werthen. "Your Herr Binder, he wouldn't happen to be about, would he?"

Breitstein consulted a large calendar laid out like a blotter on his desk. "Actually, Binder is on holidays this week. But I am sure you will find him at his small weekend garden hut. The man is an avid gardener; his roses have taken some local prizes, so I understand."

Breitstein smiled at such folly; hunting stag in the Alps was probably more along his lines for leisure-time activities, Werthen thought.

"Check with Fräulein Matthias at the front desk. She can supply you with the names and addresses of all our sales representatives. Now, can you tell me what all this is about, gentlemen? I do not mind helping out the authorities, but I also have a curiosity that needs satisfying."

Gross stood, offering his hand to the director. "Rather complicated. A matter of defective steel products. Poor imitations being sold as originals."

Breitstein showed instant concern. "I assure you, gentlemen, my firm imports directly from the source."

"Of course. In fact, we would like to use your firm as the benchmark to judge the fraudulent items against," Gross explained.

Werthen knew that Gross wanted to insure that word of his inquiries about the Harwood and Meier scalpel in connection with the Prater murders did not become public knowledge. Thus far this was the first piece of hard evidence they had discovered; there was no sense in risking such information somehow reaching the killer.

They visited the other two surgical and medical equipment suppliers in Vienna before lunch. Each of these led to a dead end. Though both represented Harwood and Meier products, neither Müller GmBh nor Leikowitz Imports dealt with the serrated or serrulate scalpel. According to each, Breitstein had done some hard dealing with Harwood and Meier to secure exclusive representation for the new product in all of Austria.

"Makes our job that bit easier," Gross said, after they had had
a quick lunch at a small *Beisl* and were headed to the garden district in Penzing where Binder's little plot of land was located.

Werthen held his own counsel, as he had much of the morning. The effects of the attack on Klimt the previous Saturday
had still not worn off; he had been in a contemplative mood ever
since.

Once in Penzing, they had to ask directions twice to find the
garden district, built on wasteland near the railway line. The settlement was constructed on a little rise overlooking the tracks and
was filled with small huts set in the middle of ten-by-forty-meter
allotments. A surprising degree of fecundity had been teased out
of these postage-stamp patches of earth; some favored fruit trees
while others enjoyed verdant vegetable gardens, and still others
focused on flowers of all sorts. The entire settlement was a riot of
colors and fragrances as a result. The one-room huts built on
each allotment were as lovingly maintained as the gardens and or-
chards: most favored the hunting-lodge look, though in a minia-
turized version: brown siding with green shutters; a rack of deer or
elk horns gracing the lintel over the front doors; potted red gera-
niums in trays under the tiny windows.

Binder's was number 55, and just as Breitstein had predicted,
the man was there tending his roses. Gross held Werthen back,
watching the man work the flowers before they announced
themselves. Werthen could see that Binder, if indeed that was
he toiling over the flowers, was methodical. He was deadheading
the plants, cutting bloomed-out flowers off the bushes and topi-
ary trees. He carried a special basket for the chore and was careful to avoid spilling petals on the neatly raked soil underneath
the plants. He wore long, rubberized gloves to protect his hands
and arms from thorns. His right hand made quick and firm cuts,
lopping off the dead flowers not with garden shears, but with a
small, hooked, and obviously sharp gardening knife.

A man of medium height and brilliantly red hair thinning in

patches, he wore an immaculately clean white apron for this task. Beneath was a lightweight summer suit.

Finally Gross had seen enough. He went to the man's gate and rapped on the wooden slats. "Herr Binder," he called.

This finally drew the man's attention away from his roses.

"Hello," he said, giving a final slash to a dead flower, sending it toppling into his basket. Werthen was reminded of images of the guillotine at work during the French Revolution.

"Fine day for the garden, no?" he said as he approached the gate. "You gentlemen from the allotment committee?"

Gross shook his head. "Sorry, other business."

"Oh. I was waiting for them, you see. The lot next door has come available. Old Frau Gimbauer died last week, don't you know. Such a sadness, to be sure, but then she has no family. No one to carry on the tradition out here, you see. And my roses do seem to want to stretch and expand. They can't be too close to one another, roses. Not like we humans all cramped in our tiny apartments. They can't stand the touch of another plant, if you want to know the truth. Wither up and die if encroached upon. Her allotment would allow me to experiment with the new hybrids out of America."

He suddenly stopped his rambling. "Do forgive. I was practicing my speech for the committee. It's not usual for one person to have two allotments. Name's Binder." He ripped the glove off his right hand. "What'd you say yours were?"

"We didn't," Gross replied. "Herr Breitstein suggested we talk with you. That perhaps you could aid us in our inquiries."

Gross offered the same cover story to the salesman, noting that the Harwood and Meier implements had been copied, using inferior steel. "If you could perhaps help us out with a list of clients who have purchased the new serrulate scalpel in recent weeks, that would help immensely."

"These counterfeit products have become a regular nuisance," Binder agreed. "I'm happy to see somebody taking the matter seriously. Cuts into everyone's profits." He grinned. "No pun intended." Another weak smile. "And it destroys customer confidence in your product."

Binder was the compulsively organized sort who took his bookwork with him even on his holidays. He made a short foray into his tiny hut and came back with a small samples bag, inside of which was his order book and schedule.

"Not a major sales item," he said, as he perused his sales chart. "Last few weeks, that it?" His hand had a slight tremor as he flipped the pages, Werthen now noticed.

"For starters," Gross said.

"Most recent sale was last week. I was in Klagenfurt Tuesday and Wednesday. I sold a pair of the scalpels to Dr. Fritz Weininger of the general hospital in Klagenfurt. Before that"—he flipped more pages, scanning with his forefinger—"before that was the end of June to a surgeon in Salzburg." Binder showed the open book to Gross.

"Nothing in Vienna?" Gross asked.

Binder shook his head, closing the sales book and returning it to the samples case. "Viennese surgeons are a conservative lot. They have not yet accepted the aseptic qualities of the serrulate blade as a trade-off for slight feathering of the incision."

Gross nodded at the salesman, covering up his obvious disappointment.

"Though . . ."

"What?"

"Well, none of the instruments have been sold here, that is a fact. But I do believe one might have been removed from my samples case. I had three of the samples when setting out week before last on a round of Viennese surgeons. Those are the original ones supplied to me by Harwood and Meier in England. But, by the end of the first day, I had only two left."

"What surgeons did you visit?" Gross demanded.

"None of them could have stolen it, I'm sure. But there was a time when I was at a coffeehouse in the afternoon that the case was left unprotected while I had to visit the men's room."

Fairly cheeky business stealing a scalpel out of a man's case in a busy coffeehouse, Werthen thought.

"We'll still need a list of the surgeons. And the name of the coffeehouse," Gross said.

"Did you believe him?" Werthen asked Gross as they walked away from the garden settlement.

"Did you notice the deft hand with the roses?" Gross said by way of answer.

Werthen nodded.

"He has a nice out-of-the-way place here to work in," Gross added.

"You mean to bring bodies back to?" Werthen looked over his shoulder at the mild-mannered salesman, who was returning to his pruning. "Seems doubtful to me. Someone would have noticed the coming and going, don't you think?"

Gross sighed. "Probably. Besides, he couldn't have killed Fräulein Landtauer."

"Or so he tells us. Seems to me he made too much of a point of inserting that alibi."

"Very good, Werthen. But I don't imagine it would be too difficult to check. Fritz Weininger. That right?"

"At the Klagenfurt general hospital."

Once, however, they had finally tracked down a post and telephone exchange and completed the trunk call to Carinthia, they were disappointed. Dr. Fritz Weininger, like most of Austria, was on holiday. He would be back in his office at the end of the week.

Events, however, overtook this line of inquiry.

EIGHT

The clock on the marble mantel rang six times; pearly pink dawn light filtered through the lace curtains, filling the room with soft luminescence. Werthen wiped at the ink that had leaked onto his middle finger, then took up the pen again.

A knock at the door stopped Werthen in midsentence.

"Herr Doktor Werthen?" Frau Blatschky's voice sounded timidly from the other side of the closed drawing-room door.

"Enter."

She did so reluctantly, rubbing her hands plaintively on her starched apron.

"What is it then?"

"A gentleman to see you."

But she had barely gotten the words out before the heavy tromp of boots sounded on the parquet outside the sitting-room door.

"Werthen!" It was Gross's voice.

"Shall I see him in, sir?"

But there was no need.

"My dear Werthen," Gross was saying even as he entered through the half-open door. "Do stop mucking about with the scribbling for now. There's work afoot."

Frau Blatschky stood by the door watching the large man with great interest.

"That'll be all, Frau Blatschky," Werthen said.

She half-curtsied and left the room.

"Come on, man. No time to lose." Gross was actually rubbing his hands at the prospect.

"What brings you here at this hour, Gross?"

Then he saw the mischievous grin on the man's face.

"There hasn't been another one?"

"No, not at all. I'm up at this ungodly hour to take you to the flower show."

Werthen was momentarily taken aback. Irony was not among the weapons he expected in Gross's intellectual arsenal.

"Yes, there's been another one," Gross said. "On with your coat, man, while the scene is still relatively unspoiled."

"But how . . . ? No, let me guess, Meindl."

Gross nodded. "He gave me a friendly call this morning at my hotel. Now off before someone steps all over my crime scene."

Werthen gathered hat, gloves, and change purse, then followed the big man as he rushed down the flights of stairs, ignoring the lift.

Gross had kept his *Fiaker*, a closed brougham carriage drawn by two gray mares, waiting outside. Climbing into it, they flew down the Josefstädterstrasse, weaving in and out of traffic with a jounce and jar that made Werthen grip his hat. Then to the mighty Ringstrasse itself and thence toward the canal. As they were crossing over the canal onto Praterstrasse, Werthen finally spoke.

"So it was found in the Prater again?"

"Precisely. And this time we're ahead of the plodders. As I said, a fresh crime scene if we make haste."

Gross hammered on the roof with the silver tip of the cane he affected today. He shouted out the window, "Ten kreuzer drink money for you, my good man, if we take less than ten more minutes."

At which there was a snapping of the reins as the driver redoubled his already prodigious efforts, and Werthen was thrust back against his seat as the horses picked up their gait to a near gallop. Looking out the window, he could see the surprised, bulging eyes and open mouths of early shoppers on the streets as their *Fiaker* sped along the cobbled Praterstrasse, an occasional blue spark flying up as they crossed tramlines.

"An elderly soul this time, I am told," Gross said as he applied white knuckles to the leather stabilizer straps by his window. "Otherwise the same *modus operandi*."

Gross looked pleased with himself at the use of the Latin. "What I like to term our murderer's preferred method of killing. We shall see presently with what degree of exactitude this method has been followed."

Gross pulled out what looked to be a leather mail pouch from under his seat. He opened the flap on the bag and began checking the contents, and Werthen couldn't help but look in as well. Writing paper, envelopes, blotting paper, a map of the city, pens and pencils bristling like quills on a porcupine, a bottle of ink, a measuring tape, a compass and a pair of drafting compasses, pedometer, bottle of plaster of paris, sealing wax, glass tubes, candles, soap, magnifying glass, gum arabic, and a large railroad watch.

"Going on safari, Gross?"

The criminologist ignored the remark, checking the seal on the bottle of plaster for freshness. Satisfied, he closed the flap once again and kept the bag on his lap, like a train passenger ready for the station.

"It's my crime-scene bag," he said finally.

They were soon in the precincts of the park itself, clattering under the giant Ferris wheel. Presently they followed a lane leading away from the amusement arcades, and Werthen looked out at the shimmering green of the early-morning trees.

"There! Over there!" Gross suddenly shouted, pointing with his cane out the right-hand side of the carriage to a group of men backlit by the rising sun, standing in a copse of trees some fifty meters from the roadside. Four horses were reined to a tall chestnut tree. They twitched their ears at the approach of the *Fiaker*. Next to the horses, a pair of police bicycles lay in a heap of metal and tires, their owners having obviously dismounted in haste.

"Thank providence it was a temperate night."

Werthen, with experience in such matters, understood the implication, but made no response.

"The body temperature, man," Gross blurted out, as if lecturing to an excessively dim student. "We must know how long he has been dead, yet chill air will cool the body down more quickly than normal upon death."

Werthen let the outburst go. Gross was never a kind or polite man when on the hunt.

"At least our friend Klimt has an alibi for last night that he can broadcast to the world," Gross added. "He was sitting in the Vienna jail."

Werthen had already made this connection himself. If in fact this victim's wounds matched the others, that should be proof positive that Klimt was innocent of the Landtauer killing, and that they were all the result of the same killer.

Gross was out of the carriage even before it had stopped, his bulky frame stumbling along on impossibly small feet until he caught his balance. He headed straight for the group of men gathered by the chestnut tree, crime-scene bag in hand.

Werthen got out and was headed for the group as well until the cabbie behind him called out, "Say there, Herr Doktor. I'll be needing my tip."

Werthen looked back at the red-nosed driver, and to the fast-departing back of Gross, then grudgingly dug into the change purse he had happily remembered to take with him. Ten kreuzers the damned fool Gross had promised, Werthen remembered. He found a coin and slapped it into the man's outstretched palm.

"And my regular fare, as well. That'll be another twenty-five."

"But that's outrageous!" Werthen thundered.

The man, however, kept his hand out, looking Werthen steadily in the eye.

Finally he dug into the change purse again and handed over the correct change.

"God preserve you," the insolent cabbie said, tipping his hat. "Should I wait?"

Now he asks, Werthen thought, and was about to explode again, but thought better of it. They would need transport back.

"Please," he said with an ironic lilt, then headed to the crime scene only to find Gross down on hands and knees, the onlookers wearing expressions of alternate amusement and amazement.

Gross made an occasional humming sound, at which point he would pull out the magnifying glass from his leather bag, inspect the ground, then, employing tweezers, pick up some nearly invisible bits and plop them into one of the envelopes from the same bag.

Werthen had the irresistible desire to start laughing as he watched the oh-so-meticulous Gross crawling about the earth, heedless of the brown stains he was making at his knees. Yet the body propped against the trunk of the tree choked off any possibility of laughter.

The victim was perhaps sixty, his head dangling severely to the right, towel-stiff gray hair combed tightly to his scalp. He was dressed in *Trachten* that recalled the hunting lodge—gray wool with loden-green piping and stag-horn buttons.

The dead man's eyes were open, peering out, frozen in wide-eyed alarm. His skin was as white as alabaster—white as that of the young Landtauer girl in the morgue. And where his nose should have been was a gaping hole that gave his face a porcine appearance.

Gross suddenly and angrily exhaled as he got to his feet.

"Who's been mucking about here?" He looked at the six men gathered together apart from Werthen.

Two of them were constables, and they coughed a laugh away, then went red. The four others were dressed in military uniform—brown tunics with bright scarlet piping, field caps on their heads with bills polished to purple-black perfection. They kept their eyes on the ground in front of their boots.

Gross wore an air of authority, and none of these questioned his right to be examining the scene, let alone gathering evidence. Finally the taller of the two constables answered Gross's question: "We had to ascertain the gentleman was dead." He wiped at a runny nose with the sleeve of his blue woolen jacket. "It's regulations."

Gross shook his head. "And is it also regulations that you provide a guided tour of the scene? There are at least six sets of footprints here all jumbled together. If you do not wish to be directing school traffic in Bukovina, I suggest you explain."

One of the army officers stood stiffly to attention, saluting Gross. "It's our fault, sir. We thought the gentleman might need help. It was first light, so we had no way to see he was beyond the need."

Red splotches were on this young officer's cheeks, making him look as if he were fresh from the country, foreign to the uniform he wore. Werthen glanced at the soldier's hands: They looked to be more comfortable grappling a plow than wielding the sword he wore at his side.

Gross gave the four soldiers a long, cool look. "And what, may I ask, brought you out here at such an unholy hour of the morning?"

This sent eyes to the ground once again and prompted the tall gendarme to jump in.

"We're looking into that, Herr Doktor. The four gentlemen here merely found the body. There was no one about at the time, as they have told me. No one at all. So they do not figure into it, if you see what I mean."

"Hmm," Gross muttered, thrusting his magnifying glass once again into the depths of his leather case. He strode over to the corpse now, knowing there was no longer any reason to be careful in the surrounding area—nothing to be found here but the footprints of soldiers and gendarmes, which most likely obscured those of the perpetrator of this latest outrage. Gross bent over the body, performing the same investigation with the head and neck as he had with the unfortunate Fräulein Landtauer.

"Aha! Just as I thought." He waved to Werthen to come over.

"You see?" Gross jabbed his finger at a sliver-thin incision over the victim's carotid. "Our man's signature," he whispered. "And the same slight feathering of the flesh as found on the Landtauer girl. Our man is still using the serrulate scalpel."

The soldiers looked on curiously, and Gross finally told the gendarmes to take the men's names and see them off to their barracks.

Thereupon Gross continued a cursory investigation of the corpse. In one of the man's clenched fists, they found the other part of the signature: the tip of the amputated nose. Gross searched the man's pockets, but seemingly found nothing, though Werthen's attention was distracted for a moment watching the policemen taking down names. The four army officers were gesticulating, making a mild protest, but, it appeared, finally and reluctantly provided their identities.

Gross's work was over. He picked a white handkerchief from the breast pocket of his jacket and patted at his filthy knees.

"You decided not to question the soldiers personally?" Werthen said.

Gross now dampened the handkerchief with the tip of his tongue and scrubbed more vigorously at the stains on his knees, with little success.

"The gendarmes have the names. The police will investigate them, though I doubt they will tie them to the murders." He finally gave up with the stains and stuffed the filthy handkerchief into a voluminous coat pocket. "But what the devil were they doing out here? Ending the night with a romp in nature?"

Werthen touched the tip of his own nose as if sharing a secret.

"Dueling, old fellow. The Prater's a favorite meeting ground. All illegal, of course, though they happen almost daily. Those young men, the officers—they'd be drubbed out of the army if they refused a challenge. But just as surely will they face demotion now they've been caught at it. Why, even our former prime minister, Count Badeni, felt it incumbent to call out a German Nationalist deputy of the Reichsrat last year. Pistols at twenty paces."

"Barbaric," Gross spluttered. "Has no one told them it is almost the twentieth century?"

But Gross was no longer interested in duels or in his own indignation. He signaled to the waiting cabbie and they climbed into the *Fiaker*.

"I blame that British blighter, you know," Gross said as he settled back in his seat and once again deposited his crime-scene bag on the floorboards.

Werthen's face showed his perplexity.

"Doyle," Gross continued. "I believe that is the fellow's name. Writes the most fantastic incidents, but insists on using my methods for his main character—this Holmes fellow. That's why the air of general amusement back there." He nodded in the direction of the two constables at the scene.

Werthen had not thought Gross noticed their amusement.

"Confound the man. He obviously read my early articles for criminal investigators. Made a complete laughingstock of me among my fellow professionals. As if I am the one pilfering the great Sherlock Holmes's techniques and not vice versa."

From the *Fiaker* window they watched as an ambulance drew up to the crime scene and white-coated medics got out. Gross sighed, whether at this sight or at his feud with Arthur Conan Doyle, Werthen could not discern.

"So, any surmises, Werthen?" Gross gave the roof a tap with his walking stick and the *Fiaker* lurched forward.

"As you say, the same modus operandi."

"Beyond that? Any observations?"

"He'd obviously been killed elsewhere."

Gross smiled. "Why do you say so?"

"Too tidy. No blood about."

Gross nodded. "Just as with the others." He fixed Werthen with a penetrating gaze. "Which tells us much, I should say. Our perpetrator may be a man of means. He has the privacy in which to drain his victims' blood. Privacy implies space, and space the wherewithal to afford it. I doubt seriously that such a process would be conducted out of doors. Too risky. Ergo, some indoor space is at his disposal. And some form of transport. Perhaps he kills wherever he has the opportunity, but then he must convey the body to the bloodletting rooms, further transport them to the Prater, and also be able to dispose of quantities of blood."

"Maybe he lives nearby?" Werthen suggested.

Gross thought for a moment. "Possible, though not essential. The Prater is a secluded area in which to deposit the victims; it has the further resonance of being located in the Second District, the largely Jewish Second District, as you yourself noted."

More silence as they jostled over the cobbled Praterstrasse. Activity had picked up since their earlier trip along the street. Shops had opened. Pedestrians bustled along the wide sidewalks, shopping baskets in hand. Normal life out there, Werthen thought. Blissfully ignorant of the most recent atrocity being committed in their fair city.

"As for this victim's identity?" Gross suddenly said.

Werthen shook his head. "I'm hardly a mind reader. Not that there was a sentient mind left in that poor man. Don't tell me you've figured out his identity from what we saw there?"

Gross shrugged. "Obviously an ex–civil servant. Perhaps even from the royal household. A faithful-retainer type. Clear as daylight."

Werthen was astounded. "How could you tell that?"

A sheepish grin. "The man was carrying a pensioner's card."

Werthen slouched back in his seat, pulled out a Gross

Glockner cigar, bit off the end, and spit it out the window of the cab, then lit it with his flint lighter.

"Brilliant," Werthen muttered as he watched blue smoke from his cigar being sucked out the *Fiaker* window.

"I suppose this completes our investigation then, Werthen?"

Gross was right, Werthen suddenly realized. The police would have to release Klimt now, and since Klimt was his client, his investigation into these horrible crimes should also come to an end. He was surprised to find himself disappointed. He had just gotten his teeth into this thing, and there was the Landtauer girl and her uncommon resemblance to his Mary.

"I suppose it does," he said reluctantly. "And I assume you'll be off for Czernowitz now."

Gross sighed. "Yes. I suppose so."

But neither of them believed it.

Gross waited for the police to notify Frau Frosch of her husband's death and to conduct their initial interview before visiting her himself.

"I want to ingratiate myself to the good lady, Werthen," he explained later that afternoon, as they approached her apartment building at Gusshausstrasse 12 in Vienna's Fourth District, just behind Karlskirche. "One does not, however, ingratiate oneself by bringing bad, nay, tragic news. I leave that for the police. It is true that they might unwittingly plant information and knowledge in the woman's brain which she later feeds back to us as her own. That is, however, the chance I take in such matters. Life is a trade-off, is it not?"

When the apartment door was answered, Werthen thought the woman must be a servant, or perhaps a friend. There were no red-rimmed eyes, no sniffles of a sorrowful widow.

"Is Frau Frosch at home, please?" Gross asked. He obviously thought the same.

"I am Frau Frosch," the lady calmly answered. "Who might you be?"

"We are assisting in the investigation," Gross said, once more producing his letter from Meindl, by now rather the worse for wear.

"The police were already here this morning," she said, staring at them both levelly as if measuring them for suits.

"They were," Gross allowed. "But if you wouldn't mind a few more questions, dear lady? I know it must seem an imposition in this time of grief, but from my extensive studies in criminalistics, I have determined that the first twenty-four hours after a crime are the most crucial."

Her expression did not change. "I expect you'll want to come in, then?"

"If at all convenient, *gnädige Frau*," Gross said with what Werthen thought excessive oiliness.

Her apartment was appointed in the epitome of middle-class decorum. Everything was as it should be; that is, as someone reading *Salonblatt* magazine about the lives of the upper class and nobles thought it should be. There was not a wilted flower, a fleck of dust, a rumpled runner, anywhere to be seen. The apartment had the unlived-in feeling of a fanatical housekeeper. It was the antithesis of the Plötzl flat in Ottakring. Even Werthen was put off by such tidiness. Though fastidious, Werthen needed a *bit* of domestic mess to make him feel comfortable.

But this was not to be found at Frau Frosch's. Instead, they were led through an entry to a sitting room that was a scene out of a Makart canvas, a heavily curtained and draped space filled with massive *alt deutsch* furnishings popular twenty years before, but which now felt stuffy and overbearing. Every table was covered with brocade or tapestry; murky oil paintings filled the walls floor to ceiling; a sideboard of impressive dimensions menaced from one corner; a *Kackelofen* or tiled heating stove glistened in another.

Frau Frosch sat gingerly on the edge of a daybed, offering them seats in straight-backed tooled leather armchairs. Werthen thought she looked as uncomfortable in these surroundings as he felt.

"I really have nothing more to add than I told the police earlier," the woman began.

"I intend to cover new ground. Sometimes it is the smallest thing, Frau Frosch. The least significant detail that is most telling."

"Gross, the good lady said she has nothing to offer," Werthen suddenly interrupted. "Surely the police have gathered any information she could supply. We should be going."

"Kindly allow me to conduct the interview, Werthen. And let Frau Frosch determine if she truly has nothing more to add."

"Please excuse my colleague, Frau Frosch," Werthen said, ignoring Gross's comment. "He is sometimes overzealous in his work. Insensitive of one's feelings."

"Feelings, Werthen, must be put aside for the moment." Then to Frau Frosch: "May I continue?"

She nodded at him stiffly.

"When did you last see your husband?"

"Really, Gross," Werthen spluttered. "Is this what you call 'new ground'?"

"Enough, Werthen." Gross's voice was a low growl, a commanding presence that made the Frau sit up more stiffly in her chair.

"Now, if you please, Frau Frosch. The last time you saw your husband?"

"Last evening. About seven. He was on his way for his usual tarok game with friends."

The police had checked this, Werthen knew. Herr Frosch was due across the Karlsplatz from this flat, at the new Café Museum, where he was to meet three other pensioners for their weekly game of cards. According to his friends, Herr Frosch never arrived.

"What was he wearing?" Gross asked.

"His suit, of course. His *Trachten*."

"A bit warm for it last night, I would think."

She shook her head. "It was what he always wore. His uniform, if you like." She all but grimaced as she said this. "You can examine his wardrobe if you like. Six more hanging there, all the same color and cut. My husband had been in service to the court, you see. A valet and manservant."

"A punctilious man, then?" Gross offered.

She nodded her head vehemently. "Very."

Gross swept his hand around the room. "*His* interior design, I imagine."

She seemed to gasp at this suggestion. "But how did you know?"

"*Gnädige Frau,* I see you perhaps in lighter surroundings. More floral, more brightness of sunlight flooding the room."

"Exactly." She warmed to Gross now, Werthen noticed. No need for more interruptions on his part.

"Pardon my asking, Frau Frosch, but you and your husband had a close marriage?"

"I don't know what you mean by that."

Werthen thought Gross may have overplayed his hand, but this was not the case. There was silence for a time.

"We had no children," Frau Frosch suddenly said. "He said his duties to the empire came first."

"I am sure that was a difficult choice for both of you."

"*His* choice."

"Yes," Gross said. "His choice. Was he a drinking man?"

The sudden change of topic caught her by surprise. A hand flew up to her left eye, touching the bone beneath gingerly. Werthen only now noticed what had probably been obvious to Gross: a bluish tint under pink powder.

"He liked his wine," she finally said. "Especially since his retirement."

"No hobbies, then? Other than cards?"

She shook her head, then paused, thinking. "Yes, in a way you might call it a hobby. He said he was writing his memoirs. But I never saw a page of it. I think it was an excuse just to lock himself away in his study all morning long. He really had no idea what to do with his life after leaving service to the court. Anyway, the police found nothing."

"Would you mind if I went through his papers?" Gross asked.

"No, not at all." She led them to a study at the far end of the hall, a room as dark and heavy as the sitting room.

"He kept all his papers here?"

Frau Frosch nodded. "No need to straighten up after yourselves," she said as she was leaving the room. "This will all be packed up anyway. Everything."

"More light?" Gross smiled at her.

"Yes, Herr Doktor Gross. Much more light."

They spent almost two hours going over every possible drawer, nook, and cranny in the study, but found nothing. Gross tapped the parquet in search of a hiding place beneath the floorboards, searched for false drawers in the desk and bookcases, examined the walls behind pictures for signs of a safe. Nothing.

"Perhaps she was right," Werthen finally said. "Maybe he just wanted to hide away and drink."

Gross made no reply. He was on his hands and knees busy tapping the exterior of a large ceramic pot holding a large palm. No hollow sounds registered. The pot was indeed filled with dirt and roots.

"There is nothing more to glean here," Gross said, standing with effort and stretching his back.

All they had discovered in their methodical search was that Herr Frosch was a man with few outside interests. One drawer of his desk held old bills that covered the last year: rates and taxes including gas, 612 crowns, 38 heller; lease, 1,475 crowns; coal, 241 crowns, 14 heller; dress, wife, 742 crowns, 69 heller;

dress, husband, 812 crowns, 98 heller. And so on. Punctilious records kept by a punctilious man.

Both Gross and Werthen had noted the discrepancy in the clothing allowance. Also that Frosch was careful to use the new denominations of crowns and heller rather than the old florin and kreuzer. Gross himself, as well as much of Austria, was still struggling with the conversion from silver to gold standard, now already six years old. In two years the old florin and kreuzer would join the garbage heap of historical currencies.

They bid Frau Frosch adieu, and the lady seemed to have a special glint in her eye as she allowed her gloved hand to be kissed by Gross.

Out on the street, Werthen said, "I think you've made a conquest, Gross."

"No little thanks to you, my friend," he replied, acknowledging Werthen's planned interruptions. "Overriding one's colleague does help to establish one's authority."

They walked for a time in silence, each marshaling his thoughts from the interview and search.

"She had reason enough to want the man dead," Werthen said.

"Yes, indeed. You noticed the bruise, I assume?"

"The blighter."

"Violence is never excused," Gross said, "but one never knows what transpires behind the conjugal doors to prompt such behavior."

"A jumped-up servant who turns into a bully."

"Perhaps. Still I highly doubt the good lady herself could have killed the man and transported his body to the Prater."

"And even so, why the others?" Werthen added. "What would her motive be?"

"Perhaps they were a diversion only, in order to hide the true victim?"

It was a theory worth pursuing, but suddenly Werthen realized there was no need for such theorizing. "We should talk with

Inspektor Meindl," he said to Gross. "Surely they can no longer hold Klimt now with this latest killing." Then, almost reluctantly, he added once again, "Our work on Klimt's behalf is at an end."

Gross, however, was not listening. He had stopped in the middle of the sidewalk near the Frosch apartment.

"Means and motive," Gross muttered, shaking his head disgustedly. "We are no closer to discovering either of those crucial elements than we were last week."

"Our commission is finished, Gross," Werthen said again. "Means and motive are now someone else's headache."

"Perhaps. But, yes, we shall visit Inspektor Meindl. First, however, I would like to pay a visit to the Café Museum. Do you know its whereabouts?"

"But the police reported that Frosch never arrived there."

"Exactly my point. Ergo, somewhere between here and there the unfortunate man disappeared. And in relative daylight. At seven in the evening this time of year, there is still another hour of daylight to be sure."

Werthen nodded, seeing his point. "Someone must have seen something."

Gross nodded. "Vienna's greatest crime-fighter is its legion of nosy old ladies hanging out their windows. At seven there must have been at least one of these en route who saw an elderly gentleman in heavy *Trachten*."

"And what of the other murders?" Werthen said, feeling the excitement of the chase. "Only the industrialist, I believe, went missing in the middle of the night. The others were last seen in the twilight or early nighttime."

"Precisely. They could hardly have been murdered on the streets of a busy capital city at such an early hour without someone witnessing the act. Yet the police scoured the neighborhoods near where the others went missing. No one saw anything unusual."

Werthen leaped ahead with this reasoning. "They were not

murdered on the streets, then. Somehow the killer enticed or forced them into his transport and killed them elsewhere." Then he shook his head. "But that can't be. As you say, no one saw anything unusual."

Gross smiled. "Which leaves us with only one conclusion, Werthen. That *someone* saw something very *usual,* very common, and made no notice of it. Come, man. Lead me in the most direct route from here to the Café Museum."

They followed the Gusshausstrasse, headed for the Karlsplatz. The traffic was heavy along this street, and windows were kept closed against the noise and smell. Just before Karlsplatz, they came to Paniglgasse. Werthen assumed that the fastidious Frosch, rather than skirting the perimeter of Karlsplatz, would instead follow the narrower and more direct line of Paniglgasse to his café.

As they made their way along this smaller lane, Gross and Werthen both kept their eyes open for possible witnesses. Lounging at the doorway to number 16 was the *Dienstmann,* or public porter, who acted as the neighborhood mover, message deliverer, and general helper. He would also be the headquarters for local gossip. Dressed in a gray field jacket with epaulets and wearing a blue kepi, this one had the appearance of an ex–military man. The tin badge on his chest enhanced this appearance. However, Werthen knew, this was no military medal, but rather the man's business license.

Gross approached the porter and tipped his bowler, introducing himself and Werthen.

"How can I be of service, governor?" the man asked. Gross moved back, assaulted by the smell of wurst and cheap wine on the man's breath.

"Is this your usual location, my good man?"

"This is where the locals know where to find me if they need assistance of any sort." The porter puffed out his chest as he spoke.

"And you were here yesterday, as well?"

"I was, and that is a fact."

"Until what hour? Do you recall?"

"Well . . ." The man took off his hot kepi and scratched at the gray bristle of hair on his head. "This time of year with the long days, I do tend to stay out of doors until seven, maybe eight. Last evening—"

"You were already on your second *viertel* of wine," came a voice from the ground-floor window to the right of the doorway.

The porter did not bother to look around in the direction of the voice. He simply raised his eyebrows at Gross and Werthen.

"Now, Frau Novotny, you're a great one for exaggeration."

The old lady appeared from behind the opaque lace curtain of her open window, a birdlike creature wearing a dust bonnet out of the eighteenth century.

"And you're a great one for the wine. There was no sign of you on this street after six last night. Otherwise Frau Ohlmeier in 26B wouldn't have had to ask me to watch her sack of potatoes as she trundled her other groceries up the stairs."

"Well, gentlemen," the porter said with heavy irony, "there you have it. Straight from the mouth of God it is. I must have left work early last night. Now what is it I can help you with?"

"Actually," Gross said, tipping his bowler in the direction of the old lady, "I was hoping to speak with someone who may have noticed the happenings on this street around seven last evening. Werthen, perhaps you could proffer a thanks to this gentleman."

As usual, Gross left such incidentals as the dispersion of funds to Werthen.

The lawyer handed the porter a florin, at which the man stared skeptically for a moment, as if expecting this only child to be joined shortly by siblings.

"Thank you for your help," Werthen said with finality.

Meanwhile, Gross had approached the old lady's window. He stood almost eye to eye with the elderly woman, who was now leaning with elbows on a bolster that usually fitted between the double windows.

"I am making inquiries, my good woman, about a gentleman who may have passed this way last evening. He was a man in his sixties wearing woolen *Trachten*."

"You a copper?" the old woman asked with obvious delight.

"I"—Gross had the courtesy to sweep his hand in Werthen's direction—"we are assisting the police in their investigation."

"Saw a couple of constables messing about the street today, talking to Herr Ignatz." She nodded with contempt at the porter, who had now taken up a new post across the street. "Knocking on doors." She shook her head so vehemently, the bonnet slipped down her forehead. Righting it, she said, "Never liked coppers. I didn't answer when they came to my door." She cast a shrewd glance. "You two don't look like police. Don't act like it, either. They never pay for nothing."

"Let us simply say that we can be appreciative of any help given," Gross said.

"What's he done, your old fella in the *Trachten*?"

"He seems to have gone missing," Gross told her.

"Important enough you got coppers bothering the citizenry, you two dandies looking around for bread crumbs that might lead to him."

"Yes." Gross offered no further explanation.

"About seven, you say."

They both nodded at her.

"I might have seen him. Can't really remember clearly, though."

Gross glanced at Werthen. "If you would be so good?"

Werthen sighed with exasperation, but dug out another florin and handed it to the lady.

She placed it on the bolster between her elbows. "Closer to seven thirty, I would say. That's the time Herr Dietrich always gets home from work. Puts in long hours, does our Herr Dietrich.

Between you and me, I think he's probably keeping a mistress somewhere. Works so much, but has so little to show for it. And Frau Dietrich always wearing last year's fashions. Put on a bit of weight, too, the Frau."

"Yes," Gross said, steering her back to the matter at hand. "And you associate the arrival of Herr Dietrich with the man in *Trachten*?"

She smiled at them, showing teeth as brown as a walnut. Then she looked down at the lone florin.

"Werthen," Gross prompted.

The lawyer was about to complain when Gross shot him a look of urgency. He added a second florin.

"Came by just after Herr Dietrich went into number fifteen, there, across the way. Walking slowly enough. Wouldn't be surprised if he wasn't sickly."

"And did anyone approach him along this street?" Gross inquired.

"Can't say that I noticed. And that's not a pitch for another coin. I'm not greedy. All's I can say is he came by here. Took little enough notice of him, other than that he was dressed for winter."

"Did you see him speak to anyone?"

She shook her head.

"Were there any vehicles parked along the street? Carriages or the like?"

"There's always a carriage or two. This isn't Ottakring, after all. We've got a respectable neighborhood here. Sort of place that the municipality keeps up. They was out that evening even, fixing the sewers."

"Did you watch him as he got to the corner of Wiedner Hauptstrasse?" Gross continued.

"I wasn't *watching* him," she protested. "Just happened to see him a bit. Couldn't tell you where he went, to be honest. The water boiled over for my tea, and I had to rush back to the kitchen."

They made their adieus and proceeded down the street, searching for other open windows that might provide further witnesses.

"We hardly got three florins' worth of information," Gross complained, as if it had been his money spent.

That evening he and Gross were the guests of honor of Gustav Klimt at the Bierklinik, an inner-city eatery known for its fresh fish and bountiful servings. Klimt, or more likely Fräulein Flöge, had thought to reserve an upstairs room for their use. Present at the meal, besides these four, were Klimt's mother and unmarried sisters, and the painter Carl Moll, an associate of Klimt's at the Secession.

The Bierklinik was one of those restaurants that disabused foreigners of the idea that Viennese cooking was all kraut and sausage. Huge fish tanks flanked the walls of the entryway, and from these was selected a trio of well-proportioned trout, poached to perfection with Madeira and a hint of lemon. These were served with parsley potatoes and greenhouse lettuce, crisp and tender, jeweled with Wachauer white-wine vinegar and fresh-pressed rapeseed oil.

Toasts were made to welcome the painter out of jail and then to the team of Gross and Werthen for helping in the matter.

But Gross was not about to take kudos for undeserved achievement.

"Circumstances saved you, Herr Klimt, not our investigation. The fact that you were locked up when the most recent murder occurred was the deciding factor in securing your release."

"But you would have proved me innocent, Doktor Gross," Klimt said with a slight slur to his voice. He was at work on his fourth beer. "Of that I am certain."

"We were pursuing various leads, to be sure," Gross said.

"And you, Werthen." Klimt raised his glass. "A loyal friend indeed."

"Who almost got you killed by Landtauer."

Klimt ignored the remark. "I imagine you two are a bit depressed, no?"

Gross cast the man a shrewd look.

"I would be," Klimt continued, "were a commission taken away from me halfway through the painting. In fact, I would be half-tempted to finish the job anyway."

"Gustl." Fräulein Flöge tugged at his sleeve. For the occasion, Klimt had donned a white suit and red cummerbund instead of his usual caftan. His left arm was dramatically supported in a sling. "I am sure these gentlemen have other obligations. We are not all free to pursue our daydreams like you."

She held on to the thick right arm, taking a deep breath. It was clear to Werthen she was in love with the man. She met the lawyer's eyes at that moment, blinking for a long moment as if to say thanks to him for not letting Klimt know she was aware of his paramour and child.

"You're right, Emilie. As usual. I will confine myself to beer consumption this evening and no more unsolicited advice.

"To freedom," Klimt said, extricating his good arm and hoisting his beer mug in a toast.

Klimt's words had only echoed their own. Leaving the Bierklinik late that evening, both Gross and Werthen knew that they were going to continue their investigation.

They walked the quiet inner-city streets.

"This time of night," Werthen said, "I could understand how someone might approach and kill another. It would take great stealth and a degree of luck, but by ten o'clock most of the good burghers of Vienna are tucked under eiderdown fast asleep."

"But the others," Gross said as their boots echoed on the cobblestones. "How to explain them?"

"Vanished into thin air, only to end up in the Prater in the morning."

"Into thin air," Gross mused. "Yes. Or as if the earth swallowed them, to borrow another saying."

NINE

Two days later, Inspektor Meindl himself took them to the scene. The victim had used a small-caliber pistol, but, inserted into his mouth, it had done the job. The back of his head had been blown off. Blood and brain matter scored the walls in back of the cot where the body lay.

The tiny garden hut had little space for furniture other than the iron cot. A large copper washtub occupied part of that limited space; a coatrack, which seemed to serve as wardrobe, stood next to it. In one corner of the hut, the floorboards had been pried up. Lying on the floor next to the opening, the treasures there unearthed by the police were on display: two scalpels, a leather harness, a siphoning hose, and a jar of chloroform.

Gross touched Binder's neck. "Still warm."

Inspektor Meindl nodded. "Neighbors heard the shot just before sunrise. Officially, you're not supposed to sleep in these huts, though obviously there are those who do. Neighbor in question is ex-army. Didn't like the sound of gunfire. But he didn't investigate until later in the morning, when he saw the door ajar. He found the body. And this."

Meindl produced a note from his coat pocket and handed

it to Gross. The criminologist visibly blanched as this was being done.

"Fingerprints, Meindl. Fingerprints."

Meindl shook his head. "Not necessary anymore, Gross. Read for yourself."

He did so, and Werthen peered over his shoulder:

The game is up, I'm afraid. I had a fine run, but they're onto me now. All because of the scalpe. Pity, really. I had grand plans still to carry out. And the roses have benefited ever so much from their unexpected meals. Such a lot of fun it's been, matching wits with the police, and now the famous criminologist, Gross. And none of you were able to figure out the wonderful clues I left behind, I'll warrant. The nose, the nose. It is all about the nose. We have seen fine examples of the noseless. Oh, the gay times they have had. I have had. There would have been more, many more, if not for my own stupidity. Cupidity. Oh, rhyme me no rhymes, tell me no tales. A leather nose is no substitute for a rose. Dig and dig and you may find clues.

From outside they could hear police officers digging in the garden at that very moment. Obviously they had already had some success in their efforts, judging from the cache discovered inside the hut.

"My God, Gross," Werthen said. "It's just as Krafft-Ebing said."

"It would appear so."

"What do you mean?" Inspektor Meindl queried.

Gross ignored the question, stroking his beard in thought. "I believe you can call your men off, Meindl. Nothing more to discover out there. Blood residue washes away soon enough in soil."

"Binder truly was mad, wasn't he?" Werthen said. "He used the victims' blood as fertilizer."

"Afraid so," Gross replied. Then to Meindl again: "And I should have that tub examined closely, using reagents to search for traces of blood. This would most likely be the place where he drained the blood."

"And the noses?" Meindl asked again.

"I'll need to consult someone about that."

Later that day Werthen and Gross met once again, for a cup of afternoon tea at the Café Landtmann.

"It was as we suspected, Werthen," Gross said. "I checked with the secretary at Breitstein and discovered the employees keep a record of the private physicians in case of emergency. I visited Binder's medical man. Herr Binder was suffering from the tertiary stage of syphilis."

"Deranged, of course."

"It would appear so," Gross agreed. "Though, as Krafft-Ebing predicted, not yet physically incapacitated."

"That would seem to be conclusive, then," Werthen said. "Inspektor Meindl told me to inform you that they had indeed found traces of blood in the washtub, just as you said. And on the scalpels, harness, and siphon, as well as on other parts of the walls. The harness was apparently used to hoist the victims, and then the siphon was employed to help drain the blood from the copper tub in order to fertilize the roses." Werthen shivered despite the warm day. "A ghoulish business, all in all."

"Yes, but one that has not yet quite been explained. One assumes the bottle of chloroform dug up at Binder's was used to drug his victims. Easy enough to lure a person to a waiting carriage by asking for directions. A quick application of the chloroform on a rag and the person would become senseless and put up no fight, offer no resistance. Which explains their seeming disappearance into thin air, as you once put it."

"My assumption, as well," Werthen noted.

"There is, however, the not insignificant matter of Herr Binder's supposed alibi for the Landtauer killing, and then there is also the knotty problem of transport. How did Herr Binder move his victims to his garden hut and thence to the Prater? He could hardly have hired a *Fiaker* for such services."

It was Werthen's turn now to appear self-important. "I believe I can help you there, Gross. You see Meindl managed to track down Dr. Weininger from Klagenfurt. Seems he was vacationing near here, in Baden. And according to the doctor, Binder was not in Klagenfurt last Tuesday and Wednesday, but rather on Tuesday morning only. Weininger met with him at ten A.M., and the salesman told him he had a train to catch at noon. Which gave Binder plenty of time to return to Vienna and kill Fräulein Landtauer."

Gross nodded his head. "And transporting the bodies?"

Werthen smiled. "In fact, I had the idea to check with Herr Direktor Breitstein while you were visiting Binder's doctor. I wondered if the firm might have a delivery wagon." Werthen paused dramatically.

"Get on with it," Gross muttered.

"Well, the short of it is, yes, they do. And when questioned by Breitstein, the warehouseman responsible for maintaining it says that Herr Binder used it overnight several times that he knew of. Binder said he had large consignments to deliver to customers outside of office hours."

Gross made a most uncouth sound, almost like flatulence, as he blew disgustedly through his lips.

"Not so sad, Gross. After all, Binder himself wrote that your discovery of his serrulate scalpel was what convinced him the game was up. You were directly responsible for putting an end to these horrible crimes."

"That, dear Werthen, is one way to look at it. More satisfying, however, to clap the handcuffs on the killer oneself."

"And you received recognition from the court," Werthen added in a vain attempt at cheering him up. Indeed, the day following Binder's suicide, an official letter arrived from the Hofburg, seat of the Habsburgs. Cutting under the red wax seal, Werthen was amazed to read a personal commendation from Prince Grunenthal, adviser to Emperor Franz Josef, thanking them both for their invaluable assistance in putting such an unwholesome matter to rest. The letter had done little to cheer Gross at the time; reminding him of it now did even less.

Gross left for his post in Czernowitz the following day. Werthen saw him off at the East Train Station. As if marking the departure, the weather too changed. A thunderstorm rolled in from the Hungarian plains, and steady rain sounded on the arched copper roof of the train station as Gross's train was readied.

They were there a half hour early, as was Gross's custom when traveling. His first-class compartment was still empty; he held a reserved window seat facing the engine. The porter finished storing his luggage; Werthen had agreed to send on several boxes once Gross was settled in Bukovina. The criminologist had saved all the items of evidence he could from this case and would use them to write up an article for his monthly journal.

"Or perhaps I'll fashion it into a melodrama like those of the Doyle chap in England." Gross attempted a smile.

"Why not, indeed?" Werthen was trying to keep a positive attitude, though Gross had been morose enough since the case was closed.

As the departure drew near, Gross settled in his seat. "No need to wait, Werthen. The train will leave with or without you here."

Werthen had promised himself he would not be put off by Gross's evil spirits. "It has been an honor working with you, Gross." He stood with his hand outstretched for several instants before Gross took notice, stood, and shook his hand.

"And I you, Werthen. I suppose we shall become dull old dogs again, now, eh?"

Werthen shrugged.

"A piece of advice," Gross said. "Go back to criminal law, man. It is clearly where your heart is."

"For the immediate future, I am afraid it is the country for me. And see what new young woman the parents have 'inadvertently' invited in hopes that their only son and heir will finally marry, settle down, and produce progeny."

"Don't laugh at the proposition, Werthen. Without my Adele, I would be lost."

The two shook hands again, and Werthen departed. He looked back once, but Gross was already settled again in his window seat, a copy of the afternoon paper open in front of him.

As Werthen was exiting the train station, an adolescent newspaper hawker called out the headlines of the day's tabloid press, his voice breaking on every stressed syllable:

"Prater murderer captured! Dramatic events bring end to ring of terror! Inspektor Meindl in on the kill. Read it all here."

Werthen shook his head. Gross's joking comment about turning the case into a melodrama had already become reality. The Viennese lived for a good bit of theater.

Deep down he had to admit that he was just that little bit peeved that he and Gross would get none of the accolades. He thought about Gross's advice to return to criminal law. Perhaps if all cases ended so successfully, he would consider it. Perhaps if next time he could be "in on the kill," as the newspaper vendor had it.

He bought one of the papers from the young vendor, watching the effete lawyer making his way out of the train station. So he would not have to kill him and the older one after all. There was no relief in the thought; simply a fact. It was obvious the meddlesome criminologist was on his way to Bukovina, where he belonged. The lawyer would surely go back to his posh law practice, also where he belonged. No more messing about in other people's business.

He looked at the headlines on the newspaper and felt a certain pride at a job well done. Others sold tram tickets or cleaned streets or drove a *Fiaeker* or even taught at fancy universities for a living.

He killed people.

He was seventeen when he killed his first man. At the time, the Major thought this demonstrated great promise, for he had made the kill with his hands, no weapons. Quiet and controlled.

They whisked him out of his cell in Linz and sent him to the elite Rollo Commando training school in Wiener Neustadt as a result. There he refined his craft of killing, learning to use a knife, a cord, his fingers, even the high part of his instep to kill. He did not leave training unscathed: his instructor, sensing his apathy one day, left a jagged scar with the thrust of a stiletto in close-fighting drill.

"You must never take an attack for granted," the trainer had told him afterward. "There is no such thing as a friendly attack."

It was a lesson worth learning. He came to love the resulting scar. He wore it like a badge.

He was just out of training when they sent him on his first commission. He remembered shivering in the snow outside the lodge, watching the to and fro of servants and drivers as the night settled around them. He and two other members of the Rollo Commandos.

An hour before dawn they went in, entering stealthily through windows. The bedroom was at the end of a long, narrow corridor, far removed from the rest of the household. The young man was there, as if waiting for them. The two others took care of him; one wrestled him to the ground and the second held a revolver to his head.

He was left with the girl, who pleaded for her life. "Don't kill me," she whimpered. "I'll do anything you want. Just don't kill me." It disgusted him. She opened her night shift and let him see her breasts, her patch of dark hair down there. In the end, he let his anger get the better of him, for the first and last time. He was not a degenerate, after all. He was only doing his duty. But she kept whimpering and thrusting herself at him. He did not use the pistol as ordered, but rather killed her with his hands, grabbing her by the neck and slamming her head hard against the bedpost until she stopped the gurgling sound in her throat.

He was sent to Serbia after that, where he rotted in a garrison for several years before being called back to Vienna. He was never sure why. He asked no questions.

There had been many others since then. The last ones had been a challenge, operating in the capital itself. He liked a challenge. He worked to instructions regarding wounds and cuts, but had chosen his own victims and decided on his own means. It took a certain bit of genius to hit on the underworld, he thought.

He never knew exactly where his orders originated, only that his service was of vital importance to the empire. Something he never told his superiors, never mentioned to another living soul: It did not matter if his orders were of vital importance. It did not matter if he was serving his fatherland by his deeds.

Unlike a street cleaner, he liked his job. It was not just a duty for him, but almost like creating a work of art. A perfect kill. The sharp snapping sound of vertebrae like lake ice cracking in the thaw. The terror in the eyes of the victims when accosted, then the peaceful, almost contented look to them after he was finished with his work. All of this was immensely pleasing to him. But that was definitely something he could never mention to his superiors.

And now he had been given the biggest assignment of all. They would not find him wanting.

PART TWO

Criminal law, like all other disciplines, must ask under what conditions and when we are entitled to say "we know."

—Dr. Hanns Gross, *Criminal Psychology*

TEN

Saturday, September 10, 1898—Vienna

The world was altered.

No longer did the horse-drawn carriages along the Kärntnerstrasse irritate with their infernal noise and smell. Instead they were a romantic invitation to an outing, perhaps at the Sacher garden restaurant in the Prater. The afternoon sun was not beating down upon his head but rather bathing him in golden light. Female pedestrians might carry parasols against its strength, but Werthen grinned bathetically at its life-giving rays. The one-legged war veteran selling lottery tickets outside the Stephansdom was no longer a sorry-looking creature, but had suddenly been transformed into a silent hero. Even the late-season tourists, many of them Americans and thus loud and disorderly, seemed charming in their cultural naïveté.

In short, *Advokat* Karl Werthen was in love.

The object of his affections sat across from him now at the Kleine Ecke, the outdoor café on the corner of Graben and Kärntnerstrasse. And wonder of wonders, all because of his parents.

Werthen had arrived at Hohelände, the family estate in Upper
Austria, the Saturday after Gross's departure, determined to give
short shrift to any young women his parents had invited this year.
This annual event, this horse show, was put on for his benefit, a
parade of all the eligible young fillies for kilometers around
under the guise of a coincidental visit. Maman and Papa were
desirous of an heir; with the death of Werthen's younger
brother, Max, the duty of continuing the Werthen name had
fallen to him. My God, what a notion, he thought. One would
think we were local aristocracy or lesser nobility the way Maman
and Papa harped on the importance of continuing the family
line.

Truth was, their money had come from the wool trade, just as
they had come, not that long ago, from Moravia, hardworking
Bohemian Jews hoping to assimilate. Grandfather Isaac had
established the fortune through a blend of shrewd business sense
and twelve-hour days. Werthen's father, Emile, had reaped the
rewards of such labor when a "von" was granted to the family in
1876, five years after the family's conversion to Protestantism.

Werthen had been twelve at the time and had always found
the use of that title offensive. Just as he had railed at his father's
insistence on his sons learning the ways of a gentleman and the
supposed joys of hunting and fencing.

This year's pick was Ariadne von Traitner, daughter of Otto,
a created peer who ran a successful pencil factory in Linz.
Werthen had to hand it to his parents, the girl was fetching
enough. She had blond hair and blue eyes and was tall and wil-
lowy. She was the sort of girl Klimt might enjoy painting. Her
family had converted to Christianity in the 1840s; one would
never know she was Jewish. Neither was she as vapid as the usual
young woman whom his parents invited.

The first afternoon at Hohelände, they all had lemonade together on the side lawn, near the croquet court, with birds twittering in the nearby copse and the sun bathing them all in

golden light. Werthen, however, was feeling far from charmed or bucolic. He was polite enough, but when Ariadne proffered the opinion that Johann Strauss was the greatest Austrian composer of all time, he determined to figure out a way to let the girl down lightly. He could not imagine himself spending the rest of his life with one who ranked Strauss above Mozart, Haydn, or even that quirky old maid Bruckner.

Then, just as he had hit on a plan of action, a further guest appeared. Berthe Meisner was introduced as Ariadne's traveling companion, an old school friend from Linz, now residing in Vienna.

Werthen's parents had been ever so solicitous of this other young woman, but clearly they felt this was noblesse oblige, chatting up such an inferior person. Werthen could not explain it if asked, but he was instantly attracted to Fräulein Meisner. She had none of the Germanic looks of her friend and was not of high social standing. Instead, she had a darkly handsome face and eyes that shone with a sort of mischief and knowing. She was twenty-five and worked for the Municipality of Vienna in one of its new day-care centers for working-class children.

"Working with the unwashed to save her soul," Ariadne pronounced in an irritatingly arch manner. Werthen's parents seemed to find this comment vastly humorous, but Berthe had been little amused. Her eyes seemed to flash at her friend, and Werthen could see that she was prepared to retort, but then thought better of it, sipping at her lemonade instead and smiling knowingly.

Werthen appreciated her reserve. After all, one could say little to such an ignorant remark. It was as if Fräulein Meisner had been embarrassed for her wealthy friend and cared not to draw further attention to such silliness. Her silence spoke volumes to Werthen.

The next day, rising early to avoid Ariadne at breakfast, Werthen set out on a walk to the nearby Lake Iglau. Sunrise was a magical time to be at the lake, with the mists rising off the water and the pike dimpling the surface in search of food. Ahead of him on the path to the lake, he discerned another figure, a female, and feared that he had been mistaken about the von Traitner girl: perhaps she was the type to arise early after all. Quickly, however, he realized that it was her companion, Berthe Meisner. For the second time in twenty-four hours he felt an immense attraction to her. He breathed in deeply and with joy just seeing her. As if sensing his presence, she turned, squinted rather myopically at him, then waved.

"Seems we both had the same idea," he said, catching her up. "Mind if I accompany you?"

"Not at all. What same idea?"

"A visit to the lake."

"Oh. I had no idea. I just came out to get some air."

"Then do allow me to introduce you to the wonders of Lake Iglau."

She smiled, shaking her head. "Do you always talk like that?"

The question took him aback. "Like what?"

"Like you were running for mayor of Vienna. Too many words. Pompous."

He felt himself reddening.

"See, there I go again. I am so sorry. Mother always told me I spoke too rashly."

"I hadn't noticed," Werthen said, feeling offended and slightly defensive.

"It must be the lawyer coming out in you. You needn't bother with me, though. Really. I love plain speech." She saw his discomfort now. "Blasted. And I do like you. Rosa is always telling me just to think twice before talking."

"Another friend of yours?" Werthen asked, hoping to change the subject and return to the warm feeling he had earlier.

"Rosa? Yes, I expect you could call her a friend. Rosa Mayreder. You've heard of her, no doubt?"

Werthen certainly had heard of the fiery Frau Mayreder, Austria's Susan B. Anthony or Emmeline Pankhurst.

"So you are a suffragette?" Werthen said.

They began strolling again, in the direction of the lake.

"You don't approve?" she asked, smiling at him.

"On the contrary. Women's suffrage is long overdue. We are fast approaching the twentieth century, but Austria still drags its feet in the Middle Ages in many respects."

She grabbed his hand suddenly. "Bravo for you. See, there was nothing stuffy about that speech. Just plain, honest talk." She grew suddenly embarrassed, letting his hand go. "Forgive me."

"No . . . I mean, there is nothing to forgive. In spite of your quick tongue, I find you—"

She put an index finger to his lips, and shook her head. "Bad luck. Let's just enjoy the morning. Tell me about that bird over there. The one with the rusty crown of feathers."

They met by "accident" the next two mornings, each enjoying the company of the other, but for Werthen it was becoming more than a mild flirtation. Fräulein Meisner had a solidness, a being in the here and now that appealed to him. Yet this was combined with a sparkling intellect that challenged him. She teased Werthen and made him laugh, and she also surprised and sometimes shocked him with her opinions on everything from Richard Wagner—"an overblown, self-congratulating anti-Semite"—to the new field of psychology—"sex, sex, all nerve disorders caused by sex; Freud theorizes like someone who gets too little of it."

The third morning, however, Fräulein Meisner was not to be found on the path to Lake Iglau. Werthen felt disappointed and was amazed at the feeling. He picked up his pace in hopes of meeting her at the breakfast table. Ariadne was there, but no Fräulein Meisner.

"Karl," Ariadne said with a chiding tone, looking up from a

plate full of cheese, wurst, and breakfast rolls. "You have been treating me very badly." She smiled archly to show she was playing with him.

Werthen was in no mood for play; neither did he like her using his first name. It assumed an intimacy they would never share. However, it was his parents' house; he would be polite.

"I did bring a deal of work with me."

"Oh, you men," Ariadne gushed. "Work is all you ever think of. But of course I respect that, too. A man should have goals and a proper position."

He smiled, pouring himself a cup of coffee and pointedly not taking a seat. "Where is your friend this morning?"

Ariadne chewed on a piece of breakfast wurst, her little, sharp teeth making distinct clacking noises. After swallowing, she wiped her heavily painted lips with a damask napkin.

"Oh, she is busy packing. No one to keep me company, it seems."

"Packing?" He hoped the urgency did not sound in his voice.

"Called away to her father in Linz, it seems. She leaves on the midday train. So tiresome. And I thought we were all going to have such fun here together."

He excused himself and fled to his room. The news of Fräulein Meisner's departure had, in fact, upset him. Just as her absence this morning on his walk had left him feeling a bit empty. My lord, he thought. If I were a doctor, I'd prescribe a bromide. He had not felt this way since the death of his fiancée, Mary, and was not sure he wanted to feel like this again.

By eleven, however, he had made his decision. When he told his parents that he had to return to Vienna to take care of a suddenly remembered legal matter, they visibly paled.

"But, Karlchen," his mother complained, "you need this annual holiday. The air of Vienna this time of year is poisonous."

"A nuisance," his father spluttered. "Riding party all arranged for this weekend. Splendid new mare for you."

He made his apologies but was adamant.

"And what about Ariadne?" his mother said.

"I am sure you can explain matters to her."

"Whole house is leaving," his father mumbled. "Coming and going like moths at a light."

In the event, Werthen was just in time for the midday local to Linz, with a transfer to Vienna. Steam vented from the undercarriage of the train as he boarded, valise in hand.

It took him fifteen minutes to find her, seated by herself in a second-class compartment; he joined her, tucking his own first-class pass into his inside jacket pocket.

"Herr Werthen." Her eyes widened in surprise as he entered the compartment.

"May I?"

"But of course." She swept her hand to the row of empty seats across from her.

"Quite a coincidence," he said, reddening at his lie.

"Yes." She closed the book she had been reading, *Lay Down Your Arms,* by Bertha von Suttner.

"Good?" He nodded at the book.

"Oh, this. I've read it so many times I could no longer say if it is good in the sense of a good story. It is rather like an old friend."

Neither said anything as the train suddenly lurched and then began pulling out of the little station.

"I thought you were home for a week," she said as the train began to pick up speed, creating a gentle rocking motion.

"That was the plan. Business," he said importantly. "Some papers to prepare."

She nodded at this.

"And I thought you were to remain with your friend Fräulein von Traitner for rather longer," Werthen said.

"Well, family business, you see."

"Yes, quite."

He was beginning to think this was all a terrible mistake on his part. Clearly his feelings were not reciprocated; how could he have been so stupid as to chase after the woman when she plainly found him a dullard or worse?

"We aren't being honest, are we?" she suddenly said.

And then everything was fine.

"No. Not at all," Werthen told her. "I heard you were leaving, and . . ."

"Ariadne is an old friend. She comes across as a dithery, superficial person, but I've known her for years. She is different underneath. Can you understand?"

Perfectly, for his relation with Gross was much the same.

"It was becoming too uncomfortable," she pressed on. "Your parents invited her to their home to meet you."

"Then you feel it, too?"

"Yes. Oh, yes, Herr Werthen. I feel it."

It was as if they had gone too far too quickly; both were silent for several more moments as the train trailed through pleasant greenery, passed by sudden lakes.

She again took the initiative.

"Come, Herr Werthen. No awkward silences now. Shall I tell you more about myself?"

Thus, as the train dawdled through the countryside toward Linz, Werthen discovered that she, like him, desired to be a writer. For Fräulein Meisner, however, journalism was the apex. She was already contributing articles on social issues to Viktor Adler's socialist newspaper, the *Arbeiter Zeitung*.

"But I can hardly call myself a socialist," she said. "After all, I live on the allowance my father gives me, which is made from his shoe manufacturing, a business made possible by the sweat and toil of mostly underpaid workers. We all live with varying degrees of hypocrisy, I fear."

Which explained her volunteer work in day-care centers, Werthen figured, but did not ask. Which also explained the second-class carriage when she clearly had the money for first.

"And now your turn. Why wills and trusts?"

He was about to make his standard reply when she said, "And don't tell me it's because of your parents' sense of propriety."

He was taken aback by her insight, by her honesty, but at the same time he bristled at the implicit criticism.

"Someone must do it. It's an honest enough profession."

"No," she hurriedly said, noting his defensive tone. "Don't misunderstand me. I am not disparaging the profession. But for you . . . I sense something else."

He was about to boast of his recent success with Gross, but instead decided to trade confidence for confidence. "I was once a criminal defense lawyer."

"Aah." She looked at him closely. "You lost a case. . . . Or was it that your passion for the law came between you and someone you loved?"

Again he was struck by her prescience, as if she could see right into him. And then he told her of his fiancée, Mary, and how he blamed himself for neglecting her in her final illness.

"She always wanted me to go into a tidier field of law," Werthen said. "I granted her that final wish."

Fräulein Meisner said nothing after this confession, merely put her hand across the space dividing them and gently patted his knee.

The train pulled into the Linz station. They descended, and as Werthen headed to platform three for the Vienna connection, she suddenly stopped.

"This is as far as I am going."

He was suddenly downcast; he had been enjoying the company. He could not remember the last time he had enjoyed the company of a woman this much. It showed on his face.

"My father really is expecting me," she explained. "A bit of family reunion before I return to work in Vienna."

"How nice for you, and him."

They stood for a moment in the middle of the busy platform as people rushed past them on each side.

She was the first to extend a hand. "It's been a pleasure, Herr Werthen."

"All mine, to be sure, Fräulein Meisner." Her hand felt smooth and warm in his, like a sturdy little bird.

"Simple words, counselor. This is not the mayoral race."

Again he blushed.

"And you really should, you know."

He shook his head, not understanding.

"Return to criminal law. It's quite clear you are smitten with it."

"Yes," he said, flustered and again put off-balance by her keen perception of him.

The stationmaster called out the train for Vienna. He made no move to leave her.

"Your train," she said finally.

"May I see you again?"

She thought for a moment. "Ariadne," she reminded him.

"She will find a much more suitable young man than I, never fear. May I?"

A second call was made for his train.

"Hurry, you'll miss it."

He lingered.

"Yes," she said. "I would like that."

He beamed at her like a schoolboy. "Fine. Good." He began to feel a fool. "That's wonderful, Fräulein Meisner."

"Go." She pushed him off, calling after him, "And it's Berthe, not Fräulein Meisner."

He tipped his city bowler at her as he hurried to his train, getting on just as it was departing.

As he took his seat, he realized he had not got her address.

He fretted about this all the way back to Vienna, trying to figure a way to track the young woman who had made such a large impression on him. He could hardly ask the von Traitners for the address of their daughter's best friend. By luck she might be on the telephone exchange, though he highly doubted it. More likely she was taking a room somewhere with some formidable landlady who would do her all to protect the morals of her renters. What was that school she worked at? But he could not remember the name. Then he did remember that she was a contributor to the socialist newspaper the *Arbeiter Zeitung.* Perhaps a visit to those offices would secure him the address of one of the correspondents.

He mooched around Vienna the first hot days of September, even opening his office, to work half days. His assistant, Dr. Wilfried Ungar, was not back from his vacation—if you could call it that—to Rome, there to study thirteenth-century documents at the Vatican library on the Albigensian heresy. Quite keen on mental improvement was young Ungar, and a stolid, practical clerk and assistant. Werthen was happy to be working with him out of the office, and as the practice had grown, Ungar had become invaluable.

Once the mahogany furniture, green wallpaper, and tasteful prints of flowers and animals had pleased Werthen; surely the surroundings were meant to reassure his clients of his eminent respectability. Now, suddenly, he felt choked by the walls, the pretense.

He finally tracked down her address by the end of the week; a journalist friend who sometimes submitted articles to the *Arbeiter Zeitung* (under a pseudonym, of course) secured it for him.

It was in a well-kept baroque building in the Seventh District, not all that far from his own residence. That they had never run into one another on the streets amazed Werthen. Or perhaps they had crossed paths and neither had noticed the other.

He rang the *Portier*'s bell. A sallow-faced woman in a long, white canvas housecoat came to the door, eyeing him suspiciously.

"What is it?"

"Fräulein Meisner."

"Not home," the lady said.

"Do you perhaps know when she is expected?"

The woman puffed her lips. "Can't say. Went to visit her father. Imagine. A young lady like that having a whole flat to herself. In my day, girls stayed home until married. The world we live in."

She looked to Werthen for confirmation of her outmoded beliefs, but he merely tipped his bowler.

"I will try again later in the week then."

He was just about to turn the corner when someone called his name. Turning, he saw Berthe, suitcase in hand.

"Aren't you clever," she said as they approached. "And all this time I have been trying to figure out how I would be able to track you down. A rather more simple task than yours. After all, a lawyer surely has an office and surely is listed with the professional societies if not with the telephone exchange."

They stood in the street for a time, smiling at one another.

"We can't simply hang about here," Berthe said. "Come on up while I put my things away. I can make you a cup of coffee."

The suggestion startled Werthen; he had never been in a young lady's rooms unchaperoned. Despite his best efforts at keeping such surprise off his face, Berthe felt his discomfort.

"Don't worry, counselor. I won't try and seduce you."

She took his hand and led him past the scandalized glances of the *Portier*. Berthe's suite of rooms were simply and elegantly furnished with Jugendstil pieces. She made coffee as he looked at the Japanese wood-block prints on her wall and glanced at the writings of Karl Marx and John Ruskin in her bookcase. She served coffee in an earthenware jug and they talked for at least an hour.

As he was leaving, she leaned toward him perceptibly. He

took her in his arms and kissed her warm lips. She smelled like fresh linen and a new day.

After that, they had been apart little. And now, here they sat in the sunshine of the outdoor café on the corner of Graben and Kärntnerstrasse.

Berthe and he were freshly returned from his parents at Hohelände, where they had announced their engagement.

Werthen's sparrowlike mother could only say, "Really, Karlschen, you do surprise one." At the same time, his father thundered at him, "Engaged! Why, man, you haven't known the girl a pair of weeks. I'll be damned."

To be honest, no little part of his initial attraction to Berthe had been the inappropriateness of the liaison. The Habsburg heir apparent, Franz Ferdinand, was also creating a stir at court with a similar romance. Sent to woo one of the several eligible daughters of the Archduchess Isabel, Franz Ferdinand had instead fallen in love with the archduchess's lady-in-waiting, Sophie Chotek, daughter of a Bohemian baron. Franz Ferdinand was said to be prepared to accept a morganatic marriage, which would mean that none of his children would be heir to the throne. The emperor was believed to have uttered an uncharacteristic obscenity when presented the news. The militaristic and bellicose Franz Ferdinand was the last man in the world Werthen would have credited with such romantic notions.

And so here he was, sitting in the September sunshine of Vienna, with his own Sophie.

Their tea came and Werthen and Berthe settled down to conversation again. She thought that perhaps they had been too precipitate, announcing their engagement as they had done. He thought not.

"A spring wedding would be quite fine, don't you think?" he

said breezily. It was not that he was not taking this seriously. Rather it was all such good fun.

"And you haven't even met my father yet." Her mother died when Berthe was ten.

"I am sure he will approve."

"Don't be so positive," she said, squeezing lemon into her tea. "Papa doesn't think much of Christian converts."

Herr Meisner, it appeared, was as stubbornly Jewish as the Werthens were passionately assimilationist. His daughter had, happily, like Werthen, given up on religion as a divisive and somewhat antiquated institution.

"Registry marriages are quite the fashion now," Werthen added brightly, dismissing the matter of parental approval. "You *will* still love me in the spring, won't you?"

She shook her head in mock disapproval. "Try to be serious for just one moment."

Suddenly from the street there arose a stir. A young boy was selling what appeared to be a special edition of the *Neue Freie Presse,* and passersby were swooping the papers out of his hands as quickly as he could produce a new one from his shoulder bag. Their waiter spoke to one of those who had just procured a paper. Werthen could see the waiter's shoulders slump, as if struck a powerful blow. He put his hand to his face, muttering, "It can't be."

"Karl?" Berthe said, grabbing his hand. "Is it war?"

Werthen called to the waiter, who came to their table.

"Please excuse the emotion. This is a terrible day."

"What is it?" Werthen said.

"Our empress is dead. Assassinated in Geneva!"

ELEVEN

The state funeral was a week later. The entire city was draped in black, and even the weather contributed to the gloom; after weeks of sunny skies, the day dawned chill and cloudy. By noon storm clouds had gathered, threatening to rain at any moment. Black umbrellas added to the funereal bleakness.

Pictures of the Empress Elisabeth, dear Sisi to the Viennese, appeared in every shop window. The populace was in mourning for the empress, who, truth be told, had been absent more than present in her capital city. "The wandering empress," some journalists had taken to calling her. She had built a villa on the Greek island of Corfu but quickly tired of it. A brilliant horsewoman, she roamed Europe and the British Isles in search of hunts. Declared the most beautiful woman in the world, Sisi was, it seemed to Werthen, also the saddest. A cousin of mad King Ludwig of Bavaria, she probably inherited some of that regent's tainted blood. Sensitive and somewhat unstable, she could not suffer the court intrigues or pomp in Vienna. Her absences made Emperor Franz Josef a straw widower, but the empress had seen to his well-being, arranging the society of a Burgtheater actress, Katharina Schratt, to entertain him in her stead. With the death of her son, Crown Prince Rudolf, in 1889, Elisabeth had completely forgone even the pretense of her imperial duties. She had not even returned to Vienna for the emperor's jubilee celebrations earlier in the summer.

And now her ceaseless wanderings were over, for she had been killed by the anarchist Luigi Luccheni in Geneva, struck low by a sharpened file. Luccheni was in custody in Switzerland, elated with the celebrity that had suddenly attached itself to him. Had he not killed an empress? Had he not sent shock waves around the world with the telegraphed news of her death? Had he not brought all of Vienna and Austria to a weeping halt by his singular blow?

What a world we live in, Werthen thought, when such a guttersnipe and lowlife as the uneducated, illegitimate stonecutter Luccheni could affect world events.

Ever since hearing the name of the assassin, Werthen had been puzzled as well as outraged. He was sure he had heard or read the name "Luccheni" somewhere recently. It was infuriating; the memory teased him, but would not come. Finally he had to force himself to stop trying to retrieve it. Perhaps he would remember without trying.

The Saturday of the funeral, Werthen had been invited by Klimt to view the cortege from the balcony windows of the new Hotel Krantz on the Neuer Markt, across from the small and severely plain Capuchin Church. In the crypt of this church, the Habsburgs had been buried for several centuries. Klimt was not actually the host for this viewing assemblage, but was a guest himself of a notable foreign visitor to Vienna, the American writer Mark Twain. As the hotel would be the new home for Twain during the winter months, Herr Krantz had invited him and his family and friends to watch the procession from what could be termed loge seats.

Klimt had made the writer's acquaintance just the week before, when Twain visited the Secession. They had hit it off—Twain had apparently mistaken Klimt for one of the workmen, and the painter had taken that as a compliment—and the result was an invitation to Klimt and a friend. With Emilie Flöge laid up with a cold, Klimt had been good enough to include Werthen as this friend.

Small enough recompense, Werthen figured, as the painter had yet to pay his legal bill.

Werthen met Klimt outside the hotel at noon. The square was already flooded with citizenry braving the occasional shower. They went up to the hotel mezzanine, a glassed-in portico overlooking Neuer Markt. Beneath was a sea of bowlers, black-feathered hats, and umbrellas. Klimt led Werthen to the American, who was holding his own court from an easy chair at one end of the room. Numerous other notables were gathered here, as well, Werthen noticed, including the writer Arthur Schnitzler, the peace activist Baroness Bertha Kinsky von Suttner, the Countess Misa Wydenbruck-Esterházy, and the musicians Theodor Leschetizky and Ossip Gabrilowitsch.

Twain was attired in his customary white suit and did not bother to stand when Klimt introduced Werthen. He merely waved a cigar at the lawyer to acknowledge his presence and confined his comments to Klimt, speaking a rather bizarre mixture of German and Yankee English. Werthen, who had studied English from a British tutor, was flummoxed by the expression "polecat," which Twain employed to describe the assassin, Luccheni. Klimt smiled and nodded his head at Twain's outburst, but as they left their host to take up a position at a window, Klimt muttered, "Couldn't understand a word the man was saying."

Below the hotel, soldiers, dressed in dazzling uniforms, cleared the Neuer Markt, pushing the crowds back to the sidewalks and forming a cordon around the entire square. Slowly the square filled again, but now not with civilians but with naval and army officers in dress uniforms and gleaming gilt helmets. Fifty Austrian generals wore bright green plumes and pale blue tunics, while other officers wore red, gold, and white uniforms, creating an immense palette of colors in contrast to the black drabness of the normal citizens who had lately stood there. Suddenly the storm clouds parted, and shafts of sunlight filled the square, illuminating the sea of color in such a flash of light that Werthen had to squint his eyes. Near the door to the church itself two groups took up position: one was the purple-robed Knights of Malta, and the other the red-clad Knights of the Order of the Golden Fleece. Werthen, who had thought to bring his opera glasses with him, identified the latter by the insignia of the small figure of a pendant sheep's fleece or skin in gold hanging from the neck of each of these iron-rigid men. He knew the figure represented the mythical fleece that Jason and the Argonauts sought, symbolizing the high ideals of the knights of the order, primary among them the preservation of the Catholic Church.

The military officers filled the square, leaving only a narrow path for carriages to come and go, delivering their aristocratic cargo at the church steps. First to arrive were the Habsburg archdukes and archduchesses, then the German kaiser, the kings of Saxony, Serbia, and Romania, and the regent of Bavaria. These were followed by over two hundred court personages and high nobility, who would be allowed to enter the church. After a full hour of such carriage traffic, a procession of priests arrived, bearing the crucifix, their golden robes touched with white lace. Finally the church was filled, but there was still a half hour to wait before the arrival of the hearse. Werthen passed the time by playing his opera glasses over the faces of those who had found space on the sidewalks of the square. He stopped when one face came dramatically into focus: Dr. Hanns Gross.

Werthen excitedly pointed out the criminologist to Klimt, who insisted they bring him up in the hotel to view the rest of the procession. Werthen began to object, noting it was hardly their place to do the inviting, but Klimt was out the door before he could finish. Werthen followed the painter's progress as he made his way around the perimeter of the crowd and finally reached Gross, who looked pleasantly surprised, then followed Klimt's raised hand as he pointed to the Hotel Krantz. He, too, seemed reluctant to intrude, but Klimt literally dragged him for a few paces to indicate his seriousness.

By the time Klimt returned with Gross, the church bells of Vienna had already begun sounding, marking the imminent arrival of the black, baroque hearse drawn by eight gray Lipizzaners and carrying the body of the Empress Elisabeth. Wherever one was in the Habsburg realms this afternoon—from Innsbruck in the west to Budapest and beyond to Transylvania in the east, and from Prague in the north to Sarajevo in the south—he or she would not be out of earshot of the bells, Werthen knew, for over ten thousand churches were now pealing their bells in unison.

As the bells continued to sound, Werthen could discern the thrumming of hooves on cobble. At precisely twelve minutes after four a body of cavalry rode into the square, four abreast, clearing a way for the funeral cortege. After the cavalry came a group of lancers, dressed in blue and gold, followed by a mourning coach drawn by six horses, bearing the emperor himself, aided by his daughters Marie Valerie and Gisela. As he descended, the old man looked bowed and broken by this final—one hoped—calamity in his long life. He had withstood assassination attempts, a troubled marriage to the aloof Elisabeth, and the tragic deaths of his brother, Maximilian, in Mexico, and his son, Crown Prince Rudolf, dead by his own hand in 1889.

Reportedly, when given the news of Sisi's death, Franz Josef had finally broken down, crying out, "Am I to be spared nothing?"

Franz Josef entered the church before the arrival of the huge black hearse, each of its eight Lipizzaners plumed with black ostrich feathers. The hearse was surrounded by outriders in black with white wigs, and by a tall, white-haired man dressed in the same bloodred cloak as the Knights of the Order of the Golden Fleece at the door of the church. This was Franz Josef's aide Prince Grunenthal, the man who was probably Inspektor Meindl's powerful sponsor in Vienna. The last of a long line of his family who had served Habsburg emperors over the centuries, Grunenthal was perhaps as old as the emperor, but seemed years younger, his body erect and proud as he preceded the coffin to the steps of the church. There, according to ritual, he knocked on the door. Werthen focused on the aged prince with his opera glasses. He knew what was being said by heart, as did every schoolboy in Austria.

With the first knock, a friar inside the church would demand, "Who is it?"

Then Grunenthal would answer, "Her Most Serene Imperial and Royal Highness, the Empress Elisabeth of Austria-Hungary."

"We know her not."

The door would remain closed until Grunenthal again knocked.

"Who is there?"

"The Empress Elisabeth."

"We know her not."

Then would come a third knock upon the door by the golden staff Grunenthal carried for the occasion.

"Who is there?"

"Your sister Elisabeth. A poor sinner."

At which the doors would, and did, open.

It could hardly be called a festive air, but after the closing of the church doors upon the coffin, the atmosphere at the Hotel Krantz lightened. The assembled could see nothing more, and now it was time for a bit of socializing.

Gross explained that he had returned from Czernowitz for

the funeral, but also because there was nothing for him to do there.

"They are still in the process of building my classrooms and laboratories," he complained. "I would have stayed on in Graz if I'd known such was the case. There will be no classes until the spring semester at this rate." His wife, Adele, was off visiting a school friend in Paris, waiting for him to get settled before coming to Bukovina.

"But that is marvelous, Gross," Werthen said. "You can stay on in Vienna now for a time. There's a room in my flat at your disposal."

"Really, Werthen, too kind of you." Gross looked as if he meant it, too. "Czernowitz is no world capital, to put it mildly."

Klimt took Gross by the arm to introduce him to Twain, but the two were already acquainted, at least by mail. Twain had consulted Gross several years earlier when writing his *Tom Sawyer, Detective.* Now the two began conversing animatedly, despite Twain's limited linguistic abilities.

After the final peeling of bells, indicating the end of the service at the Capuchin Church, sherry was served, and a half hour later, the proceedings were about to end when Twain made a pronouncement in English all of those gathered could understand.

"But of course they've got the wrong man in Switzerland. Or the right one for the wrong reason. It's all to do with the Hungarians. First Rudolf and now his mother."

"What could he have meant?" Werthen asked of Gross when, later that evening, they were settled down to a nice plate of Frau Blatschky's boiled beef and potatoes, accompanied by a chilled bottle of tart *Grüner Veltliner* from Gumpoldskirchen.

Gross, who had taken Werthen up on his invitation and was now occupying the spacious back bedroom, spooned freshly ground horseradish onto his plate. Berthe, joining them for dinner, sat primly at the other end of the table from Werthen, giving him a taste of what married life might be like. The dining room faced onto the courtyard. It was a trim little room, all in Biedermeier. Two silver candelabra lit the space in warm light.

"Twain is a man of fiction, never forget that," Gross somewhat cryptically answered. He offered the horseradish to Berthe with a dramatic flourish, but she politely declined.

"You mean he makes things up out of whole cloth, Herr Doktor Gross?" she said with a wry smile.

"Perhaps not *whole* cloth. But he takes tall tales related to him by the Hungarian nobility a little too literally. They are forever going on about their Magyar freedom, as if they would not in turn oppress every other minority in their realm if given half a chance."

"I take it you are not a fan of the dual monarchy," Berthe said, shooting Werthen a conspiratorial look. Werthen had shared his high and low opinions of Gross with her, noting especially the criminologist's tendency toward pomposity.

"I should say not, my good woman," Gross boomed. "Most idiotic bit of diplomacy Franz Josef ever came up with. Eviscerated the empire. I wouldn't doubt that Austria will be reduced to a mere shadow of herself in the matter of two decades. But that is neither here nor there. Friend Twain was merely repeating the conspiracy theories so often voiced by the Magyars. To wit, Crown Prince Rudolf was not the victim of suicide nine years ago, but of an assassination by those close to power who had no appetite for his liberal ways or his pro-Magyar views. I assume the same is now being said of his unfortunate mother, who also tended to romanticize the Hungarians."

"An intriguing theory," Werthen said, winking at Berthe. This was going to be jolly good fun, he thought, having Gross as a houseguest and having Berthe to help him poke and prod at the man's inflated ego.

"Poppycock," Gross said, cutting his beef and forking it along with a healthy dose of horseradish into his mouth. He chewed aggressively, then washed down the beef with a draft of wine.

"The man's confessed to his crime," the criminologist continued. "I fear our empress fell victim to a professed anarchist who was not sure of his intended victim until he almost literally ran into Elisabeth on the quays of Geneva. Who could not even afford a proper weapon, but had to grind down a cheap file to make a stiletto."

Gross shook his head vigorously, as if this tawdry fact added to the tragedy. "No, my friends," he said, eyeing Werthen and then Berthe, "I am afraid what we have here is not high intrigue but low and very sad comedy."

TWELVE

Gross did not bear inactivity well. Werthen had assumed this to be the case before; now that they were sharing the same roof, he perforce had to experience it firsthand.

On the Monday following the state funeral, Gross made a return visit to his beloved Brueghel room at the Kunsthistorisches Museum. Werthen, who had resumed his law practice after his return from Upper Austria, met him for lunch after a busy morning preparing the trust of Baron von Geistl. They attended the Burgtheater that evening, seeing Girardi play in Johann Nestroy's *Lumpacivagabundus,* a satirical comedy that fitted the actor's talents perfectly. Gross, however, was not amused, Werthen noted.

Nestroy had made the leap from Volkstheater to the more prestigious Burgtheater because of longevity; the play had premiered in 1833 and had confused the Habsburg censors enough so that its subtle social criticism had been overlooked even to the present day. The play chronicled the fortunes and misfortunes of Leim, a joiner, Zwirn, a tailor, and Knieriem, a cobbler, all framed by a series of supernatural events, primary of which was their holding communally a winning lottery number.

Nestroy, not only a playwright but also a skilled actor, assumed

the role of Knieriem 258 times, or so tonight's program explained. Girardi had taken on this part now for himself and performed it with great aplomb. Yet Gross could seemingly find
nothing to like in the farce. Each time the audience broke into
laughter, Gross scowled at the stage. He squirmed in his seat at
every turn of the plot, as the three journeymen pondered how to
use the money miraculously won from their shared lottery ticket.
Instead of bettering themselves, Zwirn and Knieriem squandered
their magical winnings and remained, at the end of the play,
firmly—one might say defiantly—outside the orbit of bourgeois
life. Only Leim used his winnings wisely, marrying his longtime
sweetheart and setting up a productive business.

"Absolute piffle," Gross pronounced after the houselights went
up following the third act. "Why they should be showing such
revolutionary and demoralizing prattle at the noble Burgtheater
is beyond me."

"Oh, come now, Gross," Werthen replied as they made their
way up the aisle to the coat check in the lobby. "You sound like
an old reactionary. I found it extremely clever."

"Clever," Gross spluttered. "So when you and your Fräulein
Berthe marry and begin having children, I suppose you will
want your offspring to ape such dissolute behavior. I think not,
Werthen. Speaking from personal experience, one must be ever
vigilant when it comes to one's children."

Werthen made no reply to this. Gross was of course referring
to the troubled history between himself and his gifted son, Otto.
Where Gross senior was all business and practicalities, young Otto
had a playful spirit, never one to take life too seriously. Indeed,
even as an adolescent Otto traveled in somewhat louche society,
and this more than anything else troubled his father. Young Otto
made friends of artistic bohemians and had himself become a free
thinker in matters of sex and marriage. Gross even mentioned
experimentation with drugs. Although Otto seemed to have straightened himself out and was now successfully pursuing medical studies,

son and father were still oil and water. It was a mark of Gross's disturbed equilibrium that he would mention Otto at all, even tangentially. Gross was, to put it simply, bored stiff.

The next morning they spent a painfully quiet breakfast together before Werthen departed for the office. Walking to the suite of rooms he rented in Habsburgergasse in the First District, Werthen wondered if perhaps it had been a mistake inviting Gross to stay. He was turning churlish and bearish; even fair-minded and forgiving Berthe was making herself scarce, not really caring to be around the man in such moods.

That night, however, Werthen recalled that he had received a piece of mail for the criminologist, forwarded from his former address at the Hotel Bristol. Frau Blatschky had prepared a marvelous *Zwiebelrostbraten* for dinner, which they accompanied with a bottle of Bordeaux that Werthen had taken great pains in choosing at his wine merchant's on the way home.

Gross seemed to brighten as he opened and read the letter Werthen produced for him.

"Well, that is an interesting turn of events," he uttered as he set the letter down next to his plate. He filled his glass half full of the wine, which had not yet had time to breathe, and threw it back as if it were American whiskey.

"What is it, Gross?"

"The autopsy report on Herr Frosch, the last victim in the Prater murders. Not that it matters much now. His neck was broken, just as we all assumed at the time."

"Doesn't sound so interesting to me," Werthen said, pouring himself a glass of the wine and swirling it in his goblet.

"The interesting part is that the man was at death's door when he was killed. Dying of cancer, so it appears."

"Hmm." Werthen eyed the deep ruby glints of the wine, the "legs" forming at the lip of his glass. "Wonder if he knew?"

"That, my dear friend, I hope to determine. Tomorrow."

Werthen was about to denigrate the idea. After all, the case was closed. What did it matter if the man knew he was dying or not? Idle curiosity had made Werthen posit the question, but suddenly he was happy he had. He held his tongue. No sense in discouraging Gross. Any activity was better than none.

They spent the rest of the evening in pleasant conversation.

In the morning Werthen inquired of Frau Blatschky if their guest had risen yet. Werthen was due at the office earlier than usual and did not want to wait for breakfast.

"Oh, yes, sir. The Herr Doktor was up with the birds and had his coffee and kipfel an hour earlier than usual. I believe he has already departed."

The news came as something of a relief for Werthen, who could now unfold the morning *Neue Freie Presse* and read in peace. He wondered if he should get back in the habit of writing his stories before beginning his workday; if he should bother writing them at all anymore. However, for the time being, he was content enough just sipping his coffee and scanning the paper for large chunks of white space, which would indicate a story that had been censored. This was a national sport in Austria. People would then spend the rest of the day trying to discover the juicy bits that had been cut out of the newspapers.

At five that afternoon, just as Werthen was preparing to close up for the day, Gross telephoned him, his voice vibrant and excited once again. It was a pleasure to hear that tone.

Gross invited him for a drink at the Café Central on Herrengasse, the home of Vienna's literati since the scandalous demolition of the Café Griensteidl the year before. With the building of a bank on the site of the Griensteidl, the literary world of Vienna, including Schnitzler, Peter Altenberg, Hugo von Hofmannsthal, Karl Kraus, Hermann Bahr, and Felix Salten, had migrated to the nearby Central. Werthen was somewhat amused by Gross's choice of venue, but happily agreed to meet him there in half an hour.

Gross was occupying a corner table by the time Werthen arrived and was nursing a *viertel* of white wine. Werthen ordered the same and joined his friend, surveying the other tables for anyone he knew. Only the young Hofmannsthal, sporting a wispy mustache, and his older mentor, the bohemian and sandal-wearing Altenberg, were in attendance today.

"You're looking awfully pleased with yourself, Gross," Werthen said as he took a chair. "What've you been up to?"

"It has been an intriguing day, my dear Werthen. Most intriguing."

As he sipped his wine, Gross explained to Werthen that he had first gone to Frau Frosch on the Gusshausstrasse to ascertain whether her husband knew of his illness, and to find the name of his doctor. In the event, however, the Frau had other news for Gross.

"She told me that she had been contemplating getting in touch with me," Gross noted. "I am happy to say that my earlier efforts in winning her trust thus paid off. With the assassination of the empress, Frau Frosch felt she was no longer under an obligation of secrecy."

Gross paused dramatically, seeing that he had caught Werthen's attention.

"Herr Frosch had a distinguished visitor in June," Gross finally continued. "The empress herself came to talk to him. According to Frau Frosch, they were in consultation for over an hour in his study, and when she left, she was extremely distraught. The empress made Frau Frosch pledge herself to secrecy. No one was to know of her visit to Herr Frosch."

"Whatever were they talking about, Gross?"

"Herr Frosch did not confide in his wife, but she does recall him talking of his memoirs at about this same time, and how he was finally going to tell the full truth about the Mayerling tragedy."

"You mean Crown Prince Rudolf's suicide?"

"Was there another tragedy played out there?"

Really, Gross could be insufferable when he was in his cogitating frame of mind, but Werthen let it go. This was still better than depression by inactivity.

"But what could he know?" Werthen wondered aloud. The Mayerling tragedy had rocked the court and all of Austria in January of 1889. Rudolf, heir to the throne of Franz Josef, supposedly despondent at being kept out of responsible situations in the military and government, had turned to drugs and drink. Perhaps he had inherited some of the Wittelsbach instability from his mother. There had even been talk of the young prince suffering from incurable syphilis. At any rate, one snowy night he had taken the life of his young mistress, Marie Vetsera, then shot himself.

"It turns out that Herr Frosch was in service to the crown prince himself, as a personal valet. He was at Rudolf's hunting lodge in Mayerling the very night of the deaths."

"But we found no evidence of such memoirs," Werthen said, recalling their patient search of Herr Frosch's papers following his death. "We concluded it was all hot air on his part."

"Something important brought Empress Elisabeth to see Frosch after all these years," Gross said. "Something was said behind closed doors, according to Frau Frosch, to shake the empress so that she needed a brandy to bring the color back to her cheeks before leaving."

Neither said anything for a few moments, then Gross continued, "Frau Frosch, by the way, knew nothing of her husband's terminal condition, but she was able to supply me with the name of his doctor. I visited that gentleman this afternoon, and he verified that Frosch was aware of the seriousness of his cancer. That would seem to add verity to the tale of Frosch being willing to share certain secrets with the empress."

"You mean that he no longer had anything to lose?" Werthen was quick to reply.

"Exactly. Let us surmise that his silence about certain incidents had been purchased or otherwise won—"

"By threats?"

Gross shrugged at the suggestion. "Perhaps. But facing death anyway, perhaps he decided he had no reason to hold his tongue any longer."

"I see your point. This is intriguing to be sure."

"It becomes even more intriguing once one looks at the date of the empress's visit. June twelfth."

Gross said this with a flourish, as if pulling a final rabbit out of a hat, but it took Werthen a moment to figure out why this date should be so important.

"You mean that the Prater murders began just a few days later?"

"The body of the washerwoman, Maria Müller, was found on June fifteenth," Gross concurred.

"You're saying the murders were somehow connected to what Frosch knew about the Mayerling tragedy? That seems a bit of speculative fancy."

"I am surmising nothing, merely stating certain facts. Herr Frosch was the sixth victim in that string of murders. Yet he is the first for whom we can now find a possible motive. Such motive being that he was going to release damaging information about the death of Crown Prince Rudolf. If Rudolf's death was not a suicide, then those responsible would not want such information made public. This is instructive, I believe."

Werthen's head began to spin with possibilities. If Rudolf had not killed himself, then who had murdered him? And why?

The crown prince had been known as a firebrand and a liberal. He had written surreptitiously for Moritz Szeps's liberal *Wiener Tageblatt* for several years before his death; his articles criticized the do-nothing aristocracy and the foreign policy of his father that favored alliances with Germany and Russia. Rudolf was also known to consort with powerful Magyars in Budapest seeking Hungarian independence, and to court the

French for secret treaties, both of which would have been trea-
sonable activities. The crown prince had, in fact, numerous enemies at court, in the diplomatic corps of the Ballhausplatz, and
in the military. Even the new heir apparent, Franz Ferdinand,
could be said to have a motive for Rudolf's death. It had, after
all, cleared the way for him to become emperor upon the death
of Franz Josef.

Theories about the crown prince's death had abounded at the
time, in part the fault of the clumsy handling of the matter by
the then prime minister, Count Taaffe, who had wanted to employ
Habsburg censorship to control the tragedy. The official version
had, at first, laid the cause of Rudolf's death to a heart attack, and
no mention was made of the unfortunate young Vetsera woman,
who accompanied Rudolf in death. Taaffe had, however, quickly
discovered the limits of censorship, for the foreign press got wind
of the double shooting, and wild story followed wild story: The
Hungarians assassinated him because he betrayed their plot; the
French killed him for fear he would tell of their secret negotiations; a local hunting guide had shot him for seducing the man's
wife; he was killed in a duel over the honor of a young Auersperg
princess. Finally, it had to be made public in Austria that the
crown prince had killed his young lover and then himself, but
some still blamed a Magyar or French plot, even an assassination
by the prime minister.

Such thoughts were, for Werthen, an open door to unhealthy
and unwarranted suspicions, what Krafft-Ebing and other psy-
chologists termed paranoia.

In fact, Gross was getting too far ahead of himself, making
too rapid a connection between Frosch's position as former valet
to Rudolf and his death last August. Werthen decided to temper
such thoughts with sober reality.

"You forget, Gross, that Binder confessed to those crimes.
There was no motive other than the wretched nightmares playing in the mind of a man diseased with syphilis."

"Such was the official version, yes."

"The version you subscribed to, as well," Werthen reminded him.

But Gross ignored this statement. "I recall a comment at the time of Frosch's death. Something along the lines that Frau Frosch, who had clearly been beaten by her husband, had sufficient motive to want him dead. That in fact perhaps the other deaths were committed only to cover up the real one, that of Herr Frosch. I made that statement with no small amount of levity. However, it may be a theory we now need to reexamine in light of new evidence."

"Surely you cannot be suggesting we reopen the Prater murders?"

Gross merely raised eyebrows at Werthen.

"You cannot seriously believe that those other unfortunates were killed simply to divert attention from the death of Frosch?" Werthen went on. "Besides, if Frosch were the intended victim all along and the other five only used to cover up the true crime, then why risk exposure by waiting over two months to do him in?"

"That, my dear Werthen, is something to be taken into consideration as we proceed."

But Werthen did not fully attend to this reply. Instead, he was now struck with a more serious consideration, one he was sure Gross had already thought of.

"But following these admittedly wild conjectures on your part . . ."

"Follow on," Gross encouraged.

"That would lead one to wonder about the death of the empress, as well. If Frosch were killed because of something he knew about the death of Crown Prince Rudolf, then was Empress Elisabeth's death connected to that of the former valet to her son? Was she killed because of what Frosch disclosed to her?"

Gross smiled contentedly. "Fine reasoning, Werthen."

"Outlandish reasoning. The anarchist Luccheni committed

that crime." And suddenly it was there, popping into his mind unbidden.

"What's the matter, Werthen? You look as though you'd seen a ghost."

"The man's name. That feckless Luccheni. I knew I had seen it somewhere before. Gross, remember the watch list we secured from Meindl? That of anarchists and other terrorists the police were keeping a watch on this summer?"

"Luccheni was on that list?"

"I'd swear I read his name there. 'Luccheni, Luigi, stonecutter.' He was in Vienna this summer. My god, Gross, could Luccheni have committed all the Prater murders? But what of Binder, then?"

"We are, it seems to me, Werthen, in the strangely unique situation of having too many guilty parties."

"This is all supposition, Gross."

"And supposition it will remain unless we investigate further, my friend."

Werthen knew what Gross was implicitly asking of him, and it took him no longer than an instant to answer.

"Then let us begin, Gross. *Herr Ober,*" Werthen called to the headwaiter. "Another round of wine here."

As they left the Café Central an hour later, neither Gross nor Werthen was aware of the figure sitting in the covered carriage across the street. He sat in the shadows and watched the pair as they made their way down the Herrengasse.

Not now, he thought. Too public.

So the swimmers had, as he earlier feared, floundered onto something. Amateurs with the luck of amateurs.

Their luck, however, was running out.

Soon. Very soon.

THIRTEEN

Berthe had taken his decision well.

It was during the intermission in Gustav Mahler's debut at the Musikverein at the helm of the Vienna Philharmonic. Werthen had met her for dinner and the symphony after leaving the company of Gross at the Café Central.

Mahler was making a name for himself in the city of music. The year before, he had taken over direction of Vienna's Court Opera and was transforming that house to be the leading one in Europe. Of course to assume that official court position, Mahler, a Jew (though nonpracticing) had had to convert to Christianity.

For his debut, he was conducting Beethoven's Seventh Symphony, Werthen's favorite. The evening had begun with Mozart's *Jupiter Symphony,* and in the interval Werthen explained to Berthe what Gross had discovered and his own decision to assist the criminologist once more. Werthen's legal assistant, Dr. Wilfried Ungar, three years out of Vienna law, was a capable young man, well able to take over the work at the law firm for the time being. Werthen's most important commission, the preparation of Baron von Geistl's trust, had just been completed.

"You need not explain all this to me, Karl. When I agreed to be your wife, I did so knowing I am an independent woman well able to provide for myself. I am not marrying you for your earning power. You must do in life those things that most satisfy. Otherwise, what is it all for?"

He wanted to embrace her then and there in the second-floor interval salon of the Musikverein, amid the potted palms and the tuxedoed and bejeweled patrons who were milling about during intermission, *Sekt* flutes in hand. He closed his eyes and smiled at her instead.

Once seated again in the darkness of the auditorium, she took his hand. As the music swelled during the adagio section of the Seventh, he thought he had never been happier in his life.

Meindl was surprised to see Gross back in Vienna. Gross, so he had told Werthen, was playing on instinct. They had come to the Police Presidium this morning to request a favor.

"So you intend writing up the assassination of the empress in your journal," Meindl said, when presented with the request.

"It should present a fascinating case of the terrorist personality," Gross said. "Anything we can learn about Herr Lucheni could aid in preventing such another outrage."

This implicit appeal to Meindl's professionalism finally did the trick. They were presented with the Lucheni file ten minutes later.

"But how is it you knew we had a watch file on the man?" Meindl asked.

"My colleague, Dr. Werthen, remembered a list of names you so graciously supplied when we were engaged upon . . . that other business."

Meindl nodded at Werthen, casting a weak smile. "Quite so." Then to Gross again: "I will need that file back as quickly as possible. This is all rather irregular, you realize."

Not a word of thanks for their earlier assistance; not even an acknowledgment of their participation. The man was an infernal crawler, Werthen decided. Always on the lookout for his own career.

Meindl showed them to a room normally used for interrogation, its windows so high on the wall that one could not see the outside, only imagine it. They sat at the large and rather bruised table placed in the middle of the room, dividing up the pages of the lengthy report between them.

Werthen took the first part of the report, which included a biography of the anarchist Luccheni. Born in Paris in 1873 to an unmarried laundress of Italian extraction, Luccheni never knew his father. His mother left France the year following her son's birth and placed the infant in an orphanage in Parma. From there he was cast like so much flotsam onto the streets at an early age, to become a laborer. Soon he found an easier occupation as a soldier, serving in Naples under Captain Prince Vera d'Arazona. After three years, Luccheni left the army and became a servant to the prince, but this lasted for only a few months.

Luccheni took to the road, settling for a time in Switzerland, but also roaming to various capitals, including Vienna and Budapest, and falling into the company of anarchists who supplied the pliant and barely literate young man with literature espousing the destruction of society leading to the creation of a free and classless world in its place. Soon he began, according to Swiss police informants who had infiltrated anarchist cells, to espouse his belief in the "propaganda of the deed," or letting one's actions spread the philosophy of anarchism.

From the pages before Werthen, it was apparent that Luccheni had come to Vienna in early June. Word had come from the Swiss police that Luccheni had boarded a train in Geneva bound for Vienna on June 10. The police in Vienna had not picked up his trail, however, until June 12, when he was spotted outside a known anarchist haven in the workers' district of Fünfhaus, a pension run by a Frau Geldner. Luccheni had spent the day of the twelfth in the grounds of the Volksgarten, the lovely gardens built on what were once part of the city walls, destroyed by French troops under Napoléon. Werthen himself often enjoyed a pleasant afternoon in these rose gardens, laid out to resemble Paris's Luxembourg Gardens.

Luccheni had passed the morning and afternoon moving from one bench to the other, keeping in clear sight of the entrances and exits to the park, as if expecting someone to enter the gardens at any moment. Finally at precisely 5:28 that afternoon, he was approached by a tall man wearing the clothes of a housepainter: white overalls and a boatlike hat fashioned from an old newspaper. He handed Luccheni a note and left the park. Unfortunately, just at that time, the other half of the pair of police watching Luccheni had had to retire to the nearest pissoir on the Ring. Thus the police had been unable to trace the further movements of this other man. The partner did, however, return in time to aid in the tracking of Luccheni out of the Volksgarten and onto the Ringstrasse, where he turned left, headed toward the Opera.

One watcher crossed the Ringstrasse to follow parallel while the other kept a discreet distance behind the anarchist, careful not to be noticed. Luccheni walked with speed, according to the police report, as if he knew his destination and had to be there at a certain time. Just beyond the Court Opera, he crossed the busy Ringstrasse on Kärntnerstrasse. The two police watchers now changed positions vis-à-vis their quarry. Luccheni continued onto Wiedner Hauptstrasse past the Karlsplatz. Just in back of the Technical University he suddenly turned left onto Paniglgasse, then right at the first intersection, with Argentinierstrasse, and then another left on Gusshausstrasse. The police watchers followed him to about midblock, where Luccheni stopped and seemed to assume watch himself on a building across the street. They did not know which one, either number 12 or 14.

Suddenly Werthen stopped reading. He felt a chill go through his body.

"Gross," he said. "You should look at this."

Werthen handed the criminologist the pages he had finished and continued reading from where he had left off.

Subject remained partly hidden behind a gas lamp for over two hours. At one point he appeared eager to move. A female resident of number 12, dressed in black, quickly departed, ushered out by two men into a waiting landau. The carriage pulled away quickly and the subject resumed his seeming watch. At 8:12 precisely, subject broke off watch and continued walking back to his accommodations in Fünfhaus.

Gross had already finished reading his pages, and Werthen handed him the final ones for June 12. The criminologist puffed out his lips as he read, then stabbed the paper with a forefinger.

"Hah! You see, Werthen. There is a connection!"

"That was the very night Empress Elisabeth was visiting Herr Frosch," Werthen said excitedly. "It was Frosch's apartment Luccheni was watching. Gusshausstrasse 12. It all fits."

"Lower your voice, my friend," Gross counseled. "Yes, indeed. It was to Herr Frosch the anarchist had been directed. Most likely by this message handed to him by the mysterious house-painter. Thus, he was already stalking his victim long before he struck."

"That was her the police saw leave the building, wasn't it, Gross? The lady all in black? Empress Elisabeth."

"Yes. It must have been. And for once she was traveling in the company of bodyguards, or the cowardly Luccheni may well have struck that very night. It seems, however, that the police watchers were ignorant of the empress's movements. They obviously did not know her identity."

"She often traveled incognito. I believe," added Werthen, "that she often assumed the identity of one Countess Hohenembs, though usually her marvelous looks gave her away."

"This changes things dramatically," Gross said, collecting the papers. "There is nothing of interest in the later reports. The police, in fact, lost track of Lucheni by the fifteenth. It is assumed he had already left Vienna by that time. Or did he remain in Vienna for two more months, changing addresses to evade the police watch, and commit the atrocities we all put at the door of Herr Binder?"

"But for what possible motive? He was after royalty, after all, Gross. The newspapers say he was ready to kill the Duke of Orléans, but that the unfortunate empress stumbled into his path first. He was after someone important just to get his name in the papers. Why all those other victims then, several of whom were of the working class, which he, as an anarchist, professed to be protecting? It makes no sense."

"You are, of course, correct, Werthen. Such a theory does make no sense. However, we have posited the connection between the deaths of Frosch and the empress. Therefore, the only alternative theory is that Lucheni did not kill the empress."

Werthen simply stared at Gross, unable to say anything to such an outlandish statement.

"Come, Werthen. Close your gaping mouth and help me collate these papers and return them to Meindl. We have work to do."

Frau Geldner's pension was located on Clementinengasse, not far from the Empress Elisabeth West Train Station. Werthen could hear the groan and huff of engines arriving and departing; the heavy smell of smoke was in the air. This area was part of the northern extremity of the garment district, where looms and seamstresses worked twelve hours a day, six days a week.

Opening her door on the fourth knock, Frau Geldner was a large, florid woman dressed in a gingham housedress and smoking a meerschaum pipe. She scowled at Gross as he handed her his card.

"You blokes must have gotten the wrong address. We don't cater to your class here."

"No, Frau Geldner," Gross said, inserting his booted foot in the door to keep her from closing it on them. "We have the correct address. The one, I believe, where the celebrated Signor Luccheni briefly stayed last June."

She shook her head. "Don't know any Luccheni. Don't care much for foreigners. No toffs nor foreigners. That's my motto." She chuckled, coughing wetly. Three spiky black hairs bristled from the tip of her red nose.

"That is not what the police report says."

She glanced at his card again suspiciously. "Says here you're a professor. That right? Not police?"

"That is correct, my good woman."

"And who's the stooge with you? He don't say much, do he?"

At which comment Werthen felt it necessary to introduce himself.

"A lawyer, huh? Professor and lawyer all took the trouble to come way out to Fünfhaus to visit the likes of me. Must be important, then."

"Your working-class-rustic act is not convincing," Gross said sternly, his foot still in the door. "I have read your writings in the *Daily Anarchist*, Frau Geldner. And while I hardly agree with your thesis that all the woes in the world have been brought about by the plutocrats and aristocracy, I certainly recognize a first-class mind when I encounter one. Now can we please cease with this hard-bitten whore-mistress role that you have assumed and get down to business?"

At this, the Frau smiled, opened the door fully, and ushered them in.

"A professor who can read," she said, her voice now assuming a higher and, to Werthen's ears, a more refined tone. "What a novelty. Come this way, gentlemen. Into my lair."

They followed her down a long, dark hallway into a sitting

room that was surprisingly modern and comfortable. Werthen had been expecting a jumble of cheap and aged furniture, but he found a room appointed in Jugendstil and art nouveau chic, with chairs and divan upholstered in swirls of greens and golds that Klimt himself might have painted.

"We're not such barbarians, after all, are we, *Advokat* Werthen?" she said, catching his look of amazement.

But Gross was not interested in the tedious puncturing of the balloons of class bias. He took a chair before being offered and set to business.

"There is no use prevaricating. We know Luccheni stayed here for several days in June."

"Three to be precise," she said, moving to a cherrywood sideboard fitted with stained glass that could have been the work of Koloman Moser, another of Vienna's leading lights in the decorative arts.

"Slivovitz?" she offered. "I find it just the thing to pick up one's spirits in these difficult hours between *Gabelfrühstück* and lunch." She poured herself a healthy amount in a brandy snifter without waiting for their replies and merely shrugged when they both declined. The plum brandy went down in one swig, and she sat on the divan, motioning Werthen to take a chair.

"He always so simple?" she said to Gross.

"Madam—," Werthen began, but Gross cut him off with an upraised hand.

"Please. The matter at hand, and we can let you get on with your prelunch preparations."

She chuckled again at this. "You are a wry one, aren't you? Gross . . . ? You know, I may have heard of you."

He nodded appreciatively. "My work has its followers."

"Aren't you the fellow who told the world the Jews were slaughtering Christians in Bohemia? Blood rituals and all. My, but you were off the mark on that one."

"Yes," Gross answered abruptly. "Now about Luccheni."

"What about him? Silly little man, if you ask me. The chaps call him 'the stupid one.'"

"The 'chaps'? By which you mean fellow anarchists?" Gross said.

She nodded quite cheerfully. "That is exactly what I mean."

"Why was he here?" Werthen asked, suddenly tiring of this silly sparring.

"He speaks!" Another laugh, followed by an extended bout of moist coughing. She laid the pipe down on a side table, and it slowly extinguished itself. "Sorry," she said, once the fit had passed. "I'm not usually so rude. But with you two, I find it rather amusing."

"Nonetheless, Frau Geldner, you failed to answer my associate's question," Gross persisted. "What business did Luccheni have in Vienna?"

"None at all. He was on holiday for all I know. Or care."

"The man was a near vagrant," Werthen said. "You expect us to believe he was visiting Vienna for his cultural betterment?"

"I rent rooms," she said simply. "Many times such visitors are referrals and thus I know their business. Luccheni was not such a referral. He had simply heard of my pension from his friends and showed up on my doorstep on June eleventh. I could hardly turn him away, could I?"

"You said before," Werthen quoted, "'no toffs nor foreigners.' Are we to assume that was a lie? Either you were lying then or now."

But the lady remained unflustered. "Such eloquence might do very well in front of a judge, Herr *Advokat*, but here I make the rules. I am the judge. I say things. Some are true, some are jokes, and some are that awful thing you just mentioned, lies."

Gross threw his hands in the air. "Then we have little more to discuss. Perhaps the police . . ."

"Oh, they've been over it several times with me already. But I'll tell you something for nothing. That man Luccheni couldn't manage to kill a goldfish. He was all talk and no action. The ones who do the deeds, they're all action and no talk. Believe me, I've known both types."

"What do you make of her?" Werthen asked as they left the premises and headed to the *Fiaker* rank near the train station.

"Make of her?" Gross said as if pulled reluctantly out of thought. "Why, Werthen, I make nothing of the woman whatsoever."

"I mean, was she telling the truth about Luccheni?"

"She herself confessed to being laissez-faire where truth is concerned. I see no reason to even wonder about her comments. All of them are suspect. She could be up to her eyes in the plot to kill the empress, or she could be absolutely correct about Luccheni's incompetence."

Gross sped up his pace and Werthen almost had to break into a trot to keep up.

"Gross, would you please slow down. What's the hurry, man?"

He stopped suddenly, looking at Werthen with surprise. "I would have thought that was obvious, dear Werthen. We have a train to catch. If we make haste back to Josefstädterstrasse, we can pack, pick up a few essentials, and return to the West Train Station in time to catch the Alpine Express at four. That should allow us to arrive in time for early breakfast tomorrow morning."

"Arrive? Arrive where? What are you talking about, Gross?"

"Geneva, Werthen. We're going to interview Luccheni."

FOURTEEN

Werthen watched the early-autumn landscape race by outside the spotlessly clean window of the club car. Gross was holed up in his compartment, reading accounts of the empress's assassination in a variety of newspapers, from the London *Times*, to *Le Monde* from Paris, and Milan's *Corriere della Sera*. He had secured these from the tobacconist on the corner of Josefstädterstrasse and Laudongasse, who specialized in international editions and had saved copies dealing with the death of the empress. With the censor hard at work in Vienna, foreign newspapers might include information that had been excluded from domestic papers.

After their train passed through Innsbruck, they ate together in the dining car—a farmer's omelet accompanied by a serviceable Müller-Thurgau from the Wachau, a wine region along the Danube that had until recently been best known for its wine vinegar. At first, there was little small talk, as Gross was in deep meditation.

Finally, Gross looked up from his barely touched meal. "Do you recall, Werthen, what I had to say of the empress's death just following her funeral? That is, when I dined with you and the estimable Fräulein Meisner?"

"I do very well." Werthen laid down his fork and knife between bites. "You commented unfavorably upon the idea of some form of conspiracy being at the center of the deaths of both Empress Elisabeth and her son nine years before."

"Yes. In fact I said I believed that 'what we have here is not high intrigue but low and very sad comedy.'"

Gross paused and Werthen took another bite of the omelet, enjoying the taste of the black mushrooms included in the hearty concoction. He chewed slowly, thoroughly.

"Have you now changed your opinion?"

"The ironies," Gross muttered. Then louder: "The blasted ironies."

A well-heeled couple sitting at the table behind Gross looked up from their soup disapprovingly.

"Calm yourself, Gross. What ironies are we talking of?"

"They begin, dear Werthen, with the empress's visit to Geneva itself, well-known nest of many revolutionaries of as many stripes. She was of course advised away from the city unless she had made certain security precautions. But traveling under her useless pseudonym of Countess Hohenembs—useless because her face was too well-known to afford her any anonymity—she had only a small retinue. These included her lady-in-waiting, Countess Sztaray; her private secretary, Dr. Eugene Kromar; her English reader, Mr. Barker; her chamberlain, General Beszewiczy; and a bevy of other aides and attendants that made up her court. She had come to Geneva to see the Baron and Baroness Adolphe de Rothschild, who live in the nearby château of Pregny."

Gross had obviously collected this information from the various papers he had been poring through all afternoon, and though Werthen was fully aware of such particulars, he let the criminologist continue, for thinking aloud was one of his methods of arriving at new connections. Werthen did, however, take the time to tip a finger at the waiter and order a dessert of *Palat-schinken* with chocolate drippings and nuts, and an eiswein to accompany it.

"In the event," Gross continued, after declining dessert for himself, "the empress visited the baroness on the ninth and came to Geneva that same day, putting up at the Hotel Beau-Rivage. The following day she purchased a player piano and rolls of music at Bäker's, on the rue Bonivard. You see, Werthen, though she was little at home in Vienna, she never forgot her husband. That final gift was intended for him. At any rate, by one thirty-five that afternoon, the empress was on her way from her hotel, the Beau-Rivage, and walking along the Quai du Mont-Blanc toward the steamer *Geneva*, which would take her back to her Swiss base in Territet, at the other end of Lake Geneva. She had, so the French papers reported, sent her entourage by train ahead of her as she had a horror of processions. Thus, only a valet from the hotel, carrying the empress's cloak and traveling case, and the Countess Sztaray were accompanying her as they passed the Brunswick monument on their way to the steamer. Both the valet and the countess were walking ahead, for the empress enjoyed walking on her own, taking in the lovely view of the lake afforded from the quay. And it was there and then that the man struck."

Gross paused as the waiter delivered the *Palatschinken* and dessert wine for Werthen. Gross eyed the chocolate-coated crepes greedily and sighed in resignation. "*Herr Ober*, please bring another portion of that delight."

Werthen was waiting for the story to continue, and Gross mistook this for good manners. "Do begin, Werthen. No need to wait for me and risk letting the chocolate sauce go cold."

"You were saying, Gross," Werthen prompted.

"Yes. Just past the Brunswick monument, Luccheni made his move. Another irony, for that man had come to Geneva to kill not our empress, but Philippe, Duke of Orléans, whom he had missed by a day. The *Corriere* has Luccheni simply sitting bereft on a bench along the Quai du Mont-Blanc, when the empress happened by."

Werthen considered this as the waiter brought Gross's dessert. The next few minutes were taken up with an appreciation of the palatschinken. Gross closed his eyes as he ate small bites, moving the dessert about in his mouth as if it were a fine wine.

"A guilty pleasure," he said, wiping his lips with the damask napkin, then patting his ample midsection. "Adele would surely not approve. But where were we?"

"Luccheni on the bench on the Quai du Mont-Blanc," Werthen said.

"Exactly. Thus, whether by accident or design, Luccheni was on the quay at the exact moment the empress passed on her way to the steamer. It seems he moved to her quickly, as if he perhaps were an autograph seeker. However, drawing near, he struck her a blow that sent the empress to her knees. The countess and valet turned just as the man ran away. They thought he was a thief, trying to steal the empress's watch, which she wore as a broach. The countess helped the empress to her feet, and she was apparently unhurt, but somewhat shaken. She told the countess that it was nothing, and that they must hurry or miss the boat. They proceeded to the steamer, where the empress finally collapsed, and where—in the privacy of their stateroom—the countess discovered a wound over the empress's left bosom. It was a small hole emitting a trickle of blood. By this time the steamer had already left shore and there was no doctor aboard to assist them. Appraised of the situation and the importance of the passenger, the captain turned the steamer around and returned to port, where the empress was taken on an improvised stretcher fashioned out of sailcloth and six oars back to her former suite at the Hotel Beau-Rivage. There a Doktor Golay was summoned, but there was nothing he could do. I have seen the autopsy report. The puncture wound penetrated to a depth of eight and a half centimeters, entering just above the fourth rib and breaking it with the violence of the blow. It then passed through the pericardium and struck the left ventricle of the heart. Initially, the blood released internally only, into the pericardium, and slowly enough so that the empress at first thought there was little injury to her person. But by the time she had returned to the hotel, the blood was soaking her dress. She died at ten minutes after two."

The two sat in silence for a time, as if honoring the memory of the dead empress. Werthen was hardly a royalist and had in fact been critical of the life the empress had led, shunning her responsibilities at court and to her husband. However, her tragic death had brought out a latent and surprising loyalty to the crown in him.

Gross continued, "Immediately following the empress's stabbing, a cry and alarm had arisen. Two cabmen and a boatman gave chase to Luccheni as he hurried down the nearby rue des Alpes. An electrician named Saint Martin was coming from the opposite direction and heard the shouts. When he saw Luccheni running pell-mell toward him, he simply put out his hands and caught the man. Assisted by the cabbies and the boatman, he took the struggling Luccheni to the nearest policeman and handed him over."

"But why didn't Luccheni strike out at this Saint Martin?" Werthen asked, pushing aside the dessert, half-eaten. The part he had eaten was so rich that it was sure to keep him awake for hours.

"Apt question, Werthen. From *Le Monde* I gathered the particulars of the weapon. It was a simple file that had been ground to a needle-sharp point and fitted with a wooden handle. A homemade weapon. But Luccheni did not have it on his person when apprehended. It was found the following morning by the concierge of rue des Alpes 3 in the entrance to that house. Luccheni apparently disposed of his weapon as he was running from the scene."

Gross paused, and it was not to eat his dessert, Werthen noted.

The lawyer thought for a moment. "Odd behavior for the man."

Gross beamed at him. "How so?"

"Well, it seems Luccheni had made no escape plan. He runs willy-nilly down a side street straight into the arms of an electrician. Had he wanted to effect an escape, he would have had a carriage waiting, wouldn't he? Or at least have committed the deed in the crush at the steamer entrance, where he could perhaps become lost in the crowd."

"Assuming that it *was* a plan, Werthen, and not a spur-of-the-moment decision."

Werthen waited a moment, then continued, "However, Luccheni's presence in Vienna outside Herr Frosch's apartment house when the empress was visiting is significant. I think we can assume this assassination was planned. In that case, the fact that Luccheni had made no escape contingency implies that he wanted to be caught, or was not afraid of being caught. You see his smiling face on every front page, ecstatic at being the center of attention for once in his miserable life."

"You mentioned odd behavior," Gross prompted, as if to get the lawyer back on track.

"Yes. If my suppositions are correct, then why would he throw the file away? Why not use it one more time, on the police for example, whom he sees as instruments of class oppression? And why, once apprehended, did he refuse to speak?"

"Ah, you have been reading the accounts as well," Gross said. "That bit comes from the Zürich *Post*, I believe."

Werthen ignored this. "These facts do not seem to fit together somehow. On the one hand Luccheni is proud of his crime. On the other, he tries to cover it up."

Gross nodded his head slowly. "Excellent, Werthen. Exactly what I was thinking. We must make a note of that as well. We shall have a busy time in Geneva, my friend."

After dinner, they retired to their separate sleeping compartments. Just as Werthen feared, the rich dessert kept him awake for hours as the train hurtled through the night. Usually the gentle rocking of the cars, the clacking of the wheels over the points, and the mournful sound of the whistle as the train approached crossings were a soporific for him.

Tonight, though, he lay sleepless in his narrow bed and tried reading for a time. Werthen liked to practice his English by reading British authors—he avoided American writers, such as Twain, as they tended too much to the surface of things. Instead, he had taken Thomas Hardy's *Tess of the D'Urbervilles* along for this trip, but the plight of the poor village girl paled by comparison to the real-life incidents he was investigating. He finally placed the book in the net rack overhead.

Every time he closed his eyes, the myriad of facts and events flooded his hooded vision. He saw the shorn nose of Liesel Landtauer and the exploded brains of Herr Binder. His mind's eye witnessed the assassination of Empress Elisabeth and took him into the candlelit rooms of Crown Prince Rudolf at Mayerling. Was there a connection between all these, or were his and Gross's imaginations working overtime? Were the gruesome Prater murders simply a cover-up for the killing of Frosch, and was that in turn linked to the death of the empress? Even to that of the Crown Prince almost a decade previously?

He finally fell asleep deep in the night. He awoke with a start as a conductor outside his window announced their arrival in Zürich. Werthen struggled out of bed and pulled the curtain aside on his window. Few passengers were debarking or entraining this time of night. Glancing up and down the platform, he caught the eye of a tall, gaunt man who was staring at his compartment. The man had a scar running from the corner of his mouth up to the left temple. He saw Werthen looking at him, but did not avert his eyes. If anything, he fixed him with an even closer and almost savage glare. Werthen instinctively dropped the curtain. Then, a moment later, he lifted it again, but the man was nowhere to be seen.

He nodded off again soon after the train departed the Zürich Hauptbahnhof and slept dreamlessly for a time, until the words Mark Twain had uttered at Empress Elisabeth's funeral came unbidden to mind:

But of course they've got the wrong man in Switzerland. Or the right one for the wrong reason. It's all to do with the Hungarians. First Rudolf and now his mother.

FIFTEEN

Werthen was in a nasty mood by the time they reached Geneva at half past six in the morning. He did not even bother counting how many hours he had slept; that would only make him feel more exhausted. He resolved, not for the first time in his life, to refrain from rich desserts in the future.

His last bit of sleep had been disturbed by dreams of himself and Gross being pursued by the tall, thin man with the scarred face, whom he had seen on the platform last night in Zürich. Or at least, whom he thought he had seen. He had, after all, just woken from a sound sleep before peering out of the curtain.

Perhaps he had allowed his imagination to get the better of him, thinking that the man was staring at him, when he could just as well have been staring at the conductor beneath his window, waiting for the all-aboard call.

All the same, as he and Gross detrained, he kept his eyes open for any sight of this mysterious fellow passenger, but failed to see anyone vaguely resembling the man.

"What *are* you looking for, Werthen?" Gross said.

Werthen shook himself out of his sleep-deprived paranoia.

"A porter, of course, Gross. Unless you would care to camel these bags yourself?"

But of course Gross had already secured the services of an able-bodied porter, who now quite efficiently stacked their luggage upon a small cart and followed them down the long platform.

Werthen had given little thought to their schedule once in Geneva, other than that they would interview Luccheni. Now, as they came out of the cavernous train station into the early morning sun just climbing above the rooftops to the east, he was surprised when Gross announced to a carriage driver their destination:

"Hotel Beau-Rivage, my good man."

Gross left Werthen to take care of incidentals such as paying the porter. Once installed in the carriage, Werthen voiced his surprise.

"You really think it a wise idea to stay at the same hotel as the empress?"

"But that is exactly why we will stay there, Werthen. There are witnesses to question, the scene to examine. To do otherwise would be unwise and a waste of our time."

Werthen did not want to bring up economies. Gross lived on a professor's salary, which his writings supplemented, of course, but still he was not a rich man. Werthen doubted if his colleague, though able to afford the luxury of the Hotel Bristol in Vienna, understood the elegance and expense of an establishment such as the Beau-Rivage, which catered to royalty.

"However," Gross said, after a few moments' silence, "I would not refuse to be your guest this one time. Knowing your family coffers run deep, of course."

"Please," Werthen said, hardly bothering to disguise his annoyance. "Do be my guest, Gross."

"Don't mind if I do," he said, settling back against the leather seat and smiling quite contentedly.

The Hotel Beau-Rivage, like many other buildings in Geneva, still bore black bunting, marking the passing of the empress. The large and noble-looking edifice was constructed forty years earlier on the Quai du Mont-Blanc, and each of its lavish rooms afforded marvelous views out onto Lake Geneva. The foyer was immense, with marble columns and tile floors, appointed with the finest furnishings. Fresh flowers were being put in place as they arrived, dozens of bouquets gracing marble-topped and marquetry tables.

The season was winding down, and Werthen and Gross thus had their choice of rooms. They took adjoining suites on the third floor, facing the lake. This was a luxury that would bite not insignificantly into the supplementary allowance Werthen received annually from his family estate.

For Gross, the first order of business, after cleaning up and settling into their rooms, was breakfast, which they had in the solarium tea room.

It was almost eight by the time they finished their coffee—a brew superior even to that of Frau Blatschky, Werthen thought. And the croissants accompanying it had been marvelous. French-speaking Geneva prided itself as being an outpost of French culture in Switzerland, especially for dining.

Gross appeared to know exactly where he was going as he and Werthen left the hotel and had the doorman get a carriage for them. Gross gave the cabbie an address in the southeastern district of Plainpalais: Boulevard Carl-Vogt 17.

"Right," the man answered in French. "Hôtel de Police it is."

They were treated to a miniature tour of the city, as the carriage headed south along the Quai du Mont-Blanc, and across the Pont du Mont-Blanc to the south shore of Lake Geneva. From here they traveled through pleasant residential districts, tree-lined streets interlaced with public gardens and parks, to the Boulevard Carl-Vogt, a block from the banks of the Arve River. The cabbie let them out at an imposing structure from the eighteenth century bearing the official crest of the city over the entrance. This was, as Gross quickly explained, the Direction Centrale de la Police Judiciaire.

A reception desk was in the massive entry hall; Gross inquired of the young woman working there the office of Monsieur Auberty.

She looked with interest at this request. "Is he expecting you, gentlemen?"

"I telegraphed him from Vienna. Professor Gross is my name, and this is my associate, *Advokat* Werthen. It is in regards to the Luccheni matter."

"Of course," she said. Obviously Luccheni was the most important criminal Geneva had had to deal with in decades, and Auberty was the investigating magistrate in the case. The receptionist, one of the few women working at the Direction Centrale de la Police Judiciaire, as far as Werthen could ascertain, placed a call to the officer in question.

Five minutes later, a portly man of about sixty limped down the main staircase. What hair he had left at his temples was snow-white and stood out in sharp contrast to the black suit he wore.

"My dear Gross." He held out his hand as he approached. "How good to see you after all these years. Frankfurt, was it? I still remember the paper you presented on handwriting analysis. Brilliant."

Gross barely had an opportunity to greet the man in return and to introduce Werthen before Auberty ushered them up the stairs and into his second-floor office. Here everything was action. Several male typists, who had obviously recently been posted to the office, all seated at improvised desks, were pounding away at keys. Two other men were working telephones, while a third pored through police files.

"We are going to be sure about this one," Auberty said by way of explaining all the activity. "We're preparing a case that no defense attorney will be able to attack."

He led them into his inner office, spacious and appointed in Louis XV furnishings. Light poured in from floor-to-ceiling windows, partially opened. Lace curtains fluttered in the morning breeze. Sweet-water smell from the nearby river was carried in the breeze.

"Please," he said, indicating upholstered armchairs across the desk from him. "So you came all this way just to talk to the man, eh?"

"You know my monthly journal, Auberty. I thought that such an interview would be an invaluable resource for other investigators. An index to the anarchist's mind, if you will."

"But to be published *after* my trial," Auberty said.

"That goes without saying," Gross replied.

"He is an odd one," Auberty said.

"How do you mean, odd?"

"You will see for yourself."

Luccheni was being held in a special security cell in the cellar of the same building. Auberty provided them with a pass, which allowed them to talk to the man for an hour under the supervision of a gendarme. Gross and Werthen were taken to the cell, lit by a single electric light encased behind a steel screen on the ceiling. Everything in the room—bed, table, and chairs—was constructed of poured concrete, so that nothing could be hidden in the cell. It had been specially constructed for political prisoners, the guard explained on the way down to the cellar.

"We built it last year, but had no idea it would be put to use this soon," the guard said as he unlocked the door to the cell.

"Company, Luccheni," he said to a small man huddled on the bed.

The anarchist looked up at this, his eyes bright and eager.

"Press?"

"In a sense," Gross said, quickly answering the question to

preempt the guard. "I am most eager to meet you, Signor Luc-cheni."

Gross had switched to Italian, which Werthen spoke only haltingly, though he could understand it well enough.

"In what kind of sense?" Luccheni asked, his eyes squinting in suspicion.

"I publish a journal of criminalistics, read by learned men around the world."

"A specialist, then. I like that idea. Let everyone know of my deed."

"To be sure," Gross said. "But perhaps we could retrace the events of that day." Gross nodded at the concrete chairs. "May we?"

"Be my guests, signore," Luccheni said, then broke into a cackling laugh that put Werthen on edge.

"You came to Geneva to kill the empress of Austria, is that correct?"

Luccheni looked from Gross to Werthen. "No one's taking notes. How you going to remember what I said?"

Gross glanced at Werthen. "You understand what he wants?" he asked in German.

Werthen nodded and took out his leather notebook and pencil.

"He understand Italian?" Luccheni demanded.

Gross nodded.

Luccheni smiled at this. "Be sure to get my words down like I say them. Now, what did you ask?"

"If you came to Geneva with the express purpose of killing the empress of Austria."

Luccheni shook his head. "No, not really. I thought of doing in that French chap, the Duke of Orléans. But he had already left by the time I got here. But then I heard the empress was here, and she would make an even better target. It had to be someone important enough to get in the papers." He smiled like a ferret. "I guess she was."

"Heard?" Gross interrupted. "From whom?"

Luccheni grew suspicious once again. "From the newspapers, I guess. Not much secret when the royalty comes to town."

"But there was nothing in the local papers to announce her arrival. In addition, the empress was traveling under an alias." Gross paused dramatically. "So I repeat my question, who did you hear this from?"

"Look, you want my story for your magazine or not? I did it. I killed her. Saw her prancing along the quay bold as daylight. And I knew I had to do her. Her and all the rest like her. Oppressors and parasites. Feeding off the poor of the world. We're better off with none of them. Chop all their heads, that's what I say."

Werthen had a powerful desire to slap the man. However, his feeling of revulsion at Luccheni had nothing to do with a fondness for aristocracy or privilege. Rather, he squirmed because of the man's obvious joy in his position. He was enjoying his notoriety, the infamy brought about by his cowardly action of killing a defenseless woman.

"And what did you do then?" Gross said, leaving for the time his question of how Luccheni discovered the empress's whereabouts.

"Do? Why I went up to her like this."

He leaped from the bed and moved toward Gross, but the guard quickly barred his way.

"No, no. Please leave him be, Officer."

Luccheni looked up at the policeman and sneered as he continued his pantomime.

"Perhaps, however, you could use this gentleman," Gross said, indicating the officer. "He is somewhat closer to the empress's height than I."

Seeing that the policeman was reluctant to perform the role of victim, Gross said, "If you please, sir, in the interests of science." The guard shrugged and Luccheni closed on him.

"Her fancy maid was walking ahead, and the queen—"

"Empress," Werthen blurted out in his rusty Italian. He could not help himself from correcting the lout.

"Queen, empress, all the same to me. She was all alone on the quay. So I came up to her like so." Luccheni stood directly in front of the guard now. "And I hit her like so with my special file." Luccheni made a thrust at the officer's chest with his left hand, stopping inches above it, then cackled again as he saw the policeman automatically wince.

"I knocked her down with the blow. Knew it had struck home. So I left her dying there and ran."

Werthen carefully watched the small man with his bushy mustache and wild eyes and had to restrain himself again from laying hands on the anarchist.

"I see," said Gross. "And you left the file sticking in the empress."

Luccheni smiled. "My signature." Then, looking at Werthen, he suddenly shouted, "Write! Write all my words down!"

"Really, Gross, this is too much."

"Calm yourself, Werthen. All for a good cause."

Werthen began taking notes. This pleased Luccheni, who now went back to his bed and sat on the edge of it. He was so short, his legs did not reach the floor.

"Another thing, Signor Luccheni," Gross said. "Did you act alone? Was this your assassination plot, or were you commissioned somehow?"

This angered Luccheni. "Mine. All mine. I'm the one who thought it up. I'm the one who struck the blow. They'll remember me a hundred years from now."

"Is that why you were in Vienna last June?"

The question caught Luccheni by surprise. "Last June?" He scratched his head in a poor attempt at dissimulation. "Can't remember where I was in June. I travel a lot."

"You were in Vienna from the eleventh to perhaps the

fourteenth or fifteenth. On the night of June twelfth, you took up watch on a house in the Gusshausstrasse. Or do you not recall that, either?"

"You a reporter or a prosecutor? I don't like these questions."

Gross pressed the point. Werthen knew the technique from personal experience. Flatter then fluster. Sometimes you could get valuable information from an otherwise reluctant witness.

"Were you following the empress even then, Signor Luccheni?"

"What do you mean 'following'? I saw her on the quay and killed her. It was my heroic deed for the cause of international anarchy."

"You were prepared to kill her in June, weren't you? But cowardice prevented it. When you saw the two bodyguards, you were too afraid to act. Isn't that so?"

Luccheni bristled at this suggestion. Agitation showed on his face; his breathing became more rapid.

"I'm no coward. I didn't even know she was there. He just told me to wait at that address."

"'He.' Who?"

But Luccheni realized he had said too much. "I don't want them in here no more," he said to the guard. "Get them out. I'm not talking to him."

They waited a few moments, but clearly they would get nothing more from Luccheni.

Back in Auberty's office, Gross asked the investigating magistrate about the weapon.

"He seems to believe he left the file in the empress's body."

"The man is not as stupid as he appears," Auberty replied. "In fact, he is rather cunning, in an animal sort of way. He tells a variety of stories, all in an attempt, I believe, at appearing insane. Diminished capacity could be his defense. But it won't wash. The fact is, he stabbed the empress. We have dozens of eyewitnesses to the deed. Running from the citizens afterward, he simply threw the file away in a futile attempt at appearing innocent. Now that he's been caught, he's looking for any way he can of getting out of it."

Werthen disagreed with such an assessment, and by the skeptical look on Gross's face, he thought the criminologist felt the same.

"You obviously have the weapon in your evidence bags."

Auberty nodded. "It's what killed her, all right. There were still traces of blood on it."

"I know it might sound forward of me, but I was wondering if it would be possible to view the file."

"No need, Gross. I know all about your enthusiasm for dactyloscopy. In fact I have your 1891 monograph on the subject among my files. Though fingerprinting cannot yet be used in a court of law, I was fully prepared to take prints from the file handle and compare them with Luccheni's. But there was nothing there. Or rather, too much there. The file had been handled by numerous people before being passed to the police. A jumble of prints, and mostly smeared."

Gross let out an audible sigh. "How unfortunate."

"Not to worry. The case against Luccheni is ironclad. The man is as good as convicted."

Auberty's "ironclad" case was rapidly rusting, Gross announced as they left police headquarters. "Twain was right. They do have the wrong man in custody."

Werthen did not immediately answer as they turned left out of the headquarters and walked toward the intersection of Rond-Point, there to find a *Fiaker* rank. In his rational mind, Werthen agreed with Gross, but instinctively he wanted Luccheni to be found guilty. The man was despicable.

"Luccheni could have been lying about leaving the file stuck in the empress, just like Auberty said."

"Yes," Gross allowed. "But I do not believe so, and neither, my friend, do you. However, that is of less consequence than another essential fact."

"The mysterious 'he' that Luccheni mentioned?" Werthen offered. "Presumably Luccheni was referring to his controller in the anarchist movement. All that shows is that Luccheni was not acting on his own, but was part of a wider plot."

"Indeed, but *whose* plot?" Gross asked cryptically. "Yet again," he hurried on before Werthen had time to wonder too much about that statement, "this is not the pertinent fact that disqualifies Luccheni as the assassin."

Werthen came to an abrupt halt just as they reached the busy intersection. "What then?" he said in exasperation.

"Calm yourself, Werthen. I know the man rankles, but we cannot allow personal feelings to intrude in the determination of legal matters. The fact I refer to is physical in nature. To wit, the man's size and his left-handedness."

"He is diminutive, to be sure. But that notwithstanding, he is sturdy enough in build to have dealt a death blow to the empress."

"Sturdy enough, indeed, but tall enough?"

Werthen immediately saw what Gross was getting at. Acting as stand-in for the empress in the reenactment of the assassination, the guard had stood a good head taller than the man. The empress, a woman of stature, was surely several inches taller than Luccheni.

Gross saw such understanding show on Werthen's face. "It is quite simple, really. From the autopsy report it is clear that the wound was of surgical precision. Also, it is obvious that it was created by a downward thrust through the pericardium, and with an angle that presupposes not only a much taller but also a right-handed assailant."

"My God, Gross, you mean Luccheni could not have killed her. But dozens of witnesses saw him strike the empress."

"Strike her yes. But stab her?"

"Who then?"

"Exactly my question, Werthen. Let us find a carriage and hasten back to the hotel. There are numerous witnesses to the crime on the staff of the Beau-Rivage."

When they finally found a carriage and pulled away from the curb, another carriage also jolted into sudden movement behind them. Fingers tapped nervously on the sill of the open window of the carriage door. A gruff voice sounded from within imploring the cabbie to quicken the pace.

They were in luck. Fanny Mayer, wife of the owner of the Hotel Beau-Rivage, was at the desk this morning and had commented that she had witnessed the entire event from her upstairs balcony. When Gross explained his presence in Geneva and that he was assisting Investigating Magistrate Auberty, Madame Mayer instantly summoned a clerk from in back to take over the desk.

"An awful day," she told them as they settled in the hotel lounge for midmorning coffee. She was attractive and alert, Werthen thought. The perfect combination for hostess of such an establishment.

"But it had begun so wonderfully for the empress," she recalled. "She requested a tray full of our breakfast rolls, one of every flavor and shape for her morning repast. Thereafter, she ventured to Bäker's on the rue Bonivard and made the purchase of a player piano and music scrolls. Such a thoughtful, considerate person."

Suddenly the lady began sniffling and pulled a lace cloth from the sleeve of her moss-green silk gown. "Sorry, gentlemen. But it was such a terrible thing. The world misunderstood her, I am sure. She was the kindest person. She remembered one's name, even that of serving girls. That such a thing should happen."

"Yes," Gross sympathized. "Terrible indeed. And anything

you can remember will help to bring the guilty man to proper punishment."

"I've already told the police everything I know."

"Of course. Though sometimes one recalls things after a certain time passes. The shock of the event often clouds one's memory, you see."

This seemed to make sense to Madame Mayer, and she pulled herself together, sitting upright and replacing the lace hankie.

"Anything I can do. Anything. I still carry a small piece of bloodstained ribbon from the empress. I shall always."

"You viewed it all from your balcony then," Gross said.

"Right. The empress and Countess Sztaray had gotten a late start from the hotel and were hurrying to catch the steamer. I wanted to be sure that she in fact did arrive in time, and thus I watched her departure. The countess was in front with one of our porters, young Mouleau, who was carrying the empress's case and cloak. You see, the empress had sent her entourage ahead by train . . ."

"Yes," prompted Gross. "And then what happened?"

"They were just passing the Brunswick monument, the empress walking behind the others, and the first departure bell sounded for the steamer. I was concerned that they might, in fact, miss their passage. Just then, I saw this man get up from a bench on the quay, quickly approach the empress, and then strike her a savage blow to the chest. I gasped and then cried out. The empress was knocked down and this villain ran away. The countess turned around just at that moment, perhaps hearing my scream, and she in turn raised an alarm."

"It must have been awful for you to watch," Werthen said. "I mean, so far away and unable to give assistance."

Madame Mayer nodded. "But others were there to help. A coachman rushed up and helped the empress to her feet. I remember he was so helpful, he even brushed her skirts. Then our doorman, Planner—he's an Austrian, too—ran up and assisted, but it appeared the empress was fine. A blow and nothing more. She and the countess continued on and boarded the steamer. In the meantime, they had caught the assailant and brought him here for questioning. A sniveling, cringing villain if ever I saw one. I must admit my husband, Charles Albert, grew quite agitated and even struck the man across the mouth. At that time we thought he was simply a petty thief who had tried to steal the empress's diamond watch. Imagine our distress then when some minutes later the steamer returned to the quay and the empress was brought in a makeshift stretcher back to the room she had latterly occupied. There was nothing to be done. A doctor was summoned, but she died within minutes. I remained with the countess and her dead empress for the following six hours before her court returned."

Despite her efforts at maintaining her composure, Madame Mayer once again began sobbing.

"There, there." Werthen made to pat her shoulder, but thought better of it, not wanting to give offense at being too intimate.

"And this coachman," Gross said. "He is a local man?"

She sniffed once more. "Coachman?"

"The one who assisted the empress to her feet."

"Oh." She thought a moment. "I really don't know. Planner might be able to tell you."

Planner was on duty at the door. Of medium height and undistinguished features, he nonetheless carried himself with great importance, decked out in a red uniform with gold epaulets and a shiny black kepi. He was pleased to talk to other Austrians.

"A right panic it was," he said when asked of the events of the day Elisabeth was assassinated. "She said good-bye to me personally, she did, on her way out. Called me by name and all. She knew I was Austrian, see. Always left a good tip for me in one of her embossed envelopes. We won't see her like again."

"You were at the door then when the empress departed," Gross said.

Planner nodded.

"Did you witness Luccheni, the assailant, attack the empress?" Werthen asked, tired of remaining the silent "associate."

"No, sir, I can't say I did," Planner said, turning to the lawyer. "I was busy see, fetching a carriage for the Baron and Baroness Guity-Fallour. Regulars, they are. Always come in September for the opening of the opera season. And quite a fine opera it is, nothing on the par of Vienna's Court Opera, of course—"

"I am sure it is not," Werthen interrupted, "but to the point. You were busy with other guests and did not see the blow. What did you see?"

"It was Madame Mayer's scream from above caught my attention. And then pandemonium out on the quay. I saw the empress on the ground and this bloke helping her up. I ran out to them."

"Did you get a good look at this man helping the empress?" Gross now put in. "Madame Mayer seems to think he was a coachman."

"Could have been. He was dressed common enough."

"You don't know him then?"

"Never saw him before nor since. Tall bloke. Tall and rangy. Had the empress up by the time I got there, seemed to be trying to clean her off. Only saw him from the back and side sort of before he left and let me and some other men plus the empress's lady-in-waiting attend to her."

"Anything else you can remember about the man?" Werthen queried. "Anything at all?"

"Well, one thing. Looking at the fellow from the side like I say, I thought I could see a nasty-looking scar. But I can't be certain. It was panic, like I say. Could've just been a shadow."

At the mention of the scar, Werthen felt a shiver pass through his body. He held his counsel, however, until they had interviewed several others among the staff who saw the events.

None of them, however, could recall the tall man who helped the empress.

Gross questioned Madame Mayer once again as to why she thought the man was a coachman and was given the sensible response that she had noticed him climbing into the driver's seat of a two-horse carriage parked nearby and speeding off after the empress was on her way to the steamer.

Over lunch of fresh trout and a Rhine wine, Gross and Werthen discussed their findings.

"We need to contact the Countess Sztaray, of course," Gross said. "I believe she has left for her family estates in Lower Austria. Perhaps a telegram would be the wisest. We need to ascertain what she has to offer about this mysterious coachman."

"You believe this 'coachman' killed the empress, don't you, Gross?"

"Afraid so, Werthen. Under the guise of cleaning her off, he expertly stabbed her with the stiletto-sharp file. She was still in shock from the broken rib, which Luccheni had caused with his blow."

"Do you think Luccheni meant to kill her at all?"

"Do you remember the words of Frau Geldner from Vienna, his onetime landlord? That he was incapable of killing anyone? I think that is the fact. All bluster and no skill. Perhaps he thought to throttle her, but was scared off when help came. The fact is, I believe that the unfortunate—yes, unfortunate—Signor Luccheni was made to look the guilty party, when in fact an expert and practiced assassin actually did the deed."

"In other words," Werthen said, "Luccheni was somehow tricked into attacking the empress to provide a cover for the true killer. This was not an anarchist assassination at all. Is that what you are implying?"

Gross shook his head vehemently. He had not yet tasted his poached trout.

"No implications here, Werthen. That is exactly what I am

saying happened. And this fits perfectly with the death of Frosch, which also was made to appear to be the work of some other hand, that of the Prater murderer."

"She was killed to maintain her silence," Werthen muttered, feeling suddenly queasy. They were getting into very deep water here. "To keep the events at Mayerling a secret."

"Perhaps. But let us not get ahead of ourselves." Gross picked up fork and knife and began boning his fish. "It is my opinion that this coachman simply came back to the scene later that night and tossed the file into a doorway along the route where Luccheni had run. It is the simplest thing in the world to plant such faux evidence."

"Gross. There is something I should tell you. The description of this coachman. If he indeed had a scar—"

"Then he is surely the man that has been following us," Gross finished, smiling at his friend.

"Then you knew."

"I have been conscious of someone following our movements for some days now. I believe I saw him on the platform in Zürich," Gross said. "Where, I imagine, judging from the light that fell upon the platform from your open curtain, you saw him, as well."

"But why did you say nothing?"

"For the same reason you did not. I could not be sure. Perhaps it was my nerves getting the better of me. Perhaps it was simply my imagination. Now we know it is not. Now we know that we are battling a powerful enemy, dear Werthen. An expert killer who must also realize we are onto him. We must take care, Werthen. Our lives are surely in danger now."

SIXTEEN

They were just in time for the one-o'clock steamer that stopped in nearby Pregny, location of the Rothschild estate. They had come unannounced and thus found no little difficulty in talking their way through the gate and beyond the overly conscientious butler who answered the front door. That they were now armed did not help their cause.

Gross had taken the precaution of bringing two Steyr automatic pistols. These weapons, invented by the Austrian Joseph Laumann only six years earlier, had been artifacts in Gross's crime museum in Graz, but the criminologist had for sentimental reasons taken them with him when leaving for Czernowitz.

Gross had appeared rather sheepish when presenting Werthen with one of the twin guns, but the feel of cold steel in his hand made Werthen, a crack shot, feel more comfortable. His father's desperate attempts at assimilation—the riding, shooting, and fencing lessons young Werthen was forced to take ad nauseam—did have their benefits, it seemed. Though such efforts to wipe away the image of the intellectual Jew and replace it with the modern déclassé man of action had been far from successful, there were still atavistic holdovers of the regimen.

Familiarity with pistol and sword being two of those. A knowledge of fine wines was another and more pleasing one.

Any comfort the pistols might have afforded was, however, offset by their having to keep their heavy topcoats on to conceal the bulky weapons in their jacket pockets. Today, the afternoon heat of the day at Pregny made such a subterfuge all but intolerable.

Finally, Werthen, speaking with the Rothschild butler, was able to dredge up the name of local aristocracy with whom his parents were acquainted. He stretched the point to say that the Baron and Baroness Grafstein had sent their personal regards to Baroness Julie de Rothschild.

These names swayed the earnest butler, and he sent word to his mistress, who had been taking an afternoon rest. Julie de Rothschild appeared ten minutes later, a small and finely built woman with sparkling eyes and carefully coiffed brown hair. They met in a sitting room to which the butler had directed them, and Baroness de Rothschild set their two cards down on the side table next to the armchair she threw herself into.

"So you are not anarchists, after all?" she said.

"My good lady," Werthen made to protest.

"Michel, the butler, said you looked like anarchists. Why else wear such heavy coats on a warm day? Are you carrying bombs?"

Her wry smile implied she did not for a moment suspect them, but Gross grew suddenly huffy.

"I can assure you, Baroness, we are here on the most vital business."

"Then the Grafsteins . . . that was simply a ruse."

Werthen began to apologize, but she waved it away. "Never mind. Life does get boring here. I am ready for an adventure today. What brings you gentlemen to Pregny? And please, do take off those ridiculous coats. Armed or not, it is all the same to me."

They did as they were bid, and her eyes went immediately to their bulging jacket pockets, but she said nothing.

"It is about the empress," Gross said.

"I thought as much. You wish to know her business here the day before she was killed."

Werthen appreciated the lady's directness, though he could still feel the heat in his cheeks at having been caught in his lie about the Grafsteins.

"Exactly," Gross said.

"The empress came, as you have, under the guise of mutual friendship. My husband, Baron Adolphe, once a banker in Naples, gave up that life for the refinements of Paris, where I met him. We had the occasion later to know the deposed king and queen of Naples when they lived in exile in that fair city. My husband was able to, shall we say, aid the king out of potential financial difficulties resulting from his lost kingdom. The queen of Naples, is, as I am sure you know, the sister of Empress Elisabeth, who called as a courtesy to her sister, ostensibly to personally thank us for this earlier assistance. However, she, like you gentlemen, had another motive to her visit."

"Which was?" Gross asked.

"To seek my husband's assistance in the publication of her majesty's memoirs. Adolphe has among his many other holdings a large publishing firm in Berlin. The empress wanted to ensure that her memoirs would not be censored. They were, to use her words, 'potentially inflammatory.' My husband of course said he would do everything in his power. Elisabeth apparently had not begun the writing, but was most emphatic that there should be no censorship whatsoever."

"She gave no indication of the nature of the inflammatory bits, I presume?" Werthen queried.

"No, *Advokat* Werthen. She was quite mysterious about that, I must admit. The notion did intrigue my husband. She was very nervous, almost disturbed. A condition not helped, I dare say, by her discovery upon signing our guest book. Thumbing through the leaves, she found the name of her unfortunate son, a visitor a full decade earlier when we had first settled in Pregny. She almost broke into tears seeing his signature."

"And Crown Prince Rudolf. Do you recall the purpose of his visit?"

She smiled. "Neither I nor my husband were in residence at the time. A royal request came to 'borrow' our secluded château for a few days. One does not refuse such requests."

"You do know, though, don't you?" Gross persisted.

She sighed. "It was no great secret that the marriage between Rudolf and the Princess Stephanie was far from happy. Rudolf had his assignations. I believe he was meeting a fond friend here, one of the illegitimate daughters of the Russian Czar, to be blunt. The unfortunate girl has since taken herself off to America of all places, where she in turn gave birth to another illegitimate child. Or so the gossips have it."

"Well," Gross said, standing suddenly and preparing to leave.

"We must thank you for your frankness, Baroness," Werthen said, rising now as well and trying to cover up Gross's rudeness.

"I was happy to help. You know I am no gossip myself. I have not told another soul about Rudolf's visit here. But in the aid of justice, it is of course my duty."

She seemed to glow all over, Werthen noticed. The Baroness Julie de Rothschild was enjoying her little adventure.

They now had their motive for Elisabeth's death. Like Frosch before her, she was threatening to make public certain events that someone did not want known.

Werthen and Gross were careful to watch for the tall, gaunt man on their trip back to Geneva. However, they saw no sign of him.

Before dinner, and while Gross was taking a brief rest—they would be catching the night train later that evening—Werthen decided to do some quick shopping. He could hardly return empty-handed to his fiancée. According to the deskman, some of the best shopping streets were nearby, in the rue Bonivard and rue Kleberg.

Werthen left the hotel, walked along the Quai du Mont-Blanc and past the Brunswick monument. This was exactly the route the empress had taken on the fateful day of her assassination, he remembered. He then turned right on the rue des Alpes, the street down which Luccheni had fled after striking the empress. Would they ever know the truth about that tragedy? Werthen wondered.

Rue Bonivard was the first street on the left, and inspecting the shops, he came upon Bäker's music shop. He recalled that the empress had shopped there the morning before her death. On sudden impulse, and wishing to leave no stone left unturned in their Geneva investigation, Werthen entered the shop and spoke with a young salesclerk dressed in a claret-colored velveteen suit and sporting a Vandyke beard. Werthen's French served him well enough as he asked the clerk if anyone was in the store who remembered the empress's final purchases.

"I attended the empress," the young man said in a voice drenched in self-importance. "You have a personal interest in the matter, monsieur?"

Werthen handed him his business card, and explained as best he could that he was working with the famous Austrian criminologist Professor Dr. Hanns Gross in illuminating various aspects of the assassination.

Gross's name meant nothing to the salesclerk, who now gazed at Werthen with some distrust. Werthen then mentioned that they were assisting Monsieur Auberty, and the clerk suddenly brightened.

"Ah, the esteemed investigating magistrate. There should be no difficulties in this matter. Dozens saw the anarchist chap kill the poor woman."

"Yes," Werthen agreed. "Myself and my associate are, however, attempting to put the crime in context, to give a dramatic picture of the empress's last day. I understand that she purchased one of these new pianos that play themselves."

The clerk smiled at this description. "Yes, the empress was most impressed with this model of the orchestrion, more popularly known as a player piano."

He led Werthen to a standard-looking upright piano. The brand name Pianola showed over the keyboard.

"One may play the piano as one does a normal instrument." The clerk sat at the bench, cracked his knuckles, and struck the ivory keys a fierce blow that launched him into the Beethoven Piano Concerto in B-flat major. The small, elegantly appointed shop reverberated with the strong music. As Werthen began to lose himself in the music, the clerk stopped abruptly midphrase.

"Or," he said, standing now and taking a paper scroll with punched holes and inserting it in a mechanism under the top hood of the piano, "one may let the instrument, in a sense, play itself." He sat on the bench again, pushing the pedals, which in turn operated a vacuum motor that turned the scroll. Suddenly the keys to the piano depressed themselves and struck against the internal strings, playing the same Beethoven piece.

The clerk beamed at the machine. "It works on the same principle as the Jacquard looms controlled by a punch card. The perforated paper roll passes over a cylinder containing apertures connected to tubes that are in turn connected to the piano action. When a hole in the paper passes over an aperture, a current of air passes through a tube and causes the corresponding hammer to strike the string. You will note that there is little emotion in this rendering, as a technician simply perforates the paper after it was marked up in pencil using the original music score. I believe soon, however, pianists will be able to use a recording piano that marks the paper as it is played. This will allow for nuance and individual expression in tempo and phrasing. Imagine, we shall be able to preserve the keyboard technique of say, Anton Rubinstein. People a hundred years from now will be able to marvel at the Russian's playing as we were until his death several years ago."

This was all very well, but Werthen had not come into the shop for a musical or mechanical lesson.

"The empress bought this particular model?"

"The very one. It was shipped the week following her assassination. We sought to honor her final request despite the tragedy."

"And I assume she bought music for the piano, as well?"

"Yes," the clerk said tentatively.

Werthen noted the hesitation. "What scrolls did she buy?"

"Scroll," the clerk corrected. "Just one piece of music, the choice of which I thought rather odd, as a matter of fact. We have a wide selection of composers, from Beethoven to Strauss. The empress, however, chose a single work. By Wagner." Again the hesitation.

"If you please, what was the piece?" Werthen insisted.

"A piano adaptation of the final scene of *Tristan and Isolde*," the clerk finally answered.

"You mean the 'Liebestod'?" Werthen said. "Love-death."

"A wonderful bit of musical creation," the clerk enthused. "Magnificent in its representation of struggle and resolution."

" 'How gently and quietly he smiles, how fondly he opens his eyes! Do you see, friends? Do you not see?' " Werthen spoke the words that Isolde sings as the knight Tristan, mortally wounded, lies dying in her arms. "A rather odd choice as a gift for one's husband." The words were uttered before he could stop them.

"It was not my place to judge the appropriateness of such music, monsieur. She was the empress, after all."

Werthen ended up buying Berthe a gold bracelet from Vigot's, a fashionable jewelry shop in the rue Kleberg. He had it inscribed on the inside with the message AS PURE AS GOLD IS MY LOVE FOR YOU. KARL.

The very message that the boulevard dandy Count Joachim von Hildesheim has inscribed in the bracelet he gives to the chanteuse Mirabel in Werthen's short story "After the Ball." He doubted, however, that Berthe would notice. Werthen's short stories were, after all, hardly bestsellers.

Gross and he had dinner together before leaving the hotel. The criminologist was interested in Werthen's sleuthing discovery:

"You are correct, Werthen. 'Liebestod' is an extremely odd bit of music to choose. It is as if she was sending the emperor a message."

But they put aside further discussion to fully enjoy the food fit for royalty that the Beau-Rivage chef, Fernand, had assembled that evening. They began with a half dozen oysters, followed by *pâté de foie gras de Strasbourg*. Next came *jambon du Parma au melon* and a salad of smoked highland salmon and hothouse greens. Then came a consommé of veal, succeeded by an exquisite chicken-liver mousse with port. Fresh apples and a triple-cream Camembert concluded the feast. The food was accompanied by a bottle of fine Rhine wine, an 1880 Beaune, and pear liquor with the fruit and cheese.

After all, they could not, as Gross said, come to Geneva and not appreciate the cuisine, could they?

It was almost nine o'clock by the time they finished eating. The train departed at ten thirty. Thus they made haste to have their bags brought down, while Werthen settled the bill. They set off from the Beau-Rivage with full bellies and much to contemplate on the return journey to Vienna.

The carriage jostled as they traveled along the cobbled quay. The motion, combined with the amount of wine he had drunk, began to make Werthen feel sleepy. He opened the curtain on his side of the carriage just in time to see another carriage approaching quickly from a side street. The two horses pulling this carriage were in full gallop, their shoes sending blue sparks off the cobbles as the carriage wheeled onto the quay at a terrific speed. Werthen was about to yell to their cabbie to watch out when the carriage in fact struck theirs a vicious blow on the side. Instead of reining in his horses, the driver of this other carriage whipped them on, further crashing into their own carriage.

Werthen heard their cabbie shout out something in anger, and a third crash sent their carriage careening out of control.

"Jump, Gross," Werthen shouted. "We're going off the quay!"

But it was too late. The carriage flipped once before splashing upside down into the waters of Lake Geneva. The inside quickly filled with water. Wearing their bulky coats, both Werthen and Gross were instantly weighed down. Werthen had been a strong swimmer as a youth, though he had not practiced the skill in many years. He thought to take a large breath before the carriage was completely filled with water, but could see that Gross had made no such precaution and was now flailing about in a panic.

Werthen grabbed the criminologist by the back of his collar and was struck for his troubles by one of the man's flailing arms. He shook off the blow, thrust himself feetfirst out the open window of the carriage, then began trying to tug the larger Gross out the same opening. He felt his lungs almost bursting. To save himself, he would have to let Gross go. Get to the top and suck in more air, then dive again. But Gross surely could not last that long.

Suddenly from behind a strong hand seemed to grip his own coat. Another yanked the door of the carriage open and retrieved Gross. They came spluttering and gasping for air to the surface next to a rusty metal mooring hoop. Werthen grabbed on to this and held Gross in his other hand, as he surveyed the surface of the water in search of their rescuer.

He was nowhere to be seen.

By this time, however, a hue and cry had brought others to the scene, and these men now pulled Werthen and Gross out of the chill water.

Their cabbie had jumped from the carriage before it

PART THREE

The three enemies of the criminalist are evil nature, untruth, and stupidity or foolishness. The last is not the least difficult.

—Dr. Hanns Gross, *Criminal Psychology*

SEVENTEEN

Sunday, September 25, 1898—Vienna

After being fished out of the cold waters of Lake Geneva, they had returned to the Hotel Beau-Rivage and assumed their old suites. Their clothes were dried and pressed for them by the morning, but they decided not to venture out of the hotel that Saturday. Their assailant might well be awaiting a second opportunity at squelching their investigation, and this time with means less subtle than last night.

Neither did they make an official complaint of the attack. Gross knew it would serve no real purpose other than tying them up in Switzerland for several more days, when their business now was most assuredly in Vienna.

They had reached the Austrian capital on Sunday morning, taking the night train on Saturday and sharing a sleeping compartment to ensure mutual safety—which meant a sleepless night for Werthen, listening to Gross's stentorian snores.

By the time their train pulled into the Empress Elisabeth West Train Station, a steady cold drizzle or *Niesel* had settled over the city. They were, however, traveling light, for all their cases had been lost when the carriage had spilled into Lake Geneva, and it was easier for them to navigate the arrivals platform and catch the first waiting *Fiaker*. Luckily, Werthen had been carrying the present for Berthe on his person, and that, along with his pistol and soggy leather notebook, had survived the murder attempt.

Neither of them had said that word, but both understood what had occurred in Geneva: Someone had tried to kill them.

Frau Blatschky was happy to see them when they arrived at the Josefstädterstrasse flat, and as they freshened up, she prepared them a real Sunday *Frühstück*, with coffee, slices of Schwarzwald ham and Austrian Emmentaler, yesterday's *Bauernbrot* (as bakeries did not operate on Sundays), and a moist *Gugelhupf*. Despite his lack of sleep, Werthen felt almost human after finishing his second piece of the Frau's famous pound cake.

They had agreed to give it a day before discussing the events in Geneva and how they might relate to the events in Vienna. The time had finally come for a frank discussion.

They retired to Werthen's study and sat in the Biedermeier chairs facing the fireplace, which was lit for the first time this year. Outside, the day was growing even grayer, and the drizzle had turned to full-scale rain.

"Item one," Gross began without further ado. "We assume that our friend with the scar was the driver of that carriage that struck ours and drove us into the water."

"I could not see his face," Werthen said, "but he was a tall man and appeared rather thin. So, yes, I believe that is a safe enough assumption."

"Which brings us to item two. Someone is trying to stop us from investigating the death of Empress Elisabeth. Ergo, that means that we are correct in assuming Luccheni is innocent."

Werthen nodded in agreement. This had been his reasoning as well.

"Which in turn opens further questions," Gross continued. "Item three, I am increasingly convinced that the murders of Herr Frosch and the Empress Elisabeth are connected, as we suspected. We have the common thread of Luccheni, as well as the fact that both were attempting to make very public certain facts that would prove uncomfortable, embarrassing, or dangerous for certain parties as yet undetermined."

"I would think that is self-evident."

"Nothing, Werthen, is self-evident. We must painstakingly gather support to prove such theses. I thus see our course of action as twofold. First, we must, as the Chinese say, walk the camel back to its camp in order to set a new course. That is, the Binder investigation must be reopened. All evidence in that case must be thoroughly reexamined in light of our thesis that Frosch was the intended victim, and that the other unfortunates were simply sacrificed to establish a false lead, to make everyone believe that an insane person was murdering innocent and random victims. Such a reinvestigation includes the death of Binder himself, his medical records, alibis, or lack thereof. Everything."

Another nod from Werthen. With just the two of them, this could take weeks if not months. However, his blood was up now. This investigation had, by the attempt on their lives, become personal. It was fortunate that Werthen had not yet sent Gross's papers on to Bukovina. Thus all materials concerning the Prater murders were still in his flat.

"At the same time," Gross pushed on, "we must examine the other side of our thesis. If not Binder and Luccheni, then who?"

"The logical starting point is a reevaluation of Crown Prince Rudolf's death." Werthen had been giving much thought to this aspect of the case.

"Agreed."

"Frosch was supposedly going to publish the truth of that unfortunate young man's death, presumably that it was not, in fact, due to suicide. Frosch, we assume, was killed to keep the secret of Mayerling, whatever it is, intact. And the empress, I fear to say, was killed for the same reason. Having learned the truth from Frosch, she, too, was prepared to go public with it."

"Which brings up two further questions," Gross said. "First, as you queried when we first learned of Frosch's connection to the tragedy at Mayerling, Werthen, why the delay with Frosch's death? After all, the killings began in June. Why would they, whoever *they* are, wait more than two months and risk having such information made public?"

"It makes sense that Frosch was not the first victim," Werthen offered, "for that would have been too obvious. However, why not the second, third, or fourth? Such a positioning would have functioned to hide the real reason for his death. Why was he the last one? To my mind, it only makes sense if his death fits some schedule of events we are not yet aware of."

"Agreed. And we shall uncover that hidden schedule in due course, Werthen. Now for the second question. Cui bono? That is a first principle in criminalistics. Find the motive—who benefits. No reason to vary from that principle with these deaths."

Werthen leaned back in his chair, putting his fingers to his temples. This single aspect had occupied his thought for several days, and he did not like the conclusions he was coming to.

"In the case of Crown Prince Rudolf," Gross said, "I can see one direct and very immediate beneficiary to his death, a person whose motive would outweigh petty rivalries and political squabbles. His cousin." Gross clasped his hands, looking straight into the fire. "Archduke Franz Ferdinand, the heir apparent."

Now that the words had been uttered by Gross, they took on a new reality for Werthen. No longer were they his private fears or delusions. Franz Ferdinand had been in line to inherit the throne of the Austrian-Hungarian Empire once Rudolf was dead, as Franz Josef had only one son. The emperor's younger brother, Karl Ludwig, and Franz Ferdinand's father, thus stood to inherit the throne upon Franz Josef's death. Franz Ferdinand, as the oldest son, was groomed to follow in succession after his father, never a very healthy individual. In 1896, Karl Ludwig, a highly religious man, had died of typhus after drinking contaminated water from the river Jordan. Nothing, now, stood in the way of Franz Ferdinand directly inheriting the Habsburg crown from the aged Franz Josef. Becoming emperor of 50 million subjects occupying much of the European continent would surely count as a motive for murder. Even for a royal murder.

They were both silent for a few more moments. The involvement of the heir apparent would surely explain how the killer of Frosch and Empress Elisabeth had been able to discover the intentions of those two. He could have well-placed spies, perhaps even an agent who had infiltrated the anarchists and was able to manipulate Luccheni. Franz Ferdinand was, in fact, even now busy installing what was often referred to as the Clandestine Cabinet at his Viennese residence, the Lower Belvedere. There he was, with the emperor's reluctant approval, establishing the Military Chancellery. He and his aides fought tooth and nail in opposition to many of the policies of the government, in particular the stance vis-à-vis Hungary.

Franz Ferdinand was, as Werthen and most Viennese who read a newspaper knew, an ardent opponent to increased Magyar independence. Instead of allowing the empire to be split in half by Hungarian ambitions for separatism, he favored shoring it up by creation of a third power, a Slav kingdom in the south, dominated by the Croats. Rudolf and Elisabeth had both been ardent friends of Hungary's, promoting the cause of Magyar independence at court. Such a difference of opinion could have added to the archduke's disdain for the both of them. Franz Ferdinand, however, was kept at arm's length by the emperor, and this only made the blustery archduke angrier and more frustrated. His bellicose nature and thwarted ambitions were the subject of avid Viennese gossip. He was an ardent hunter, perhaps relieving the frustration of waiting in the wings by killing animals. Some credited him personally with the slaughter of over one hundred thousand deer, pheasants, and other game animals at his battues held on his estates in Bohemia and Austria. This tally was all the more gruesome noting that the fellow was only thirty-four and had, most probably, several decades more hunting in him. One of the richest men in Europe, Franz Ferdinand was not a lovable sort, being gruff and brusque to servants and ministers alike.

But was he also a cold-blooded killer who had arranged the deaths of his cousin, the crown prince, his aunt, the empress, and seven others in a brutal attempt at concealing his crimes?

The sound of the doorbell made both Werthen and Gross start. They looked at each other in alarm; clearly, the same thought was uppermost in both their minds: Was it the killer come to finish his work? They had foolishly taken no precautions against such an eventuality, thinking they were safe in the apartment. But what if the killer had become desperate and no longer cared to make their deaths appear an accident? Neither of them was even armed, and before they could spring into action, Werthen could hear Frau Blatschky already opening the door.

It was too late to call out and stop her. A sudden wave of guilt washed over him, fearing that he had brought such danger to their doorstep, involving even the unfortunate and quite unwitting Frau Blatschky.

Then he heard Berthe's voice at the door, and he breathed easily.

As he stood to greet his fiancée, Gross cautioned, "Tell her nothing. The less she knows, the safer she is."

The words chilled Werthen, making him realize just how perilous their investigations had become. Gross was right. He could not risk endangering Berthe. But how much had he already told her? He would have to somehow convince her that all had come to naught with their Swiss investigation.

Frau Blatschky showed Berthe into the study, and Werthen felt his heart quicken seeing his betrothed, her cheeks red from the suddenly chill weather, her hands busy with the hatpins and then removing her damp hat.

"What a pleasant surprise," Werthen said.

"Is it?" she responded with a smile. "Good to see you again, Doktor Gross."

"Fräulein Meisner."

Werthen drew a chair up to the fire for her.

"You honestly don't remember, do you?" she said, taking a seat next to him.

"Remember?" Then it came to him. He had arranged to take her to the midday Sunday concert of the Philharmonic. But with everything else going on, he had completely forgotten.

"I am an idiot. Please forgive me."

"I thought as much when there was no word from you. So you went to Geneva?"

"Whatever would make you think that, Fräulein?" Gross cut in before Werthen had a chance to respond.

"Well, it would be the logical next step, wouldn't it? If you were investigating a connection between the death of the empress and the Prater murders."

Gross shot Werthen a fierce look. "I am afraid your fiancé has been rather overstating the case. It's the fiction writer in him, I assume."

"Actually, Berthe," Werthen joined in, "we did travel to Geneva, but it all came to nothing. Wild speculation on our part. A coincidence and little more about the empress seeing Herr Frosch. But," he hurried on, giving her no chance to comment, "I did have a chance to do some shopping while there."

He went to his desk and fetched the box containing the gold bracelet from the center drawer.

"For you." He smiled at her warmly.

"Awfully kind of you," she said, "but it won't put me off the scent. You two are hiding something. One needn't be a detective or famous criminalist to sense that."

She opened the box and took the bracelet out. "Oh, Karl, you really shouldn't . . ."

Then she saw the inscription on the inside and took the bracelet to the light of the window to read.

He watched her facial expression turn from pleasant surprise to perplexity. Finally she nodded her head, handing the bracelet back.

"You can keep your bribe, Karl. And next time, be more original. You should have known that I would look up every story you ever published and learn them by heart. At least have the decency to use quotation marks if you are going to quote yourself."

"Berthe, you don't understand," Werthen began.

"Oh, I think I do," she said, heading for the door. "It's not the inscription on the bracelet I resent. That is simply lazy of you and almost comical. But you don't trust me, and that hurts. I know you are lying about this case. Both of you look dreadful, as if you were pulled headfirst out of Lake Geneva or something. Yet you tell me it was all imaginary. Perhaps you are afraid that I, just a silly little woman, will gossip and babble and undo your good work. Or perhaps you are trying somehow to protect me by keeping me in the dark. Which also reduces me to a silly little woman incapable of taking care of herself."

"It is not the way you think it is," Werthen protested.

She stopped at the door. "Then tell me how it is, Karl. Now."

Werthen glanced at Gross.

"You don't need his permission," she said.

Werthen hesitated.

"Fine." She opened the door. "When you are ready to treat me like an equal, you know where to contact me."

She went to the front door.

"Berthe!"

Gross grabbed his arm. "Let her go, Werthen. It is the best thing for now."

Werthen tugged his arm free.

"If you truly love her," Gross said, "protect her by keeping her in the dark. Do not make her another target."

Werthen felt his shoulders slump. Gross was right, of course. He watched as she opened the apartment door and stormed out. He did love her. But could he ever convince her of that again?

They spent the rest of the day mapping out their next steps. Werthen forced himself to take his mind off Berthe and concentrate on the urgent matter at hand. He hoped there would be time to repair the damage to their relationship when all of this nightmare was settled. Berthe was a sensible girl; surely she would understand that it had all been for the best. For now, he knew he could not afford divided loyalties. His primary duty at the moment was to solve these murders and to bring the killer and his controller to justice.

Their first order of business, as Gross had pointed out, was to work back through the evidence against Binder and reexamine the facts concerning the other deaths.

"You have, I believe, been keeping a journal of our investigation, is that correct, Werthen?"

"I have indeed."

"Thorough?"

"As much as I could make it."

"I would like to take a look at that, if you do not mind. It may open some new avenue of inquiry for us."

"But of course."

Werthen fetched the journal from his desk. He had written up his notes every morning and was able to present Gross with a very readable account of matters.

"Impressive," Gross muttered as he leafed through the leather-bound notebook.

The criminologist holed himself up in his bedroom after lunch, reading Werthen's account. Meanwhile Werthen attempted to outline a course of action for the investigation of a new suspect, the heir apparent. One could not simply interview Franz

Ferdinand, he assumed. Or perhaps, posing as a journalist, one could gain access to the Lower Belvedere. But of course, this was absurd, he suddenly realized. If Franz Ferdinand was the power behind all these killings, then he would also be aware of the identity of Gross and Werthen. After all, he would have been the one to order the attempt on their lives. So Werthen could thus hardly beard the man in his own den; he might very well not leave such a meeting alive. Still, part of him wanted to confront the archduke, and to look into his eyes to see if he was really the mastermind behind all this human misery.

Failing a direct approach to the heir apparent, Werthen began trying to develop an indirect approach. Through one of his ministers, perhaps, or his servants. However, he had only begun such considerations when Gross came storming out of his bedroom.

"My God, Werthen, how could I have been so foolish? Do I not have ears? Do I not know how to listen to witnesses? You have it here in black and white. The solution to how these people were seemingly whisked away with no one seeing a thing."

"And what would that be?" Werthen was skeptical; after all, he had written the notes himself and had not noticed any such solution.

"You recall our interview with Frau Novotny? She of the pair of watchful eyes on the Paniglgasse?"

Werthen nodded, recalling the old woman who seemed to know the goings-on of all the inhabitants on her street. "She saw Frosch passing her window about seven thirty the night he was murdered."

"Exactly," Gross said, collapsing into one of the chairs by the fire, now reduced to glowing ash. "And do you recall what else the good woman told us?"

"Inconsequential titbits. Neighborhood gossip. Nothing to do with our case."

Gross was beaming his well-fed-cat smile.

"Well, what did she say, Gross?"

"According to your account—I assume you did not make up such dialogue on the spot?"

Werthen bristled at the suggestion. "I recorded speech as closely as I could to the original, taking notes as we went along."

"And right you were to do so, Werthen. This is your record of Frau Novotny's answer to my question as to whether there were any carriages parked in Paniglgasse the night of Frosch's murder." Gross cleared his throat and read, "'There's always a carriage or two. This isn't Ottakring, after all. We've got a respectable neighborhood here. Sort of place that the municipality keeps up. They was out that evening even, fixing the sewers.'"

"The carriages, is that it?" Werthen said. "Should we question the lady further about those carriages she saw?"

"Not the carriages, Werthen. Something so usual that it escaped even our attention at the time."

"The sewer workers!"

Gross thrust himself out of the chair and began pacing about the room. "You see, Werthen, that is how the killer could make his victims disappear."

"By taking them into the sewers."

Like a small child at a birthday party, Gross clapped his hands in excitement.

"You are onto something here, Gross," Werthen said, suddenly infected by the criminologist's enthusiasm. "Beneath this city is a positive rabbit warren of tunnels connecting cellars and sewers, all left over from the days of the Turkish sieges. For someone with knowledge of the system, such pathways provide an excellent means of traveling unseen through the city, or rather, under the city."

"We must check with the public works department first thing in the morning," Gross said. "We can ascertain if there was actually a crew at work the night of August twenty-second. If not, it is safe to assume that our new theory is workable. That in fact the killer assumed the guise of a sewer worker and was thus able to ensnare his victims without anyone noticing."

"What about the other murders?" Werthen suggested. "Perhaps someone saw sewer workers near the scene."

"Yes," Gross reluctantly said. "Tedious, however. With Frosch, we could trace his footsteps from home. The other victims present a more difficult problem. One does not know where they were taken. A safe assumption is that our killer simply set up his little trap—a tent over an open manhole cover—and waited for the next likely person. Evening and late-night hours would have been the easiest, of course, with fewer possible witnesses. That he so brazenly operated in the early evening with Herr Frosch is further indication that the former valet to Crown Prince Rudolf was the intended victim all along. The killer did not have the luxury of choosing his time and place with Frosch. Rather, he had to fit his crime to the victim's schedule."

Werthen, despite his enthusiasm, decided to play devil's advocate.

"That does not rule out Binder, however. He could have impersonated a sewer worker, chloroformed his victims, and then carried them through the sewers to where he had left his firm's carriage. Then he took them back to his garden hut to perform his grisly surgery and thence to the Prater to dump the corpses."

"Plausible," Gross allowed, sitting again. "Which means that we need to focus very closely on Herr Binder now. Before, we examined him with an eye to proving his guilt. Now we will do the opposite. We are looking for any reason to pronounce the man innocent."

EIGHTEEN

Their first bit of business was easily dispensed with next morning. A visit to the public works department on Schottenring quickly provided what they were looking for. Posing as a leaseholder on properties in Paniglgasse, Gross and his attorney, Werthen, were shown maintenance schedules and emergency-repair records from the past year and for the year to come. For the evening of August 22, 1898, there was no record of any repair crew working on the street.

"And this is the only bureau which keeps such records?" Gross inquired of the clerk, a pimply youth who looked as if he had still not completed his *Matura*.

"Well, of course it is," the truculent clerk said with the hauteur of the born civil servant. "I would have told you otherwise, wouldn't I?"

Gross was about to give the insolent youth a tongue-lashing, but Werthen wisely led him away and out of the office. There was no need to make a scene that could possibly lead to more public knowledge of the new direction their investigation was headed.

They carried umbrellas this morning, along with their pistols.

The rain had stopped, but the streets were still glistening with yesterday's drenching.

The next stop, close by, would take more finesse. They needed to examine the suicide note Herr Binder had left behind and test it against other script that he had surely written. Gross remembered the order book the man had carried with him.

They entered the Police Presidium and, after speaking to the reception sergeant, were shown up to Inspektor Meindl's office.

"This is becoming a habit," the inspector joked when seeing the pair. But his wary gaze denied his bluff good humor. Werthen wondered if higher powers had not, perhaps, got to the man.

His suspicions were proven correct when Meindl, presented with Gross's tale of further articles for his *Archive of Criminalistics*, simply threw his hands in the air and told them point-blank there was nothing more he could do for them.

"But why ever not, man?" Gross pleaded.

"It is just not on, Professor Gross. This must come to an end."

"What must? Our collegial relationship?"

"Come now," Meindl spluttered. "You know what I am speaking of. You two seem to have a bee in your bonnet. Attempting to make all manner of absurd connections between the Prater murders and other matters of, shall we say, more global import."

Neither Gross nor Werthen rose to this bait.

"You must understand," Meindl insisted. "The case is closed. We have more important things to spend our time on. I am sure you both do, as well."

More silence from Gross and Werthen.

"It is simply out of the question."

The ticking of a standard clock on the wall behind them was the only sound.

"Enough!" Meindl finally blurted out. "But this is positively the last request. Understood?"

"But of course, my friend," Gross said.

Ten minutes later they were in possession of Binder's suicide note, neatly preserved in a vellum envelope, and the salesman's order and appointment book, with a white tag glued to it, bearing the case number A14. Unlike the police log concerning Luccheni, which pertained to a still active case, the evidence against Binder was from a closed file. Thus Meindl allowed them to take the documents with them with a final and pained caveat: "Tell no one about this!"

"To work," Gross said to Werthen as they left the Police Presidium and hurried along the Ring back to the lawyer's flat.

Gross had devoted much of his first book, *Criminal Investigations*, to a careful study of handwriting analysis.

"The principles are relatively simple," he told Werthen as he set the two samples of Binder's handwriting on the desk in the lawyer's study. "We are trying to ascertain if Herr Binder's suicide note was either a forgery or a message written under duress. To do so, we need a copy of his actual handwriting." At this, Gross tapped the oilskin-covered order and appointment book. "What we are looking for are both structural, graphical differences in the writing—a letter 'g' for example with a swooping tail in one and a very truncated one in the other—and also content differences—perhaps Herr Binder had the unfortunate habit of misspelling certain words or enjoyed certain locutions overmuch. We must therefore submit both these specimens to the closest possible scrutiny."

Werthen felt he was sitting in one of Gross's as-yet-nonexistent classrooms and was being offered a lecture in Basic Criminology. Without explanation, Gross suddenly left the study, only to return several minutes later with both a magnifying glass and microscope in hand.

"It is amazing, Werthen, what a person's handwriting reveals. That of learned men, for example, is often almost illegible, though the individual letters bear a striking resemblance to print, with which they are so much in contact. The chicken scrawl of the physician I believe we are all familiar with, written in haste as befits a busy and urgent schedule. Or there is the rapid, light, uniform, and always legible script of the tradesman, as that of our Herr Binder. Writing, you see, is not simply done with the hand, but also with the brain. It is a representation of the whole man or woman. We have only to divine the various aspects of it, to study over and over various hands, to see patterns revealed."

Opening the dead man's order and appointment book, Gross was immediately pleased.

"You see what I say about the uniform and legible script of the tradesman, Werthen? Even these notes written for himself portray Herr Binder as an organized sort, fastidious even."

Gross picked up his magnifying glass, examining the script in the order book, then moving to the suicide letter, making quick deliberations.

"Interesting. There is indeed a wealth of detail to be discovered in these two documents." He took the magnifying glass away from his eye. "I shall be at it most of the day. I do not want to bore you."

"You mean you want me to leave. Gross, you forget whose apartment this is."

"Some things are best done in solitude, my friend."

"You are hopeless, Gross. How your good wife ever puts up with you, I'll never know."

But Gross was not listening. He had already put the suicide note under the microscope.

Dispossessed of his study, Werthen decided to go for a walk. The day had brightened and the wet streets of the morning had dried. He kept a sharp eye out for anybody following him, but doubted the killer would dare to make a move against him in broad daylight.

Still, having to continually look over one's shoulder was dismaying. Perhaps the killer would feel frustrated by his failure in Geneva and resort to more direct means: a marksman's rifle could bring him low from a hundred meters. Werthen's eyes suddenly went to the windows above him on both sides of the street. A carriage approached from behind him, the horses' hooves clopping on the cobbles. He tensed, moving closer to the wall of a building in case the assassin might be inside the carriage ready to strike with a thrown knife, a blown poison dart.

Would he ever be able to enjoy a leisurely walk in his city again? Had he and Gross gotten in over their heads with this affair? Perhaps it was time to turn this investigation over to the professionals. Problem was, if this went as high as the heir apparent, then the professionals could well be complicit. Clearly, they were no longer welcome guests with Inspektor Meindl; had word actually reached him to discourage any further investigation into the Prater murders? More likely, it was simply complacency. Meindl had other fish to fry now; the Prater murders were, for him, a closed case.

Werthen felt a hand at his left arm and jerked around suddenly, his right hand going to the gun in the inside pocket of his suit coat.

"Werthen, old man. You look as though you'd seen a ghost. It's just me. How *are* you?"

Werthen quickly covered up his alarm. "Excellent, Klimt. Couldn't be better."

But the painter scowled and did not seem convinced by this. He carried a string shopping bag full of pastries; the neck of a bottle of Inländer rum stuck out between the strings of the bag.

"Not in the office? Playing hooky, then. Well, come on." He took Werthen's free arm. "Just in time to join me for *jause.*"

Werthen had not indulged in afternoon tea for years, usually being far too busy for such *gemütlich* traditions.

"Why not?" he said. "A fine idea."

They were just outside the street entrance to the painter's courtyard studio, and Klimt led him through the entryway and into the bucolic courtyard. Klimt had created a bit of the wild here in the very heart of urban Vienna, with tall grasses joining flowering bushes and all shaded by two glorious chestnut trees. His ocher-painted studio was on the far side of this wild garden; a large, black-and-white cat was hunting in the grass. Klimt buzzed his lips at the animal, but it ignored him.

"Cuddles is quite a serious hunter," Klimt said as he opened the unlocked door to his studio. "Totally ignores me when a mouse is about."

Werthen had never been to Klimt's studio. From gossip, he imagined it to be populated by numerous sylphlike models swanning about in various stages of undress. Instead, a charwoman, squat, about fifty, and badly in need of a bath, was just finishing up washing the floor and chided the painter for bringing company in.

Klimt ignored her and shoved some charcoal sketches aside on a large central table, then deposited his shopping there. As Klimt lovingly unpacked the pastries, and the cleaning lady huffily departed, Werthen gazed at the work in progress on several easels: portraits of several women whom he knew personally, from the best levels of society. Klimt was a dab hand at giving these matrons an air of mystery and employing gilding, bright floral colors, and strange iconography to make these otherwise quite unremarkable ladies appear downright exotic. Werthen was startled to find the beginnings of what appeared to be another portrait. At least the subject was sitting in the classic pose of a portrait, but she had no clothes on.

Klimt followed Werthen's eyes to the work. "Overpainting does the trick. They'll never know she was in the buff to begin with."

"You mean you paint these women in . . . in . . ."

"The nude, Werthen. The nude." Klimt broke off a bit of *Nusstorte* and plopped it in his mouth, munching quite happily. "Don't look so outraged," Klimt said, now pouring out some of the rum into two cloudy glasses. "It's not for any prurient reason. Having them nude to begin with gives me a better insight to their soul. It allows me to see their true character and portray them as they should be, not necessarily as they would like to be seen."

Werthen looked more closely at one of the portraits nearing completion. It was impossible to tell that the painting had begun as a nude.

"Cheers," Klimt said, handing him one of the glasses. "You look as though you could use this."

Werthen suddenly felt like one of Klimt's models, stripped bare of artifice. He downed the rum and made his way through part of the *Nusstorte* and part of a poppy-seed roll. Klimt replenished Werthan's glass several times as the afternoon wore on.

Finally Klimt asked him, "What is bothering you, Werthen? We are friends, after all. I hope you believe that. You came to my aid when I desperately needed someone to believe me. Now tell me."

Werthen looked into the smoky brown depths of the rum.

"It's the bill, isn't it? I've been meaning to call on you and explain that. Several portrait fees are long past overdue, and until they arrive, I am rather strapped for funds. That's the problem with working for people with a 'von' attached to their names. One can hardly send a bill collector to their door. But as soon as I am paid, I shall send along my remittance."

"It's not that, Klimt," Werthen finally said, rather touched by the painter's explanation. Werthen took another sip of the rum and felt the warmth course through him. He and Gross had been going it alone for too long; he suddenly felt the need for an objective ear, if only to confirm that their theories were not fantastical.

Thus, he decided to take the painter into his confidence, laying out the course of events since they had last seen one another the day of Empress Elisabeth's funeral.

Werthen left nothing out, not even his spat with Berthe, and when he finished, Klimt sat very still, saying nothing. The cat had come in now through an open window and was weaving itself in and out of the painter's legs. Klimt absently broke off a piece of pastry and gave it to the animal, who sniffed at it for a moment, then moved off to a far corner of the studio.

"My God, man," Klimt suddenly exploded. "You could've been killed. What are you doing playing at policeman? Leave painting to the painters. Leave catching criminals to the cops."

"But what if the police are prevented from doing their work? What then?"

"You actually suspect the archduke?"

"It is one avenue of inquiry."

This was followed by another extended silence. There came a crunching sound from the corner to which the cat had retired.

"One thing is for sure," Klimt finally said. "You two need help."

"Leave painting to the painters, Klimt. You said so yourself."

"But that is exactly what I intend to do. My father was a master engraver, and I grew up working with him. As a result, there is nothing I do not know about the imprint of signatures and the delicate individual characteristics of the hand at work sketching or writing. You do not know how many times I had to forge my own father's signature on those engravings."

When they arrived at the flat, Gross was still hard at work on a close examination of the writings of Herr Binder.

"See who I ran into, Gross," Werthen announced upon entering the study.

Gross looked up from his microscope with a scowl on his face. He barely muttered a salutation to the painter.

"Don't be such a gruff bear, Gross. Klimt has come to help."

"With what?" Gross said, gazing once again into the lens.

"With Binder's handwriting analysis, of course."

This time when Gross looked up from the instrument, anger rather than mere peevishness showed in his face.

"What have you been discussing, Werthen?"

"It's all right, Professor," Klimt interrupted. "Werthen here's told me all about your adventures in Switzerland. No need to worry, I won't be spreading news of it all over Vienna. And it's time you fellows got some help in your endeavors. It's the least I can do to repay your earlier kindness to me."

Klimt quickly explained his unique training in engraving to the criminologist, who slowly lost his anger. Instead, he seemed almost amused.

"And so you believe that you can tell me about this writing?" Gross said. "Granted, *Ames on Forgery* lists the occupation of engraver as one of those which could provide insight to handwriting identification, but I have yet to see it of any worth."

The criminologist stood upright now, putting his palms in the small of his back and stretching. "However, this could be a mild diversion. My mind needs one. A sort of competition. I must warn you, though, Klimt. I have made a close study of graphology and handwriting."

"I'm sure you have, Professor. Now, if I could take a look at the documents."

Gross handed him both the order book and the suicide note. He no longer bothered with the vellum envelope for the note, for he had examined it minutely for fingerprints and found a bewildering jumble, far too many for identification purposes. One day, the criminologist continually complained, the police would awaken to the value of fingerprinting and handle evidence with care.

Klimt took the two samples, the book in his left hand, and the note in his right. He squinted at them for a time, then set them down and pulled out a pair of reading glasses from the frock coat he now wore. Werthen assumed the more ostentatious and breezier caftan had been put in mothballs for the colder months. Fixing the wire arms of the glasses around his ears, Klimt picked up the two samples once again, working his lips as if reading aloud. He flipped through the pages of the order book, examining each against the note. He sniffed once, sucked his teeth, then handed the two samples back to Gross.

"Simple enough, I should say."

"Oh, should you?" Gross said with heavy irony. "Do tell."

"Well, first off, the suicide note's a clear forgery."

Gross's sense of levity was exchanged for interest.

"How so?" Werthen asked.

"Several things," Klimt said, addressing them both. "Not that it isn't a good job of penmanship. Obviously, the forger knows his business and had a sense for Herr Binder's eccentricities. You can see he has the letter 'e' down. Binder writes it in the Greek fashion, like an epsilon. And the curious spelling of 'scalpel.' Binder inverts the final 'l' and 'e.' You can see it all throughout the order book and also in the suicide note. Our man's done his homework, all right."

"So you discern a male hand at work in the suicide note?" Gross said excitedly.

"Oh, most definitely, Professor. No way to disguise that, is there?"

Gross shook his head in agreement, looking now with a new-found respect for Klimt.

"But if it is so accurate in the details," Werthen said, "how can you know it is a forgery?"

"*Because* of the likeness. The writing in the order book and that on the suicide note are far too similar," Klimt answered. "The upward slant of the line, the clear penmanship, the careful spacing between letters. I ask you," he turned to Werthen, "if you were writing your farewell letter, about to put a revolver in your mouth and blow your brains out, would your hand be as steady as when leisurely filling out an order for three dozen scalpels?"

Werthen did not bother with an answer. "You mean the absence of signs of nervousness in the suicide note make it a forgery."

Klimt shrugged. "That about sums it up. Your conclusion, too, Professor?"

"Bravo, Klimt," Gross said, clapping his hands noiselessly. "Exactly my conclusions. I, too, noticed the absence of a sense of urgency in the suicide note. Observe that it was written with a steel-nib pen, a number two, I should think. When writing with such a pen and dipping it into the inkpot at intervals, a certain number of words can be written before the line becomes too light and illegible. I compared both texts for such a detail and discovered that, while the order book displays a regular variation between blacker letters and paler ones, denoting the spot where the writer had to dip the pen again, no such breaks occur in the suicide note. All the letters are of a uniform darkness; pale letters are in fact missing altogether. Which tells me that the note was not written out spontaneously, but rather copied meticulously to disguise the writing. The writer was constantly dipping his pen to create the perfect lettering, not waiting for the line to begin to pale before doing so. Ergo, this is a forgery, a well-constructed copy of Binder's hand."

Werthen looked now at both samples and could see for himself what Gross was talking about; it was so obvious once explained.

"Moreover," Gross continued, "I have made one further discovery while examining Herr Binder's order and schedule book. He could not possibly have killed Fräulein Landtauer, for he had an alibi for that evening after all."

"But the doctor in Klagenfurt—," Werthen began.

228 :: J. Sydney Jones

"*Not* in Klagenfurt, but in Graz," Gross said. "Binder's mind must have begun to play tricks on him, the effects of syphilis. He in fact noted his visit to Graz, but in the wrong month. I only caught it as he wrote the date '16-8-98' next to the doctor's name, though it was in the July section of the schedule. He must have taken the train from Klagenfurt to Graz on the Tuesday, for he was conferring with a doctor there at the end of the evening surgery. It turns out I am personally acquainted with the chap, a capital surgeon, one Doktor Bernhard Engels. I went to the local exchange and confirmed by telephone the fact that Binder was, indeed, in our old hometown the very night of the Landtauer girl's murder. He had to wait until the doctor's evening surgery was finished before presenting his wares. Engels says that Herr Binder was at his office until at least nine in the evening. Consulting the k. und k. Railway Timetable you keep in your desk, I discovered that the last train for Vienna departs from Graz at eight thirty in the evening; the first in the morning leaves at six thirty and does not arrive until long after the police had already discovered the body of Fräulein Landtauer. Thus, Binder was indeed innocent of her murder. Which, in turn, means he was innocent of them all."

Though they had speculated such, this proof came as a shock to Werthen. Suddenly they were no longer working with hypothesis. Binder's innocence set all their other assumptions into place now. Werthen felt a chill go over his body and shivered.

"Looks like you fellows are onto something big," Klimt said.

"Now we are left with the question of why Binder," Gross said, moving to the window and looking out at the afternoon street. The light had already changed to the golden soft rays of fall.

"Scalpels?" Werthen offered. "They were involved in the murders, and he could thus have a logical linking to the crimes."

Gross nodded. "That is, if the person responsible for all these outrages was trying to direct us toward Binder. And I believe he was. Binder was chosen early on as the sacrificial lamb for these crimes. There is also the matter of the noses."

Klimt jumped in now. "Now that Binder is not your man, the whole affair of syphilitic rage at those without the disease no longer washes."

"Exactly," Gross said. "Yet those mutilations were a signature. We examined the idea of anti-Semitism and decided that was a false lead. What other symbols concern the nose?"

"Conceit," Werthen said. "Being *hochnäsig*, or having one's nose in the air."

"Nosy," Klimt quickly added. "Sticking your nose in other people's business."

Gross closed his eyes in contemplation. He heard the offerings but made no immediate response. "Something to do with Frosch, for he was the real victim," he said absently. "It is teasing me, this connection. Infuriating."

"Something to do with smell," Klimt said, thrashing about now for connections.

Suddenly Gross slapped his hand on the windowsill. "That's it!"

"A smell?" Werthen said.

Gross looked at him in bewilderment. "Of course not. No, it has to do with American Indian lore. The Sioux of the Plains tribes, if I am not mistaken, cut off the noses of squaws unfaithful to their husbands. And Frosch—"

"Was about to be unfaithful and reveal the truth about the death of Crown Prince Rudolf," Werthen finished for him.

"Who would do such a thing?" Klimt said in disgust.

"Someone for whom symbols are terribly important," Gross answered. "For whom loyalty is a be-all and end-all. And someone with enough power to strike at the very heart of the empire, brazen enough to assassinate a crown prince and the empress."

Gross turned his back to them once again, gazing out the window. "Also, someone who thinks he is very clever. We shall see about that."

He could see the criminologist standing in the window of the flat across the street. If he had a rifle with him, the man would be dead.

He was still fuming about the catastrophe in Geneva. "Make it look like an accident," he had been ordered. That was a mistake; instead of killing the lawyer and the professor outright, he had to try to arrange a traffic accident and ended up wasting the lives of a perfectly good pair of horses.

All the mystery and false leads. All the drama with mutilation of the Prater victims. He had done his best to create *eine schöne Leiche,* or a beautiful corpse, with each of those, but why all the extra trouble? He'd had to arrange an underground surgery to accommodate that tall order; outfitting a *Keller* in the Third District with surgical instruments and vats for siphoning off the blood, which he subsequently leached into the nearby sewer channel. He had used maps of the sewers and catacombs supplied to him by his controller to become an expert at navigating the underground world of Vienna and was careful to avoid any of the squatter cities established underground by the homeless. Such a lot of bother for death. The only satisfying part of all of those had been the initial contact, the odor of fear as he took them from the back, his hands in a viselike grip on their head and a quick twist to break their neck. The satisfying sound of it.

He was never given anything but orders: no explanations, no reasons. Of course he was a soldier; orders were orders. But one wondered, what were they playing at? Even with the empress he had had to play the role of a coachman rushing to the scene in assistance. And why the charade with the idiot Italian? Orchestrating that had taken more effort than ten clean kills.

Even meeting with his controllers had turned into an opera. At the last meeting with his Major—actually a lieutenant colonel now, but he would always be the Major to him—another person was there to make sure the orders were set out clearly. Dressed like a monk in a hooded cassock, he was, his face hidden in the shadows. All he could discern in the dimness of the room was the figure of a small golden sheep dangling from the man's neck. Why all the drama? It was only killing, after all.

Now he had to make up for the fiasco in Geneva with the lawyer and the professor. It had been the first time he'd failed. It would not happen again. He didn't care what the Major told him, next time he would make no mistakes. Subtlety was for pastry chefs. A bullet to the brain would do the trick, and let the constabulary try to piece together the crime.

NINETEEN

They were to meet with Professor Krafft-Ebing the next morning in his university office, for Werthen, going over his notes the night before, had come across a possible link in the murders to Franz Ferdinand. The brother of the heir apparent, Archduke Otto, was, as Krafft-Ebing had described during their first meeting, a member of the notorious One Hundred Club, those sufferers of syphilis who regularly debauched young virgins. Thus, perhaps the matter of the nose mutilations still involved syphilis, but not Herr Binder. Perhaps it was somehow connected to Franz Ferdinand and his brother. In any case, this link, albeit tenuous, to Franz Ferdinand was too tantalizing to pass up.

Gross was skeptical, but came along anyway.

Before they left the flat, Werthen noticed the early mail on the table by the door. On the very top was a letter with Berthe's handwriting. He opened it quickly and with Gross breathing impatiently over his shoulder read her note:

Dear Karl,

Please forgive the histrionics Sunday. I do love you. But we must also learn to trust one another. To hold nothing back from each other. And please tell Dr. Gross to stop reading this over your shoulder!

Werthen turned around, and indeed Gross had been perusing the letter, but showed not a whit of remorse.

"Clever girl, that one" was all he said.

Werthen returned to the note, this time facing Gross:

This is a hellish busy week for me, and I am sure for you as well. Let us meet on Friday night and have a celebration. Kisses, darling. Sorry to sound like a schoolgirl, but I miss you. And I do love the bracelet.

Love, B

Werthen sighed with relief. How he loved her. Her angry words had been plaguing him; now he felt that he could truly move ahead with their investigation once again.

"What are you waiting for, Gross? Time's wasting."

Krafft-Ebing had a corner office on the third floor of the new Ringstrasse building completed by the famous architect Heinrich von Ferstel a dozen years earlier. The immense limestone facade of the building dominated the boulevard. Werthen knew that five years earlier Klimt had been commissioned to create a series of ceiling paintings for the entrance, but that after much haggling no themes had yet been agreed upon. The ceiling still looked awfully bare. As they climbed the broad stairs to the third floor, Werthan was surprised to see a female student in braids and a pale blue navy dress hurrying to a lecture, then remembered females had been granted entrance to the university—in the philosophy faculty only—the previous year.

Krafft-Ebing was waiting for them as arranged this morning by *Rohrpost*, the pneumatic underground post that was often as fast as using the telephone, and glanced at the silver-tipped walking stick Werthen was affecting today. A razor-sharp sword was inside, and Werthen knew how to wield it.

Krafft-Ebing's office was utilitarian in appointment: glass-fronted lawyer's bookcases lined the walls and framed large windows overlooking the Ringstrasse. His desk resembled a schoolmaster's, small—literally dwarfed by the large room—and piled high with notebooks and hefty tomes generously bookmarked with slips of blue paper.

They made small talk for a few moments, the psychologist expressing surprise that Gross was not in Bukovina, then got down to business.

"I really do not see how I can help you regarding the One Hundred Club. I shared with you what information I had regarding that infamous society at our last meeting." Krafft-Ebing leaned back in his leather chair. "But why the continued interest, gentlemen? I understood that the Prater murders had been solved." His supercilious grin let them know that the psychologist did not for a moment believe that the real culprit in those murders had been brought to justice.

"We have discovered new evidence," Gross said, informing Krafft-Ebing of the alibi discovered for Herr Binder, but not of the connection between the Prater murders and the assassination of Empress Elisabeth or her son. Gross did not want to endanger his old friend, and knowing too much about this case was to put oneself at risk. Werthen, after the departure of Klimt the evening before, had roundly been chastised by the criminologist for having given the painter too much damning information. Werthen's ears were still ringing from that dressing-down.

Krafft-Ebing nodded sagely as Gross imparted the new facts. "Then you are looking for a new profile. But you can hardly suspect Archduke Otto. I mean, the man is a flamboyant fool, but hardly a murderer. Besides, I would imagine that you would now be looking for other connections than those having to do with syphilis. If Binder is innocent, it means that someone wanted to make him look guilty and was thus using the unfortunate man's infection as part of that charade."

"Or was using Binder's syphilis to cover up his own," Werthen quickly offered.

Gross made no response to this, but Krafft-Ebing pursed his lips and said, "Possibly," without much conviction. "I was reminded of our earlier conversation," the psychologist went on, "at news of the death of the empress."

Gross and Werthen exchanged glances at this non sequitur, but by this time Werthen was aware of the psychologist's roundabout way of discussion.

"At first I heard only that she had died in Geneva, poor woman. I had not seen the newspapers yet and read of her assassination. Thus I thought—and this is what reminded me of our earlier conversation—that she had finally succumbed to her illness."

Gross and Werthen sat in silence, but this very silence was a question.

"You see, she was a sufferer, as well."

"The Empress Elisabeth had syphilis?" Werthen all but choked on the question.

Krafft-Ebing nodded solemnly. "Not many knew. It was a very well kept imperial secret. Which explains her estrangement from her husband and her continual travels. She was forever seeking a cure, forever trying to run far from the memory of that disease."

Gross was finally nudged back into speech: "How do you come by this information, Krafft-Ebing?"

"I was, during the final years of his life, the personal physician of Crown Prince Rudolf, if you recall."

"Of course." Gross nodded. "You were much away from Graz then. A most prestigious appointment."

"Yes, it was. And it was also a burden in many ways. For you see, that sad young man was also infected. Had been at birth, as a matter of fact. Congenital syphilis."

"But where . . . ?" Werthen left his question half-spoken, for the answer was obvious. Franz Josef, the kindly father figure of the empire, *Der Alte*, the bewhiskered gentleman who ruled the empire with punctilious efficiency, who had been at the helm for half a century. He had infected his young wife with the disease, who in turn gave birth to a child who carried the deadly bacteria in his blood. Werthen suddenly understood the empress's final gift to her husband: the player piano with the single scroll: "Liebestod."

"The first child, Archduchess Sophie," Krafft-Ebing continued, "lived only a pair of years until succumbing to the inherited disease. The second child, Gisela, managed to escape its effects, as did the fourth child, Marie Valerie, born about a decade later. But the third child, the long-awaited heir to the throne, Crown Prince Rudolf, was born with syphilis. By the time of his death, it had gone beyond the second stage."

"Tragic," Werthen muttered. He was also confronted with a totally different picture of Franz Josef than he had ever had before. "But what of the emperor?"

"I have never examined him, but apparently he is one of those lucky enough to escape the ravages of the illness, thus far. He is far from a young man and there is very little visible effect from the disease, so far as I can make out. Her majesty, however, was a different matter. By the time of her death, she was afflicted with tremors, her legendary beauty had gone, and she preferred to cover her face as if living in Islam."

"Was the crown prince in his right mind at the time of his death?" Gross asked.

"I should say so. He had not yet reached the tertiary stage; you might say he was in a sort of remission. In some, this time between the early stages and the tertiary can last decades. But it preyed on him; he knew he was living in the shadow of the gallows."

"Was he suicidal?" Werthen now asked.

But Krafft-Ebing showed sudden suspicion at all this interest so far removed from their stated investigation. "Gross," he said, and then nodded at Werthen, "Herr *Advokat*, I think you are not being forthright with me."

"Idle curiosity," Werthen said, trying to smooth it over. It sounded insincere even to his own ears.

"Your choice to know or not," Gross finally said. "But let me warn you, knowledge can be dangerous. We ourselves have narrowly avoided death once as a result of our investigations. I do not want to involve others if not absolutely necessary."

"Nonsense," Krafft-Ebing spluttered. "Now you have got *my* curiosity up. How can I know how to help you if I am kept ignorant of the facts?"

Gross exchanged a glance with Werthen, then sighed deeply before outlining the connection between the Prater murders, including that of Herr Frosch, and the death of Empress Elisabeth and Rudolf a decade earlier. He did not, however, provide any details about the direction their investigation was currently taking—toward Archduke Franz Ferdinand.

The psychologist sat in stunned silence for a time after Gross finished.

"My God, it sounds like something the American writer Poe might come up with," he finally said. His mind worked quickly, piecing together this information with Werthen's earlier questions regarding Archduke Otto. "So you suspect Otto . . . No. You suspect his brother, Franz Ferdinand! He would be the one to stand to gain most by Rudolf's death."

"A kingdom," Werthen said.

Krafft-Ebing shook his head violently. "No. Completely wrongheaded." He focused on Gross. "You believe this?"

"He has motive," Gross allowed. "And whomever we are battling—for it is a life-and-death battle, make no mistake—has terrific power, that is clear from the way he has controlled the investigation into the Prater murders from the very outset."

"Nonsense," Krafft-Ebing insisted. "Franz Ferdinand is

sometimes a blustering fool, frustrated at being kept out of policy-making, just as his cousin Rudolf had been. But I have met him. He is actually quite a knowledgeable chap. He has even written a book about his travels, visiting the warmer climates in an attempt to cure his tuberculosis. I had cause to examine him in March, as a matter of fact. I pronounced him cured and able to take on full duties of heir apparent. You should have seen him once I made the pronouncement. He danced around like a small child. The man grows roses, for Lord sake. How can he be a cold-blooded killer?"

"Roses?" Gross said. "Interesting. The same hobby as our Herr Binder."

When Gross glanced at him, Werthen noted for the first time that the criminologist might be taking his theory about Franz Ferdinand seriously.

"I should keep my opinions to myself then," Krafft-Ebing said, "and simply help you two create a new profile of the killer. Like you, Gross, I believe that our killer created the signature wounds on the victims of the Prater murders for a reason. The mutilations were not done simply to make the perpetrator look insane. I think they are all significant and all help to sketch a picture of the killer. The nose first."

"Settled?" Gross suggested.

"Yes," Krafft-Ebing said. "I very much like your theory about Indian lore. The unfaithful servant gets his nose chopped off, just like an unfaithful wife. The fact that it is an American Indian practice is also a signpost. It means the killer has perhaps had the luxury of travel to the United States and back. We Austrians have not sent many immigrants to the New World. More likely it would be someone with the means to travel, or at least someone educated enough to read of such practices. This points to wealth, possibly even aristocracy."

"The middle classes are well enough educated these days," Werthen objected.

"Of course they can read," Krafft-Ebing said. "Any shopkeeper could pick up the adventure books of Karl May and possibly find a reference to such practices in the Indians of the American Plains. But it is the use of such information I am referring to. Honor and faithfulness are terrifically important to this person. Most of us do not live by such symbolic acts. For our killer, such symbolism is important, no, vital. We see that if we look more closely at the other markers."

"The blood," Gross said. "After deciding against the Jewish angle, we did let that detail lapse."

"It is as important as the nose," Krafft-Ebing said. "Blood symbolizes so many things: life, fecundity, sexuality, breeding. But the draining of the blood is telling. Linked with the mutilated nose, I would say that the blood in this case indicates a lack of breeding, or of good blood, as the aristocrats might say."

Werthen found this discussion somewhat ironic given that Krafft-Ebing himself was a *Ritter*, a member of the lower aristocracy, but the aristocracy nonetheless.

"Excellent," Gross said, rubbing his hands. "And the placement of the bodies?"

"That is the third marker," Krafft-Ebing agreed. "The Prater. Now an amusement park, and thus one thinks it is a symbol of the common man. Or perhaps it was merely a handy place to dump the bodies. Deserted enough in the middle of the night so that no one would notice."

"Yet the killer took these people off the streets of Vienna, some even when it was still light," Gross said. "No, I do not think it was the remoteness of the place that determined the use of the Prater."

"It was a royal hunting preserve in the time of Joseph I," Werthen said.

"Once again to the aristocratic connection," Krafft-Ebing said. "And these victims were left as if they were trophies of the hunt."

Werthen thought quickly of Franz Ferdinand's reputation as a hunter who had slaughtered thousands of game animals, but said nothing. There was no reason to derail Krafft-Ebing from his speculations.

"We are coming closer to a full picture of the perpetrator, gentlemen," the psychologist said. "A man of power and wealth able to most probably hire someone to do his killing for him. Someone for whom loyalty and breeding are all important. A soldier perhaps, or a member even of one of our illustrious knightly orders, such as the Austrian Imperial Leopold Order, the Maria Theresa Order, the Order of St. Stephen, or even the Order of the Golden Fleece. Those all have a code of honor which demands members to censure other knights for treason or heresy. Such a code could be extended in the man's mind to a servant of the empire as Herr Frosch. Even to the empress herself."

"I believe all members of the royal family are automatically members of some orders," Werthen added.

"The Golden Fleece," Gross said with a sly grin at his display of arcane knowledge. "But there is nothing saying our perpetrator must belong to such an order, merely that he wield power of some sort. Which leaves a wide assortment to choose from. First we have the eighty living descendants of Empress Maria Theresa and her son, Emperor Leopold II. Archdukes, archduchesses, princes, princesses, counts, and countesses."

"The First Society," Krafft-Ebing added.

"Quite. Any of those could wield the sort of power we are looking for. Then comes the lower hereditary titles from the other parts of the empire, many of which are Hungarian, I remind you. Most of these, with some prominent exceptions such as Esterhazy, Schwarzenberg, Grunenthal, and Thurn and Taxis, have titles no higher than count. Then comes the third tier of *Dienstadel,* who earned their titles, such as knight or baron, through service to the crown."

"As with my own family," Krafft-Ebing said.

"And let us not forget," Gross continued, "the vast array of civil servants, military men, advisers, and even servants who are in positions of power at the court. I have read estimates of the number constituting the court as high as forty thousand."

But Werthen had stopped listening. Franz Ferdinand was surely a member of the Golden Fleece, as had been Crown Prince Rudolf. Had Franz Ferdinand needed a rationalization to kill his older cousin, he could have told himself he was doing it for the good of the country, to save Austria from Rudolf's love of the Magyars, who wanted to break from the dual monarchy. Franz Ferdinand would have been twenty-six at the time of Rudolf's death, with enough allies to pull off such a coup as assassinating the crown prince and making it look like suicide.

"Do you agree, Werthen?"

Gross's voice finally brought Werthen out of his thoughts. He did not know how long he had been out of their conversation.

"Sorry, my mind was wandering. Agree with what?"

"Our next step should be to determine if our central theory is correct."

"And that is?"

"That all of this revolves around the death, no, the murder, of Crown Prince Rudolf a decade ago."

"Short of finding a copy of Frosch's memoirs, how do you propose to do that?" Werthen asked. "We can hardly reopen that investigation, as well. The crime scene exists no longer, as Rudolf's bedroom was literally torn apart to renovate the Mayerling hunting lodge into a Carmelite nunnery. Many of those who were present at Mayerling that night, including Rudolf's driver, Bratfisch, and now Frosch, are dead. So how to proceed?"

"By examining the body."

"But the crown prince is in the crypt of the Capuchin Church," Werthen argued. He did not like being diverted from this present investigation by Gross to waste time on a ten-year-old murder. "They would never let us open his sarcophagus."

"Not the crown prince, Werthen, but the girl. Marie Vetsera, whom he supposedly shot before killing himself."

"What could you possibly hope to prove by looking at that rotting corpse?"

"I am not certain, Werthen. Perhaps we shall only succeed in stirring up the killer even more. Enough, perhaps, to act unwisely. Or perhaps there is indeed something to be found in the cold, damp earth besides worms."

Gross rose from his chair, nodding at the psychologist. "Krafft-Ebing, as always, it has been a delight. Many thanks for your assistance, and do look both ways before crossing the Ringstrasse tonight."

The psychologist shot Gross a look. "You as well, Gross. We shouldn't want to lose you, just yet."

What they found so blasted humorous about the prospect of death, Werthen did not know.

"And let me know if the Vetsera clan agree to the exhumation," Krafft-Ebing said as they were on the way out the door. "You'll need a medical doctor present for the examination, I assume?"

TWENTY

Outside, Klimt was still waiting for them. He had insisted on playing bodyguard, and—with the assistance of his former cellmate Hugo from the Landesgericht prison—he had recruited three hulking and rather unsavory-looking individuals, under whose bulging jackets Werthen imagined there to be an assortment of pistols, truncheons, knives, and brass knuckles. Each of these men wore a derby hat atop a medicine-ball-sized head. Klimt made no effort at introductions, and neither Werthen nor Gross insisted on formalities. Though Gross had scoffed at the idea last night, he was not, Werthen noticed, complaining of the company today.

They were sandwiched by their escorts as they made their way along the Ring.

"You seem to be a bit of an amateur historian of your adopted city, Werthen," Gross said as they walked toward the nearest fiacre rank, at Schottentor. "Tell me, what became of the Vetsera girl's mother?"

"Well, the court banished her, as you could quite imagine. She was blamed for throwing her beautiful young daughter at the crown prince. Fact of the matter was, however, though

Helene Vetsera was a social climber and not beyond arranging an affair between her seventeen-year-old daughter and Rudolf—indeed, rumor has it she herself as a younger and married woman tried to bed the crown prince—she was innocent this time. It was the empress's niece Marie, Countess Larisch, who acted as go-between for her cousin and the Vetsera girl. She, too, was banished from court as a result of her involvement. I believe she recently married a Bavarian singer and is living in Munich."

"Yes, yes, Werthen," Gross said impatiently. "But the mother, that's the one I am interested in."

"She was dropped by all good society, though her brothers, the Baltazzi boys as they are known, have managed to remain in society's good graces. Great racing gents, they are. You can find them at Freudenau in the racing season."

"Werthen!"

"Yes, the mother. Last I knew Helene Vetsera was still living in the family mansion on Salesianergasse."

"The so-called Noble Quarter. Then let us be off."

"But, Gross, we cannot simply go calling on the baroness. There is etiquette to follow. One must present one's card beforehand and wait to be invited."

"Nonsense, Werthen. The lady is probably pining away, eager for any visitation. If she is the pariah you say she is, she will be only too happy to greet us. Quickly, man," Gross said as he flagged a passing *Fiaker*, "we have no time to waste."

He and Werthen jumped in the *Fiaker*, leaving Klimt and his crew scrambling for the next available carriage.

Arriving at Salesianergasse 12, Werthen was surprised to find that Gross was right about the baroness's eagerness for company. They delivered their professional cards to the aged butler who answered the door, and within five minutes Helene Vetsera received them. Werthen saw Klimt and his bulldogs draw up in a *Fiaker* just as he and Gross were entering the house.

The baroness was seated in a large and rather dark room when the butler showed them in. In her day, Helene Vetsera had been known as a beauty, Werthen knew. Her Levantine good looks came from her father, Themistocles Baltazzi, who came from Asia Minor and embraced the ideal of empire to such an extent that he grew rich off bridge tolls and other such government concessions. She was one of four children; the other three were boys, who had made names for themselves in England racing horses. Helene married an Austrian diplomat and had several children, most notably a daughter, Marie, who became infamous for her early death at Mayerling.

"I have, of course, heard of your work, Herr Doktor Gross," the baroness said after introductions were made.

The light was so poor in the room that Werthen could not make out her features clearly; he imagined that was the intention. Gossip had it that she had aged horribly after the death of her daughter and banishment from society.

"That pleases me, Baroness," Gross said with courtly grace. "I must apologize for our unannounced visit. I explained to *Advokat* Werthen that such behavior was not quite *au fait,* but he would not be convinced. My sincere apologies on his behalf."

Werthen rolled his eyes at Gross.

The baroness cast Werthen a reproachful look, then turned again to Gross.

"This must be a matter of some urgency, then," she said. Clearly her curiosity had been piqued.

"It is, Baroness. But to you, it may prove also a somewhat painful one. You see, my colleague and I are writing a review of police procedures in the tragic affair at Mayerling."

An audible sigh came from her at the mention of that name.

"It will be published in my journal, the *Archive of Criminalistics.* A professional organ, you understand, read by criminologists around the world. We hope to put all gossip to rest regarding the death of your daughter and the crown prince. To that end, we require your assistance."

"My baby." A sniffle came from the dusk surrounding the baroness. "So misunderstood."

"That is exactly why we have come to you, dear Baroness," Gross continued. "We hope to clear up any misunderstandings regarding your daughter. It is my contention that she was, in fact, an innocent victim. That she was merely at the wrong place at the wrong time. Far from being part of a romantic suicide pact, young Marie was, sadly, an accidental casualty of other machinations. I believe we can prove this if we had the opportunity to view the remains."

Gross left his pronouncement dangling without further explanation. Werthen assumed the woman would, after having time to collect herself, welcome any attempt to clear her daughter's name and gladly sign an exhumation form for the body.

"That is quite impossible," the baroness said, standing suddenly. "Do you know how long I have lived in exile from society? Almost a decade. And only now are things beginning to thaw. I received an invitation from the Princess Metternich for a soiree just last week. Perhaps my tragic loneliness is coming to an end. And you wish me to jeopardize that by opening up all those old wounds?"

Werthen was surprised but not amazed. He had dealt with people for too many years to be amazed anymore. The baroness was more concerned with her social standing than clearing the name of her dead daughter, which meant that they had to attempt a different approach now.

"Perhaps it is time to inform the good lady," the lawyer suddenly said.

Gross had the good sense to display no wonderment at this. "I will leave that up to you, *Advokat* Werthen."

"Baroness," Werthen began, "I must tell you that our investigation has been commissioned by the highest powers."

"You mean—," the baroness began, but Werthen cut her off.

"We are not at liberty to mention our sponsor, but rest assured that our mission has been sanctioned at the highest level of the court. Your cooperation in this matter would not go unnoticed."

"But you should have said so earlier. It is my patriotic duty to aid you in this. Of course I can see that. Please, please, get to the bottom of all this. Tell the world that my dear Marie was an innocent."

"A simple note, Baroness, with your signature," Werthen said. "That should suffice."

"Anything. Anything. And please let your . . . sponsor know my deepest devotion to the House of Habsburg."

Werthen did not respond. Writing materials were gathered and a note penned to the abbot of the Heiligenkreuz Monastery, where Marie Vetsera was buried.

As if in a cheap melodrama, lightning and thunder greeted them that evening at the Heiligenkreuz Monastery. The abbot, a feminine-looking soul in his brown robe and tonsured head, took the Baroness Helene Vetsera's note in his plump fingers and sucked his teeth.

"Most unusual," he said after reading it.

"The lady wishes her daughter's body exhumed," Gross said. "We have brought along workmen"—he nodded at Klimt's crew, gathered, hats in hand, in the reception hall—"a notary"—another nod, to Werthen—"and a medical doctor"—a final nod, at Krafft-Ebing, who had had to leave his schnitzel half-eaten at his apartment to join the group.

A jagged line lit the sky outside, followed by a roaring clap of thunder. Rain pelted the roof.

"This is all too reminiscent of that awful night she was brought here." The abbot shook his head, handing the note back to Gross. "We had to wait several hours to bury her, for the ground was flooded."

Gross ignored this remark, anxious to get down to business.

"Do you have an outbuilding where we might conduct an examination?"

While Krafft-Ebing changed into his examination clothing, Klimt and his men saw to the slogging work of digging up the coffin from the unmarked grave in the monastery cemetery. Werthen held a lantern as the men put their backs into it, the rain falling steadily now. The abbot, draped in a cloak and with an umbrella held over his head by one of the novitiates, kept up a steady stream of chatter as the men dug. By the time the first spade struck wood, Werthen had been informed about the miserable conditions on the night of the burial, the last-minute permission by the bishop to allow for the burial of a suicide on consecrated ground (for though the official police report noted that the crown prince had shot her, her death was deemed part of a suicide pact). The abbot had also told him of the distressed state of the girl's uncles, who had accompanied the corpse to Heiligenkreuz that stormy night in 1889.

The digging continued for ten more minutes until Klimt and his men were finally able to slide a rope under the coffin and begin hoisting it out of the moist, clay earth. Werthen was relieved to see that it was a simple wooden coffin. That meant that it would not be airtight, that air and insects would have done their job. With an airtight coffin, the corpse was likely to still be in putrefied liquefaction. Also, from what the abbot had said, the body had obviously been buried in haste and not been embalmed.

Werthen followed the men as they manhandled the coffin up a slippery slope, their way led by dim lantern light. They finally reached the small stone toolshed that had been set up for the exhumation. Gross was waiting with Krafft-Ebing, both of them in white gowns, rubber gloves, and surgical masks. A crude examination table had been made out of a spare door and two sawhorses. Krafft-Ebing directed the men to this table, and they set the coffin atop it.

Gross took up a crowbar and began opening the lid, the nails squealing as they were dislodged. It took several minutes to loosen the lid, and when it was finally opened, a rush of foul air filled the room, quite overwhelming Werthen and the others. Two of the toughs Klimt had hired had to rush outside to be sick. So much for Werthen's theories about the coffin not being airtight. He slung an arm over his mouth and nose, breathing in the wet wool of his overcoat.

"It's all right now," Krafft-Ebing said. "Just accumulated gases escaping from the coffin. The corpse itself has quite decomposed."

Werthen and the others slowly took arms away from mouths to discover the psychologist was right. The door to the outbuilding had been left open, and fresh air now rushed in. Werthen dangled his lantern over the coffin, as did Gross, while Krafft-Ebing got down to forensic work. The pitiful girl's frock was still draped on the skeletal remains. A strand of golden hair was visible here and there.

Krafft-Ebing muttered unintelligibly into his surgical mask as he examined the corpse, nodding his head occasionally as if agreeing with himself. Suddenly a loud "Hmmm" from him and a shake of the head.

He stood upright, pulling his mask down. "Most odd," he said. "There are no traces of a perforating bullet wound to the cranium as the police reports had it. Rather, the cranial cavity shows signs of extreme trauma."

Gross was instantly captivated by this pronouncement, but Werthen, with less experience in forensic medicine, was unsure what this meant until Gross offered an explanation:

"Consistent with a beating, perhaps?"

Krafft-Ebing nodded. "I should say so. She was either struck with a large blunt instrument repeatedly, or alternately her head was battered against such a blunt object."

"As in a bedpost, for example?" Gross said.

"So she was not shot?" Werthen finally found his voice.

"Decidedly not," Krafft-Ebing said. "And I must tell you, having known the crown prince, I cannot believe he would have been capable of such a deed."

More lightning lit up the sky dramatically outside the small building, and when the thunder came, it was followed close upon by a bellowing voice.

"Just what the Hades do you think you are doing?"

The voice belonged to a tall, dark gentleman standing in the doorway. Werthen immediately recognized him from his brash mustaches and the lively checked pattern of his topcoat. Alexander Baltazzi, uncle of the slain Marie. King of the Turf, as he was known in Vienna, for his racehorses that seemed to take every race.

"Baron Baltazzi—," Werthen began, but the tall, angry-looking man cut him off.

"Close that coffin at once. My sister rescinds her permission. At once, do you hear? You have cruelly misled her."

No one made a move. Instead, Gross calmly said, "Our work here is done. Would you care to know the results?"

"Out," Baltazzi shouted. "This matter is closed. The past is the past."

"She was murdered, Herr Baron," Gross said. "If that matters to you. Not a suicide, but a homicide."

"Enough!" Baltazzi drew a pistol from his jacket pocket, but one of the toughs immediately knocked it from his hand with a well-placed boot.

"Did you hear me?" Gross asked. "A homicide. Your niece was murdered, and not by the crown prince."

The man looked at Gross with sudden loathing. "You presume to tell me news of my niece? It was I who brought her here to be secretly buried. I who stuck a broom handle between her dress and body to hold her body upright as we left Mayerling so that any curious onlooker would be none the wiser. I who helped personally to dig the hole you just took her from. And you presume to tell me of her death? Enough now, I say. Our family has suffered enough. We have finally regained some of our lost influence, and not you or anybody else will put that at risk."

Gross nodded his head at Klimt, and the men put the lid on the coffin once more, then lifted it to rebury it. Baltazzi followed them silently on their task. He said not another word as the dirt was filled in once again. Then he returned to his waiting carriage and left the monastery.

"The man is a cad," Werthen said as they sped back toward Vienna in their carriage. Krafft-Ebing had come in his own brougham and had left first; Werthen and Gross had followed with Klimt and his men in the last carriage.

"Don't be so quick to judge, Werthen," Gross said with sudden, and for him, uncommon empathy. "It must have been a harrowing experience burying his niece. The full force of the House of Habsburg came to bear upon him. I imagine I would want to put it behind me, too."

The rain had let up, but the roads were wet. Their driver was taking it slowly. Werthen, poking his head out at one point, could no longer see the lantern on the rear of Krafft-Ebing's carriage.

"So what do we do now, Gross?" Werthen finally said. "If Marie Vetsera's death was a homicide instead of suicide, does that not suggest at least that the crown prince was also murdered? Shouldn't we take this new evidence to the father? To Kaiser Franz Josef himself?"

But there was no time for a response. From in back of them came the crack of a tree splitting at its trunk. Werthen looked out in the gloom and thought he saw the tree blocking the roadway in back of them. Klimt and his men were on the other side. He was about to tell the coachman to turn around and help them clear the tree, but suddenly the man gave the horses the whip, and Werthen and Gross were jolted back against their leather seats.

"Slow down, man," Werthen shouted. "We're losing the others."

The carriage jolted off the main road now and down a dirt and mud trail.

"I believe that is the man's intention," Gross said, pulling his pistol from his coat pocket and nodding for Werthen to do the same.

Before they had a chance to ready themselves, however, the carriage suddenly braked, the horses snorting. The doors flew open on both sides, and Werthen only managed the barest glimpse of his attacker as a strong hand was clamped over his nose and mouth, the noxious odor of chloroform overcoming him. As he slipped into blackness, he saw again the scar on the man's face. Then nothing.

TWENTY-ONE

The woman walking ahead of him looked familiar. She wore a slate blue dress with a small bustle and a waist cut severely enough to create an hourglass effect. It was the Empress Elisabeth, Werthen was sure. He wanted to run to her, to tell her to beware. But before he could do so, the woman turned. It was his fiancée, Berthe Meisner, and seeing him, she smiled. Her bodice was undone, and her left breast dangled out of the dress, pendulous and soft.

"You silly man," she said. "Come to me."

He was about to do so when he felt hot breath in his face. The sour smell of the breath finally awoke him.

"Werthen, are you all right?"

He opened his eyes and stared into the face of Hanns Gross. Werthen had experienced the same sense of shock as a young boy sleeping rough under the stars for the first time with his older cousins. In the morning they had been awakened by a herd of cows that had wandered into the field; the humid, chlorophyll breath of one of the beasts had greeted him upon waking.

He tried to sit up, but felt suddenly nauseous. He looked at Gross and realized the criminologist was dressed only in his underclothes. Peeling back the comforter covering him, Werthen discovered he was also undressed.

"Where are we, Gross?" he finally managed to ask, looking around the sumptuously appointed room, Flemish tapestries on the high walls, crystal chandeliers on the ceiling, mahogany and rosewood furniture.

"Well, I am hardly the best one to ask regarding such questions, as I am a relative stranger to your city. But I should hazard to say we are in a bedroom of the Lower Belvedere."

"What?" Werthen leaped out of what was a four-poster bed and almost fell over. Dizziness overcame him, but breathing deeply several times, he felt better. They had obviously been dosed several times with chloroform for his head to feel so badly today. And Gross's breath announced that the criminologist had been sick sometime in the night.

Werthen went to the window and pulled back brocade drapes. Sure enough, several stories beneath him was the sweep of gardens and graveled walking paths laid out in the grand manner of Versailles leading up to the elegant expanse of the Upper Belvedere, a summer retreat for Prince Eugene of Savoy, who had commissioned the famous baroque architect Johann Lukas von Hildebrandt to construct both it and the building they were obviously standing in now, the Lower Belvedere.

The headquarters of Archduke Franz Ferdinand.

That thought sent Werthen's mind racing, no longer leisurely taking in the pleasant view.

"We've got to get out of here, Gross."

"That does not seem to be a problem," the criminologist said. "Though it would be a long drop out of this window, the bedroom door is unlocked."

"Why didn't you say so before?"

Just then the door in question opened and liveried servants delivered a tray with breakfast coffee and rolls as well as their clothes, freshly laundered and pressed. The sight of these two servants in blue-and-gold uniforms, periwigs, and long stockings was so startling that, for the moment, both Gross and Werthen lost a sense of urgency to escape. Surely they could not be meant harm with unlocked doors and gussied-up servants delivering coffee. Or was this all intended to lull them, or worse yet, as a final meal before execution?

Werthen quickly dressed, ready to make a run for it. His pistol was not with the clothes, and he assumed Gross's had been confiscated, as well. But they had returned his silver-tipped walking stick with the hidden sword. They would not be defenseless. Then he noticed that Gross, still in his undervest and long underwear, had made himself comfortable in a Louis XV chair and was sipping coffee from fine porcelain.

"That may be drugged, Gross."

"I highly doubt it, my friend. There are so many other and more economical means of controlling us. Sit. There is no hurry. We shall see what our host intends."

Confound the man, Werthen thought, feeling out of sorts and none too eager to test his tender insides with coffee. Finally, however, the rich aroma of the blend won him over, and he joined Gross for a light repast, after which Gross leisurely dressed.

They did not have long to wait, for the same servants, accompanied this time by a pair of armed guards, came for them.

"Would you please come with us, gentlemen?" one of the guards requested.

"Where are you taking us?" Werthen queried.

"You will soon see." The guard swept his arm to the door.

Werthen and Gross followed the servants and were in turn followed by the guards as they made their way down a carpeted hallway and to a magnificent main stairway. However, they did not take these stairs, but instead continued on to the opposite wing to a smaller servants' staircase that led them down narrow flights of steps to a back entrance to the palace. Outside, the fresh air began to revive Werthen. Last night's rain had left the air clear and sweet-smelling; the sun shone brightly in their faces. The servants stopped and bowed to them, then departed.

Ahead of them, Franz Ferdinand, dressed in a light blue cavalry tunic and red breeches, was busily deadheading flowers in one of the rose gardens of the palace. As they approached, Werthen could see that the man wore a chestful of military medals. He also realized that the archduke was much smaller than he had thought, for he had only seen him on an upraised platform at celebrations, or in the back of his speeding motorcar. The future emperor finally saw them approaching and put down his secateurs.

"Gentlemen," he said. "I see you are none the worse for wear."

Werthen was about to explode in anger, but Gross headed him off.

"The accommodations were acceptable, yes. Not that either of us were aware of them."

Franz Ferdinand looked from one to the other, a slight smile on his lips. Werthen had never assumed the man had a sense of humor.

"I must apologize for Duncan's zeal," he said.

Suddenly the tall, scar-faced man appeared from behind a rosebush. Werthen automatically gripped his walking stick, but the release was jammed. He could not pull his sword.

"I am afraid we have disabled your weapon, Herr *Advokat*. I feared that your blood might be high, and I want no further complications. As I was saying, Duncan took my orders to bring you here immediately rather too much to heart. It is the Scots in him, you see." Then to scar-face, in schoolroom English: "Right, Duncan?"

"If Your Highness says so," the man replied, also in English, but of a glottal nature that tested Werthen's linguistic skills.

Franz Ferdinand turned again to Werthen and Gross. "He has been with me for years, ever since my visit to Scotland in

1892. He was a mountain guide on a shoot. Saved my life when a Highland pony slipped on scree. I would have toppled to my death had it not been for Duncan. But he does go in for drama. A simple invitation would have done, I should imagine. When I learned that Duncan had bribed your coachman to take his place and of your chloroformed kidnapping, I was sorely put out, I assure you. However, according to Duncan, such measures were necessary, as assassins were waiting for your carriage just a kilometer down the road."

Neither Gross nor Werthen responded to this.

"Duncan, in fact, has been a watchdog for you for several weeks."

"Are you telling us that he was the one who pulled us out of Lake Geneva?" Gross asked.

"The very one," Franz Ferdinand said with pride. "Actually, Duncan is hardly as ferocious as he looks. The scar is a result of a terrier bite and an incompetent surgeon when he was a mere boy. It lends a certain cachet, don't you think? And it makes him stand out in a crowd. I wanted you chaps to know you were being followed, to be on guard. You two have made yourselves some very powerful enemies. That happens when one wants to shine light in the darkness. When one wants to bring reform to a benighted empire."

"Why are we here, Your Highness?" Gross finally asked.

"I like directness, Professor Gross. I am pleased that you asked." The archduke now waved away the two other guards, leaving just Duncan and three of them. "Have you ever heard of the Rollo Commandos?"

Werthen and Gross exchanged questioning glances.

"No, I thought not. It is not one of those secrets a government likes to get about. The Rollo Commandos are an elite squad. They are at the beck and call of the highest powers. Their mission is to eliminate the enemies of the empire."

"Assassins," Werthen said.

"If you like," the archduke replied. He picked up his secateurs again and began cleaning out the spent roses, leaving Gross and Werthen to mull his revelation.

"I have followed your investigation from afar, as it were," Franz Ferdinand said, carefully inching down the stalk of a tea rose to find a five-leafed junction where he could snip. "From what has been reported to me, it is clear that you are on the right path. That you have linked the Prater atrocities with the deaths of both Crown Prince Rudolf and the Empress Elisabeth. And if I know that, surely they know it, as well."

"They?" Gross said.

"Your nemesis."

"And who would that be?"

"Oh, I can give you the name of the man who pulled the trigger or struck the knife. He is Sergeant Manfred Tod. An ironic name, no?" Then to Duncan: "*Tod* means 'death.'"

"Yes, Your Highness."

"Tod is a longtime member of the Rollo Commandos. He, like Duncan, bears a menacing scar, though slightly less visible, on his neck. The result, they say, of a fight to the death with his training instructor. The infamous Tod was, as a matter of fact, freshly recruited in January of 1889."

The date was not lost on Gross. "The month of Rudolf's death at Mayerling. Are you saying Sergeant Tod was the assassin?"

"Among them. There were three, according to my sources." The archduke looked hard at Werthen. "I know, I make a much better suspect in the killing, right? So much to gain. And everyone knows how much I disliked my cousin. It was all the gossip." He breathed deeply. "Of course the truth is far different than the gossip. In fact, I admired and looked up to Rudolf. He was my mentor in many ways, and my protector from his father and my uncle, Franz Josef. He guided me through youthful indiscretions, showed me what my true responsibilities were as third in line to the throne. I may not have agreed with him on his Hungarian adventure, but I loved him like a brother nonetheless."

"What Hungarian adventure are you referring to, Your Highness?" Werthen asked.

"Come now, gentlemen." The archduke sounded disappointed. "If you have come this far in your investigations, I am sure you have also uncovered the source of all this misery." He waited a moment for a reply, but when none was offered, he plunged on. "Rudolf was to be made king of an independent Hungary. Poor Rudolf, he had grown so frustrated with being kept in the wings by his father that he allowed himself to be manipulated by the Magyars into accepting such a fanciful proposition. He died for it."

"You mean—," Werthen began.

"Yes, I mean he was assassinated for treason. But not by me, gentlemen. That is why I brought you here. To tell you that. And that I did not kill Frosch or my aunt or any of those unfortunate victims found in the Prater. Again, I may not have agreed with her close relations to the Hungarians, but I admired her courage. She would not allow herself to be controlled by the emperor as the rest of the court does. She built a life on her own terms. I can appreciate that, especially now."

Werthen knew that the archduke was referring to his own love for Sophie Chotek, who, though of noble birth, was deemed below the standard for Habsburgs.

Looking at him and listening to him in person, Werthen was almost convinced of his innocence.

"Who is the real nemesis, then?" Gross persisted. "This Sergeant Tod is only the instrument of death. A puppet. Who is pulling the strings?"

"That, gentlemen, is for you to discover. I must warn you, however, you have entered dangerous waters. Your quarry is among the most powerful men in the land. Duncan will no longer be able to protect you, nor will that painter chap and his band of ruffians. You must strike and strike quickly or all is lost."

"An interesting personality," Werthen said as they left the palace and headed for the Ringstrasse. It was midmorning now and the Schwarzenbergplatz was filled with carriage traffic and several noisy automobiles that frightened horses. Pedestrians were bustling on the streets, as well, and such a flurry of activity gave Werthen a sense of safety. Tod could hardly strike in such circumstances. If there really was a Sergeant Manfred Tod. At least they were armed now. The archduke had had their pistols returned to them before they left the Lower Belvedere, and the pistols were loaded. However, Werthen's cane-sword was still jammed.

"I found him a very forthright individual," Gross pronounced after a short hesitation. "He also serves a fine cup of coffee."

"But what of his revelations?"

"Plausible."

Werthen stopped in the middle of the busy sidewalk. "Come, Gross. Not so laconic, please."

"I am ruminating, Werthen. You noticed the pendant of a sheep's fleece Franz Ferdinand wears among his other medals?"

Werthen, in fact, had not, but recalled from their earlier conversation that all Habsburg archdukes automatically became members of the order.

"As Krafft-Ebing said," Gross went on, "the man we are searching for may be bound by the rules of such an order."

"I suppose that cozying up to the Magyars could be considered treasonous behavior. But that could mean any of over fifty members of the order, not just Franz Ferdinand."

Gross nodded. "There of course is a further possibility," he said, taking Werthen's arm and urging him forward. "The crown prince, according to Krafft-Ebing, suffered from syphilis, though it appeared to have halted its deadly advance. What would happen were he to become emperor and the disease recur?"

"A tragedy, certainly," Werthen said. "Both for the empire and for the House of Habsburg."

"Exactly. It would hardly take Rudolf's supposed treason with the Magyars for someone powerful to want to eliminate him. His death could be seen in so many ways and by so many people as a salvation to the empire."

"Even for Franz Ferdinand?"

"Yes," Gross said. "But I have a feeling about the man. We criminologists cannot proceed by objective facts alone. Sometimes we need to let our instincts speak. Mine say that he is a misunderstood individual, hardly so unsympathetic as court gossip would have him be. I believe that he knows exactly who is responsible for all these deaths, but that he cannot confront the man himself. Rather, he wants us to thrash around and solve the problem for him. Which means that this nemesis is very powerful indeed, just as Franz Ferdinand said. I take his advice to heart. We must strike now or risk all."

Suddenly Gross sped up his stride, pulling out his watch from his vest pocket. "Come, Werthen. We must make haste. We need to be there before eleven."

"Where, Gross. And why before eleven?"

"That is the witching hour, my friend. The end of registration for royal audiences."

"Gross, you must be insane. Are you seriously considering what I think you are?"

"We are loyal subjects, Werthen, you and I. Upstanding individuals. Like the rest of his fifty million subjects, we have the right to a personal audience with the emperor. We have much to tell him. Now hurry, man."

TWENTY-TWO

The Hofburg, the city residence of the Habsburgs, was at once fortress, seat of government, and private home. A sprawling warren of tracts built higgledy-piggledy over the centuries, in a mixture of styles from Gothic to Renaissance to baroque to neo-Classicist, the Hofburg housed the apartments of the emperor, the State Chancellery, the Imperial Library, the Winter Riding School, and thousands of apartments for everyone from little-known Habsburg archdukes and archduchesses to pensioned ministers and several thousand servants, who slept in cramped quarters under the eaves and scurried about back stairs and along hidden corridors keeping the whole miniature city functioning.

Cutting through the Inner City rather than following the Ringstrasse, Werthen and Gross entered the complex through the Michaeler Tor, leading to the oldest tract, the Schweizerhof, from the late thirteenth century. Werthen never failed to be awed by the sheer history and longevity as represented by the Hofburg, seat of the Habsburgs for six hundred years. To the left was the red-and-black gate to the Schweizerhof; the insignia of the Order of the Golden Fleece was displayed over this gate, for within lay the Imperial-Royal Treasury, among whose most fabulous artifacts was the treasury of the Order of the Golden Fleece, including the very lance that had pierced the side of Jesus on the cross. After the Spanish and Austrian lines of Habsburgs split in 1794, it took thirty carts and three years to move that treasury from Burgundy, thus keeping it out of the hands of the French.

Gross said nothing as he led the way past these reminders to a wing perpendicular to the Schweizerhof, forming an inner courtyard with it. This was the Imperial Chancellery, where Franz Josef resided and worked. The Habsburgs were a superstitious lot; new rulers refused to live in a portion of the Hofburg where an earlier ruler had lived. Thus a strange game of musical chambers was played. Empress Maria Theresa had resided in rooms facing the inner court of the Leopoldine wing; her son, Josef II, lived on the opposite side of the same wing; Francis II chose the oldest tract, the Schweizerhof, while his son, Ferdinand, who had suffered from epilepsy and whom the Viennese had loved as something of a simpleton, moved the entourage back to the Leopoldine wing. Now that unfortunate Habsburg's successor, his nephew Franz Josef, had taken up residence opposite that in the newer Reichskanzlei, the first emperor to do so.

Werthen's study of Vienna's past had become an avocation for him, an enjoyable pastime, a cozy, leisurely investigation of bygone times.

But suddenly he himself had been caught up in the maw of history, and it no longer seemed so gemütlich. The massive gray buildings all around now bore down upon him; he could feel the weight of their stones, their secrets.

"What do you intend telling him, Gross?" Werthen asked as they took the small flight of steps up to the main entrance.

"I haven't quite decided, Werthen. I suppose we shall have time once we have registered for an audience to consider that."

Gross was right: They were the last to be registered that day, and they would thus have a long wait to speak with the emperor.

A young adjutant took their name and looked rather skeptically at Gross as the criminologist described the ostensible reason for their visit: a formal thank-you for his post in Bukovina.

They took up uncomfortable seats on a marble bench against one wall of the large and ornate waiting room. Except that no women were present, the sixty or so other prospective visitors included a complete cross-section of Viennese society, from a foppish-looking young man in a yellow waistcoat and robin's-egg-blue coat, to a muttonchopped, heavyset burgher in a rumpled brown woolen suit and the bright red nose of a tippler.

Werthen, like all Viennese, knew the myth of Franz Josef. The boy emperor who took the reigns of government in the difficult year of 1848, who faced the crowds demanding democratic reforms and turned them away. Concessions were made, but nothing lasting, for Franz Josef, a true Habsburg, believed fervently in the monarchy and deeply mistrusted the voice of the people. A constitution had finally been granted, and a parliament established, but both were more theoretical institutions than practical ones. Even Hungary had been granted more power in the empire via the *Ausgleich,* or compromise, of 1867.

Werthen, like everyone else in the empire, also knew the real power still lay in the hands of Franz Josef and his close circle of advisers and handpicked prime ministers. The emperor continually canceled the power of parliament, ruling instead by the loophole of Paragraph 14 of the constitution, which allowed for rule by emergency decree. Universal male suffrage—let alone the vote for women—was a long way off. These twice-weekly audiences were as close to democracy as the old emperor cared to come. Such individual meetings, *Angesicht zu Angesicht sehen,* as they were called, or face-to-face, lasted only a few moments at best, enough time for a few practiced words, but they served as a release valve for the people. After all, what need had they of a functioning parliament when they could speak to the emperor himself whenever they pleased?

The most famous bureaucrat in Europe, Franz Josef personally saw to the running of his vast empire. Rising at five in the morning, he worked steadily until eight, when he met with his ministers. Then came a simple lunch, and more work that often took him deep into the night. His diversions were few: a summer holiday at Bad Ischl, where he hunted in the mountains, and an occasional visit from his special friend, Die Schratt, as the Burgtheater actress was affectionately called by the Viennese.

However, twice a week, at ten in the morning, Emperor Franz Josef set aside several hours for personal audiences with his subjects. He heard complaints, received gifts, and kissed the occasional baby at such meetings with the common folk.

Then back to his reading of files and signing of documents. That he maintained this arduous schedule even in face of the tragedy that had so recently befallen him was a mark of the old man's resilience. It made Werthen almost like the man, despite his autocratic ways.

But suddenly it struck Werthen: "You've come to accuse him, haven't you?"

Gross had been busy twiddling his thumbs, first one direction then another. The question seemed to jolt him out of his thoughts, yet he made no immediate response.

"Franz Ferdinand said that we must strike quickly. Is that what you plan to do? If not Franz Ferdinand, then who would be powerful enough to order murders and assassinations? Who else would have the motive? But his own son and wife?"

Werthen had grown so excited with this line of questioning that his voice rose in volume, drawing the disapproving glances of several in the room.

"Steady, Werthen," Gross counseled. "I do not believe we are at that extreme point as yet. I have, however, given some thought to our unexpected visit with Archduke Franz Ferdinand. His man Duncan was indeed the one we both saw from the train on the way to Geneva. His scar is, as the Archduke explained, immensely noticeable, almost defining. I wonder, perhaps, if it was not too defining for us, as well."

"I don't follow you, Gross."

"The hotel porter in Geneva, the young Austrian . . ."

"Planner," Werthen offered.

"Yes. He described to us the man he saw helping the empress up after her attack. Tall, as I recall. And he mentioned the possibility of a scar. I believe we both jumped to the same conclusion without further questioning Herr Planner. The mere mention of a scar conjured Duncan's visage in both our minds. Yet Franz Ferdinand insists that the real murderer, this Sergeant Tod, also bears a scar, but on his neck, not his face."

"I see where you are going with this. We need to requestion Planner. He never described exactly where this scar was on the man he described." They had, in their earlier investigation, also contacted the lady-in-waiting to Elisabeth, Countess Sztaray, but she had been no help in describing the mysterious coachman.

"A telegram should do, I believe. Unless we dare to chance an international call."

Werthen shook his head. "We could wait hours for the call. Better to stop at a post office once we are finished here. We could have his reply by evening."

Gross's attention was suddenly drawn to the doorway, where the young adjutant sat. He was conferring now with a tall and forceful-looking old soldier, dressed in military blue, his snow-white hair giving him an aura of power rather than age. Werthen recognized him at once: Prince Grunenthal, the emperor's principal aide and longtime adviser. The prince looked up occasionally as he spoke to the adjutant, looking into the waiting room, surveying those awaiting an audience. His eyes locked on Gross and Werthen and held them for several seconds before moving on to others. In the next instant, he was gone.

Gross, too, had noticed the prince's stare and suddenly rose. "Come, Werthen. I believe we are premature in this."

He strode out of the waiting room, not bothering to speak with the adjutant, leaving Werthen to simply straggle behind as best he could. Hailed by the adjutant, Werthen told the young officer that something urgent had come up and to please pardon their hasty departure. Gross was already out the main door to the Reichskanzlei by the time Werthen caught him up.

"What is all this, Gross? Have you taken leave of your senses?"

"No." Gross spun around, facing him. "In fact, I believe, dear Werthen, that I have finally *come* to my senses. We need more before we have a face-to-face with the emperor."

"Was it Prince Grunenthal's presence? It did seem as if he recognized us."

But Gross did not bother to answer. Instead, he turned and strode forward, passing the Schweizer Tor again and now passing under the archway of the Leopoldine wing and through a passageway leading to the newest section of the Hofburg, still under construction. The proposed Heldenplatz with its new additions was still mostly bare ground bristling with surveyor's sticks. To their right lay the Volksgarten, ahead the Ringstrasse, and on the other side of that boulevard the twin museums—art and natural history—which were to form the other axis of the huge Heldenplatz.

Gross finally favored Werthen with a bit of an explanation as they walked hurriedly toward a fiacre rank on the Ring.

"I've been a fool, Werthen. This is a two-pronged investigation, and I have left the trail of Herr Binder too long. Someone chose that unfortunate man as the sacrificial lamb. We need to know who. Once we ascertain that, we can work our way up higher. Our two investigations will have become one."

Gross was lost in thought as their *Fiaker* drove them around the Ring to the address in the Third District Gross had given the driver. Gross spoke only after they had left the *Fiaker* on Erdbergstrasse, not far from the surgical-equipment firm of Breitstein und Söhne.

"Herr Binder's doctor," Gross said by way of explanation. "As good a place as any to begin." By chance a post office was on the next corner, and before going to the doctor's office, they dashed off a telegram to Planner in Geneva asking specifically where on the coachman's body the scar was and requesting a reply as soon as possible.

Dr. Gerhardt Thonau had his office across the street, on the top floor of the house at number 14. A large, rather forbidding woman, dressed in blue with a starched white apron, opened the door at their third ring and appeared to recognize Gross from his previous visit inquiring about Herr Binder's medical condition.

"Are you seeking medical attention this time?" she said as she let them in. A strong smell of roses was in the entryway, but none were to be seen. Indeed, the scent was so cloying it could only have come from a bottle, Werthen decided. "This is a doctor's office, after all," the woman said with heavy irony, "not an information booth."

"It is good to see you again, too, Frau Doktor Thonau. And I should be happy to pay your husband's usual fee for a consultation." He peered at the empty waiting room. "That is," he said with an irony to match hers, "if I would not be displacing a more needy patient."

"We were about to sit down to lunch," she replied, "but I am sure the doctor can find time for you gentlemen. That will be fifteen crowns."

Werthen was about to splutter a complaint: The best of the Ninth District surgeons would never dare demand such an exorbitant fee. However, Gross stopped him with a pat on the back.

"Excellent. Perhaps you could see to that, *Advokat?*"

Werthen shot Gross a look, but it was no use. He brought out his change purse and extracted a ten- and a five-crown coin, hefted them for weight, then handed the money over to the doctor's wife, who duly noted the charge in a large and somewhat dusty ledger. Werthen was sure she noted no more than five of the crowns given to her.

"Go on in," she said, slamming the large ledger closed. "You remember the way, I expect?"

Gross led the way through the threadbare waiting room and into a surgery at once dark and evil-smelling. Dr. Thonau, reed-thin, was busily washing medical instruments in a basin in one corner.

"Professor Gross, good to see you again."

He did not, however, looked pleased. Werthen thought Thonau, could, in fact, do with a visit to a doctor himself. His skin was the pallor of old milk; his red-rimmed eyes squinted without benefit of pince-nez.

"Have a seat," he said with false heartiness. "I was just cleaning up from the morning consultations. Have you come for an examination?"

Gross did not take the proffered seat. Neither did he bother introducing Werthen.

"No, Dr. Thonau," Gross all but thundered. "I have come for the truth."

Thonau shook his head. "What truth would that be, Professor?"

"Please, no insouciance. I haven't the stomach for it today. Who did you tell about Binder's syphilis?"

"Aside from yourself, you mean?"

"Yes."

"No one, of course. A patient's records are private. What do you take me for?"

"A poor man, a mediocre physician, and a henpecked husband whose wife would dearly love to see you earning more, and no questions asked. That, Dr. Thonau, is what I take you for. A man desperate for a little extra cash. A man who would not stop at such niceties as patient confidentiality."

Thonau tried to bluff it out for a moment, puffing up his hollow chest and blustering about false accusations and solicitors.

Werthen put a stop to that nonsense quickly enough, announcing himself as Professor Gross's lawyer. At that Thonau suddenly slumped down in his chair like a deflated balloon.

"You won't tell . . ."

He hesitated, and Werthen imagined he was referring to the physicians' professional ethics board.

". . . my wife, will you? She doesn't know about my little arrangement with Direktor Breitstein. It's the only spare change I get my hands on."

"Breitstein!" Gross said.

"Yes." Thonau shook his head, sniffling now. "I am or was doctor to several of his employees. He arranged a reduced rate for them and then paid me a regular allowance to keep him abreast of his employees' health. It was all aboveboard, though."

Gross snorted at this. "I am sure it was."

"No, I mean, Herr Breitstein only wanted to know if his employees were healthy. It is important to him to have the best representatives he could. The 'face of Breitstein and Son,' he called his sales force."

"Then why keep Herr Binder?" Werthen asked. "The man had syphilis, after all."

Thonau turned to Werthen now, smiling as if to ingratiate himself with his other interrogator.

"That is what I mean about it being all aboveboard. Herr Breitstein did not use the information against his employees. He had their best interests at heart, too."

"That is what he told you," Gross said, "or that is what you assume?"

Thonau shrugged. "I can't remember. But please, gentlemen, I implore you, do not tell my wife."

"That, Dr. Thonau, is one promise I assure you I will keep. When did you first report Binder's condition?"

"Several months ago. Perhaps late May? I would have to look at my records. It was after my first consultation with Herr Binder. He came complaining of dizziness and loss of appetite. It was obvious to me what was wrong with the man, but I ran certain tests. Then when I told Herr Breitstein, he told me not to tell Binder of his condition. I treated him with Epsom salts. There was little else to be done for the man at that stage of the illness."

"Binder did not know he had syphilis?"

Thonau shook his head. "Not from me, at any rate."

"And what explanation did Breitstein have for this?" Gross demanded.

"He said he did not want the poor man to worry. There was nothing to be done for him at that stage of the disease anyway. It may sound unorthodox, but Herr Breitstein does have—"

"We know," Gross interrupted. "The best interests of his employees at heart."

There was nothing more to be learned from Thonau, and they left. Happily, Frau Thonau had retired to the dining room, and they let themselves out.

Breitstein und Söhne was just two blocks away. They lost no time in getting there, but were surprised at the lack of activity. Last time they were here, a delivery van was being loaded and salesmen were bustling about. Now, even the secretary was missing from the desk outside Breitstein's office.

Gross knocked on the door to the man's office and entered without waiting for a reply. Inside, the teary-eyed secretary was arranging flowers, several bouquets of them, all with a black ribbon.

Gross and Werthen exchanged glances; each knew what this meant.

"Excuse us, Fräulein," Gross said. "We have come to speak to Herr Direktor Breitstein."

At which the young secretary's tears flowed afresh, and she searched for a hankie stuck up the sleeve of her white blouse.

"You haven't heard, sir?" she finally managed.

"Heard what?"

"Herr Direktor Breitstein is dead. Killed he was, just yesterday." She blubbered for a time, then regained composure. "A hunting accident, it was. At his lodge in Styria for his annual vacation. The poor man. What'll ever become of us now?"

Gross went farther into the room. For a moment Werthen thought he was actually going to solace the young woman. Instead, he went past her to the row of pictures behind the desk, looking at them closely.

"Has anyone been in this room today?" he asked.

The secretary looked up from her hankie. "No. Just me, sir. Arranging the flowers."

"And who delivered the flowers?"

"A man, sir."

"Did he leave them outside, or did he bring them in here?"

"In here, sir." More tears flowed at this, as if she thought she was in trouble.

"Please, Fräulein. This is important. Think now. What did the man look like?"

She sniffled, bit her lip, and daubed the hankie at her watery eyes. "Like a delivery person, sir."

The muscle in Gross's cheek began to work, but he kept his impatience hidden. "Was he tall?"

"Yes, sir."

"Any distinguishing marks?"

"Marks, sir?"

"Scars," Werthen all but shouted, less successful than Gross at disguising his impatience.

"Oh, yes, sir. That he did. I noticed it, and that is true." She drew a forefinger across her throat. "Like someone had tried to kill him or something."

Gross turned his attention back to the photos. "Look, Werthen. Do you see here? We have a missing photo."

Werthen crossed the room now and saw, indeed, a rectangle of lighter wall in the line of photos where one had clearly once hung and was now missing.

"I was looking at those photographs the day we interviewed Breitstein," Werthen said. "I thought I recognized someone in one of the photos."

"Who?"

Werthen sighed. "I have no idea, Gross. It was just one of those fleeting impressions one gets. I was too far away to make out the pictures clearly, and whoever it was had a hunting hat on. It wasn't the face anyway that I recognized, but something about the way the man stood. His bearing."

"Think, man."

"It's no use, Gross. It's not there."

"Are you gentlemen from the police?"

It was the teary-eyed secretary; they had completely forgotten about her, so concerned were they with the missing picture.

"No, Fräulein," Gross said, turning to her. "Merely customers of your former employer. We will leave you to your arranging now."

As they left the office, Gross gripped Werthen's arm. "Could it have been Franz Ferdinand? He is a fearful hunter, so it is said."

Werthen shook his head, frustrated. "I simply do not know, Gross. If only I had paid more attention that day. You think it is so important?"

"I think Herr Direktor Breitstein was killed because of it."

They returned to Werthen's Josefstädterstrasse apartment at midafternoon and were barely in the door before both of them were enfolded in the delighted arms of Gustav Klimt. Krafft-Ebing was waiting there as well and clapped them on their backs as a homecoming gesture.

"We thought you were dead for sure," the painter said as he finally let Werthen and Gross struggle out of his grip.

By "we," Klimt obviously meant his trio of hired thugs, for they had made themselves quite at home and had Frau Blatschky bustling in and out of the kitchen, delivering up generous helpings of her boiled beef and fresh horseradish. Werthen suddenly realized he and Gross had had nothing to eat since breakfast at the Lower Belvedere. The smell of the food made him salivate like a dog.

Frau Blatschky was as happy to see them as Klimt, but the three toughs simply tipped a fork or knife at them by way of greeting. There was plenty of food to go round, and Werthen and Gross joined in with hearty appetites. Krafft-Ebing, however, had had enough adventures for the time and left as the others were tucking into their meal. He did not even bother to inquire about what had happened to them the night before.

Gross refused to discuss the new developments until they had finished and Klimt had sent his men on their way for the night. However, before they could begin to discuss anything, the doorbell sounded. Klimt stopped Frau Blatschky on her way to open it and instead opened it himself, taking the precaution of keeping the chain on.

It was the telegraph from Geneva they had been expecting. Gross quickly opened it while Werthen fished out some change as a tip for the delivery boy.

"Aha," the criminologist said. "Just as I thought."

He handed the telegram to Werthen. Planner proved to be a miserly correspondent, for the message was only two words in length: "On neck."

TWENTY-THREE

Werthen and Gross were at breakfast. It was nine thirty, a time when most self-respecting Viennese were already on to their second breakfast, *Gabelfrühstück,* of a wurst semmel and a glass of tart white wine. But last night had been a late one for the pair. It was midnight before they had convinced Klimt that he should go home. With their pair of pistols for protection and a stout front door, they were well protected, they told him.

"It surely proves the archduke right," Werthen said now, between nibbles of the butter kipfel on his plate. He had little appetite this morning, still too excited by last night's news.

"Hmm." Gross made his comment from behind the pages of this morning's *Neue Freie Presse.*

"Does that mean you concur, Gross, or simply that you are bored with the conversation?"

"Hmm."

"Blast it, Gross. You are being far too blasé about all this. The scar on the man's neck means it was not Franz Ferdinand's man who killed the empress."

Gross put down his paper, lifting his eyebrows at Werthen.

"We have been through all this, my friend. Until midnight last night, as a matter of fact."

"But sleeping on it, does that not make it seem of more import to you?"

"As I said last night, it is a strong indication, but there are other possibilities to explore."

"What? Surely you do not believe that the archduke had a second scarred cohort in his employ just to throw us off?"

"A possibility, Werthen. I believe I categorized such a theory last night as possible though not probable."

Werthen took a sip of his coffee, and when he looked back at Gross, he was confronted with the palisade of the newspaper in front of the criminologist's face.

"Really, Gross, you can be infuriating at times. We have Breitstein newly dead, and now this news from Planner in Geneva that implicates Sergeant Tod—"

"According to Franz Ferdinand," Gross said in a muffled voice from behind his paper.

"And you just sit there reading the damnable news."

Gross set the paper down once more. "What would you have me do, Werthen?"

"Action, Gross. Now is the time for action."

"And what exactly does that mean?"

"Alert the authorities in Styria for one. They should be treating Breitstein's death as a homicide and not an accident. The police need to reinvestigate the scene before it becomes totally polluted, interview the other witnesses before their memory becomes fogged by time and preconceived notions of accidental death."

Gross beamed at him. "Bravo, Werthen. You are learning my techniques at long last."

Werthen gazed at him a moment longer. "You've already done it, haven't you?"

"You did insist on sleeping in, Werthen. I thus had a fair amount of time on my hands this morning."

"And the mysterious Sergeant Tod?"

"Alas, I have few connections with the military. But I did contact Krafft-Ebing, who knows a former member of the General Staff."

"Professionally?"

Gross shrugged the ironic question off. "It is important that the man is no longer actively involved in the military. I am sure you understand why."

"So that he, in fact, is not part of the cabal."

"Ah, it is now a cabal? Yes. Conspiracy, cabal. Give it what name you like, it would appear that members of the state itself are involved in these crimes. Krafft-Ebing assured me absolute secrecy. His man will ask discreet questions regarding the existence or nonexistence of one Sergeant Tod and the Rollo Commandos. Nothing that will raise eyebrows or red flags."

"So what do *we* do?"

"Wait, Werthen. And finish our breakfast."

At that moment there came a loud and insistent rapping at the apartment door. Whoever their visitor was, he or she was too impatient even to use the bell. Frau Blatschky had been given strict instructions not to answer the door. Instead, both Werthen and Gross moved to the foyer, where their pistols were kept in the umbrella stand. They drew the guns out; Werthen peered through the fish-eye peephole in the door and saw a large, portly man with a long, gray beard and wearing a brown bowler. He was dressed in an expensive-looking brown suit to match the hat.

"Do you know him?" Gross whispered.

Werthen shook his head. "But he looks all right."

"Looks?" Gross hissed, as if appalled at such a suggestion.

"I know," Werthen whispered back. "Books and covers and all that. But he doesn't appear to be an enemy."

A violent rapping at the door made Gross cock his pistol. "Slowly then," he said. "With the chain still on."

Gross took up position to one side of the door while Werthen cautiously opened it a crack.

278 :: J. Sydney Jones

"What have you done with my daughter?" the man outside shouted as soon as he caught sight of Werthen.

"I am sorry. Who are you, sir?"

"Damn it all, man, I am Joseph Meisner, father of Berthe."

Werthen fell over himself to put his pistol away and get the chain off and invite the gentleman in. Gross likewise uncocked his weapon and stuck it in the outer pocket of his morning jacket.

Meisner huffed in, burly and worried-looking. He and Werthen had not yet met, though Berthe had of course apprised him of the engagement. Meisner looked him up and down, then shifted his attention to Gross, still standing by the door.

"Herr Meisner." Werthen put his hand out. "It is a great pleasure, sir."

Meisner did not take the proffered hand. "I only wish I could say the same. Now, what is all this about my daughter?"

"Well . . ." Werthen felt for once a lack of words. He was not prepared for such an altercation. "We intend to be married, sir. That is—"

"I know that, you dunderhead! Where is my daughter?"

"You have freshly arrived from Linz, sir?" Gross said now.

"And who would you be?"

Gross introduced himself, and Meisner squinted at the sound of the name. "As in the criminologist? So you already know." He turned to Werthen. "You brought him in then, without consulting me first?"

"Sir," Werthen said, "I have absolutely no idea what you are talking about."

"Berthe, you dunce. My daughter. Your betrothed. She's been abducted. Or don't you bother to keep track of your fiancées?"

"Abducted." Werthen felt the air go out of him. They had been so painstaking about precautions for their own safety, and meanwhile his one love had been left unprotected, shunted aside, in fact.

"How do you know this, sir?" Gross asked, taking charge.

"A note. Whoever perpetrated this outrage sent me a note telling me that my daughter would be returned only if I spoke with the *Advokat* here."

"You have the note with you, sir?"

Meisner groped into several pockets before finally finding it. Gross made no effort to stop him, Werthen noticed. Little good would fingerprints do them with none on file to check against.

Gross unfolded the note, which looked to be on expensive paper. He read it once, sniffed, then read it again. "The blackguards," he sputtered, handing the note to Werthen, who now perused it:

Dear Sir,

Your daughter will come to no harm if you act promptly. You must convince Advokat Werthen to cease his investigations. That is your duty now. Once it is clear that such investigations have been brought to a close, Berthe Meisner will be returned to her home and life.

Sincerely, a Friend.

Werthen's blood ran cold reading this. My God, what could he have been thinking to put her in harm's way like this? It was the story of his first love, Mary, all over again: She had lain dying while Werthen busily pursued his studies. Now, given a second chance at love, he had committed the same sin. He had been so wrapped up in the investigation that he had not given proper thought to Berthe's safety. If he was able to get her back safely, Werthen vowed never again to ignore the person who should be uppermost in his life.

"Have you checked your daughter's lodgings?" Gross asked.

"Of course I have. I took the early train from Linz after receiving this note—"

"In what manner?" Gross said.

"What do you mean?"

"He means how did you receive the note," Werthen said, finally shaking off the initial shock and willing himself into action once again.

"A street youth simply knocked at my door and said a man paid him a half crown to deliver it."

"Did you perhaps inquire after this man?" Werthen asked.

"Why should I have? I had no idea what was in the note at first. By the time I'd read it, the child had vanished."

"Your daughter's lodgings?" Gross prompted him.

"Yes. Well, arriving in Vienna, I went straight to her flat, but there was no answer. The *Portier* had not seen her since Tuesday. Then I went to the school where she volunteers. They told me she did not come to work yesterday and they had had no word from her. The children at the school missed her, that was what they told me."

Werthen and Gross exchanged glances. "We will find her, Werthen," Gross promised.

"What is all this about?" Meisner said, his voice no longer full of outrage, but now tinged with fear and grief. "What investigation is this fiend talking of?"

Another exchange of looks between the two. Gross nodded.

"We should sit, Herr Meisner," Werthen said, taking the older man by the arm. "There is much to tell."

As Werthen explained the investigation of the Prater murders that had eventually led to the very doors of the Hofburg, Gross used his magnifying glass to minutely examine the paper upon which the note to Herr Meisner had been written. Gross finished his labors first and sat quietly—uncommonly so, Werthen thought—as the lawyer finished his disquisition.

"So somebody powerful wants to protect himself," Herr Meisner said. "What a foolish way to go about it, kidnapping my daughter. Why not just kill you two?"

The blatancy as well as the pure logic of the question took Werthen aback momentarily.

Gross replied, "Not for lack of trying, Herr Meisner. But an apt question. One that I have just now been giving thought to myself."

"And double the fool," Meisner continued, shaking his head. "For how can they be assured you will not pursue your investigations once Berthe has been returned?"

"Exactly," Werthen said.

"I expect we shall discover that presently," Gross said, holding up the note. "This piece of paper is, in effect, an invitation."

"What are you talking about?" Meisner said, regaining his former belligerent attitude. "It's an extortionist's bill of change, nothing more, nothing less."

"Is that so?" Gross said. "Then where are the conditions?"

"It says clearly enough here that once your infernal investigations have come to a halt, Berthe will be released."

"Those are no conditions, Herr Meisner. Those are demands. How, for example, can it be made clear 'such investigations have been brought to a close,' as herein demanded? Do we take a full-page advertisement out in the *Wiener Zeitung* saying Professor Doktor Gross and *Advokat* Werthen are pleased to announce that their investigations of the Prater murders have now been closed? Do we seek an audience with the emperor and say the same? Pahh." Gross made a dismissive sound somewhere between a sneeze and a cough. "I tell you, Herr Meisner, this is not an extortionist's letter, but a clear invitation to a meeting."

Werthen watched the two men square off against one another; they were too alike to ever find common ground, that was clear.

"Now you are a clairvoyant, is that it, Professor Gross?"

"There are no psychical tricks to my conclusion. It is all here." He waved the note in the air. "Not in the text, but in the very paper upon which it is printed. I have made an exhaustive study of paper, you see, Herr Meisner."

"I suppose you have even written a monograph on the subject," the man said with heavy irony.

"Indeed I have. And I can tell you that this piece of paper has a footprint to it every bit as exact as that of a man. Firstly, the paper is of the finest linen content available. That immediately separates the writer from the mass of people. Then the watermark is very distinctive: the letter 'W' inside a circle, *Kreis,* which is the monogram for 'Wernerkreis,' the premier papermaker in Austria, with its main outlet on the Graben in the First District. Moreover, this particular watermark bears what appears to be a personal symbol at the very bottom, hardly legible to the naked eye, but which I could discern with the aid of a magnifying glass."

Gross stopped, looking awfully pleased with himself.

"Well, out with it," Meisner demanded. "What is it you found?"

"The letters 'AEIOU.' "

"Austriae est imperare orbi universo," Werthen said. " 'It is Austria's destiny to rule the world.' "

"Very good, Werthen."

"Actually," Herr Meisner said, "that simple series of vowels commissioned by Friedrich the third for his state carriage and churches and public buildings in Vienna, Graz, and Wiener Neustadt are hardly so simple of interpretation. Others have decoded their meaning as *Austria erit in orbe ultima,* 'Austria will exist eternally.' Or even *Alles Erdreich ist Österreich untertan,* 'All the earth is subordinate to Austria.' But whatever the translation, the higher meaning is the same, a belief in the historical calling of the House of Habsburg."

Gross and Werthen both looked at this Herr Meisner with new appreciation.

"What?" he said. "Because a man manufactures shoes he cannot cultivate his mind? I will have you know I am, in addition to being an amateur historian, one of the foremost Talmudic scholars in Austria." Then a pause and a shaking of his head. "I must apologize, gentlemen. It is not my usual manner to trumpet my achievements. I am distraught. The matter at hand is Berthe's freedom and how to effect it."

"I appreciate the added information, Herr Meisner," Gross said, also moderating his tone. "And you are correct, all interpre-

THE EMPTY MIRROR :: 283

tations of the insignia point to a member of or someone close to the House of Habsburg. We shall discover exactly who after a visit to Wernerkreis on the Graben."

They were shown into his office, an opulent space overlooking the newest tract of the Hofburg, the Heldenplatz, with the plane trees on the Ringstrasse beyond now beginning to turn yellow and orange. This was the room of a man who exerted ultimate power. You could feel the self-confidence in the enormous rosewood desk, the six Louis XV chairs gathered in a small conversation circle at one end of the room, in the abundance of Flemish tapestries of hunting scenes hanging from the walls, in the elegantly crafted star-parquet floor, in the Meissen fireplace, in the green brocade curtains framing floor-to-ceiling windows, in the rows of books that filled one wall. Gross examined the books as they waited; Werthen fidgeted with his tiepin.

They had, with relative ease, discovered the identity of the person who used the AEIOU stationery. Gross had simply ordered a gift box of specialized stationery from the firm of Wernerkreis in the Graben, using those exact initials in the watermark, and when the clerk politely informed him that such an insignia was already in use, Gross feigned vague interest as to the identity of his doppelgänger. The clerk quite proudly announced the name, at which point Gross muttered, "Just as I thought."

They had taken what precautions they could. Herr Meisner was sent to stay with Klimt until they returned from their visit. If they did not return, then Meisner and Klimt would be sure to report them missing, and to supply the name of the guilty party to newspapers throughout Europe.

Gross was certain they would make such a return, but Werthen was sure of nothing anymore. All of his fondest certainties had been turned on their heads by their investigation. But he would do whatever necessary now to see that Berthe was released unharmed. It was his fault she had been placed in danger in the first place. If he had only had the common sense to take her into his confidence as she had demanded, then she, too, would have been on guard. But he had hoped to shield her by simply keeping her in the dark, thinking her ignorance would be her protection, and never realizing that she would be used as a bargaining chip by a ruthless Machiavellian monster.

Werthen's ruminations were interrupted by an exclamation from Gross.

"Ah. As I expected." He pulled a thin pamphlet out of a section of the bookcase. "My monograph on the identification of paper types and watermarks. This is indeed a formal invitation, Werthen."

At that moment the double doors to the office were thrust open, and a tall, white-haired man swept into the room, dressed in the formal red robes and ermine collar of a Knight of the Golden Fleece.

"Sorry to keep you gentlemen waiting," Prince Grunenthal said as he crossed to his desk. He also wore the formal chain of the order, whose motto, engraved on the precious metals of the links, was "Not a bad reward for labor." Werthen had always been mildly amused by the motto, the baseness, the crassness of it, in juxtaposition to the stated purposes of the Order of the Golden Fleece, to defend the Roman Catholic religion and to uphold the chivalric code of honor of knights. Grunenthal sat in a rather regal chair behind his desk, leaving Gross and Werthen to stand. Gross, however, replaced his monograph on paper and was quick to take a seat in one of the Louis XV chairs, distant from the desk. Werthen followed suit.

"I forget my manners," Grunenthal said, rising and crossing to join them. "I have been looking forward to this meeting for quite some time, though I do find myself torn in my emotions."

"You could have simply invited us, Prince Grunenthal," Gross said, not bothering with small talk. "It was not necessary to kidnap Fräulein Meisner in order to get our attention."

"Hardly kidnap, Professor Gross. Let us say she is a guest of the state."

"Let us say that you are desperate, Prince Grunenthal." Gross looked at him with his piercing eyes as if he could bore a hole through the man. Grunenthal returned the stare with equal intensity.

"I want my fiancée back, Grunenthal," Werthen said, purposely dropping the man's title. He had forfeited any right to it, in Werthen's opinion.

"And you shall have her back, *Advokat*," the prince said, now turning his stone-cold gaze upon Werthen, "directly we come to an agreement."

"Desperate," Gross repeated. "Otherwise you would simply have had us killed, as you did all the others. But things are getting out of hand, aren't they? Too many people are involved now. Who knows whom I or Werthen have told about this investigation? Who knows how many copies of our investigation notes I have sent to colleagues throughout Europe? Those questions are our life insurance, no? They are keeping us alive, for our very deaths would prove our investigations were correct."

Grunenthal clapped his surprisingly tiny and well-manicured hands together slowly, menacingly. "Bravo, Professor Gross. It is a pleasure to finally confer with a man whose mind is equal to the task at hand. I would, of course, rather you were both . . . disposed of. But you are correct. That is no longer practicable. Therefore"—the prince shrugged, with palms upraised—"an agreement. A truce, as it were."

"Treaties are your forte, are they not, Prince?"

"I pride myself that I have been of some use to the empire during my decades of service."

Werthen wanted simply to throttle the man, but knew that would not help the fate of Berthe. He understood that he had to keep himself under control and let Gross handle these matters.

"A good diplomat knows about give-and-take," Gross went on.

"You have something we want, that is clear. Berthe Meisner. We, on the other hand, have something you badly need, our silence. I expect you will explain how we can guarantee our silence."

"Oh, indeed, I shall, sir. It is quite simple, really. You drop your investigations, tell your colleagues of your mistaken direction, refute any prior claims to knowledge of the identity of the killer and his master, or you shall find yourselves accused of the crimes."

The prince smiled with absolutely mirthless eyes. Werthen thought he had never seen a living man's eyes so completely void of life.

"I assume you have gathered certain 'evidence' that will further such a preposterous claim," Gross said.

"Of course. A bit of a hobby of mine, you know, criminology."

"I noticed." Gross nodded toward the section of the bookshelves he had been perusing.

"Yes. I possess all the basic texts on the subject," Grunenthal said, "as well as some of the finest fabulists, Poe, Collins, even this new chap Conan Doyle and his Sherlock Holmes. I have made an intensive study, you see. Your motive is quite wonderful, if you don't mind my saying so. Hubris. Professional pride. You commit the most heinous series of murders so that you can solve them and gain international fame. That is, you and your henchman, *Advokat* Werthen."

"So we have mutual insurance?" Gross said.

"I should hope so."

"Why not simply proceed then?" Werthen blurted out. "Accuse us. Create another smoke screen."

"Were I a younger man, I might. But all games must come to an end. I find this is perhaps the optimum result. A draw rather than outright victory."

"It is no game!" Werthen felt himself go red in the face; the heat went down to his stomach. If he had a gun with him, he would have shot the man like the sick animal he was. "You and your creature have butchered innocent citizens."

"Werthen," Gross cautioned.

"No, no," Grunenthal said. "Your colleague is right. This is no game, though it must be played with the cunning of a chess master and the courage of an equestrian. We are talking about nothing less than the survival of the Habsburg Empire."

Werthen was about to comment again, but Gross placed a hand on his arm in restraint.

"You see me as a monster," Prince Grunenthal went on, "but I see myself as the protector of this country and all she stands for. I have made difficult decisions, heart-wrenching decisions, but they have all been in the service of Austria and the greater good."

For a moment, Prince Grunenthal sat still, staring off to some distant horizon or thought, as if unaware of their presence.

"It all began with Rudolf, did it not?" Gross prompted.

Grunenthal's gaze was jerked back to Gross and the present. "Rudolf. The crown prince, yes. Such a promising boy. So much native intelligence. But his tutors, especially Latour, corrupted him. Turned him into an archliberal. And he was impatient. So impatient. He should never have become involved with the Hungarians. They convinced the boy to accept the crown of Hungary. The crown. Preposterous. As if he would be king, usurping his father's role. Far too Shakespearean for my tastes."

"And he had to die for that."

"Had to? No. But it was decided. There are fifty-one of us. All knights dedicated to the preservation of the Church and the empire. I am the chancellor of the Order of the Golden Fleece. It was my duty to bring the matter to the others. Knights have a right to trial by their fellows for charges of treason, and that was what Rudolf had committed by accepting the Hungarians' offer. It was they found him guilty. I was then responsible for carrying out the sentence."

" 'They,' " Gross said. "The emperor is also a knight of the Golden Fleece. Was the verdict unanimous?"

Grunenthal shook his head. "All but that weakling cousin,

Franz Ferdinand. We gave the crown prince the option of killing himself. He was to repair to his hunting lodge at Mayerling to do the deed. After all, the romantic youth talked often enough about suicide to his various lovers, but in the end he could not do it. Instead he found solace in one of those lovers, the Vetsera girl. It was found necessary to carry out judgment by other means."

"The Rollo Commandos stormed the place and assassinated him, brutally killing the Vetsera girl."

"That did not go exactly as planned. Where humans are involved, there is always human fallibility."

"In effect, you staged the double suicide."

Again, Grunenthal shrugged with his palms spread upward as if these were events beyond his control. Werthen felt that the prince actually believed that he himself was a victim: of his duty, his honor, his ties to the emperor.

"And after the initial furor died down, there were no more complications for almost a decade," Gross said.

"There is no need to lead me like a donkey, sir," Prince Grunenthal said. "I am only too happy to discuss this with a man of your erudition, Professor Gross. Indeed, this next part should interest you no end. . . . Yes, for nine years there was no difficulty regarding the unfortunate business at Mayerling. Many of the principals had died or had been convinced that silence was the best course. Then Herr Frosch, the crown prince's valet, discovered he was dying of cancer and that he had nothing more to gain or to lose with his silence. He wrote to the empress. We monitor . . . monitored her mail, you see. It was clear from the letter we intercepted that we had, in fact, missed an earlier communiqué outlining Frosch's allegations vis-à-vis the death of her son—"

"He knew the truth?" Gross asked.

"Enough to piece the rest together. We had paid him a significant pension in hopes of maintaining his secrecy. Thus, when it was discovered that he was going to bring his information to a public forum, certain calculations needed to be made."

"About Frosch or the empress?"

"I regret to say both. As the American humorist Mark Twain, our distinguished guest at the moment, might say, 'The cat was out of the bag.' It was my duty to put it back in again, a task which could not be achieved without injury to someone."

"But why the delay?" Gross asked. "Why wait so long to kill Frosch when he was your primary target?"

The prince smiled like a particularly unpleasant lizard. "Ah, that was indeed a risk, but you see we could not deal with him immediately. That would surely have alerted the empress and perhaps forced her into some rash action. Also, we had to somehow secure the manuscript Frosch told the empress about as well as insure that it was the only copy. We, in fact, entered into negotiations with Herr Frosch in mid-June. I sent my adjutant to the man, posing as a German publisher anxious to purchase any memoirs dealing with Mayerling. Frosch took the bait, but in the event proved a capable negotiator, haggling over terms, promising a time for the handover and then breaking his promise in order to extract an ever-larger price. It seems he wanted to leave a large bequest to have a statue of himself erected in his hometown. Arrogant upstart. Meanwhile, we traced any possible safe-deposit boxes or other secret places he might have where he could sequester a second copy. All of this took time. But by August twenty-second we finally took possession of the material. Thereafter the way was clear to eliminate the man."

"And the empress?" Gross said.

"We received word from abroad that she was attempting to place her own memoirs with a reputable publishing house. We could not allow that to happen."

Werthen, who had had a fair amount of experience with heartless killers in his career, was nonetheless amazed and appalled at the sangfroid that Grunenthal displayed as he recounted his twin plans: the killing of Frosch and of the empress. Herr Breitstein, it appeared, had accidentally inspired in the prince the idea of the series of brutal murders to be used as a smoke

290 :: J. Sydney Jones

screen to conceal the killing of Frosch. Several months before the letter from Frosch was intercepted, Breitstein had been among those seeking an audience with the emperor. He wanted to be the purveyor of razors to the court; the matter was handed over to Grunenthal, who met with the man. In small talk, the managing director of Breitstein und Söhne attempted to ingratiate himself and to make himself seem like a humanitarian and model employer, and Grunenthal found out about the illness of Herr Binder, one of the firm's top salesmen, whom Breitstein was carrying despite his illness.

"Then when the crisis came over the Frosch letter," Prince Grunenthal explained, "it all just fell into place. Breitstein with his surgical instruments, and the unfortunate Binder dying of syphilis. I saw a modus operandi to a series of killings that would have the police and perhaps even eminent criminologists scratching their heads in an attempt to understand the symbolic meaning of the wounds, a meaning, which once gleaned, would lead directly to Binder's door."

"I noticed a book on American Indian ethnography among your other volumes," Gross suddenly said. "It was all about loyalty, was it not? The syphilitic nose was your attempt at misdirecting the investigation, pointing to Binder."

Grunenthal smiled as he nodded at Gross.

Werthen could no longer control himself. "Why kill all those innocents? Why not just make Frosch's death look like an accident and be done with it?"

Grunenthal turned to Werthen, fixing him with cold eyes. "In part so as not to make the empress suspicious. However, that, as you see, was unnecessary, for she had her own plans to make the Mayerling secret public."

"It won't wash," Werthen charged on. "All these senseless murders . . . abominations."

"*And* in part," Prince Grunenthal continued calmly despite Werthen's agitated state, "because of the great game, setting a conundrum for minds such as yours to wrap around. One likes to eschew the commonplace. Arranging an accidental death for Herr Frosch would have been so . . . so mundane, so tawdry."

"Why, you're mad as a hatter," Werthen said.

Suddenly the languid facade Prince Grunenthal had maintained was broken, and they were allowed a glimpse inside the man. His ice-cold gaze chilled Werthen to his very soul, and he knew for certain that they would never be safe as long as Grunenthal lived. The man truly was insane, but still commanded an evil cunning. Perhaps he had always been thus, or perhaps the power he had wielded for decades had ultimately undone him. But the origins of the prince's mental instability were not Werthen's concern. What *was* his concern was that Grunenthal's depravity would always threaten them and those they loved.

Gross placed a calming hand on Werthen's shoulder, then, speaking to Prince Grunenthal, returned the conversation to its former course: "The nose gambit."

Grunenthal came back to himself, a small shiver returning the controlled expression to his face. "Yes, that worked quite well to point to Binder in the first instance. But once you began poking into the matter again, uncovering the truth about Binder, then I realized we had to tie up all loose ends. Breitstein had to die, as well. And the picture of me on a shoot at his Styrian estate had to disappear from his office."

"Was Sergeant Tod responsible for all those deaths?" Gross demanded.

"I see you have been talking to the archduke. I cannot imagine from what other quarter you would discover that name. But, yes, Tod has proved a dexterous agent."

"He must have also infiltrated the Swiss anarchist cell and learned of Luccheni's desire to make himself famous by killing some nobility," Gross said.

"In fact that was another officer, but once we had an inroad there, I utilized Tod to control the anarchist, to point him in the

292 :: J. Sydney Jones

right direction. Luccheni began following the empress when she made her surprise visit to Vienna last June. Such behavior, once it comes out at his trial, will help to hang him. He was meant to kill the empress in Geneva, but just as with Crown Prince Rudolf, I had a contingency plan. Tod was there to make sure the bumbling fool actually did kill her. In the event, as you know, Luccheni proved incapable of the deed. He became flustered once he knocked the empress down, and Tod had to do the job as he helped to pick her up and apparently dust her off. And that should have put an end to it, except for the curiosity of a criminologist and his attorney friend."

Werthen spoke up again: "You say the emperor knew of the fate of his son. Was he also aware of the assassination of his wife? Of the series of senseless murders committed in order to cover up the killing of Herr Frosch?"

Grunenthal answered this with silence and an expression on his face that gave nothing away.

Finally he said, "I realize that all of this must shock you two. Perhaps it even revolts you. But keeping an empire together is not child's play. What are the lives of a few inconsequential men and women as compared with that goal?"

Neither Werthen nor Gross attempted to answer this.

"So now your suspicions have been confirmed," Grunenthal went on. "You are part of the secret sharers. I offer you the life of Fräulein Meisner in return for your silence. And I will add a small bonus. You thirst for justice, I am sure. Or is it simple vengeance you desire? Whatever the case may be, I offer you partial satisfaction. The life of Sergeant Tod shall also be forfeit. Ours is an imperfect world, gentlemen. Partial justice is better than none at all."

To which Gross calmly replied, "And how shall all this be effected?"

TWENTY-FOUR

I don't like it," Werthen said.

"Neither do I," concurred Herr Meisner. "Far too risky."

"The only risk is doing nothing," Gross insisted. "It will work. You shall see."

They were back at Werthen's flat, planning their movements for tonight. Grunenthal had arranged an appropriately ironic location for the handover of Berthe Meisner: at the Casa d'Illusion, a house of mirrors in Venice in Vienna, the canal-riddled reproduction of several blocks of the Italian city in Vienna's Prater. The amusement park had been closed down as a sign of mourning since the assassination of the empress; it would provide a secluded rendezvous.

Grunenthal had further insisted that Gross and Werthen come alone and unarmed, otherwise Tod would, in the prince's chillingly euphemistic words, "dispose of his charge."

Gross continued, "It is all a matter of psychology, gentlemen. Grunenthal is sure that I and Werthen are completely unable to take the law into our own hands. Remember his final words this afternoon: 'You are honorable men. You believe in the rule of law. It is not in you to play the role of vigilante.'"

Werthen also remembered what the prince had said next, *And that is the difference between us, gentlemen. I am not afraid to accept such a burden. I am a prince; you are mere citizens.*

"Being honorable implies weakness in his cosmos," Gross continued. "But that ego of his, his hubris and supreme self-confidence, will be his undoing, for he cannot imagine us having the initiative or pure animal cunning and courage to lay such a trap."

"And what of Tod?" Werthen asked.

"Again, it is a matter of psychology. Here is a man who has been trained to kill from the time he was a young adult. He has been dangled on a string like a very puppet. It is only right that he will rebel someday against such perfidy. I will simply give him the reason and opportunity by bringing up the fact that Grunenthal has offered us his head as part of the bargain."

"He will never believe you," Herr Meisner countered.

"It is not necessary he believe me, only that he begin to doubt his master. The seed will be sown, the two vipers will turn on each other."

"You make it sound far too simple, Gross," Werthen said. "But there is the life of Berthe in the balance. We cannot forget that."

"It is *her* life I am considering, Werthen," Gross said, exasperated. "Do you seriously believe that she, or any of us for that matter, will be safe after tonight? That the prince will keep his bargain? No. He will simply wait for the passage of time to blur the import of events. Then he and his minions will seek the perfect opportunity to eliminate us all one by one. Do you want to live the rest of your life looking over your shoulder?"

Werthen sank down into one of the Biedermeier chairs. Gross was right, but he hated to admit it. One look into the unguarded eyes of Grunenthal this afternoon had been enough to convince him the man was a monster capable of anything. Yet he could not stand the thought of endangering Berthe further by this wild scheme. He simply wanted her back, to hold her and to never let her go again. Suddenly another thought came to mind.

"Gross," he said. "Grunenthal never did answer my question this afternoon."

"No, he did not," Gross said, not bothering to ask which one.

"Did the emperor know of all this bloodshed? Even of his own wife's assassination?"

"I believe the more apposite question is, Werthen, whether or not the emperor ordered such bloodshed. Grunenthal, by his own admission, was responsible for organizing the entire sordid affair. It was most definitely his hand at work in the painfully convoluted series of killings that were meant to conceal the deaths of Frosch and the empress."

"But?" Werthen said.

"Yes, the infernal 'but.' I suppose we shall never know if Grunenthal was working on his own initiative or was marching to the orders of his emperor. By directing full attention to himself, he may be falling on his sword, just as he would have Sergeant Tod do."

"But then eliminating Grunenthal and Tod may not eliminate the danger to all of us."

"On the contrary," Gross said. "It is the only way to do so. Once Grunenthal is gone, the emperor, if he actually was involved in these murders, will surely not wish to pursue a losing cause. I have thought long and hard about this, Werthen. Franz Josef, whatever else he may be, is a consummate realist. He knows when to call a truce. If, and that is a big 'if,' he was really the person who ordered all these deaths."

"I sincerely doubt he did," Herr Meisner said. "Franz Josef may be the emperor, but he is still a man. He loved that Wittelsbach woman, that is clear. He allowed her the ultimate gift in a marriage: total freedom. Only deep love could allow such a gift from a man who badly needed his empress at home. But this is

beside the point. I agree with you, Gross. We must deal with
Grunenthal. A man of that twisted a nature, who could concoct
such vicious crimes—he will never keep his word."

Gross was silent for a moment, then asked, "Werthen?"

"Yes." He finally nodded. "I agree also."

"Good." Gross clapped his hands together. "Then we must
hurry. First we contact Klimt. There is much to plan for tonight."

They were there early. Gross hoped this would give them time to
examine the vicinity, to acquaint themselves better with the lay-
out of the park. *Venedig in Wien* was not the sort of entertain-
ment that any of them regularly indulged in.

Black flags draped the fun-house concessions. Instead of
crowds of Viennese milling about and cheering the strong man,
screaming as the demons leaped out of hiding in the grotto ride,
or drinking mugs of beer in the garden cafés, the entire Wurstel-
prater, or amusement park, was eerily still. Not a person was in
sight.

They made their way through the silent streets and over the
artificial canal of the Venice-in-Vienna section beyond the foot
of the Riesenrad, to the building where Prince Grunenthal had
instructed them to meet.

Werthen was impressed: It was actually as if they were standing on the quai of Venice's Grand Canal. This elaborate theme
park had over a kilometer of canals, and somehow the builders
had even managed to get the smell of the water right: a mixture
of sweetness and decay. The buildings surrounding the canal had
elaborate Venetian facades; their fundaments appeared, in the
dim light, to be centuries old rather than just three years, for
Venice in Vienna had only been built in 1895.

They stopped outside the Casa d'Illusion; their instructions
were not to enter but to await Grunenthal at the water's edge.
A poorly tethered gondola knocked repeatedly against the

balustrade lining the canal. Werthen cast an irritated glance at the boat. A crumpled sheet of tarp lay in the bow.

They arrived alone, as instructed. They had also come unarmed, as agreed upon. In other respects, however, they had not complied with the prince's demands.

It was a full moon tonight; clouds scudded in front of the moon, then blew away, casting a huge shadow of the Ferris wheel over them. That ride had been built to celebrate Franz Josef's golden jubilee, Werthen knew, but its opening had been inauspicious. A working-class woman, Marie Kindl, had hung herself from one of the thirty gondolas to protest poverty in Vienna.

This evening the Riesenrad, like the rest of the rides, was silent. A noise to his left made Werthen spin around. A cat slunk through the silent lanes.

There was little to be learned from their early arrival. Werthen shivered as a gust of wind curled around his legs. He felt alone and vulnerable in the open spaces of the empty Prater. Gross, however, appeared undaunted, puffing out his chest and pacing back and forth along the canal.

They waited for over an hour before Werthen, growing suspicious, said, "They are not coming."

"Nonsense," hissed Gross. "It is a test merely. They are most likely watching us to make sure we have no associates hidden away."

"But we do, Gross."

"However, they do not know that, Werthen."

They waited another half hour. The night had grown bitterly cold now. The time for the meeting was well past now.

"Gross?"

The criminologist did not at first answer.

Finally: "Yes. It is time."

They raced to the entrance to the house of mirrors.

"Come out, men," Gross called. But there was no answer from inside.

"My God, Gross," Werthen wailed. "What have you done?"

The lawyer tugged at the door to the Casa d'Illusion, but it was chained shut. Behind them the knocking of the tethered gondola had grown more insistent, as if not caused by the mere motion of water.

"The boat, Gross."

Werthen leaped over the side of the balustrade, landing neatly in the tethered gondola. Throwing aside the tarp, he uncovered Klimt, bound and gagged, his eyes bulging in panic.

It had been their plan for Klimt and Herr Meisner to hide in the Casa d'Illusion in the afternoon, before any watchers might catch them. They took weapons with them: an old shotgun and hunting rifle Werthen had from the time his father was attempting to turn him into a proper country squire. Klimt and Meisner would thus be their insurance in case something went wrong with Gross's scheme to turn Tod and Grunenthal against one another after the handoff of Berthe.

"It was as if he knew we would be there," Klimt said, once they had released him from his bonds. "He came for us only minutes after we arrived."

"He?" Gross said.

"Tall, with a face like walking death. And the scar."

Werthen was still in shock; he knew what this meant. Berthe was dead. And all because of him and clever, clever Gross. But, no, he could not blame Gross. They had all agreed to the plan. What the criminologist had said about Prince Grunenthal not keeping his word in the long run was true. They had had to act. But what now? How could he live without Berthe? How could he live with her death on his conscience?

"So he was watching all afternoon," Gross said.

"We didn't have a chance. No sooner had we broken into the house of mirrors than it appeared to be on fire. We leaped out of an open window into his waiting arms. It had only been one small flame reflected a hundred times in all shapes and sizes through the mirrors, but we had no way to know that. He forced Meisner to tie me up and then Tod took the man with him."

"There is hope, then, Werthen," Gross said excitedly. "Why not simply kill them then and there? She may still be alive."

"I do not need your false hope, Gross."

"Tod gave me a message from Prince Grunenthal," Klimt said. "So he must have been watching, too."

"A message?" Gross asked.

"He said he was sparing my life because I owed the empire paintings for the new university aula." The painter stopped abruptly as if not wanting to say any more.

"Go on, Klimt," Werthen urged. "I must know."

"He also said to tell you that you failed to live up to your end of the bargain. He said you would know the price for disloyalty."

"Oh, Christ," Werthen moaned. "I've killed her."

"Easy, Werthen," Gross counseled. "We can't know that."

The wind whipped around them as they stood in silence in the shadow of the Riesenrad, water lapping at the edges of the canal.

"I want to leave this evil place," Werthen said. "Now."

"Not so quick, *Advokat*."

The voice came from one of the darkened alleyways.

Werthen and the others spun round at the sound. Then came the sound of footsteps from the opposite direction. Three figures came into view from that direction. Werthen could feel his heart racing, hoping against hope for what he knew could not be true.

But it was.

"I have granted clemency," the voice from behind them boomed.

Werthen did not turn to it, however, but kept watching in awe as Herr Meisner and Berthe were shepherded in front of Tod, who held a pistol to her head.

"I still need your spoken guarantee," Prince Grunenthal said from behind them. He stayed in the darkness, but his voice carried. "I hope that it will be worth something this time. I have given you a second chance, for you must now see how senseless it is to try to outmaneuver me. Your lives will be forfeit if you ever dare to betray me again. Herr Meisner has apprised us of your plans, Professor Gross. It would be futile trying to turn Sergeant Tod against his master. He is a soldier; he knows his duty."

"I would not dream of it," Gross said.

"Fine," Grunenthal said, still in the shadows. "First, the formalities. Your promise, gentlemen."

"Yes," Werthen said. "You have it. Total secrecy regarding the . . . affair."

"I as well," Klimt said.

"And professor?"

"I, too, give my word," Gross said.

"What is this?" Berthe suddenly blurted out.

"A bargain, young lady," Prince Grunenthal said calmly. "One to which we also need your assent."

"Karl?"

"It's all right, Berthe. Give him your word not to talk of any of this."

"Simply give him your word, Berthe," Herr Meisner, visibly shaken by his ordeal, said.

"What's going on? Who are these men?"

"Even better," Grunenthal observed.

"Is this to do with your investigation?"

"Please, Berthe," Werthen said. "I am sorry about before. I should have told you everything, but now you will have to trust me. Please." He sought out her eyes and held them. "Please."

"She knows nothing about this," Gross added. "We purposely kept Fräulein Meisner in the dark, hoping it would in turn keep her safe."

"Please," Werthen repeated.

She nodded. "All right. I promise. You have my word I will not speak of being kidnapped or of this meeting. I know nothing more."

Grunenthal nodded to Tod, who released Berthe and her father. She ran to Werthen and they embraced for a long moment.

"That, gentlemen, is that," Grunenthal intoned importantly. "You may be gone now."

Werthen shuffled off with the others, like a repentant servant. But he knew this was not the end of the matter. As he had come to realize this afternoon, the affair could never end if Prince Grunenthal was still in power or, indeed, alive.

TWENTY-FIVE

Saturday–Sunday, October 22–23, 1898—Vienna

Several weeks went by, and Werthen had ample time to make his plans. He descended the carriage outside the Palais Kinsky, its windows brightly lit for the monthly soiree, and showed an embossed letter to a footman attired in periwig, knee pants, and stockings—a stubborn relic out of Mozart's time. The monogram of the Archduke Franz Ferdinand at the top of the letter was sufficient to gain him access to the exclusive gathering. Once inside, he wasted no time, fearful watchers would spot him and evict him. He hurried up the wide marble staircase to the ballroom with its ornate chandeliers and star-patterned parquet floor. Tonight the famous pianist Paderewski was giving a recital. Werthen was relieved to see that the guests were still milling about, exchanging gossip and false cheer.

Prince Grunenthal was there, just as the archduke had told him he would be. He stood head and shoulders over a clutch of society women, diamonds in their hair. The prince was saying something quite amusing, for the ladies began twittering into their fans just as Werthen reached the group.

"You, sir, are a cad," Werthen pronounced. "You have interfered with my fiancée and I publicly challenge you."

The angry red face of Prince Grunenthal turned just in time to receive a slap from Werthen's white gloves, purchased specially for the occasion.

"I await your seconds. The choice of weapons shall be yours." It was a calculated risk, but surely the age of the prince would limit him to pistols.

"This is an outrage," Prince Grunenthal began.

"Yes, it is. And you have committed it. Do you have the courage to seek redress or are you simply going to bluster? Or perhaps you will have me thrown into irons to save your honor."

The women whispered excitedly to one another at this comment. Otherwise, the entire room had gone absolutely silent. All eyes were on Prince Grunenthal. Werthen had backed him into a corner publicly, as was the plan.

"I will see you in hell, *Advokat*."

"Do I take that as an acceptance of my challenge?"

Another moment of tension-filled silence. "Yes, damn you."

Werthen had spent the last weeks, ever since deciding on this course of action, practicing his marksmanship. Finally there was something for which he could be grateful to his father. The endless hours as a youth on the firing range would, he hoped, be his salvation.

Berthe had simply left Vienna with her father after learning of his plan.

"I cannot stop you and I cannot watch you die. I'm sorry, Karl, but we almost lost one another once. Twice is more than I can bear."

His explanations to her were unsatisfactory. He knew, however, that in time she would understand. This was the only way they could be together. They would never be entirely safe as long as Grunenthal was alive.

Prince Grunenthal's second was the young adjutant who had

304 :: J. Sydney Jones

been on duty at the Reichskanzlei the day Werthen and Gross had gone to have an audience with the emperor. He arrived at Werthen's flat a little over an hour after the lawyer's altercation with Grunenthal.

So far, so good, for the adjutant announced that the prince's choice of weapons was pistols, with one shot from each side. There was no way that Grunenthal could expect Werthen to be even a fair shot; his innate anti-Semitism would simply disallow such a notion. The adjutant also noted the location for the duel: the Prater meadowland, just beyond the Riesenrad. This was the place the bodies had been dumped by Grunenthal's henchman, Tod. Again, the prince was being melodramatic, something that Werthen had counted on.

"At first light," the adjutant said as he was leaving Werthen's apartment. "Six thirty tomorrow."

After he was gone, Gross looked at his friend with sympathetic eyes. "You are sure you wish to go through with this, Werthen?"

He felt anything but sure. In fact, he wanted at that moment simply to catch the next train to Linz and hide away with Berthe.

"Yes, Gross. It is the only way."

"Not the only way, Werthen. We have been through this a dozen times. Not the only way, at all. But your way."

"He is a fiend, a mad dog. He needs to be put down."

Werthen did not sleep that night. Neither did Gross, for he was busy with last-minute preparations. It must all go according to plan, every piece of it, or death awaited Werthen.

Instead of sleeping, Werthen thought of the morning to come, reviewing all aspects of his plan. Archduke Franz Ferdinand himself had become an essential part of this, for, when approached, he found Werthen's strategy inspired. It could rid him of one of his archenemies at no personal cost. And if the scheme failed, neither would he be compromised by it.

Werthen's one regret was that he had had to invoke the name of his beloved in his challenge to the prince. However, it was the one offense that would be universally understood. Its very plausibility would provide Werthen with protection if he succeeded in the duel. After all, what man would not fight for his ladylove? What man would not want to seek redress for another besmirching the good name of his lady? That Grunenthal was widely known as a roué helped Werthen's cause. The emperor himself could hardly punish a man for fighting such a duel.

Werthen was dressed by five. Frau Blatschky sniffled all through breakfast; her coffee was thin and weak.

"It will be fine, Frau Blatschky," Werthen said at one point.

"Oh, Herr Doktor Werthen, sir, I sincerely hope so. It is a cruel world indeed when one such as you must bear arms."

He knew it was meant kindly, but the comment did little to instill confidence in him.

Gross, who was to act as his second, arrived with the carriage at five thirty.

"All is in readiness?" Werthen asked.

"I sincerely hope so," the criminologist said, his eyes bloodshot from lack of sleep.

They set off in the darkness, the metal-rimmed wheels of the carriage clicking against the cobbles in the otherwise stillness of predawn.

Prince Grunenthal, hatless, and his second were already at the meadow when Werthen and Gross arrived. Werthen, suffering the effects of a sleepless night, felt a sudden fog in his brain. He took deep breaths, hoping to clear his thoughts and vision for what lay ahead.

As he and Grunenthal exchanged glares, the adjutant and Gross spoke of final arrangements.

"It is my duty," the adjutant said, "to offer your man the opportunity to apologize for his insult. Otherwise, we shall proceed."

306 :: J. Sydney Jones

"My man, good sir, has nothing to apologize for. It is your master who is at fault, and your master who will pay."

Then came the choosing of weapons. Grunenthal supplied, for the occasion, matching Webley and Scott .45 caliber revolvers, with ivory grips. The large caliber indicated that despite the rule of one shot this was still a duel to the death. Both seconds inspected the guns, insuring that each had a single bullet in their chambers.

Werthen felt the heft of his. He had been practicing with a much lighter Enfield revolver. As he was getting the feel of the pistol, Grunenthal called to him, "There will be no more chances for you—for any of you."

Werthen made no reply. From the beginning he knew this would be a do-or-die gambit. All the others involved had agreed. All that is, but Berthe.

The horses at Gross's carriage whinnied as the first rays of the sun broke over the eastern horizon.

"Gentlemen," the adjutant said. "Time."

He placed them back-to-back; Werthen felt the man's rump in the small of his back, he was that much shorter than Grunenthal.

"When I command, you shall each take fifteen paces. At my next command, you may turn and fire at will."

"You will all die now," Grunenthal hissed at him.

"Ready, begin," the adjutant shouted.

Werthen kept himself focused on the paces; he made each a long stride, for the farther apart the better. A trickle of sweat slid down his shirt collar in the chill morning air. Birdsong from the woods in back of him broke his concentration for an instant, and he lost count of his steps. Then he remembered that imitated birdsong was the agreed-upon signal. He took a deep breath. Or was it actual birdsong?

He took several more paces before the adjutant again called out:

"Turn and fire at will!"

Werthen half-turned as directed by the dueling instructor Franz Ferdinand had supplied. He did not offer his full body, but a profile only. He held his fire, also as instructed, allowing Grunenthal the first shot, but the prince seemed to have had the same instructor, presenting Werthen with his profile as well, and holding his fire.

"Fire at will," the adjutant repeated.

This seemed to spur Grunenthal into action. He took careful aim and fired. It happened so quickly, Werthen did not even realize he had been shot. It was as if a loaded cart had slammed into his right leg, spilling him onto the ground.

"Werthen!" Gross yelled.

Werthen lay on his back for a moment, watching birds flap out of the trees at the sudden slap of the shot. He felt ridiculous lying there, like a character in a Tolstoy novel.

Suddenly Gross's face filled his field of vision. "We need to get you to a doctor."

Werthen closed his eyes for a moment. He knew the pain and nausea would soon strike. He needed to act now.

"Help me up. I still have my shot."

"It is over, Werthen. Don't be a fool. We will find another way."

"Help me up, damn you. You are my second. Act like one."

Werthen's sudden fury startled Gross, and the criminologist did as he was told.

Werthen hobbled helplessly on his good left leg for an instant. Across the stretch of thirty paces, Grunenthal held the gun at his side, his face ashen now, seeing Werthen again on his feet. The shot should have killed him, the prince knew. Not his own, of course, but that of the marksman, Tod, hiding in the woods in back of him. So the birdsong *had* been their prearranged signal, after all. Meaning that Klimt and Duncan had taken Tod. He would in turn be dealt with appropriately. The sentence had already been delivered.

"Is your man in any condition to continue?" called the adjutant.

"Yes, I am," Werthen shouted.

Grunenthal still looked in amazement as Werthen took careful aim. His would not be a body shot. He wanted to finish this, for once and for all. He planted his wounded right leg solidly in front of him and felt a wave of pain wash over his entire body. His shirt was drenched in sweat as he held the Webley and Scott in front of him, supported by his left hand.

Grunenthal jerked suddenly, as if fear had overcome him, but then forced himself to stand still and receive the shot.

"You haven't the courage to do it," he cried out suddenly. "You will always be a mere citizen."

The crack of the shot stirred the remaining birds out of their nests and into the rose-colored dawn. The bullet struck Grunenthal over his left eye, toppling him and taking off the back of his head. His once white hair was now a mess of pink brain matter and blood.

EPILOGUE

Werthen was still groggy from morphine; tomorrow he would cut back on the dosage of that painkiller. Meanwhile, he floated in a cozy fog.

He had a private room in the General Hospital; flowers filled every possible space. At times, the smell was almost overwhelming. Several of the bouquets were from Gross, who had had to leave suddenly for Bukovina; the university chancellor himself sent for him, as they had found temporary classroom quarters. Gross had visited yesterday before catching his train and had given Werthen an autographed copy of *Criminal Psychology*.

"Perhaps we will have the opportunity to work together again one fine day," Gross had said before leaving.

Drugged and unable to speak, Werthen had simply nodded. Strangely, he felt tears build in back of his eyes as the criminologist was shepherded out of the room by Berthe.

Yes, Berthe, for she had returned. In fact, she had been there when he awoke from surgery last Monday. And she had remained at his side since, policing the frequency and duration of visits.

Now she was speaking to his most recent visitor: "Make it brief, Herr Klimt. He needs his sleep."

"It will be very short," Klimt said. "And might I say, it is good to see you again, Fräulein Meisner."

She smiled at this. "Charm will do you no good, Klimt. You have a pair of minutes, no longer."

Klimt bent over Werthen's bed so that she would not hear their conversation.

"From what I hear there was another suicide last night. Terrible. Vienna has become the suicide capital of Europe, according to the foreign papers. A jumper this time. Seems to have climbed to the top of the Riesenrad and made a swan dive."

Werthen breathed deeply. He was not a vindictive man, but neither was he sorry to hear of the death of Sergeant Tod.

"Actually," Klimt whispered, leaning over more closely to Werthen's ear, "Duncan had to kill him at the Prater before the duel. I would not want to be a deer stalked by that Scot, I can tell you. We kept the body on ice for a time, so that nobody would make the connection between his death and Grunenthal's."

With great effort, Werthen focused his mind and speech. "Thank you, Klimt. You are a true friend."

Klimt shook his big head. "It was nothing, *Advokat*. Anyway, it makes me feel less guilty about not getting your fee to you yet. Never do business with the aristocracy."

Werthen could not agree with the man more.

"Enough, Klimt," Berthe said. "Karl needs his sleep."

It felt good to be fussed over, Werthen thought, as he drifted off to sleep.